D0196584

FULFILLMENT . . .

Without a backward glance, Rob swept Arianna into his arms and carried her from the hall. He began the long climb up the spiral staircase to the tower room, then into the circular chamber at the very top of the stairs. Arianna gasped in awe. Animal skins, stretched over the windows, darkened the room, but thousands of fireflies lit it up again, twinkling magically like tiny candles.

The fireflies floated around the lovers, circling them with their fairy light, while Arianna's eyes rivaled their brightness.

"How lovely," she cried. "You've made my day complete."

"Not quite complete, my love," he answered in a deep, husky voice. Setting her down, he drew her into his arms and his lips sought hers.

Arianna's arms crept around his neck, holding him tight. When the kiss ended, he looked down at her, his need showing clearly in his eyes. "Shall I summon your handmaidens to help you ready for bed?"

She spoke softly, her lashes lowered. "I need no help but yours." She turned her back to him. "My love," she whispered, her flesh trembling in anticipation, "begin with the laces . . ."

LET ARCHER AND CLEARY
AWAKEN AND CAPTURE YOUR HEART!

CAPTIVE DESIRE (2612, $3.75)
by Jane Archer

Victoria Malone fancied herself a great adventuress and student of life, but being kidnapped by handsome Cord Cordova was too much excitement for even her! Convincing her kidnapper that she had been an innocent bystander when the stagecoach was robbed was futile when he was kissing her until she was senseless!

REBEL SEDUCTION (3249, $4.25)
by Jane Archer

"Stop that train!" came Lacey Whitmore's terrified warning as she rushed toward the locomotive that carried wounded Confederates and her own beloved father. But no one paid heed, least of all the Union spy Clint McCullough, who pinned her to the ground as the train suddenly exploded into flames.

DREAM'S DESIRE (3093, $4.50)
by Gwen Cleary

Desperate to escape an arranged marriage, Antonia Winston y Ortega fled her father's hacienda to the arms of the arrogant Captain Domino. She would spend the night with him and would be free for no gentleman wants a ruined bride. And ruined she would be, for Tonia would never forget his searing kisses!

VICTORIA'S ECSTASY (2906, $4.25)
by Gwen Cleary

Proud Victoria Torrington was short of cash to run her shipping empire, so she traveled to America to meet her partner for the first time. Expecting a withered, ancient cowhand, Victoria didn't know what to do when she met virile, muscular Judge Colston and her body budded with desire.

Available wherever paperbacks are sold, or order direct from the Publisher. Send cover price plus 50¢ per copy for mailing and handling to Zebra Books, Dept. 3785, 475 Park Avenue South, New York, N.Y. 10016. Residents of New York and Tennessee must include sales tax. DO NOT SEND CASH. For a free Zebra/ Pinnacle catalog please write to the above address.

SANDRA DAVIDSON

ROSEFIRE

ZEBRA BOOKS
KENSINGTON PUBLISHING CORP.

To the three fantastic "A" women who helped me realize my dream: Alice Orr, my agent, Ann La Farge, my editor, and Arianna Warwick, the heroine of my story.

And to my husband, Bill, for giving me the chance to write in the first place, keeping me supplied with plenty of computer paper and printer ribbons, and believing in my dream.

ZEBRA BOOKS

are published by

Kensington Publishing Corp.
475 Park Avenue South
New York, NY 10016

Copyright © 1992 by Sandra Davidson

All rights reserved. No part of this book may be reproduced in any form or by any means without the prior written consent of the Publisher, excepting brief quotes used in reviews.

If you purchased this book without a cover you should be aware that this book is stolen property. It was reported as "unsold and destroyed" to the Publisher and neither the Author nor the Publisher has received any payment for this "stripped book."

First printing: June, 1992

Printed in the United States of America

Prologue

The dragonfly spread its crystal wings and dipped its tail into the forest pool, disturbing the naked femininity reflected there. Arianna waited impatiently for the delicate ripples to disappear, in need of one more glimpse. Magically, her image returned and she drank deeply of it, imprinting it on her brain so that she might conjure it up again when she was sorely troubled over the deceptive life she was forced to live.

Sighing forlornly, she reached for her hose and breeches and pulled them on. Then, taking the long strip of cloth, she wound it tightly around her chest to bind and flatten her breasts. She quickly put on her shirt and jerkin and tucked her golden hair into a cap.

Staring back into the water, she saw a delicate young boy instead of the small curvaceous female she had seen moments ago. She sighed again. How long must she live like this? How long must she be deprived of feminine clothing? Deprived of ribbons and garlands of flowers for her hair, petticoats to flounce prettily at the boys? How long must she suffer so?

She started down the path that led to the main road to Norbridge, resenting every step. Emerging from the woods, she reached the road, so deep in misery she didn't hear the rough masculine voice call out to her until it repeated the command, "Make way."

Looking up, she saw the party of richly-clad knights and elegantly dressed ladies riding upon velvet-coated, high-stepping horses. Her misery was now complete.

Standing by the side of the road, she watched as the entourage passed by, envious of the beautiful garments the ladies wore—envious of the luxurious life they led. What did it matter if she was disguised as a boy? Dressed as a female she would still be forced to wear the plain coarse fabric of a peasant.

For all her nearly sixteen years she had dreamed of being a fine lady, of riding a beautiful white stallion whilst everyone looked at her in admiration. It was a dream that would not die, no matter the reality of her dismal life. Watching the entourage move down the road, hearing the gay laughter of the ladies drifting back to taunt her, she wanted that dream all the more and vowed she would do anything, risk anything to become part of that world.

Chapter One

Norbridge, England, July 1583

Arianna's spirits soared as they always did when she entered the castle mews. It was here that she spent her days as an apprentice to her father, the duke's master falconer, in the guise of his son. Here that she could escape for awhile the life that she hated, tending the precious hawks and falcons in her care.

Adjusting her eyes to the dimmer light inside the wooden building, she saw a stranger standing in front of the gyrfalcon's perch—a boy not much older than she, by the looks of him, dressed in the garb of a huntsman. Angry at having her only sanctuary violated—the one place where she could forget for a time her dismal life—she cried out in frustration, "What are you doing in here? It's forbidden to all but the duke's family and his falconers."

Robert turned to gaze at the diminutive boy, a look of amusement on his handsome, boyish face. "By whose authority do you speak to me thus?"

Arianna faltered, gazing into the warmest brown eyes she had ever seen. "By my own—Aaron Trilby—apprentice to the duke's master falconer. It's my duty to care for these valuable birds."

7

"Is that so? Such a large task for such a small being." Robert reached out slowly, deliberately, to caress the bird's downy chest feathers. "What if I told you I intend to ignore your warning and go hawking with the rarest of your precious birds, the gyrfalcon?"

Arianna swallowed hard. The gyrfalcon was indeed a rare specimen. Snow white in color, it could be found only in the most northern climes and was worth a king's ransom. She hadn't expected this young upstart to challenge her authority. No one had before, but she couldn't back down now. Her father had warned her she must never back down to anyone, man or boy, or they would bully her forever.

Sizing up the young man, she determined whether she could hold her own. Tall, gangly-legged, and thin, he was no more than a year or two older than she, with hair the color of rich sable. As his eyes drew her into their depths, she thought that no one with such eyes would ever harm her. Shaping her hands into fists, she took a cautious step toward him. "Then I shall have to stop you."

Raising her fists, she advanced another step, then stopped when the boy began to laugh.

"And what are your thumbs sticking up for? Do you mean to gouge my eyes out?"

Arianna looked down at her hands and flushed a deep red — her thumbs were sticking straight up like maypoles. She opened her mouth to speak, then shut it when the boy proceeded to clasp her hands in his, tucking her thumbs down properly.

A tingling sensation shot through her at his touch, traveling down to her belly and below. He must have felt it, too, for he dropped her hands as if he had been burned and looked at her strangely.

"Who the devil are you?"

Struggling to regain her composure, she answered.

8

"Are you deaf as well as rude? I said before I am apprentice to the master falconer. I train the hawks and peregrines for the duke. Is that so hard to fathom?"

Shrugging off the unsettling feeling in his groin, Robert asked, "Falcons? Hawks? One so small as you could train nothing larger than a sparrow hawk. Nay, not even them. Sparrows are more to your liking. Yes . . . Sparrow, an apt name for you."

Taking a dagger from his waist, he tapped the apprentice's shoulder. "I dub thee Sir Sparrow, champion of falcons and hawks and fierce defender of the duke's mews."

Arianna pushed the dagger off her shoulder. "Sparrow is it? And you, you are nothing more than a dirty old mynah bird, for verily, they chatter away incessantly, repeating human speech, but without any understanding. And furthermore . . ."

"Whoa, there!" The voice came from the doorway. "I see you two have already met. But I must say, Aaron, that's hardly the way to speak to Lord Warwick of Everly."

Arianna's mouth dropped open.

Robert laughed heartily, enjoying Aaron's embarrassment. "The lad has mettle. He was going to take me on, though I'm twice his size." Robert's gaze traveled over Aaron's small form, an eyebrow raised cockily. "So. This is the legendary falconer you've told me so much about, Will. You didn't mention his disagreeable nature."

William Ludlow, son of the Duke of Norbridge, slapped Arianna on the shoulder. "In sooth, until this moment, I have never seen that side of him. Methinks you bring out the worst in him, Rob."

Arianna was deeply humiliated. This arrogant young boy was Lord Warwick? She had thought him to be much older, not this fuzz-faced boy with the legs of a

9

colt. But no matter, this youth had the power to have her punished for being rude to him.

"Forgive me, Lord Warwick. Dressed as you are, I had no idea you were anything more than an annoying huntsman. I mean . . . oh, fiddlesticks, I don't know what I mean."

Rob laughed again, offering his hand to the apprentice. "Will has sung your praises often." Sparrow reached out and when they touched, the same tingling sensation coursed through Rob once again. What was happening to him he wondered. Why should the touch of a boy affect him so strongly?

He had heard of boys his age becoming interested in other boys as sexual partners, but it couldn't happen to him. He had no reason to doubt his masculinity. He certainly had a healthy interest in females, though so far, he hadn't found one to fire his loins. Brushing off the feeling, he forced himself to speak casually. "There now, Sparrow, Will. Now that we've been properly introduced, shall we go a-hawking? 'Tis what I came to Norbridge for, is it not? To learn from this diminutive flyer of hawks."

Will looked curiously from Rob to Aaron. "Sparrow? Is that to be your name then, Aaron? I like it. The Sparrow who flies with the hawks. Yes, yes, I like it well."

Lord Warwick had come to Norbridge to learn from her? Arianna stood a little taller with that knowledge, happy that there was one way that she could achieve the admiration she so fervently desired.

Feeling the need to live up to her reputation, she tried hard to impress Lord Warwick with her expertise, flying a peregrine falcon from the top of a nearby hill and manning it with all the skill at her command. She knew it must be working from the way he looked at her. But, oh, it was unsettling. His intense gaze had her flustered in a way she couldn't begin to understand. She had never felt this way before.

She had flown many a hawk and falcon in front of dukes and earls and barons with the greatest of confidence, which came with the knowledge that she was indeed good at the craft. But here, now, with Robert Warwick, she could barely walk without tripping. What was it about him?

Watching as he strode toward her, his long, lanky legs eating up the ground, his tightly muscled shoulders jutting forward with each step, she knew the answer: he was the one she desired as her mate. That revelation surprised her, startling her with its forcefulness, for she had never before thought about exactly what she wanted or needed in a man.

"Well, how was that, Sparrow? I thought my hawk responded faster to my signals this time. What do you think?"

Arianna's face grew red. She mustn't think of him that way. She could never be anything more to this nobleman than Sparrow, a boy who flies hawks. "I think, Lord Warwick, that you're off to a good start."

"Excellent. Did you hear that, Will? By the end of the summer, when I return to Everly, I shall no doubt impress even my father with my skills, thanks to our little Sparrow. And now, if I may have your attention, I propose that as long as we three are alone, Sparrow shall call us by our given names. We'll all be more comfortable for it. Agreed?" Rob eyed Will to see how he would react.

Will nodded back, surprised. It was not like Rob to make friends so fast, and certainly not with a peasant. "Agreed."

"Sparrow?" Rob said, gazing into dazzling blue eyes that stirred him in ways he found increasingly disturbing. "Do we have a pact then? Will you be our instructor in the art of hawking, our comrade, and our confidant?"

11

Arianna couldn't breathe. Comrade? Confidant? It was more than she had ever dared dream. Her face lit up. "Agreed."

Will laughed heartily. "Don't be so quick to agree, Sparrow. Rob expects a great deal from his friends. Even so much as your very blood. When we were but nine or ten, he took his dagger and sliced his finger and then mine, wanting an oath in blood to back up our allegiance. Do you remember, Rob? I bled so much I ruined a new velvet doublet. Father was furious."

Arianna's eyes opened wide. Surely he didn't expect . . .

Rob smiled at Sparrow's frightened look. "Don't worry, I've outgrown the need for blood oaths."

Arianna and Will saw the mischievous glint that came to Robert's eyes. "But . . ." Rob deliberately hesitated.

Will and Sparrow remained quiet, waiting to see what Rob would say.

Rob took his dagger from a sheath at his waist and with a grand gesture laid the blade on his arm, the point facing Sparrow. "To seal our pact of friendship, you must take the oath of the sword."

Arianna looked at Rob's puzzled expression.

"Kiss the blade of the dagger," Will instructed. " 'Tis a sacred oath."

Moving closer to Rob, Arianna looked into his eyes, then lowered her head to solemnly kiss the blade. The steel was warm from Rob's body. "I swear by this sword — dagger, I mean — to be a loyal comrade to you and to Will."

"Here, here!" Will shouted. "Mark this day well, for 'tis the beginning of an alliance among the son of a duke, the lord of a faraway castle, and . . . an apprentice falconer."

Apprentice boy, Arianna added to herself.

12

* * *

Arianna stood in the doorway of the mews scanning the inner ward for Rob. In the two all-too-short months that had passed since she first laid eyes on him, it seemed she spent every waking moment thinking of him. She knew it was foolish, but she couldn't help herself. Not only was he tall and handsome, but kind and gentle; even if he had been born a peasant like herself instead of a nobleman, she would have wanted him above all others.

Sighing deeply, she hoped she'd see him. He and Will had been too busy these past few days to seek the company of their apprentice falconer. A flash of purple caught her eye, causing her to frown. Only one person she knew had a garment that color — Lady Judith, Will's raven-haired sister.

A twinge of jealousy stabbed through her as Judith drew closer and she could see clearly every elegant detail of the velvet gown. Why, of why had fate made her a peasant doomed to wear dull clothing while this heartless girl enjoyed so much?

Shifting her gaze to the pearl-trimmed headdress Judith wore over her dark hair, she imagined it on her own head and her hand moved up to touch her hair, falling back to her side dejectedly when she touched the harsh material of the hood that hid her long tresses.

Judith looked neither to the left nor to the right as she headed for the mews, Will and Rob following closely behind. Roses of all colors and gillyflowers to match grew in splendid profusion there, but Lady Judith took no notice of their beauty or their delicious aroma.

Arianna hated it when Lady Judith deigned to visit the mews. The haughty girl three years her senior had no understanding of raptors, yet insisted on hawking with her brother and father whenever she was allowed.

Because of her carelessness and ignorance, two birds had already been lost.

"Ah, there you are, Sparrow. We've come to see the new fledgling peregrine," Judith called out. "I'm tired of the ancient one I'm beset with now."

"May we take a look?" Rob asked, knowing how protective Sparrow was of the hawks.

"Really, Robert. There's no need to ask permission of a servant. It's my bird, after all, not his."

Arianna was used to Judith's curt words and insulting manner and had learned long ago not to be riled. "The fledgling's by the gyrfalcon's perch, but mind you don't get too close, or it'll take a chunk out of you quick as a wink. I know—he's already gouged my finger."

"Oh, pooh, it's only a baby, isn't it? You coming, Robbie?" Judith snaked her arm through Robert's and steered him over to the fledgling's perch.

Robbie? So that's the way it is, thought Arianna. *The witch is out to win Robert, and by the looks of it, he doesn't mind one little bit. Look at the way she rubs her hand up and down his arm, gazing up at him with such adoring eyes. Disgusting, that's what it is, purely disgusting.*

Arianna's fingers gripped the rough door frame hard, unaware of what she was doing or of the wetness between her fingers as the wound inflicted by the fledgling broke open again. Her eyes followed Robert and Judith. Why did Judith have to ruin the happy times she had with Rob and Will? Happy, despite the constant struggle to keep her identity a secret.

It was her low station in life that saved her from being discovered. Will and Rob thought Sparrow to be a boy who never dared mingle freely with his highborn friends, and they accepted the limits Sparrow put on their friendship.

14

As the summer months rolled by, Arianna's breasts continued to blossom and her mother bound them tighter and tighter with strips of cloth. Then, there was the matter of her voice. Will and Rob kidded her about it, asking when it was going to change to a rich baritone as theirs had. To fool them, she started talking in lower tones, forcing the unnatural timbre, but it made her throat sore and raspy.

She couldn't deny, though, how much she enjoyed being with them. She loved the casual way they treated her, teasing her about her size, but respecting her for the skillful and graceful way she manned the hawks.

She soon learned a lot about the male animal. Some of it was amusing, some of it was shocking, but all of it was fascinating, and she adjusted to their ways. But there was one thing to which she could never adjust.

Seeing them naked.

On those occasions she diverted her gaze from Will's nakedness, but couldn't keep her eyes off Rob's slim-hipped, golden body and the part of him that swayed between his legs when he walked. Each time she saw it was like seeing it for the first time, and she wondered at the restless yearnings that always crept through her at the wondrous sight.

Her yearnings grew stronger as the summer wore on, making it all the harder to play a boy. As her feelings toward Rob grew stronger and stronger, she wanted to touch him, hold him; she memorized every detail so she might conjure him up in her dreams each night, for then she could be with him in the intimate way denied her in the light of day.

If only Rob could know. She knew he agonized over his attraction to Sparrow. Each time they touched, however casual it might be, she knew he felt what she did — the physical attraction of a man for a woman. If only she could ease his mind, tell him it was all right, that the

15

boy he knew as Sparrow was, in truth, a girl. Mayhap, then, he wouldn't feel the need to flirt with Lady Judith.

Judith's voice broke through her reverie and she winced at the soreness of her hurt finger pressing into the door frame.

"He'll do, I suppose. One hawk's as good as the next. Shall we go? I can't bear the smell in here any longer." Judith pulled a potpourri sack from her bodice and inhaled the aromatic mixture of spice and herbs. "Robbie? Will?"

Leading the way, Judith headed toward the door and was the first to notice the blood dripping down Sparrow's hand.

"Sparrow, are you aware your finger is oozing blood all over my father's property?"

Will and Rob saw the blood and made their way over. "What happened?" asked Will.

Arianna was embarrassed. " 'Tis nothing."

"Here, let me see that," Rob said, taking Sparrow's hand.

"You'd think it was a mortal wound by the way you carry on, Robbie." Judith knew she sounded like a witch but she couldn't help it. Every time Sparrow was around, Rob seemed to forget she existed. What was it about males that made them stick together like that? The only time they were sure to pay attention to her was when they wanted sexual favors.

Judith's face suddenly took on an angelic expression and in a sweet voice she crooned, "Why don't you suck on it, Sparrow? Stick it in your mouth and suck on it."

She knew her words had a double meaning and she was eager for Robbie to be titillated. Anything to get him to show interest in her. It was becoming tiresome being treated as if she were his sister. If she was ever going to become the Countess of Everly, she would have to step up her campaign.

She had never considered him in the role of husband before, but her father had convinced her that he would make a good one, since he was heir to considerable land and holdings. Yes, she thought, gazing at Robbie's slim form. He would make a good enough husband.

Robert watched as Sparrow sucked on his wound, his finger moving slowly in and out of his pouty, perfectly formed mouth, and he felt a tightening in his breeches. Oh God, this had to stop, he thought in near-panic. He couldn't go on feeling this way about another boy.

Reaching out blindly, he wrapped an arm around Judith's waist and pulled her to his side. "I think Sparrow can manage on his own. Shall we go? I feel like taking a long hard ride on my charger. What say you, Judith?"

Judith's eyes lit up. Robert was finally taking notice. Her sensual, suggestive words must have worked. "Why, Robbie, what a delicious idea. I'd love it. Just the two of . . ."

"Whoa, there," Will chimed in. "There'll be none of this 'just the two of us.' If you go riding with Rob, you'll take a chaperon along, understand? We wouldn't want your sterling reputation to be sullied."

"Oh, Will. Stop being an old poop. Father doesn't mind."

"And we both know why, don't we? No—until the day you two make up your minds and become officially betrothed, you'll not spend a minute alone."

Betrothed? Arianna felt a lump in her throat and a larger one in her heart. Rob was thinking of marrying this . . . She couldn't think of a word bad enough to describe Lady Judith. Everyone knew she lay with any man who could grow a beard, and some who couldn't. Robert deserved better than that.

"Well, then, if you're going to be that way, you'll just have to come along, but I hope you fall from your horse and break your stubborn head. I shan't lift a finger to

17

help you."

Robert laughed, extricating himself from Judith's firm grasp. "If that's settled, go and make ready. I'll be right along. I want another look at Sparrow's finger. We can't have our apprentice falconer too incapacitated to do his chores."

Judith gave Sparrow a lethal look, then left with Will, calling over her shoulder. "Don't be long, Robbie."

Robert waited until they left, then turned to look at Sparrow with a serious expression. "I'm sorry about your finger. How did it happen?"

"Judith's new fledgling. He's got a bite as sharp as Judith's tongue," she said, smiling. "Don't mind about it."

Robert lifted Sparrow's hand and examined the finger still wet from his mouth, trying to take his mind off the sensation that coursed through his body at the hot, moist touch. What was wrong with him? Why did this happen every time he touched Sparrow? And why couldn't he stay away from him?

Arianna watched Robert closely as he examined her finger, her heart pounding faster at his nearness. She hated the lie that kept her from telling him how much she wanted to be kissed this very moment. She wanted to move into the curve of his body as Judith had, nestle up to him and feel his warmth. She wanted to absorb his strength, delight in his maleness. It was an actual need, and she had a hard time fighting it.

Robert gazed down at Sparrow. His lips were so tantalizingly near, the scent of his breath drawing him closer and closer. He caught himself just in time, forcing himself to keep from doing what his lips ached to do and cursing the fickle gods for making Sparrow a boy.

"It'll be fine in a few days," he said, clearing his throat. Reluctantly, he dropped Sparrow's hand. "Well, uh, I better be going. You know how Lady Judith is." He took a few slow steps away , then stopped and turned to gaze at him again, reluctant to be parted from him. "Why don't you join us? I'm sure Judith wouldn't mind another male along to flatter her."

Arianna shook her head, her throat too tight to speak, then turned her back, pretending to look for something. She knew when he finally left. The world seemed suddenly colder.

Chapter Two

Supper that night was pigeon pie. Arianna knew only because her mother told her so. She couldn't taste a thing and had lost her appetite completely since seeing Robert and Judith together. Her stomach churned at the thought of Rob holding Judith in his arms. Leaving the table without excusing herself, she ran to her room and began to cry.

Sybille and Peter exchanged worried glances.

"Peter, how long must we keep this up? This double life is taking its toll on Arianna."

"I know. I hate it, too, but until our Queen is freed and back safely in Scotland, Arianna must stay a boy. Her freedom, if not her very life, depend on it."

"What you say is true, but it's hard living like this, keeping such a secret. Oh, Peter, I miss my beloved Highlands. We're Scottish born and Scottish bred, and I yearn to breathe of its sweet air again."

"Shhh. The child mustn't hear."

"What harm? She knows we love our homeland. The whole village knows of it. They think as she does that we cannot return because of a clan feud."

"And so everyone must continue to think."

Arianna heard the whispered voices of her parents, as she had on so many evenings, and wondered what they had to talk of after so many years together. It gave her a good feeling to know husbands and wives could be like that—loving, caring, and gentle with each other. She hoped someday to enjoy the same kind of relationship with a man. No, not any man. Robert. She wanted no one but him, but she might as well ask for the moon, for his life was just as far removed from hers.

Kneeling beside her bed, she began her prayers, then stopped, a frown creasing her pale forehead. What was the use in praying to a God who never listened? Not even when she had been fourteen, innocent and joyous at turning into a young woman with graceful curves, breasts like ripe plums, and long hair the color of spun gold. How proud she had been of her beautiful hair. Closing her eyes, she called forth that day when her hated life as a boy had begun:

"Papa, no! Don't cut off my hair! It's the only beautiful thing I own."

Peter Trilby raised the sharpened knife to the thick golden braid he held in his rough hand. "I told you, child, it's for your own good. Someday you'll understand and thank me for this."

Gazing into her tear-filled eyes, Peter softened his voice. "Better the duke think you a lad when we go to Norbridge Castle. Better you never have to endure the deflowering by a man notorious for claiming every virgin in his domain whom he finds attractive."

"No, Papa! I would rather bed him than lose my beautiful hair! Anything is better than that."

Peter yanked on Arianna's braid. "I forgive you your harlot words, since I know how truly innocent you be. You have no idea what it would be like. The man carries the pox that turns men blind or crazy, and the women, too, who have concourse with him. I'll not condemn you to such a fate. You will become my son, and the duke will never know his new master falconer has a beautiful young daughter. In that way you will be spared."

Arianna gasped in horror as her father began to saw through the thickness of her braid, and again when he laid it on her lap. She looked down at it as one would a dead child. Tears spilled onto her cheeks as her hands flew up to touch her hair that now reached just below her ears. It was strange and alien, and her head felt so light she was sure it would float away. "I cannot bear it. I want to die."

Sybille Trilby moved quickly to gather her child in her arms. "Arianna, Rose Petal, don't be so sad. You'll not have to be a boy for very long. In a few years . . ."

"A few years! I cannot bear it even for a few hours. Why, Papa, why? If you hadn't become the falconer for the duke this wouldn't have happened."

" 'Tis a great honor, child, to be chosen master falconer to such a man. How could I turn down such an offer? You're unhappy now, but later, when we are living a more comfortable life in Norbridge, you'll be happy."

Arianna saw the forlorn look in her father's eyes. She knew he had another, stronger reason for her disguise and knew also it was useless to ask about it.

Arianna looked from her father's rugged face to her mother's gentle one. Papa, chestnut-haired and copper-bearded, with a barrel chest and stout arms that artfully commanded the beautiful peregrines—and Mama, tall, lithe, raven-haired, her own very opposite. She favored neither, for she had none of their blood.

As a small child she had been told the north wind brought her to Sybille and Peter on the petal of a rose. That had sounded so wondrous, so magical, that it satisfied her curiosity for years. But once she was no longer a child, she wanted to know the truth, for without it she felt truly a daughter of the wind, without roots, without substance.

She had been told that her real mother was a dear friend forced to give up her child because of circumstances that Peter and Sybille would not, or could not, explain.

Through the years, Arianna often wondered what her mother looked like, imagining her to be a grand and beautiful lady like the one in the rhyme Sybille recited to her so often when she was small. A fine lady with rings on her fingers and bells on her toes, riding a sleek white cock horse.

Life was so unfair. If she could but dress as a noblewoman, she would command attention and everyone would admire and love her, including the mother who had given birth to her, then abandoned her like an unwanted kitten.

"Psst! Sparrow!"

The whispered voice pulled Arianna from her reverie. Her heart leapt. Could it be Robert? He often brought her tidbits of meat and sweetbreads from his supper plate. Arianna flew to the window.

"It's me, Will."

Will's blond head popped up and Arianna swallowed her disappointment. "Will, what are you doing here?"

Robert's head appeared next to Will's. "I asked him the same thing. He insisted you join us."

"For what?" Arianna asked, her heart soaring at the sight of Rob.

"For my present. It's never too late in the evening to receive a present. Don't you agree, Sparrow? Father told me at supper that a birthday present awaits me in the stable. We're going to see what it is. Want to come along?"

"Another present? Your birthday was three days ago."

Arianna envied the festive celebrations held each year on Will's birthday. Her own birthday was September 7, just two days away, but no one knew or cared.

"So it was. My father is still celebrating it. Coming?"

Arianna smelled the faint aroma of wine on Will's breath and knew he was a little tipsy, but at least he wasn't drunk, a condition she had seen him in too often of late. What harm in going with them? More to the point, how could she pass up the opportunity to be with Rob? She had thought he would be spending the evening with the clinging, clawing Lady Judith after her disgusting performance that afternoon. The fact that he wasn't gave her hope the betrothal might never happen.

"Very well. Let's see this mysterious present of yours. A charger, I warrant, seventeen hands high." Arianna climbed out the window. "But how will we ever see it in the dark?"

24

"All taken care of. Father says there will be light aplenty to see by."

And so there was. Copper lanterns punched with tiny holes were set on the stable floor, emitting light through their myriad holes. The threesome glanced about in wonder, looking for Will's present. They didn't have long to wait.

A scratchy female voice called out to them from a stall in the darkest corner. "It's about time, your lordship. I'm about to catch me death."

The three looked from one to the other, then shrugged and made their way down to the dark stall. They stopped dead at the strange sight that greeted them. A buxom young female was standing on the straw-covered ground, stark naked except for the paper horse's ears tied around her head and a leather strap around her waist that held a coarse horsehair tail at her backside. Reddish blonde hair tumbled to her shoulders, a tangled mess of curls.

"I wasn't expecting three of ya," Buttercup wailed. "The duke said I was to entertain his son, is all. I'd of asked for more if I'd a known there was to be so many."

Recuperating from the shock, Will and Rob began to laugh, but Arianna stood with her mouth open, unable to say a word.

Buttercup joined in the laughing, wriggling her behind to make the tail swish back and forth seductively. "Who's to be the first to ride the mare, me hot-blooded stallions?"

"Have a go, Rob. By the looks of her, she'll give you a fine ride."

Robert laughed all the harder. "No, Will, this one's all yours. But I wouldn't miss this spectacle for a king's ransom. Go to it, man. Ride your strawberry mare.

'Tis your present. Sparrow and I will watch and take note of your prowess."

Will gazed at his friend, suddenly becoming sober. "I'm thinking you should have a go at it, Rob. Exercise that thing you carry between your legs. It'll make a man out of you."

Robert bristled. "When I feel the need, I'll not want your permission, Will, or any other man's."

Will heard the strain in Rob's voice and said no more. Rob was his best friend and the subject at hand was delicate at best, what with the way Rob acted whenever Sparrow was present.

"Fair enough. Stand and watch. It'll be an education for the two of you, I'm thinking."

Robert moved up behind Sparrow in the close stall as Will removed the mask and planted a wet kiss on Buttercup's lips.

Arianna was still in shock. Since her first glimpse of the *exotic strawberry mare,* as Rob called her, her stomach felt queasy. She wanted to turn and run, but when she felt Rob's hand on her shoulders, she knew she would have to stay.

She tried to relax. An impossible chore, what with Will peeling off his clothes and flinging them far and wide, the naked female helping him along, and Rob's hands pressing on her shoulders, his hot breath on the back of her neck. Will laughed when he was shed of his garments and playfully galloped around the stall like a stallion.

Arianna was astonished to see his manhood hardened to twice its normal size. She watched, helpless to look away as Will played with the girl, his hands moving over her large breasts, squeezing them and laughing when the nipples stood out taut and straight. She watched, too, as his hand slid down the girl's body,

26

disappearing between her plump thighs.

A strange feeling crept over her seeing that and it must have been the same for Buttercup, for she began to croon to Will at his touch, urging him on.

At the same time, Arianna felt something against the small of her back that hadn't been there a moment ago, something that seemed to grow and stiffen. Realizing what it must be, her heart began to pound.

All sense of time and place disappeared as she watched Will pull Buttercup to the ground, then fall on top of her. And when he began to move his hips, plunging in and out of her and making strange noises all the while, Arianna felt a tightening in her belly.

She had a sudden urge to move against Robert's hard body, and, unable to stop herself, felt her hips wriggle closer to him, pushing his hardness up against her. Rob's grip on her shoulders tightened painfully. Then suddenly, she was propelled forward.

When she regained her balance, Rob was gone.

She knew what he had been feeling. How could she help but know with his body up against her? And she knew she could never tell him the truth. Not after what she just witnessed, not after she realized what she could expect if she revealed her true identity.

Tears filled her eyes, and through their mist she saw Will pulling on his breeches and dismissing Buttercup with a pat on her round bottom. The naked girl wrapped a cloak around her and left, her horse's tail and mask still lying on the ground where they had been discarded.

Will pulled on his boots, thinking carefully of what he would say to Sparrow. As he stood up, he spoke. "Rob couldn't watch, hey? What are we going to do with him, Sparrow? Him and his . . . unnatural feelings for you?"

Moving closer, he saw the tears. "Hey, what's this? Are you crying like a female?"

Sobbing loudly, Arianna said, "Yes, like a female. Exactly like a female, for that's what I was born."

Will's expression didn't change as he reached out to cradle Sparrow's chin with his hand, tilting it up so he might gaze into her eyes. "Damned if I don't believe you. When I saw the way you looked at our naked strawberry mare it occurred to me you must be a female, but I quickly dismissed it thinking it too incredible. I don't understand. Why, Sparrow? Why have you pretended to be a boy?"

Freed from the lie she had been forced to keep so long, Arianna's sobbing grew even louder. "It wasn't my choice. My father made me dress like a boy to keep me safe from . . . your lecherous father and the terrible pox he carries."

A sad expression suddenly clouded Will's face. "So . . . that's it, is it? And here am I, following in his tainted footsteps even now, though I vowed I never would. God, Sparrow, I never realized before this minute how far I've sunk—how much like my father I am."

"Will, that's not true. You're not like your father at all. It's not too late for you. You've just turned seventeen. You've a long life ahead of you."

"And what of you, sweet Sparrow? Life is too short to deny yourself the love you so obviously feel for Rob, and he for you. Tell him—tonight. Put the poor man out of his misery."

Arianna wiped the tears from her eyes. "No, I can never tell him and you mustn't either. Not after seeing you with Buttercup. I don't want to be like her, mating on a stable floor. I want to marry the man I love and that's not possible with Robert. He's a nobleman and someday he'll be an earl. He can't marry beneath him. It just isn't done. I could never be more than his mistress and bear him bastard children. I won't live that way for anyone, not even Rob. Better he never know so I can be spared that fate. Do you understand?"

"Aye, I do, and it boils my blood to think of Rob wed to my harlot sister. He deserves a wife of pure thoughts and deeds to match his own. Though he's all of eighteen, the man is still a virgin. Can you imagine him married to someone who has slept with numerous men, and, still not satisfied, climbed into my bed as well?"

Arianna gasped in horror. "Will, you can't mean it! Surely Lady Judith would never sleep with her own brother."

"Your innocence shames me, little one. I wish it were not so, but it is. She seduced me when I was but fourteen and I've been doomed ever since."

"Oh Will, is that the sadness I see so often in your eyes? You mustn't blame yourself. You were too young to know what you were doing."

"Enough—I don't want to speak of it." Will forced a smile. "I've an idea I think you'll like. We'll go to my bedchamber and . . ."

"Bedchamber! Oh, Will!"

"No, no, that's not what I had in mind. I want to see you dressed as a lady. We'll borrow my sister's clothing, and . . ."

Arianna threw her arms around Will. "Your sister's clothing? Truly? A velvet gown trimmed with pearls or a dress made from cloth of gold? Yes, let's do it. Now!"

Will laughed softly. "Didn't I tell you you'd like my idea?" Grabbing Sparrow's hand, he pulled her out of the stall, through the stable and out the door, taking such long strides Arianna had a hard time keeping pace.

Arianna's heart raced as they sped across the courtyard to the castle entrance, then up the winding staircase to Will's bedchamber. She entered it with trepidation, jumping when Will closed the heavy wooden door behind him.

Her eyes darted to every corner, then lighted on the ornate canopy bed. A bed! A real feather bed. What luxury! Fear left her face as she gazed at the splendid trappings surrounding her and she ran to the bed to finger the rich coverlet.

Will laughed, seeing the awe in Sparrow's eyes. "Go ahead, try it out. Bounce on it if you wish. I'll be right back."

Making his way to a huge tapestry that completely covered a wall, he disappeared behind it.

"Wait—don't go. What if someone comes while you're gone? What if . . ."

Will poked his head out from behind the tapestry. "Be at ease. No one enters my room without permission. I won't be gone long. There's a passageway behind here connecting with Judith's chamber. We've used it ever since we were children."

"But won't she see you? How will you explain your need of her clothing?"

"She won't be abed yet. Not with Rob in the castle. They're probably walking in the moonlight at this very moment."

Will's words were not very comforting. After the scene in the stable, Rob would be vulnerable—easy prey for Judith. That thought made her restless and she walked over to the large arched windows and looked out at the night sky. Her eyes were soon drawn to the garden below. Was Robert there this very moment? Was he holding Judith in his arms, proving his masculinity to himself? Her eyes strained to see through the darkness, but she couldn't make anything out. Feeling a hand on her shoulder, she spun around.

"Here. Try this on."

Will held out a rich velvet gown of crimson trimmed with gold and Arianna felt weak in the knees. She had never seen anything so beautiful. "Ooooh, Will, you picked the perfect gown. I've dreamed of such as this every night of my life. I can hardly wait to . . . Oh! You . . . you'll have to help me. The laces on the gown and the cloths that bind my breasts. They'll, uh, have to be undone."

"So, that's how you've hidden your femininity, ha? Let's have a see." Will grabbed the hem of her shirt without further ado and before she knew it, the shirt was over her head and sailing toward the bed. Then, untying the strips of cloth impatiently, he began to unwind her bonds. "Poor Sparrow, having to wear these every day. It must be very uncomfortable."

When the last of the bonds fell from Arianna's body, Will sucked in his breath at the enchanting glimpse of her breasts before Arianna hid them from view with her arm. "With breasts such as that, 'tis a grave sin to hide them. Upon my sword, Sparrow, they're exquisite. You're exquisite. May I look upon them for just a moment? I promise not to touch them."

Arianna was moved by Will's fervent words and by the adoration she saw in his eyes — adoration of a male toward an attractive female. So that's what it feels like to be a girl! Swallowing hard, she nodded — wanting, needing to continue feeling so completely feminine. Taking a deep shuddering breath, her arm dropped to her side, revealing her breasts.

31

Contentment washed over her as she saw the reverent admiration in Will's eyes. For one brief moment she could glory in her femininity, could know what it felt like to be admired by the opposite sex. She would be sixteen in two days and for the first time in her life she could know how wondrous it was to be a woman.

Will turned his gaze to Arianna's eyes, forcing his hands to stay at his side. Though he wanted more than anything to touch her breasts, he could not betray her trust. "Thank you, Sparrow. You honor me."

Smiling shyly, she said, "My name is Arianna."

"Arianna . . . lovely, lovely, Arianna." His eyes moved over her once more, drinking her in for the last time before she covered herself with crimson velvet. And when the dress fell into place, he moved behind her to lace her up, his hands shaking a little.

Arianna felt the gown tighten. First at the waist, then higher and higher until her breasts were pushed upward. She could hardly breathe, but it didn't matter. Nothing mattered but the feel of the gown around her, the heavy weight of it, the sleek touch of it. She smoothed the skirt with her hands, then turned to face Will with an expectant smile.

Will stepped back to get a better look. "God have mercy on us all, Arianna. No man could resist you. No man on God's earth. No wonder your father hid you under boy's garments."

Arianna's heart swelled at Will's words and tears glistened in her eyes, falling to her cheeks when he produced a bronzed mirror and held it up.

She stared in awe at the image, her cheeks suddenly flaming as bright as her gown. Was that truly she? That beautiful young lady? "This is a dream, isn't it? I'll wake up soon and find myself dressed in breeches and shirt again. Oh, Will, I don't want to wake up. I don't want ever, ever to wake up."

Will gazed at the exquisite beauty, her face flushed with excitement, and gathered her in his arms. "I wish I could make it so, but even a duke's son cannot change the world in a day."

Lifting her head from Will's shoulder, she looked into his pale blue eyes. "Thank you, Will, for letting me have my dream, even if only for one night."

"One night? No, Sparrow, whenever you've a mind to, you can come to my chamber to try on Judith's clothes. Next time, the new violet dress, and pearls, yes, we'll weave pearls through your hair and . . ."

Arianna laid her head back on his shoulder, hugging him tight. "Lord William, you're a better man than you know. Someday you'll be the finest duke Norbridge has ever known." Will heard the trust and love in Arianna's voice and felt he could be that man. Maybe it wasn't too late.

Visions of herself in the beautiful gown flashed over and over in Arianna's head, making it difficult to fall asleep. When her brain wearied of images of crimson satin, it shifted to Will and the incredible moment when he gazed at her breasts. Her face flamed thinking of it. How brazen she had been, baring herself like that. Why had she done it?

Why indeed? Caught up in the magic of the moment, in that wonderful, soul-satisfying moment of feeling completely female, she could do nothing else.

And Rob, his touch so light and yet so potent at the small of her back, had stirred up feelings she had never experienced before, sensations only his touch could produce. Her heart ached for him, reliving the terrible moment when he had pushed her away thinking himself aroused by another boy. He was such a good and honorable person, how it must have shamed him! If only he could know. If only . . .

The euphoria faded like the morning mist, leaving her feeling dismal and alone. It was not to be. She could never belong to Robert—or to his world. Knowing that, she drifted off to sleep, escaping the pain that engulfed her, the pain that returned too soon in a vivid dream.

Robert sat tall and regal on his ebony stallion, dressed in silver armor that glinted brightly in the morning sun, almost blinding her. He looked down as she stood by the side of the dusty road and smiled at her forlornly before spurring his horse and riding swiftly away. She could hear the pounding of hoofbeats and the unmistakable clink of metal on metal as he rode. But instead of fading away, the sound grew louder and louder until it woke her with a start.

It wasn't a dream! She heard it still!

Running to the window, she looked out to see a column of men in armor riding by with Robert in the lead, dressed as she had seen him in her dream. Banners of blue and gold, held by knights on horses bedecked in colorful trappings, flew above them.

Hurriedly, she dressed in her boy's garb and ran outside, but it was too late. He was almost out of sight. He was gone and she never had a chance to say goodbye. She stood watching until they disappeared and would have stood there longer, but for the touch of her father's hand on her shoulder.

"So, Rose Petal, Lord Robert came to us a fledgling hawk and leaves a proud tercel. Did you see the way he sat his horse? He's a man now, with a man's responsibility. Word has come that his father had a bad fall from his horse and has died. Lord Warwick is now

34

the new Earl of Everly. 'Tis an awesome position, that, but he's a likely lad—he'll manage well."

Looking down, Peter saw the sorrow etched on Arianna's face. "Come, there are chores to be done. Hawks to attend. They have a need of you, lass."

Arianna moved with leaden feet, allowing her father to guide her back to the small cottage and over to the table where her mother set a bowl of porridge in front of her. She ate at Sybille's urging, but couldn't taste and could barely swallow. She was deep in shock and sorrow. Did he hate her after what happened in the stable? Is that why he didn't say goodbye? Couldn't he bear the sight of Sparrow anymore?

After breakfast, she went about her chores in the aviary, welcoming the familiar pungent smell and the satisfying sounds the birds made ruffling their feathers and scraping their talons on the wooden perches. Here she could forget about the cruel world that forced her to dress as a boy and kept her from living the life she desired.

Immersing herself in her work, she didn't hear the light, hesitant footsteps behind her until she felt a gentle tap on her shoulder.

Spinning around, she faced Buttercup, dressed now more suitably in the simple clothing of a milkmaid.

"I'm sorry. Did I frighten ye, Sparrow? I wouldna come, but I was told to give you this."

Arianna gazed at the object in Buttercup's hand and her heart beat wildly. "Robert's dagger! How did you come by it?"

"Lord Robert give it to me this morning . . . before he left."

"You were with Robert this morning? Where? In his bedchamber?"

Buttercup's mouth opened wide with shock. Blinking back tears, she cried, "It's not what ye think. I happened to be in the stable when he was saddling his horse. He told me to give it to you. I asked him if there was a message to go along with it, and he said no and that you would understand what it meant. That's all that happened, I swear."

Jubilant, Arianna took the dagger from Buttercup's hand and clutched it to her breast, not caring that it was a strange thing for a boy to do. Robert had said goodbye after all. He didn't hate her. He wanted Sparrow to know they were still friends. Tears sprang to her eyes and she turned away abruptly so Buttercup couldn't see them.

"Well, I'll leave ye be. I know you've got more important things to do than to talk to the likes of me."

Arianna heard the hurt in Buttercup's voice and turned to face her. "Buttercup . . ."

"You don't have to say nothing. I know what you must think of me, after . . . last night. But believe me, I'd a never done it in front of you if I'd a known you was a girl."

Arianna opened her mouth in amazement. "What? How . . ."

Looking down at the floor, Buttercup's bare foot shuffled restlessly through the coarse straw. "I, uh, didn't leave the stable last night, but snuck into the stall next to you and Lord William. Heard everything, I did. But don't ye worry. I won't tell a soul and I'll try and stay out of your way. I know how you must feel about me."

Arianna grasped Buttercup's hand. "Buttercup, I don't look down on you. How could I? We each must do what we must do to survive. I know how hard you work to help your mother with all the little ones, and no man to provide for them."

36

Buttercup's eyes welled with tears. "That be true. Me Ma drops babes as easy as a cat her kits. And each with a different father. I don't want to be like her, I swear. But the coins I get from men puts food on the table." Buttercup took the corner of her apron and dabbed at her wet eyes. "You don't know how many times I've started to run away. But where can I go? What can I do to make my way? I'm a milkmaid. That's all I'll ever be."

Brushing away her tears, Buttercup suddenly stiffened her back. "I've got to go. Time to salt the cheese."

Arianna reached out and touched Buttercup's arm. "It's all right to cry. You have reason enough. If you ever have need of a friend—I'm here. Remember that."

Looking deep into Sparrow's eyes, Buttercup saw she meant it and smiled shyly. "Thank you, Sparrow. I'll remember."

"Please—call me . . ."

"No. Don't tell me your name. That way I can never slip and give you away."

Alone in the mews, Arianna's jubilance turned to bitter sorrow. She was no better off than Buttercup. What use was it to dream over Robert when she could never know his love?

Chapter Three

Still thinking of her encounter with Buttercup,
Arianna entered the open door to her cottage and
stopped dead, startled at seeing a stranger sitting at
the table with her mother and father. The heads of
all three were bent close to each other; they were
speaking softly, but seriously, unaware that she was
there. Who was this stranger? Why did the scene
seem so secretive?

Before she could think further, a bundle of blue-
grey fur was at her feet, barking as if she were an
intruder.

The three looked up, startled.

Something *was* going on. It wasn't her imagination. To hide her bewilderment, she knelt down and
picked up the small dog, stroking its back and soothing it with her voice. "Where did you come from,
laddie?"

The stranger rose from the table and spoke, his
eyes staring at her intently. "I found him begging for
food on the long road from Nottingham."

"Truly? By the looks of him, I'd say he came from
a fine home. He's a Skye terrier, isn't he?"

"You know your breeds well. Yes, a Skye terrier,
but alas, not from a fine home. His owner, though,

couldn't be finer. He belongs to the Queen."

Arianna gasped loudly. "Queen Elizabeth?"

"Nay, Rose Petal," Peter answered. *"Our* Queen. Mary, Queen of all Scotland and the Isles."

"But how can that be, Papa? The Scottish Queen is in prison. At Sheffield, it's been said."

"Aye, that she is, but those terrible stone walls couldn't hold our little friend here. He escaped, brave lad that he is. Haven't you heard? The news was spread far and wide that whoever finds the Queen's dog may have a private audience in her chambers at Sheffield. My friend here was the lucky person to find him."

"Unfortunately, I cannot take advantage of the offer to meet the Queen of Scots, much as I'd like to see her again after so long a time. I have pressing business elsewhere and must take my leave. I've asked my old friend, your father, to fill in for me and return the Queen's favorite dog to her. He thought you'd like to go along."

Arianna couldn't believe her ears. A chance to see the Queen of Scotland in her private chambers was more than she could imagine. Hugging the small terrier tightly, she said, "May I, Papa? May I go with you?"

"Well . . . seeing as it's your birthday tomorrow, I don't see how I could say no. Not if I were to get a hug just about now."

Arianna set the dog on the floor and ran to her father, hugging him tightly. "Oh, Papa, thank you. It shall be the finest birthday present anyone ever had."

Peter laughed, filling the small cottage with the warm sound of his voice. "Now, my sweetest rose," he said, rising. "Meet my good friend, Mowsby. He was one of the Queen's personal guards, along with me. Mowsby, this joyous young person is my daughter, Arianna, though her garb would lead you to believe otherwise."

Mowsby hadn't taken his eyes from Arianna since she entered the cottage. He walked over to where she stood by her father's chair, his expression solemn. "My lady," he said, bowing low. Then, standing straight, he took Arianna's hand in his and kissed it.

Arianna was startled. He seemed so serious, treating her as if she were a real lady dressed in silks and satins. Then remembering the way she had felt in the crimson gown, she lifted her head, standing as tall as her small frame allowed, and accepted his tribute as if she deserved it.

Seeing her regal stance, Mowsby exchanged glances with Peter and Sybille, his face breaking out in a huge grin. "It seems I shall be leaving this animal in good hands. Ah, how I wish I could be there when you meet with the Queen. You must tell me all about it when next I travel this way."

Saying his goodbyes, Mowsby left, leaving Arianna with a thousand questions for her mother and father.

"Papa, were you truly one of the Scottish Queen's guards? You never told me that before, and how did Mowsby know where to find you after all these years?"

Peter sat down at the table and Arianna sat next to him on the wooden bench. In her enthusiasm, she didn't see the creamy white rose lying there until her hand brushed against it. "What a beauty," she cried, picking it up gently. "Where did

40

such a treasure come from?"

She lowered her head to smell the rose, noticing for the first time the drop of red that adorned its otherwise pristine petals. "Is that blood on the rose, Papa? How . . ."

"Blood?" Peter asked, feigning surprise. "So it is, so it is. Mowsby must have pricked his finger on a thorn. He brought the rose for your mother. Plucked it from some burgher's garden in Nottingham, I warrant." Peter hated to lie, but he had no choice. He couldn't tell her the ivory rose with the drop of blood was a secret signal to him from his beloved Queen—a signal he had awaited for a very long time. He looked at his wife for reinforcement and she nodded her head reassuringly, knowing the agony he felt at the pretense.

Arianna didn't miss the exchange between her parents, but said nothing. They were deliberately hiding something, but what? Why? What need to hide anything from her, their own daughter?

The little terrier jumped up on her lap and began licking her face, and Arianna forgot everything but the thought that she was going to meet the Scottish Queen. That . . . and one more curious thing: for the first time, her father had introduced her as a female. How strange.

Ivory chess pieces swam before Mary's eyes as she tried to concentrate on the game at hand. Moving her long slender fingers, she daintily clasped the white queen and slid it forward deep into the black queen's territory.

"I have you now," Edmund shouted, slapping his

41

knee vigorously and removing the white queen from the board. "I was hoping you'd do that, though in truth, I thought you too clever to make that mistake. You're not in your customary good form. Usually you beat me quite handily."

Mary glanced over at the handsome young man across from her and smiled brightly, praying he couldn't see the restlessness behind her eyes and the agitation she felt having to suffer his company on this of all days. "Mayhap, Edmund, you are getting better at the game, or I too old and feebleminded. Take your pick."

"Then I choose the first, for it would be impossible to believe such a vital, beautiful woman as Your Grace could be too old or feebleminded."

"Save your flattery for my sister queen, Lord Deveraux. I am told Elizabeth needs so very much of it, insecure as she is over her failing beauty."

"How unkind of you to say such a thing about your dear cousin, especially upon this day — her birthday."

"Is it September 7 again?" Mary asked pretending surprise. "In this place, and the other manors and castles I am forced to stay at in this inhospitable country, I lose track of the days. One is as bad as the next. Sad the days of chivalry are over, else some brave young knight would rescue me from Elizabeth's bony clutch." Mary spoke the words in a joking manner, but her eyes took in Edmund Deveraux's every blink, every muscle movement, looking for a sign that she might look to him for help.

A hard look came into his eyes and she knew before he spoke there would be no help from that quarter. Edmund was ambitious and a man rapidly gaining favor with Queen Elizabeth. He would never do anything to harm his standing. It wouldn't surprise her if he reported everything she said and did to the English Queen.

"I'm sure there are a few such chivalrous knights left, but they would be most foolhardy to commit such a treasonous act. Would you have their blood on your conscience, madame?"

Mary bit back the words she longed to reply. Yes, she thought, is not the blood of a queen more valuable than that of a mere knight's? She was saved from having to come up with an acceptable answer when a sudden cry from one of her ladies-in-waiting commanded her attention.

"Your Grace, there are two travelers on the road. Do you suppose . . ." Janet stopped suddenly, remembering Edmund.

Mary's heart caught at Janet's slip. Foolish girl. She hadn't been with her very long, hadn't yet learned to play the games necessary to survive with the perfidious English.

Mary, Queen of all Scotland and the Isles, stood and took on her queenly aura, turning toward Edmund. "My handmaiden is expecting company. A suitor, no doubt. Excuse me a moment while I take a look at the lad. I'm most curious to see what foolish man has captured her heart."

Mary walked slowly over to the arched window, aware of each step and of Edmund's eyes following her. She scanned the horizon until she made out the two riders in the distance. One, large and barrel-chested; the other, small and delicate. At last. After sixteen long years, she was here — Arianna, the daughter she had never known.

Mary watched as the two figures drew closer, tears glistening in her eyes at the sight of the graceful young lady astride her horse. Imagine, a Princess of Scotland riding that way! But then she, too, had ridden astride on many occasions, offending the delicate sensibilities of the ladies who escorted her. It seemed that Arianna took after her mother.

Or did she? How could she, raised by such simple folk. Curse the Scottish lords who imprisoned her first, not caring one whit that she was pregnant. There was no mercy in their souls, no mercy in Elizabeth's either. She had written immediately after the Scots had taken her, asking the Queen to intervene on her behalf, and how had Elizabeth responded? By offering—no, demanding—that she send her infant to Elizabeth after its birth so she might raise it as her own.

Mary's blood ran cold remembering that horrible day. Her child raised by that ice queen? While she rotted away in some dank castle? Never! In the end, she had fooled them all. She had not uttered one word, one cry, one moan when she was in labor. She held it all in so no one would know and come to take the baby and give it to Elizabeth. She would have killed the child before handing it over to that bloody Queen.

How ironic that the child should be born on Elizabeth's birthday. If Elizabeth had known she would have thought it an omen that she was meant to raise the child. But Mary wasn't born a Queen for nothing. She bore the pain in silence and after the babe was born and she had put it to her breast for a short while, her most trusted servant carried it out of the

44

castle in a basket, covered with clothing in need of mending, and gave it to Peter Trilby and his wife. It was several days before anyone but her ladies-in-waiting knew of the birth, and by that time the child was safe.

Mary watched as Peter dismounted, then helped Arianna down. She saw the protective way he watched over her as they made their way to the guard house. He had been the perfect choice to raise her daughter and had served her faithfully and without complaint all these long years. Whenever she was moved from one manor to another, one castle to another, he had picked up and moved his small family, too, so she could see her daughter on occasion.

But she was never any closer than the restricted and distant view from the window. On those rare occasions, Peter would ride by the castle slowly, without stopping, so no one would suspect Arianna was anything more than a burgher's child out for an afternoon ride with her father.

How she had yearned to hold her child in her arms! And now, thanks to a scheme she had carefully planned, she would finally meet her daughter face to face and no one would suspect a thing. Arianna would simply be the young woman who had found her lost dog and returned it for the promised private audience.

It was perfect. Her servant had carried the small dog out in a basket, just as Arianna had been taken away so many years ago. Then, Mowsby had taken the dog to Norbridge and handed it over to Peter. So simple — who would ever suspect?

No one but Edmund.

Damn him! Why had he chosen this day to visit?

It was Queen Elizabeth's birthday. Why wasn't he with her, where he belonged?

Edmund moved up beside her and saw the tears in Mary's eyes. Surely the sight of Janet's suitor could not have caused such emotion. Curious, he followed her gaze, seeing two riders at the castle gate. His brow furrowed until he made out the tiny form in the young peasant girl's arms. So that's it! Her precious dog has been found. Strange, he would never have thought the Scottish Queen so sentimental. How touching that she should cry with joy at its return. What an amusing story to relate to Elizabeth.

Realizing Edmund was standing beside her, Mary turned and favored him with a smile, forcing it to hide her true feelings. "As you can see, my petite babe is found. I've promised a private audience with the finder. Pray, leave me now, so that I may fulfill my promise."

Taking Mary's hand, he brushed his lips slowly over it. "As you wish, madame."

Edmund left the chamber without further ado, slightly irritated that he hadn't been invited to stay. But he would get the details later, of that he was sure. Flattery worked as easily on common women as it did on the highborn.

Once Edmund was gone, Mary called out to Janet to fetch her green gown. She would not receive her daughter in the somber black she wore every day. She wanted to look her best for what might possibly be their only visit. Arianna had no idea, of course, that she would be meeting her mother, but someday she would know and she wanted Arianna to remember her favorably.

She barely had time to dress before hearing footsteps echo along the corridor. Quickly, she sat on the window seat, posing serenely in the streaming sunlight. Clasped tightly in her lap, her hands shook slightly, the only visible sign that she wasn't completely composed.

Arianna stood in the doorway, holding the terrier in her arms and looking back to Peter for support. "Come in, come in, my dear. Don't be frightened. I'm made of flesh and blood, just like you."

Arianna stared at the vision before her, unable to move or speak. She had never seen anything so lovely in her life. The Scottish Queen was dressed in a velvet gown of forest green, embellished with pearls and gold, with delicate lace on the ruff at her neck and on her sleeves. Her hair was brownish red with streaks of gold to show it had once been much lighter. It framed her face like a halo, reminding Arianna of a painting of a beautiful madonna she had seen in a cathedral. Her eyes were golden, large and expressive, her face long and oval with high cheekbones that flamed with color. In sooth, she was a woman who would stand out anywhere, no matter her station in life.

Peter prodded Arianna gently, bringing her to her senses. Timidly, she stepped into the chamber and took a hesitant step forward. Seeing his mistress, the little dog immediately came to life and wriggled furiously, trying to get to her.

"So—you are the one to find my bonny dog. I would thank you if I thought you were going to hand him over to me, but by the firm grip you have on him, I fear you'll not give him up."

"Oh, no, Your Majesty. I mean, Your Grace, I

47

mean, no, I have brought your dog back to you. Here!" Arianna held the dog out at arm's length, afraid of moving any closer. The terrier became more and more excited. Her reach wasn't far enough. She would have to move closer. Taking a few more steps, she held the dog at arm's length again.

"Come closer, child. I won't bite, I promise you. You will come to no harm in my company."

"Yes, Your Highness," Arianna answered obediently, then stepped up close to the Queen's chair. "He's, he's . . . quite a nice little dog. I'm sure you missed him very much." Arianna placed the dog in Mary's lap, then stepped quickly back, curtsying as she had been taught.

The dog clamored for attention, and Mary absentmindedly stroked his back. But her eyes and mind were focused on one thing only: the sight of her daughter, Arianna. "Please — stay close, my dear. It isn't every day I get to visit with one so young and charming."

Arianna heard the catch in the Queen's throat and her heart went out to her, making it easier to forget her own discomfort. Feeling the cool touch of slender fingers on her own, a shiver went through Arianna. She had felt that touch before. But how? When?

With her free hand, Mary patted the seat beside her. "Sit. Keep me company for a while."

Arianna sat next to the Queen, her hand still held tightly — so tightly, Arianna felt the blood throbbing through her hand and the queen's as well, but she didn't mind. In some strange way, it was a comfort to her.

The Skye terrier, failing to attract his mistress's attention, climbed off her lap and sniffed around the chamber, contented to be home. Peter and Mary's ladies-in-waiting watched from the doorway, far enough away to afford mother and daughter a degree of privacy.

Peter's eyes were shining; he was deeply touched as he watched Mary and Arianna speaking quietly to each other, each looking into the eyes of the other with reverence and adoration. He hadn't been aware of how closely they resembled each other, but seeing them together, it was obvious. Even the timbre of their voices was similar, he thought, listening to their mingled murmur.

Dressed as she was in Sybille's simple dress, Arianna looked lovelier than he had ever seen her. It broke his heart that she was forced to wear boy's clothing—not for the reason he had given her, but to keep Queen Elizabeth from finding her. In all the long years the English Queen had been searching for Mary's daughter, she never thought to look for a boy. Arianna's masculine garb had served her well, protecting her from the English Queen.

It had been risky, allowing her to dress as a female today, but he had taken the chance so that Mary could see her daughter as she truly was. But to be safe he had waited until they were almost at Sheffield before he let her change, knowing there was little possibility of being recognized so far from Norbridge.

"And are you happy in your life, Arianna?"

"I . . . I'm happy—now—here with you, Your Grace."

Mary felt a tug at her heart. It was obvious the

49

child was not content. But then, how could anyone of royal blood be happy anywhere but where they were born to be? It saddened her to know she couldn't come to Arianna's aid, couldn't give her the heritage she deserved. A curse on you, Elizabeth, she thought bitterly. May you grow old and wrinkled, never feeling life quicken inside you. May you never cradle a child in your womb, never suckle it with milk from your breast, or feel its tender arms around your neck.

Mary reached up to touch Arianna's cheek, needing to give her comfort of a sort. "You must make your own happiness, my child. Life is too short, too uncertain to allow anything but joy and happiness to rule your life. I've always believed that, always acted on that principle, and though I'm locked away from everything I hold dear, I believe it still. My downfall came because of my high station. I've been a pawn all my life, no different from those on my chess set. Used by the French and English, even by my own brother for his greedy ends. But you, Arianna, you will never have to experience that pain. Take comfort in your simple life and you will be far happier than ever I was."

Arianna listened to the passion-filled words, hearing the pain and anguish in the Queen's voice. Joy? Happiness in a simple life? How could the Queen know anything of that? Even now, imprisoned, she had much more than Arianna could ever dream of having: servants to see to her every need, rich Turkish carpets under her feet instead of straw, and fine clothes and jewels instead of plain clothing. She went hawking when she wished, rode sleek horses over sculptured grounds, and was always surrounded by

50

people who adored her. No, this royal being could never know how miserable Arianna was in her simple life.

Arianna choked back a sob. Stop it!, she thought. Stop feeling sorry for yourself. This woman has lost more than you'll ever know. How can you compare your misery to hers?

Peter could see Arianna was about to burst into tears. Though she didn't know the Queen was her mother, she had to feel emotions she couldn't begin to understand. Mary, too, seemed close to the breaking point, overwhelmed by the emotion of being with her daughter. Soon she would be in tears and that mustn't happen. Arianna mustn't suspect there was anything unusual about this visit. "Forgive me, Your Grace, but we must leave soon. We have many miles to travel."

Mary looked up, bemused, focusing on Peter's beloved face. "Ah, Peter, I had quite forgotten you were here. Forgive me, but as you can see I was taken with my . . . your . . . daughter. Before you go, I would talk with you alone. Arianna, child, would you mind waiting downstairs? Better yet, go feed the swans by the lake. Janet will show you the way."

Arianna started to rise, but Mary stopped her. "Would you embrace me before you go? I crave the feel of youthful arms around me."

Strangely moved, Arianna circled the older woman's neck with her arms, a strong feeling very like homesickness sweeping over her. Suddenly she couldn't bear to leave this queenly woman, this motherly woman who held her so tight. But in a moment Mary's arms fell away and Arianna rose, her heart pounding. Tears welled in her eyes though she did not know why.

"I would give you a memento to remember me by." Taking a ring from her finger, Mary handed it to Arianna. "This ring was given to me by someone very special as a symbol of the love we shared. I want you to have it."

Arianna looked down at the ring and her eyes widened. It was gold with a perfect rose carved from ivory and set with a tiny blood-red ruby on one of the petals. The image of the rose Mowsby brought her mother flashed through her head. The ivory rose with the drop of blood!

"Your Majesty, I couldn't . . . it must be very precious to you."

"It is that. But it would give me great pleasure to pass it on to you. I know you would cherish it as much as I."

"Oh, I would, truly, but you may have need of it someday. It must be very valuable."

Mary laughed softly. "Do not worry so. I receive a pension from the French every year. I shall never want for anything. Take it, please."

Arianna curtsied prettily. "Thank you, Your Grace. I shall cherish it and . . . my memory of you . . . forever."

Peter led Arianna from the chamber, then returned alone as the Queen had requested.

In a daze, Arianna followed Janet down the stairs and out the huge armored door. She took the bowl of bread crumbs Janet offered and followed her directions to the lake. In an emotional state she couldn't fathom, she was glad for the solitude. She felt a heightened sense of awareness that set her nerves on end. Why had meeting the Queen left her feeling so emotional?

Hearing the sound of someone clearing his throat, she whirled around to see a handsome young nobleman observing her.

"Oh! You frightened me, my lord. I thought I was alone."

Edmund Deveraux's gaze swept over the young peasant girl with an appreciative eye. What a tasty morsel to warm his bed. "Beauty such as yours deserves an audience. It would be a pity to waste it on the swans." Sweeping his plumed hat from his head, he continued. "I'm Edmund Deveraux, at your service."

Arianna was amazed that a nobleman would introduce himself in such an intimate way. He obviously held some title, whether baron, earl or duke she could not say, but he chose to address her as a common burgher would.

"I've been visiting the Queen."

"I know," Edmund said, his eyes still roaming over her body. "I was with her when you rode up with her dog."

"Oh? Are you the Queen's friend or her foe? I mean to say, do you guard her or . . ."

"I'm merely a friend who visits her from time to time to entertain her and help her wile away the empty hours here."

"Forgive me for speaking boldly, sir, but 'tis doubtful any Englishman could be a true friend of the Queen of Scots."

"Hmmm, you speak like a Scots, and yet I hear no Scottish burr."

"It's been my fate to reside in this country since I

was a wee babe, but I am a Scots. Just like the Queen."

"More so, too, I'll wager, since your visit with her. Did she fill your pretty little head with dramatic tales of her beloved homeland? Did you know she, too, is a stranger to her own country? Her childhood was spent in France, not Scotland, and most of her adult life here in England as Elizabeth's captive."

Arianna's eyes sparked when she spoke, yet she kept her voice soft. She couldn't forget she was talking to a nobleman. "Neither was her choice, was it, my lord?"

"Touché! You've a sharp wit about you for such a young thing. A truce. Let's speak no more of countries or of queens. I would know more of you. I confess, you intrigue me. There's something about you . . . something familiar, and yet mysterious. What do you suppose it is?"

"Perchance you are not used to girls of my class, Lord Deveraux. Perchance you have been sorely deprived of that great privilege."

Edmund laughed heartily. "Perchance you are right. I would remedy that this very moment. Tell me, are you married? Betrothed? What lucky lads have you taken to bed? I would join their ranks."

Arianna was shocked by Lord Deveraux's bold words, and angry that he could presume so much. Is this the way peasant females were treated by noblemen? "Sir, be glad my father is not present or he would . . ."

"Or he would what? Dare strike a nobleman? I think not. Look—he comes. Tell him if you wish."

Arianna glanced over her shoulder and saw her father heading her way with their horses. As large

54

and strong as he was, he had never looked more vulnerable than at that moment. She would not risk harming him for anything in the world—least of all for this arrogant Englishman.

"Since I shall never see you again, I feel no need to involve my father."

"You are as wise as you are beautiful."

Peter made his way up to Arianna, eager to get her away from Edmund Deveraux. Mary had warned him how dangerous the man was. "Rose Petal, it's time to go. We have a long ride ahead of us before dark."

Edmund sized up the burly man, taking in his words. "Long ride, you say?"

Peter looked at the strutting peacock and felt a chill. "To Nottingham. Our home."

Arianna stared at her father in astonishment. Why did he tell Edmund they lived in Nottingham? Things were getting more mysterious by the minute, but she was relieved to know Lord Deveraux could never find her. "I'm ready, Father."

Turning to Edmund, she could hardly hide her smirk. "If you're in Nottingham, be sure to stop in. Like all good English folk, our door is always open to wayfarers."

Edmund was puzzled by the vixen's sudden change of mood, then the realization hit him: she had been attracted to him all along. She had been playing coy to spur his interest. "Thank you, I certainly shall. If you'll allow me . . ." Edmund locked his hands together and lowered them for Arianna's foot. He was rewarded with a flash of bare leg as he boosted her into the saddle. Yes, this Rose Petal was a tasty bit indeed, he mused.

Arianna dug her knees into the horse and started toward the gate. Then, remembering the Madonna Queen, she looked up to her window and waved.

Mary had been waiting, watching in fear as Edmund talked to her daughter. If he learned Arianna's true identity, he'd . . . but all was fine. Arianna was waving to her, riding away, leaving Edmund alone by the water's edge.

She watched until Arianna was out of sight, a terrible ache settling in her heart. Then, hearing someone sobbing loudly, she realized the sobs were her own.

Chapter Four

"She's gone. Come away from the window."

Mary Seton, the last of the four Marys who served her, guided the stricken Queen to a chair by the chess table. "Have some wine. It'll make you feel a wee bit bitter."

Mary glanced up at her beloved servant. "Do you really believe that? Do you really believe anything but freedom can make me feel better? For if I were free nothing under heaven could separate me from my children. Why has fate decreed that both James and Arianna be torn from my arms?"

Seeing the pain on her friend's face, Mary's voice softened. "Ah, but I shouldn't be taking it out on you or any of the devoted friends who have stayed with me all these years. It would have been a much lonelier world without you."

"Enough of this sad talk," Mary Seton said, sitting down at the table. "You have seen your daughter at last. Held her in your arms. Be happy for that, and proud of the beautiful young woman who shares your blood."

"I am that. Oh, yes," Mary said, patting her friend's hand. "Have you ever seen a lovelier lass?

And the way she opened up to me as if she had known me for years. It was a lovely visit, marred only by Edmund Deveraux. How frightening it was to look down from the window and see him talking to Arianna. If he ever suspected the truth, her life would be in danger. Oh, why did he choose this particular day to visit? You don't think he suspects . . ."

"Hush, don't even think it. Edmund was just being Edmund, flirting with yet another pretty young thing. That's all there was to it. Take your mind off such things. Phoebe, tell our Mary what you told Janet and me in the hall."

"I told them how much I thought Arianna resembled you when you were her age. And the way she moves—like a queen. Blood will tell, I always say."

"Ah, me, was I ever that beautiful?"

"Indeed you were. If you had not been born a queen you could have had any man of your choosing. That lovely you were."

"Choose? I never chose my husbands. I was a child when sent to France to marry Francis. Poor dear thing. If he had lived, my life would have been so different. As for Darnley, I can't bear to think of him. Such a frivolous fool."

"That may be true," Phoebe said cheerfully, "but you did choose Lord Bothwell for your third husband. At least you had your way then."

"It wasn't I who had my way, but he. Can you forget he raped me, then held me captive? I had to marry him to save my honor. What choice did I have? I thank fortune's star that barbarian is not Arianna's father, or that fool Darnley either.

Arianna was fathered by a man cut from finer cloth."

Mary heard a gasp from the three gentlewomen, and realized what she had said. "My dearest friends, I've wanted to tell you a hundred times, but couldn't, afraid of what you'd think of me. Now, after seeing my daughter full-grown, I want you to know."

Mary Seton stared at the Queen as if she had never seen her before. "You've kept this secret for sixteen years? I wouldn'a believed it of you. I've been with you since all five of us Marys were small children. Traveled to France with you and back again. I thought I knew everything there was to know about you."

"And now you do. My very last secret. I have no others."

"Tell us who Arianna's father is, Your Grace," Janet said eagerly. "I can't begin to guess."

"I doubt it not. Arianna was conceived at Sterling Castle, the night of my son James's baptism. You were there, Mary. You remember the terrible times I had before and after it. The baptism had been delayed so many times I despaired it would ever happen. Then, six months after James's birth, the date was settled. But still Darnley was being stubborn. He wanted to make it uncomfortable for me, you see, wanted to put a doubt in the minds of all who attended as to the parentage of his own son."

Janet's eyes grew large with excitement. "You don't mean it!"

" 'Tis true. There I was with a castle full of the most important personages of three countries, and he, fool that he was, decided to stay in his chambers, refusing to attend the celebration. It was a terrible time for me. I was still out of my mind with grief over the murder of poor Rizzio and completely disenchanted with my weak husband, and yet, I had to act the gay hostess to my guests. Lord Bothwell stood in for Darnley and acted as host, but it was most awkward, and Bothwell took his role too seriously, acting as if he owned me."

Mary paused and gazed into the eyes of each of her attendants, smiling sweetly. "And then, like a cool welcoming breeze on a hot summer day, Robert Dudley, Earl of Leicester, appeared. At the last moment he had decided to attend the celebration with the Earl of Bedford, Queen Elizabeth's official representative."

"The Earl of Leicester? Is he . . ."

"Yes, oh yes. My daughter's sire was lover to two queens."

"My God! If Elizabeth ever found out . . ."

"Find out? I made sure she did. Months later, after I had sought refuge from Elizabeth following my escape from the Scottish lords, and after she betrayed me most miserably, imprisoning me instead, I could contain my anger no longer. I had Lord Shrewsbury's son surreptitiously deliver a letter to Elizabeth. In it I told her the truth, that the child she had wanted to raise as her own, the daughter she would never lay hands on, was fathered by the man she loved most in the world. I'm told when she read the letter, she fell to her knees and pulled large clumps of hair from her head. In that way I had my revenge."

"You were very brave to tell her," Janet said, her young voice full of awe. "You were in her custody. She could have . . ."

"Had her own revenge? In sooth, she did. I've paid dearly for the letter I sent her, and my child pays, too. Why do you suppose she's kept me prisoner all these years? Not for the reason she proclaims to the world, but to avenge herself for my taking her lover to bed and bearing his child. It was no queenly act, but the act of a petty, jealous, barren woman. God in heaven! I pray she never discovers Arianna's true identity."

Later, when the candles had been extinguished and the others had fallen asleep, Mary lay awake looking out at the night sky, her mind reliving the day's events. She remembered every little detail of her visit with Arianna, every expression on her lovely face. And then, with memories stirred up that had been buried for years, she thought back to the night Arianna had been conceived.

It had been an unusually warm night for December, with a full moon lighting the sky. How glorious the castle looked with hundreds of candles making the great hall festive for the celebration. And how lonely she had felt, though surrounded by hundreds of people. She had gone to Darnley's chambers twice to beg him to come down for his son's christening, but he had refused. She would have to face the knowing looks and suggestive glances alone, an ever-present smile on her face.

Because she had worked so hard at it, she succeeded in turning the evening around and having a celebration worth remembering. Even the elderly statesmen had given themselves up to the gaiety and had taken part in the games that started late that night.

In a devilish mood, she suggested playing the game of *Fox and All After*, right there inside the castle walls. The Earl of Bothwel took her hand, proclaiming himself her partner, but she thwarted him. Weary of his possessive behavior, she decided to put him in his proper place and grabbed the arm of the tall, lean, and eminently handsome Robert Dudley, Earl of Leicester, declaring him to be her partner in the game. They would be the foxes, the others the hounds chasing them.

Leicester was as surprised as Bothwell at her move, but gallant that he was, he joined in. While the others waited in the great hall to a count of a hundred, she and the Earl ran away to hide. Mary smiled, remembering how she led Leicester to her own chambers—the one place in the castle no one was allowed to enter without her permission.

She hadn't planned it, but oh, how glad she was that it happened.

Closing the heavy door behind them, Mary had bolted it, then quickly locked the door leading to her ladies-in-waiting's chamber, too. Taking Leicester's hand, she led him to the window seat where they sat laughing and looking at the twinkling lights below. It was as if they were god and goddess, gazing down at the world they ruled.

"You don't mind, do you, Leicester, spending a little time in here alone? I'm afraid I needed to get away from everyone for a bit."

"Mind? How could any man mind spending time alone with a queen. A very beautiful one at that."

"Beautiful, you say? More beautiful than even your precious Elizabeth?"

Leicester smiled. He reached for her hand, bringing it to his lips. "Here, away from wagging tongues, I can say what I dare not say in public, lest Elizabeth hear. Yes, you are far lovelier than your cousin. And more, there is an aura about you, bright and full of life, that Elizabeth does not possess."

Mary was triumphant. For years she had pondered whether she was prettier than the English Queen. It was a topic discussed often amongst her attendants.

Jumping to her feet, she cried. "I knew it! I always knew it. That's why she has never met with me in person. She's afraid to see I am the greater beauty. She who treasures her beauty above all else."

Leicester stood up, remembering never to sit when a queen stands. "One of the reasons, I have no doubt."

"I would hear more," Mary said, grasping the Earl's hand. "Tell me. Is my hair more lustrous, are my lips softer and more kissable? I have a great need to know."

Leicester looked down at Mary's full lips and drew her closer, caught up in her excitement. "Your Grace, dare I . . ."

Mary saw the desire on his face and her breathing quickened. "Don't use that formal address, Robin. At this moment, I am merely a woman."

Leicester's face flushed with excitement as his arms reached out to pull Mary close, his lips coming down on hers in a kiss that grew more and more passionate.

Mary was unprepared for so bold a kiss. It sent her head reeling. No man had ever dared kiss her like that. When the kiss finally ended, she gasped for breath, then looked deep into his eyes, the brightest thing in the dark chamber. "God-a-mercy, I wasn't expecting that. I never knew a kiss could be so dangerous."

"Dangerous . . . and contagious, for I fear the passion of it has spread to parts of me I cannot long control. Mary, beautiful Mary, I must have more of your sweet lips."

Leicester crushed his mouth to hers again, slipping his tongue between her lips, searching, seeking, until she thought she would faint with desire. Pushing him away, she cried, "God's teeth, Robin, is that what it can be like—would have been like between us if I hadn't turned down Elizabeth's offer to have you as my husband? What fool I."

"What fool I, not to pursue you," Leicester answered, his hot breath against her cheek. "But Elizabeth told me you were deeply insulted at the offer, and I couldn't blame you. How could you want me, a man without a drop of royal blood?"

"That wasn't it, Robin. That was never it. The insult was that Elizabeth should deliberately offer me her cast-off lover. But I was wrong to think that, wasn't I? For she never cast you off, but loves you still."

"Aye. You misunderstood her motives, as the

whole world has. Her offer was the one truly unselfish thing she has ever done."

"Unselfish? Elizabeth? Never!"

"Yes — Elizabeth. If you remember, there was a time when she was going to marry me herself. When she decided never to marry, it bothered her that she had taken that high position away from me. To make up for it, she tried to replace what was lost with the throne of Scotland. She wanted the marriage *for me,* not to belittle you."

"If I had only known . . ."

"If I had only known how it would feel to touch you, Mary, hold you . . ." Leicester's lips brushed her cheek, then found the nape of her neck. He kissed her there, then moved down to kiss the exposed part of her breasts, while Mary's heart beat out of control and the ache inside her became unbearable.

"Robin . . . would it be so wrong . . . to pretend for just a little while . . . that we had married? That this is the bedchamber we share each night? I want to know, need to know what might have been."

"Oh, God, Mary, I . . ."

"No need to worry. The doors are bolted."

"God's teeth, Mary. If you only knew how much I want you, but . . ."

"Then don't waste precious time talking. Unlace me, strip away all evidence of a queenly nature and make me a woman naked as Eve to lie under you."

"Mary, lovely Mary, how can I deny you?" With shaking hands, Leicester unlaced the gown, then quickly dropped his hands, unsure of what would happen next. He watched in awe as Mary stepped out of the heavy garment, his chest heaving as she removed the rest of her clothing, slowly, one piece at a time, until she stood naked before him.

Overcome with emotion, he fell to his knees to pay homage, bending down to kiss one bare foot and then the other. Then, gazing up to her flushed and beautiful face, he murmured, "You are more than a Queen, you are a goddess, and I your grateful slave."

Taking his hand, Mary beckoned him to stand. "No, please, I would not have you that way. I have need of a masterful lover this night. One who can make me forget I'm a Queen, make me believe I am a desirable woman."

Scooping her up in his arms, he carried her over to the bed, then hesitating, set her down on the floor.

"Don't stop now, Robin. Don't leave me in such need."

Leicester laughed softly. "My boots. They don't belong in a Queen's bed."

Mary looked puzzled a moment, then laughed. She knelt down and removed his boots while he worked swiftly at unbuttoning his doublet. He flung it aside, and then his shirt, and was unbuttoning his velvet trunkhose when Mary stood again. Their eyes locked as he pulled off the rest of his clothing, releasing the last barrier between them.

Mary stared at him, her eyes ablaze with passion, taking in the wondrous instrument that would please her.

A murmur of voices, clearly perceptible in the air between Mary and Leicester, drifted into the chamber, from the hallway, growing louder and louder until the din was just outside the door.

Leicester was oblivious to all but the naked Queen. The beings on the other side of the door were inconsequential to his need, his great desire, to make love to this wondrous woman.

Mary heard the voices, too, and stared into Leicester's eyes afraid—not of the people outside her door, but that his passion would die because of them. Her eyes brightened at what she saw. There was no fear in Robin's eyes, no lessening of desire. Here was a man she could truly love, a man to admire for all time. Lesser men would quake in his tenuous situation, for if he were discovered naked in her chamber, he would surely die.

Leicester pulled her into his arms with a gruff noise and gave himself up to the moment—sensuously, gloriously—his hands caressing her body in a way that made her feverish with excitement.

In a moment they were on the bed, body to body, skin to skin, his hands moving freely over her. Here was a man who knew how to give her what she needed.

He entered her, hard and fast, making her blink at the strong thrust, then moved against her masterfully, in exactly the way she wanted.

A loud knock sounded on the heavy wooden door, and Bothwell's muted voice called out. "I know you're in there, Mary. Open the door this minute."

Mary laughed out loud, thrusting against Leicester with all her strength, and he reciprocated, using his body as he never had before, uninhibited and wild. They came together over and over, the passion between them building to a frenzy, their bodies slicked with sweat in the cool room. Rather than inhibit their lovemaking, the pounding of fists on wood increased their desire, increased the intensity of Robert's thrusts, until Mary thought she would die of ecstasy. When her release came, she cried out with pleasure, her voice unheard in the fierce pounding that resounded through the castle walls.

In that passionate act, a daughter had been conceived. She could never regret that or the ecstatic night with the Earl of Leicester — husband that might have been. For once, it had been her choice whom to love, her choice whom to bed, and knowing that had added greatly to her pleasure.

And . . . if she were to be completely truthful, deep in the dark recesses of her mind, she knew it had increased her pleasure knowing she was making love to the man Elizabeth loved most in this world. He had betrayed Elizabeth, her cousin, her sister Queen, to be with her. He had betrayed the woman who deigned never, even in common courtesy, to meet with Mary. And he had deigned to come to her son's baptism, though the child was next in line for the throne of England, as well as Scotland. For those reasons, and more, she could have no regrets about the Earl of Leicester.

Chapter Five

"You did it!" Arianna cried. "You convinced Judith to have the green gown made, even though she professes to hate the color."

Will stood in his bedchamber, holding the gown in front of him, an impish grin on his face. " 'Twas simple enough, after I told her the color transformed her eyes into priceless emeralds."

Arianna threw her arms around Will's neck, kissing him heartily. "Oh, thank you, thank you, thank you. It looks just like the one the Scottish Queen wore, truly it does."

Laughing, Will slapped her behind. "Well, you have it now, so what are you waiting for? Try it on. I have another surprise when you've finished."

"Another? Oh, Will. I need no other. You've made my dream come true." Arianna kissed Will once again, then took the gown from him and ran behind the tapestry to put it on. When she was ready she pushed the tapestry aside and stepped out, her mouth agape at the sight of the full-length mirror of Venetian glass that stood by the window.

"Oh, I never thought such a marvelous thing existed. Where did it come from?"

"Where indeed? I had it made especially for you. Now when you come to try on Judith's garments I won't have to break my arms holding that confounded heavy brass mirror. Does it please you, now that you can see yourself in all your feminine glory?"

"Please me? I don't know what to say. I . . . I'm overwhelmed." Arianna blinked back her tears.

"Here, enough of that. Turn around. Let me lace you up so you can see how beautiful you look."

Arianna spun around, her back to Will. "Lace me tight, really tight, so my waist is no larger than the span of a man's hand."

Will laughed joyously as he always did with Arianna. She was the one good thing in his life, the one person who could make him feel worthy. He enjoyed their times together in his chamber, away from Judith and his father, away from the rest of the world. Here he could relax and talk of things that truly interested him. She was his greatest friend.

"There—it's done. Let's see if it was worth all the trouble I went through convincing Judith that she needed this gown."

Arianna turned slowly and gazed in the wondrous mirror in awe, seeing herself as she never had before, from the top of her head to the hem of the green gown, and with no distortion. The image in the mirror took her breath away. She turned her gaze upward to Will's reflection in the mirror as he stood behind her. "Oh, Will, you'll think me vainglorious, but dressed like this, I resemble the Queen greatly."

Will's arms crept around Arianna's waist. "Vainglorious? No, sweet one, I think you're a fantastically feminine girl who desperately wants to burst from her male cocoon and become the beautiful woman she can be."

"Yes, I do. I . . ." Arianna froze. Someone was knocking at the secret panel behind the tapestry.

"Judith," Will whispered. "Go to the other end of the tapestry. Stand behind it. It's dark there and she won't be able to see you."

"Are you certain?"

"Yes—it's too dark to see anything back there. I'll get rid of her as fast as I can."

Arianna made her way down to the farthest edge of the tapestry and stood behind it, trembling. If Judith found her in one of her gowns, she would have her hands cut off.

Will unbolted the door and Judith pushed her way in. "Why is the door bolted? Do you have some little chambermaid in your bed?"

"Not anymore, love. She left hours ago. I simply forgot to unbolt the door afterward. What's wrong? Surely you're not jealous?"

"No, but I have news that shall evoke that very feeling in you. It seems I'll not be coming to your bed much longer, dearest brother. Before long, I'll be climbing into the bed of . . . my husband."

Will's heart lurched. "Who?"

"Who else but your dear friend Robert, the Earl of Everly."

"Is it under wax? When did you hear from him?"

"So, darling brother, it does bother you."

Will grabbed Judith's arm roughly, shaking her. "Is the contract under wax? Is it official?"

"Really, Will. I didn't think you'd be so upset. In sooth, I thought you'd feel some relief. You agonize so over our close relationship. No, it's not under wax yet, but will be in a matter of days. Father got word this morning that Robert was coming and that if conditions were favorable, meaning if he and I both still want this union, we will become betrothed."

"The fool. The bloody fool."

"Robbie's no fool. He knows very well what he will gain by our marriage. Father will be very generous."

"I'm sure he will. He's never denied you anything. But . . . truly, I wonder at Father's haste in seeing you married."

"What do you mean? I'm not overly young, to be sure. Only my devotion to you has kept me from marrying sooner."

"And because of my devotion to you, I want you to choose a man who can give you the most comfortable life."

"What do you mean to do, auction me off to the highest bidder? Really, Will. There is no need. Robert will do fine."

"Still, wouldn't you like to be able to pick and choose? Verily, I remember a time when you showed no interest at all in Robert."

"Before Father opened my eyes to the advantages of marrying him. I see no reason to wait any longer. But I must say, I'm pleasantly surprised to see how solicitous you are of my future happiness." Judith gave her brother a fond embrace. "You know, mayhap you're right. Mayhap I should entertain other young men as well. It would be beneficial for Robert to know he is not my only suitor. 'Twill help speed his decision. Now, if you'll excuse me, I've much to do before he comes."

In the darkness of the corner, Arianna stood frozen, her heart stricken. She heard Judith leave and let the tears flow unhindered. Robert marry Judith? Making love to her, sharing his life with her? It was too much to bear. She hadn't seen him since he left so suddenly two years ago, but her feelings toward him had not diminished. She wanted to die, to escape the pain that enveloped her heart.

Will came to her, pulling her out from behind the tapestry and taking her into his arms. "I know, I know. I feel the same way."

Comforted by Will's arms around her, she sobbed loudly, while Will patted her lightly on the back. "Oh Will, how can I bear it? How can I bear the pain?"

"You'll find a way, sweet girl. You'll find a way. But Rob, feel sorry for him. He deserves so much better. My God, he's still a virgin, saving himself to be worthy of his wife's love. He deserves a woman of impeccable virtue to match his own, not a whore like Judith who's slept with her own brother. He deserves a woman like you, Arianna."

"If only it could be. If only I had been born a noblewoman, I'd make him love me."

Will held Arianna away from him and stared into her eyes, his face lighting up as an idea came to him. Taking her hand, he pulled her over to the mirror and studied her reflection intently. "Yes, it will work. It can be. Arianna, you shall be a noblewoman. You shall win Robert's love."

"Are you mad? That's not possible, Will. You know that. I was born a peasant, and everyone knows such a . . ."

"*Sparrow* was born a peasant. But what does anyone know of Arianna, the exquisite lady in the looking-glass? We'll make up a story about your background.

73

Dressed as you are now, who would doubt it?"

"That's impossible. It would be too easy to disprove. What nobleman would claim me as kin?"

"None, to be sure, but no matter. We'll say you were born out of wedlock. Your father wanted to keep your identity a secret. Let's see, we can make you the daughter of an earl—no, a baron, harder to trace. A rich border baron who sent you to a convent to be raised. Yes, that'll work. You hated it there and escaped. Made your way here, where you sought refuge in my castle. Don't you see? You never have to declare who your parents are. We'll keep your background as mysterious as possible."

Arianna's heart constricted as the realization crept through her that it might indeed work. "Is it possible? But what reason would I have for coming to your castle?"

"Because . . . because you met me once. I treated you with kindness. I don't know. We'll make up some reason."

"You're forgetting one thing, Will. Rob may become betrothed to Judith right away. How could I possibly win him so quickly? He may not even be attracted to me."

"Not attracted to you? Even dressed as a boy he couldn't resist you. How could he resist you now, looking like an angel? No, that won't be a problem, but you are right about one thing: we'll have to move fast. The fool is liable to become betrothed to Judith right away. Unless . . . he meets you ere he comes to the castle."

"What? How?"

"Leave it to me. You have only one task at hand— to look as lovely as you do this moment. I'll have a

74

gown made up for you right away. You can't wear one of Judith's. White, of course, and a white steed to ride. Aren't you glad you listened to me and let your hair grow these past two years? You'll not have to hide it under your hooded jerkin anymore, or stuff it in your cap. You can let it flow free, a golden mane to frame your beautiful face."

Arianna's hands flew up to feel her hair. It wasn't nearly as long as it had been when she was fourteen, but now it did reach below her shoulder a goodly length. "Oh, Will. Is it possible? I want to believe you so much. But how can I, such an innocent, compete with a woman who knows well how to use her charms? I've had no experience in that at all, wrapped in my masculine clothing."

"Don't you know your very innocence is your most powerful weapon? Combined with the beauty of your face and form, 'tis potent indeed. Add to that the story of your being raised in a convent, and Rob will think your seductive ways are utterly without guile."

"Seductive ways? What do you mean?"

"I mean, you must use your body to entice him. Favor him with a glimpse of your exquisite breasts or legs — in seeming innocence, of course — and . . ."

"Will! You can't be serious!"

Will shook his head slowly. "I see the few short days we have till Rob comes must be spent instructing you in the art of seduction. But, 'twill be time well spent."

A week later, Arianna sat sidesaddle on a white stallion, dressed in a simple but elegant white velvet gown. Robert's entourage had been spotted and he would be coming along the road at any moment.

She looked around guiltily, as if expecting Judith to jump out at her from the woods at any moment. In front of her was the road to the village and beyond that Norbridge Castle, sitting high on a lush green hill. The scene was tranquil, but still her heart beat wildly. After two long years she would see Robert's familiar, beloved face, but he would be seeing a stranger. How odd that felt, knowing he would gaze at her as if he had never seen her before.

"This is it, Arianna. Are you ready?"

"No. I feel ill at ease in this ridiculous saddle. I'm not used to riding like this, Will. How do women do it? Riding astride is so much easier."

"Get used to it, milady. It's the way you'll be riding from this day on."

In the distance, Arianna heard the pounding of hooves and the unmistakable clinking of armor. Breathless with anticipation, she whispered, "Will, I'll never be able to remember everything you've taught me. He'll see right through me."

"He'll love you at first sight," Will replied as he gazed admiringly up at Arianna. Garbed in white velvet, unadorned and uncorseted, she had an air of exceptional natural beauty and innocence. How could any man resist? How could any man help but fall in love with her? God knows he'd fallen in love with her himself. Seeing the fear on her face as the horses drew closer, he called out, "Forget everything I've taught you. Be yourself and he can't help but love you."

As the pounding of hooves grew louder and louder, Arianna's heart kept time with every beat. Gripping the mare's mane, she cried, "I can't do it, I can't . . ."

"Too late," Will cried, slapping her horse's flank. "Hang on, your ladyship! You have a date with destiny!"

The horse bolted and Arianna had all she could do to stay in the saddle as it burst through the trees onto the road, right in the path of Robert's entourage. She pulled hard on the reins, trying to stop the animal before it collided with the others. The horse reared, spilling her onto the ground.

The impact knocked the wind out of her and she lay aching all over, gasping for breath. She started to rise, then sank back to the ground, giving into the pain that swept over her.

Before she knew it she was surrounded by men, and Robert was pushing his way through them to reach her. Kneeling beside her, his words echoed through her heart. "My lady, are you hurt?"

Arianna lifted her head and gazed into the eyes of the man she loved. Tears spilled down her cheeks at the sight of his beloved face, ten times more handsome than the last time she saw it. He was a man now, without a doubt, with a man's build and stature. And mayhap . . . if the gods decreed it . . . he would be hers.

Chapter Six

Robert gazed at the angelic face and his head jerked back as if struck by a blow. Here was the one he had been waiting for, the one for whom he had been saving his passion.

And she had been well worth the wait. Just gazing at her made him weak, and yet, it wasn't her beauty alone that devastated him. It was much more, though he couldn't fathom what it might be. He knew he had never met her before, and yet . . . he felt a closeness he couldn't explain. "My lady, are you injured?"

Tears spilled down her cheeks as she heard Rob address her as a lady, and she began to sob loudly from relief and joy at seeing him after so long a time.

Robert was deeply distressed by the tears and wanted to pull her into his arms, but that would be unseemly. "I beg of you, my lady, tell me where it hurts. I have a physician with me. He'll . . ."

"I have no need of a physician, sir. It's only that I am so happy to be rescued. I've been riding for two days, trying to find the castle of Lord William Ludlow, son of the Duke of Norbridge, and despaired of . . ."

"Will? You know Will? You've been traveling to see him? But surely you're not alone. Where is your entourage?"

"I am alone, sir, but please, don't make me speak of it."

Robert knew something terrible must have happened to her, and that thought bothered him greatly. He had a strong urge to protect her, and protect her he would. "You're in luck, my lady. William's castle is but a league down the road. I shall be happy to take you there."

Arianna smiled shyly, lowering her lashes. "I am most grateful to you, sir, but who do I thank for this kindness?"

"Forgive me for forgetting my manners. I'm Robert Warwick, Earl of Everly, and great friend to William. And you are . . ."

"I dare not tell you my full name, but you may call me Arianna if you wish."

"Arianna. A lovely name for a lovely lady." Robert took her hand in his and kissed it softly, astonished at the heat he felt in his groin at her touch. Who was this mysterious woman? "If you'll allow me, I'll carry you to my horse."

Reaching beneath her, Rob picked her up and carried her toward his horse, feeling her arms tighten around his neck. Her face was so close he could taste her breath. She looked up at him trustingly, innocently, her eyes still shiny with tears.

He staggered, not from her weight, for she was light as goose feathers, but from the thrill her closeness brought to his heart. Sitting her on his horse, he climbed up behind her, knowing in advance how good it would feel. He wasn't disappointed. Circling her waist with his hands, he picked up the reins and started down the road.

His body rubbed against hers with every swaying movement of the animal beneath them, putting him into a state of excitement he had a hard time containing. Who was this woman to make him feel this way? He despaired of ever being attracted so strongly to a woman, and it was a relief knowing that after his strong attraction to Sparrow, he could feel that way about a female.

"Arianna, what circumstances caused you to travel alone? If you have need of a knight, I beseech you to call on me."

"You're very kind, but I'll be fine once I've reached Norbridge Castle. Will shall offer me the protection I seek."

A pang of jealousy shot through Robert and for the first time in his life he resented his friend. What was she to him that she should trust him so deeply? He couldn't bear it if she belonged to Will or to any other man.

"Then ask me to be your friend and I will most sincerely do so."

"Lord Warwick, you are very gallant. If ever I have need . . ."

"Please, call me Robert."

"Robert." Sighing with happiness, Arianna leaned back against his broad chest, utterly content.

"Are you feeling faint?"

Realizing the too-familiar way she was leaning on him, she stammered, "Yes, I . . . feel weak with thirst and weariness."

"Then put all your weight against me. I'll not let you fall. See there, ahead. We have but a short distance to go. Will is riding out now to meet us."

Arianna watched as Will rode up. He must have cut through the woods to come out ahead of Robert's party. She saw the wide grin on his face when he saw her ensconced in Robert's arms.

"Robert, you mangy dog, you're here at last," Will shouted. "It's been too long. And who is that with you? Arianna? Can it be? How do you come to be with Robert? I didn't know the two of you were acquainted."

Arianna couldn't help smiling at Will's act and she put herself into her part. " 'Tis a long story, Lord William. One I prefer to relate to you in private."

"I understand. Arianna, I can't tell you how happy I am to see you again. I despaired it would ever happen, what with you being in the convent so long."

Robert's brow lifted. Convent? This beautiful woman in a convent? What a sweet innocent angel. She most certainly had need of his protection and he would make sure she had it.

"Please, Will, don't speak of it. No one here knows my story. I would have it that way."

"Of course. As you wish."

Hearing the murmur of voices, Arianna looked up to see they were on the narrow street leading to the castle. Clusters of people had gathered to watch them parade by. From the corner of her eyes she saw her father and the shocked look that crossed his face when he saw her. She had told him of her plan the day before and he had forbidden her, telling her it was too dangerous. She had pretended to concede, knowing if she didn't, he would find a way to stop her. Now, seeing the look on his face, she felt sick at heart. It was the first time in her life she had deliberately disobeyed him.

In a moment they were over the drawbridge and through the gate, coming to a halt in front of the castle door. A large gathering of men and women on horses were waiting there. Arianna's heart began to race and she suddenly felt numb with fear. How could she get away with her act in front of all these people?

Robert called out to the Duke. "I knew you were ex-

81

pecting me, sir, but I never expected such a large welcoming party."

The Duke laughed heartily. "To be sure, you deserve a large welcome, but in sooth, we were about to depart for my hunting lodge. But happy I am to see you safely arrived." The Duke lifted an eyebrow and his voice took on a knowing tone. "But I never thought to see a sweet damsel in your arms. Have you forgotten the purpose of your visit?"

Arianna's heart beat wildly. The Duke looked at her attentively and she was suddenly afraid.

Robert stammered, suddenly unsure of himself. "Certainly not. This lady was in distress. I was merely escorting her here. She . . ."

"What Rob is trying to say, Father, is Lady Arianna is my guest. She was on her way to see me when she fell from her horse. Rob found her just moments before I arrived."

The Duke's face lit up. "Your guest, my boy? Ah! How delightful. Welcome, my lady. My house is your house. 'Tis sad I am that I must leave before we get acquainted, but I'm sure we can make up for that when I return."

Arianna felt the color drain from her face. This was the man she had been avoiding for the past four years, the lecher she hid behind boy's garb to avoid. She suddenly felt faint.

Sensing her uneasiness, Robert dismounted and reached up to lift her down. Her leaden feet touched the ground but her knees gave way, buckling under her.

Robert felt her crumple, and scooped her up quickly. "Fear not, little one, you're safe in my arms." With one great stride he carried her through the castle door, oblivious to the shocked murmurs of the spectators.

Judith's face turned to ice when she saw Arianna on

Robert's horse, and when he lifted her in his arms and began carrying her into the castle, she was enraged. She watched in astonishment as he strode past her without so much as a glance in her direction.

Robert climbed the winding staircase, taking the steps two at a time, then made his way down the hall toward the bedchambers. Will followed closely behind. He had a hard time hiding his jubilation. His plan was working beautifully, so far.

"Put her in my chambers, Rob. I'll find another place to sleep." Will ran ahead to open the door, standing aside as Robert strode in and placed Arianna on the bed.

"Will, get some water for Arianna and ask my physician to come up and tend to her."

"Right away." Will hurried out the door and down the stairs, happy to leave Rob alone with Arianna. He walked over to where Judith still stood, by her father's horse.

Judith grabbed his arm. "Who is she? How dare Robert bring another woman to my home."

"Judith, calm down. Arianna is a friend of mine, not Rob's. She came to me for refuge. Rob is just being the gallant knight he has always been."

"Is he up there with her alone?" she cried, her tone escalating. Looking around frantically, she spotted Buttercup walking by. "Buttercup, get up there and tend to Will's guest. Immediately! And don't leave Lord Warwick alone with her for a moment."

"But milady, I'm not a chambermaid."

"You are now!"

Buttercup couldn't believe her luck. A chambermaid. Wait till Ma heard.

Will chuckled to himself. This was getting interesting. "Buttercup, bring water up to Lady Arianna, and a wet cloth to wipe her brow. While you're at it, you might as well bring her some bread and cheese." There, he thought with a smile. That ought to keep Buttercup occupied for a while. Now to keep Judith in the same condition. "If I were you, Judith, I'd take that hateful look off my face and make myself beautiful for Robert."

Ignoring Will, Judith said, "Father, speak to Will. Tell him to remove that woman from the castle. She'll spoil everything."

The Duke of Norbridge looked at his children with a knowing smile. "Now, now, Judith. If the young woman is Will's guest, we shall have to be kind to her. After all, it's not every day a pretty little thing like that comes calling."

"You men always stick together. Well, I won't have it. I don't want her here."

"Judith, you have nothing to fear. Arianna is here to see Will. I'm sure, hot-blooded male that he is, he'll keep her occupied. Isn't that right, Will?"

"To be sure. And Judith, Robert is no fool. He'll not seek a baron's daughter when he can have a duke's. A beautiful one at that, I might add."

Judith looked at Will warily. It wasn't like him to use flattery so freely. What was he up to?

Upstairs in Will's bedchamber, Robert gazed down at the lovely creature on the bed, her hair splayed out like a golden halo, surrounding her perfect face. And her eyes, yes, her eyes—so blue, shimmering like sunbeams on an azure lake, looked up at him so trustingly, so innocently, he wanted to take her in his arms and protect her from the world. Those eyes reminded him of someone, but for the life of him he couldn't think of who. Surely he would remember a pair of eyes like that.

Groaning a little from the pain in her bruised back,

Arianna sat up and swung her legs off the bed. "Thank you for your chivalry, Robert, but really, I'll be all right now. No need for you to stay and tend me. Will will be back soon with water."

Was she dismissing him already? When all he wanted in this world was to be with her. "My lady, it pleasures me to wait upon you. I am merely a mortal man, after all, and take great joy in the company of so beauteous a lady."

Arianna nearly fainted with pleasure at Rob's sweet words. So this is what it was like being a lady. Heaven, sheer heaven. "Please, sir. Remember I've spent my life in a convent. I'm not used to such attentions from men. I fear I shall blush if you say any more."

Kneeling down on one knee, Robert took her hand in his, feeling the heat in his groin once more. "Forgive me, Arianna, but every man who gazes upon you will speak the same. I pray, in your sweet innocence, you are not taken in by their flattering words and allow them to take advantage of your innocence."

"Oh, sir, does that mean I should be wary of your flattering words, too?"

"Never of me, Arianna, for I shall be your sworn protector." Robert pressed his lips to her hand, kissing it fervently. Hearing the door open, he jumped to his feet and straightened his doublet.

Buttercup peeked her head in the door. "Is it all right to enter, your ladyship? I've brung your water, like Lord William asked, and some food to eat."

Arianna smiled to herself. Buttercup! What was she doing acting like a ladies' maid? "Yes, please come in."

Buttercup walked toward the bed on wobbly legs, her mind in a whirl. She had no idea of how she was supposed to act. Concentrating hard on juggling the wooden tray, she didn't see the lady's face until she was

85

halfway across the floor.

"Lor'! I don't believe it!" The tray went crashing to the floor. "Forgive me, Sp . . . I mean, your ladyship. This be my first day as a chambermaid." Kneeling, she retrieved the bread and cheese from the floor.

"No need to apologize. I understand well. This is my first day as a lady. I've come from a convent, you see," she said pointedly. "We shall have to learn from each other."

Standing up, Buttercup looked from Sparrow to Lord Warwick, then back to Sparrow. "A convent? I see. Yes, I understand. Here—" she said, wiping the bread and cheese on her apron, then thrusting them into Arianna's hand. "Eat, whilst I go fetch another goblet of water and a rag to clean up the spill."

Buttercup ran from the room before her giggling could give her away. Sparrow a lady? If she hadn't seen Sparrow dressed as a lady once before, in this very chamber, she'd never have recognized her. She'd gone to Will's chamber on an errand for the Duke and when Will let her in, Sparrow had stepped out from behind the tapestry dressed in one of Lady Judith's best gowns. What a shock it had been seeing her like that, and how happy Sparrow had been, her eyes lit up like evening stars.

Will had been shocked, too, that Sparrow would reveal herself to Buttercup dressed like that, until Sparrow had assured him she was already in on their little secret.

It thrilled Buttercup still, remembering the way Will had looked at her then, respect showing in his eyes for the first time. She was no longer the tart in the stable, the erotic strawberry mare, but a woman who could be trusted with important secrets. And now, she would be sharing yet another secret, Sparrow becoming Lady

Arianna. To what end? Why, to marry Lord Robert, of course. How thrilling!

Robert looked at Arianna with a puzzled expression. "Why did you tell Buttercup this was your first day as a lady?"

"Because in truth, Robert, it is. Raised in a convent as I was, I was given no special privileges, but treated like everyone else." Moving to a small table by the window, Arianna set the bread and cheese down.

Rob watched the graceful way she moved and was enthralled at the sight of her uncorseted form. "Did you dress as you are now in the convent?"

Arianna looked down at the white velvet she wore. "I hesitate to tell you, sir, but I stole this lovely garment from a noblewoman on a retreat at the convent. I had no choice. I wouldn't have gotten very far dressed in my habit. They were searching for me everywhere. Oh, I cannot talk of it."

"God's blood! I can't bear this. What monster pursues you so relentlessly? Who is it who would treat you so ill? Tell me his name and I will seek him out and slay him."

"No, please. I want to forget my past. I beg of you not to speak of it again. It makes me ill. Oh, I suddenly feel faint." Arianna's arm went to her forehead, and she began to sway back and forth. In an instant, Robert's arms were closing around her.

"Arianna, I . . ." Robert felt the shock wave of excitement shoot through his body, and his lips came down on hers. The softness of her mouth excited him even more than he expected and he wanted to sink into her, become part of her.

Arianna drowned in his kiss and the incredible sensation that swept over her. This was what she had been dreaming of for so long. She wanted to stay locked in his embrace forever. Her arms went around his neck, needing to feel him closer. Then she remembered who she was supposed to be and released her hold, pushing him away. She was a lady—she couldn't act like the wanton woman she so desperately wanted to be.

"Please, Robert, surely you don't treat other ladies so disrespectfully. Have I done anything to invite such attentions? Tell me, please, so I may change my ways. I don't want other men to misunderstand."

"Forgive me, Arianna. I don't know what came over me. Believe me, I mean no disrespect. You've done nothing wrong. It's just . . ."

"Yes?"

"Just a surplus of affection that I feel, felt, for you. Will you forgive me?"

Arianna lowered her lashes. "If you can forgive me for being so ignorant of worldly ways."

"Sweet lady, don't apologize for being so innocent and pure. I admire you all the more for it."

Arianna closed her eyes, feeling suddenly sick. How could she go on playing this deceitful game? It was beneath contempt. Robert was too good for her; she would never be worthy of his love. "Robert, I . . ." Hearing the swish of taffeta, she opened her eyes and saw Judith walking toward her.

"Ah, there you are, Robbie. I've come to take you away, you bad boy. You've neglected me long enough."

Arianna watched as the raven-haired woman undulated toward Robert, and her resolve returned.

She had a noble mission: to save Robert from marrying this evil woman.

And she would do whatever it took to accomplish that goal.

Chapter Seven

From the balcony overlooking the great hall, Arianna gazed at the proceedings below, eagerly drinking in every detail to preserve it in her memory forever.

Torches were lit in every corner of the hall and servants could be seen scurrying to and from the table seeing to the needs of gentlefolk and commoners alike. Silver goblets, filled to the brim with wine and mead, were held in ornately adorned hands.

Long, empty benches lined the wall while supper was being served, to be used later when the planks were taken from the table to make room for dancing. Hugging herself with excitement, her heart soared at the thought that this could be her world!

Arianna's gaze skimmed past the faces of the people gathered at the long table. She was searching for Robert, and found him seated next to Judith. She had expected that, but she hadn't expected to see him looking so wonderfully masculine and yet so elegant, dressed in soft gray velvet touched with gold. He looked for all the world like her vision of Sir Lancelot and her heart ached looking at him, knowing him to be every bit as noble as that fabled knight.

Suddenly skittish, her gaze shifted to Will, needing to know he would be there for her if she made a wrong move, and her hand automatically smoothed the skirt of her new gown. Will had brought it to her earlier in the day, declaring it was made especially for her. It was a beautiful taffeta done in a delicate shade of pink called 'lady blush', and was so feminine in detail and design it fairly took her breath away.

Will looked up just then and caught her eye. "Lady Arianna. Join us, please."

All heads turned to look up at her.

This was it. Gathering her courage, she started down the stairs.

Instantly, the room became silent except for the rustling of her taffeta skirts as she glided down the stairs, her eyes locked with Robert's a seemingly endless distance away. She knew she was the center of attention; and she knew, too, that the way she conducted herself would determine how she was treated henceforth. But how could she convince others when she still felt caught up in an impossible dream?

Remembering the Scottish Queen — still regal, still courageous after years of being locked away — she was imbued with the confidence she needed and was transformed. She stood taller, her chin high, taking on the aura of a princess royal.

Robert watched Arianna glide down the torchlit stairway and across the floor, an angel with the bearings of a queen. A large lump formed in his throat and he knew without a doubt this was the woman he wanted to be with for all eternity. Because he knew it, he was suddenly afraid. Afraid he could never have her. Afraid she would not love him. Afraid if she did love him, he would somehow lose her. For the first time in his life he felt vulnerable.

The men at the table rose as one when Arianna drew close; two young knights moved quickly to her side, escorting her to the chair between them.

"Will shall have to share you with Sir Lionel and Sir James tonight," Judith said sweetly. "But don't despair — their company is quite charming."

Arianna had underestimated Judith's cleverness. Obviously, Judith had arranged for these two young knights to keep her occupied and away from Rob. There was nothing she could do about it but smile and go along.

Arianna glanced over at Will, hoping he would somehow help her, but he didn't seem perturbed by Judith's ploy at all. In fact, he seemed quite pleased. But why? From her vantage point she could not talk to Rob, let alone work her wiles on him. Did Will think the fond attentions of James of Fotheringay and Lionel of Tutbury would make Rob jealous? Was that the game she was to play this evening?

As the meal progressed, Arianna became more relaxed in the young knights' company. They were indeed charming, spending the evening close by her side, flattering her shamelessly and speaking to her in low intimate voices so no one else could hear. They treated her as if she were a princess and she enjoyed every minute.

From time to time she would lean back in her chair to gaze beyond everyone's backs in Robert's direction invariably finding him doing the same to her. Those few intense glances reassured her Rob was more than interested, for his face held a look of such desire it made her ache to touch him.

Judith devoted her attention to Rob, laughing gaily at everything he said and leaning against him coquettishly until Arianna wanted to choke her. How could Judith and Will be so different, fathered by the same man? And how could Judith seduce her own brother? She shuddered suddenly, conjuring up the image of Robert married to that evil woman. She couldn't let that happen.

When supper was finished and the table cleared and dismantled, the dancing began. Arianna watched as Judith rose, taking Rob's hand and pulling him out to dance with her. How was she going to separate Judith and Robert?

"Lady Arianna, I would be honored if you would dance with me," Sir Lionel said, rising.

Forcing her attention back to the table, she realized what Lionel was saying and quaked. What did she know of these fancy dances? She had seen them before, of course, had even memorized the steps, dancing by herself in the forest. But never had she danced to music or with other people. Will had not thought to instruct her, so intent had he been on his ultimate goal. But then, this could be the opportunity she had been waiting for.

"I fear my dancing shall be clumsy, unused as I am to such a frivolous activity, but if you are still game, then I shall attempt not to make a fool of you."

"Ah, fair lady, if you dance half as pleasingly as you walk, 'twill be an enchanting sight to behold."

Arianna blushed at Lionel's words and took the hand he held out to her. He led her to join the other couples waiting for the music to begin.

Two lines were formed the length of the hall, men on one side, women on the other, and when the music started, Arianna was surprised to find she could manage the steps quite easily. Giving herself up to the music, she forgot about being nervous and danced around the hall in happy abandonment, enjoying the lively interplay.

Rob watched the bewitching creature, fascinated by her every move. He couldn't take his eyes from her. Her body swayed to the music so seductively and yet at the same time so innocently, his reactions to her kept changing from sensual intensity to child-like delight then back again.

"Robbie, did you hear me? I said you keep missing a step. Stop making a fool of me."

Rob reluctantly returned his attention to Judith and

tried to concentrate on the steps, but hearing Arianna's laughter, his eyes were drawn to her once again. Did ever such a woman as this walk this earth? He was privileged indeed to be in her presence and vowed he'd earn the right to make her his.

Aware of Rob's constant attention, Arianna looked across the room at him through fringed eyelashes, her stomach tightening at the sexual tension she felt. Was ever a man born as handsome and desirable as he? He had grown quite tall in the two years since last she saw him, and his body had filled out quite wonderfully. His lean profile contained the grace of a panther.

Smiling shyly when he nodded to her from across the way, she lowered her gaze, afraid he'd see the hunger in her eyes. *Dear God, if you let me have Robert, I'll be the best wife any man ever had and I'll never lie again or pretend to be anyone but myself.* Then, fearing that was not enough, she added, *and I promise to say my prayers each night before bed.*

The music suddenly ended, as if God had wished it so that he might better hear her prayers, and she looked up to the ceiling as if expecting to see his awesome visage staring down at her.

"What is it, my lady? Are you ill?"

Lionel's words pulled her back to earth.

"Mayhap a breath of fresh air would do you good. Will you join me for a walk in the moonlight?"

Arianna didn't know what to say. Glancing over at Robert, she saw him watching her. "I'd be delighted, sir." If Rob was truly worried about her innocence, he would surely be concerned about her moonlight walk with this young, well-built, redheaded giant of a man. Too worried, perchance, to think about Judith.

Taking Lionel's hand she stepped outside, feeling the cool evening breeze caress her hair and move her skirt around her. The sweet fragrance of roses and the pungent, spicy smell of gilly flowers wafted past them and

93

she inhaled deeply of their fragrance.

"My lady, I didn't realize it was so windy out here. If it's too much for you, we can go back in."

"No, I'm fine. I love the feel of wind through my hair."

"Truly? That's a rare trait in a lady. Most gentle-women would be too concerned that a strand of hair was out of place. I . . . I admire you very much, Arianna."

Arianna smiled to herself. If he only knew. "Thank you, Sir Lionel. Shall we begin?"

"Begin?" Lionel's heart began to race and he stepped closer.

"Our walk."

"Oh, yes, of course."

Back inside the hall, Robert was having a hard time concentrating on his dancing again. Why had Arianna consented to a walk with Sir Lionel? Didn't she know where that could lead? She truly needed him to watch over her. "I don't seem to be much in the mood for dancing tonight, Judith. Shall we sit the next one out and take a walk in the moonlight?"

"What a lovely idea. I had despaired of you ever beginning our courtship."

Judith's words forced him to remember the purpose of his visit to Norbridge and he felt a sudden sense of dread. How could he have ever contemplated marrying Judith? If he had known of Arianna's existence, he never would have considered it. But he had truly never thought to find a woman who could fulfill his dreams so wondrously or create such passionate yearnings and desires within him.

When the dance ended, he took Judith's hand and escorted her outside. Here was the perfect opportunity to tell her that there would be no contract between them. But first, he had to assure himself that Arianna was safe.

Judith was thrilled with Robert's sudden eagerness to get her alone in the moonlight. Mayhap he was planning to ask for her hand this very evening. But why, she wondered, did he seem so distracted, and why, for heaven sakes, was he looking around so frantically?

Robert's eyes searched for Arianna, his brow furrowing when he found her standing close to Lionel under the shelter of a huge oak tree. That scoundrel was putting his arm around her! In a second, the bastard would be kissing her! Damn him for taking advantage of her innocence. Grabbing Judith's hand, he began taking long strides toward the tree.

The wind carried Judith's and Robert's voices to Lionel and he quickly pulled Arianna behind the tree. "Arianna, forgive my haste, but all evening I've wanted to . . ."

Arianna heard Judith complaining and knew Rob was near. She moved closer to Lionel and gazed up at him, saying sweetly, "Yes, Lionel?"

"Arianna!" Lionel's lips came down on hers.

Arianna was shocked at Lionel's boldness and pushed him away. She wanted to make Rob jealous, but not this way. God's teeth, but it was exceedingly easy to arouse the male animal!

"One more kiss, I beg of you."

"Lionel, please . . ."

Lionel pulled her into his arms, holding her so she couldn't move. Once again his lips came down hard on hers.

Judith was becoming annoyed at Robert. He was walking so fast she could hardly keep up with him, and why was he heading for that tree and Lionel and Arianna? The truth hit her then, infuriating her even more. The only reason he asked her to walk with him was to spy on Arianna. The devil take him—he was smitten by her! His actions tonight left no doubt.

Judith yanked on his arm, stopping him in his tracks.
"Robert!"

Hearing Judith's strident voice so close, Lionel released Arianna and she quickly moved out of his reach, greeting Rob and Judith with a grateful smile. Thank goodness they were here. Lionel was more than she could handle. "Robert, Lady Judith. I see you two had the same idea. Come join Sir Lionel and me in our walk. It's such a lovely evening."

Robert could easily see that Arianna was trying to make the best of an awkward situation and forced himself to stay calm. He was Arianna's sworn protector and would cause her no further discomfort. She had been subjected to enough for one day. He would pretend nothing happened, for her sake, but when next he saw Lionel, he'd thrash him soundly. "That sounds good to me. Judith, shall we join them?"

Judith stomped down hard on Robert's foot, and without further ado, walked away.

What was that all about, Rob wondered. What had he done to rile Judith but take her for a walk in the night air?

Standing in the doorway of the mews, Peter Trilby watched the figures under the tree. He had been about to advance on Lionel when he saw Rob make his way over to them. Good lad.

Carrying the gyrfalcon on his fist, he walked over to the small group in time to see Judith stomp on Robert's foot and storm off, leaving Robert and Lionel to stare after her in amazement.

On the pretext of showing her the falcon, Peter drew Arianna aside and whispered. "Well, young lady. I hope you know what you're doing. It's a dangerous game you're playing. If you'd only waited just a little while longer . . ."

"Papa, I'm sorry. I know how you feel, but I just couldn't wait. I love Robert, and I want to marry him. Will has given me the chance and I'm taking it, and not you or Mama or the Queen of England can stop me."

Peter saw the determination in her eyes, the same determination he had seen so often in Mary's. So much alike. "Rose Petal, I can't fight you on this. I'm not sure I even want to. Robert is a fine lad and if you marry him, you'll have the kind of life you deserve. But remember, if things don't work out I'll always be here for you."

"Oh, Papa, I love you. I'll always love you and Mama. And somehow I'll find a way for us to be together."

"Arianna?"

Arianna whirled at the sound of Rob's voice and forced a smile. "Robert, I've been admiring this beautiful creature. You say it is a gyrfalcon, Peter?"

"Peter! I thought I recognized you. How is Sparrow? I shall have need of a falconer at Everly soon; do you think he'd be interested?"

"Ah, Lord Warwick, indeed he would, but alas, he's not here anymore." Peter looked directly at Arianna. "He's off seeking his fortune . . . in the company of Drake."

"With Drake, ha? Somehow, I can't picture little Sparrow soldiering."

"Yes, well, you know our Sparrow, not one to let anything stop him from doing what he wants." Peter gave Arianna another potent look. "Now, if you'll excuse me, I have to get this fine fellow back to the aviary. It was nice seeing you again Lord Warwick."

"And you, Peter."

Looking around, Arianna said, "Where's Sir Lionel?"

"Gone."

"Well, then, I'll say good night. I'm too weary for anything but a soft feather bed."

"So soon?" Rob asked, his eyes begging her to stay.

"Yes, truly I must. I'm afraid everything has been a little overwhelming."

"Forgive me, I wasn't thinking. Of course you're

weary. I'll just see you to your chamber door."

More than anything, Arianna wanted just that, but she instinctively knew that she should leave him now while he wanted more. "No, please. I can find the way."

"That isn't what I was worried about. There may be other amorous knights afoot this evening. You may have need of my protection."

Arianna's willpower was fading fast; she had to leave now before it became too obvious how much she loved him. "That's very gallant of you, Robert, but I think it's time I learned how to take care of myself. After all, you won't be by my side forever, will you?" Staring into his warm brown eyes, she smiled ever so sadly to emphasize her point, then glided away.

Chapter Eight

Something woke Arianna. All was quiet, yet she sensed something . . . no, someone . . . in her chamber. Her eyes flew open, focusing on Buttercup's plump form sitting on a stool beside the bed, her thumbs twirling restlessly in her lap.

"Buttercup, you frightened me. What are you doing?"

"Waitin' for ye to wake up, Your Ladyship. So's I can get on with me duties."

Arianna stretched her limbs, groaning softly. "Buttercup, you take your new position much too seriously. Surely, there are other things you could be doing other than waiting for me to rise?"

"Not as far as I know. Been up since dawn, I have, dusting every blessed thing in the chamber and setting your clothes aright. Been to the kitchen, too, to see about your breakfast and I've run out of things to do."

"Far be it from me to keep you from your duties then," Arianna said, stretching again. Now fully awake, she climbed out of bed and walked to the window, looking down at the town nestled against the castle. She breathed the morning air in deeply, contentedly, and thought that in all her years she had never truly believed she would one day be gazing down at her village from such a lofty height.

Stretching one last time, she said, "Very well, Buttercup. You can dress me, then comb my hair if you wish, but after that you're on your own. For heaven sakes, how did you occupy your time after your chores as a milkmaid were done?"

"If the truth be known, me lady, on hot days such as this I'd walk down to the little pond in the woods, strip me clothes off, and jump into the water."

"Mmm, that sounds inviting. I'm tempted to do that very thing."

"That would never do, Sparrow—Arianna. Since ye've become a fine lady, ye'll have to act like one. Besides, if Lord Warwick or some other man was to see you all naked, why, you'd be ravaged on the spot."

Picturing Robert caressing her naked body and kissing her passionately, Arianna didn't think it would be so terrible. So involved was she in that sensuous image she failed to hear the light rap on the door until Buttercup proclaimed, "Why, Lord Warwick, how are you this fine morning?"

Arianna's face flamed. Robert! If he knew what she had been thinking . . .

Robert peered around Buttercup, his eyes seeking Arianna and finding her standing by the window in her nightshift. "I came to see how Lady Arianna is faring. "Ah, there she is." Pushing Buttercup aside, Rob strode in.

Flustered, Arianna took a couple of steps backward. "Robert!"

She was directly in front of the window, caught in the rays of light that illuminated her shapely form enticingly through her thin nightshift. Rob came to a halt, his throat constricted, his eyes unable to leave the delectable and revealing sight. Then, realizing in the long silence that followed that he was expected to say something, he spoke, clearing his throat several times in the process.

100

"I, uh, wanted to see how you were doing this morning. You left so abruptly last evening . . ."

"I . . . I'm fine. Thank you for asking." Arianna noticed the intense way Rob looked at her, his eyes seeming to penetrate her very clothing . . . Oooh . . . so that's it. She felt the warmth of the sun on her back and realized what held his interest.

"Milady," Buttercup said, picking up the velvet robe from the bed and handing it to Arianna. "Your robe."

"I have no need of it, Buttercup. Not on a day as warm as this. The sun feels so good against my back." Will had said a glimpse of breast or leg would perk Robert's interest. Well, he was getting that glimpse and more.

"But, uh . . ." Buttercup had the same view that Robert was enjoying, but didn't want to embarrass Arianna by saying so. Arianna seemed completely unaware of what she was doing to Robert. "Since Lady Judith was kind enough to lend it to you, milady, why don't you wear it?"

"Really, Buttercup, didn't I just inform you that you take your duties much too seriously? I'm fine, thank you."

Robert's eyes moved over Arianna, completely enthralled and taking in every beautiful curve. What agony. What sweet, sweet agony. God's blood, how he wanted her . . . wanted to tear the nightshift from her body so the vision would be complete, wanted to . . .

Rob's thoughts were interrupted by Will's cheerful voice from the doorway . . . "Rob, Judith and I have been looking all over for you."

Rob quickly grabbed the robe from Buttercup and wrapped it around Arianna. "I just came to see how our brave little Arianna is."

"And how is she, Robbie?" Judith appeared in the doorway, a poisonously sweet expression on her face. "Why is it whenever I seek your company I find you in

Lady Arianna's bedchamber? Am I deluded in thinking it was I you came to Norbridge to see?"

Will was enjoying himself. "Now Judith, Rob is only being hospitable to our guest, as you should be."

"Please, Will," Arianna said, speaking softly. "Don't deride your dear sister. Not on my account. As you all can see, I'm fine. Thanks to Judith's kindness in giving me Buttercup for a chambermaid, I have everything I need and am quite comfortable.

Judith was taken aback by Arianna's kind words. "Yes, well, I was happy to do it. And now, gentlemen, what about that game of pall mall you promised? Mayhap you'll join us later, Arianna. I imagine even fugitives from convents know how to play *that* game. Robbie, Will, are you coming?" She beckoned to the men and they reluctantly started for the door, stopping dead in their tracks as Arianna spoke.

"I beg you to forgive my absence, Lady Judith, but I'm off to frolic in the forest pool."

Judith's mouth flew open. She spun around to face Arianna. "Surely you jest. It would be most unseemly for a lady to bathe naked in a public place."

"Public? The forest? I hardly think there'll be anyone there."

"Arianna," Rob said, "what Judith means is that the countryside is full of miscreants who might happen upon you. You might be . . ."

"Oh!" Arianna said as sweetly as she could. "I hadn't thought of that. I had no such worries in the convent. Why, I often went to the pond there, swimming naked. Ohhh, I do so want to enjoy the water. It would feel so good upon my thirsty skin."

Rob felt a throbbing in his groin at Arianna's words. "It would be most unwise, Arianna. Without someone to guard you, you would be in great danger. And since that is quite impossible under the circumstances . . ."

"Impossible? But why? Surely there are trustworthy knights in this castle who could keep watch over me. Mayhap . . . if I may be so bold, you and Will would do me that honor?"

"Splendid idea," Will responded, seeing what Arianna had in mind. Where did she learn such trickery?

"You can't be serious, Will. How could we protect Arianna's privacy? I'm sure she doesn't want you gaping at her," Rob added, more sharply than he intended.

"Nor you, Rob. Simple enough. We'll wear blindfolds!"

"Oh, Will, what a wonderful solution," Arianna said sweetly.

Robert swallowed hard. "But . . ."

"What say you, Robert? Are you game? With two such trusted and noble knights guarding me whilst I'm in the water, I'll have nothing to fear."

"It's out of the question, Arianna," Judith declared, her voice shrill. "I've never heard such an outrageous idea in my life. You have a lot to learn about being a lady, it seems, but unfortunately, I haven't the time or inclination to teach you. Are you coming, Rob? Will?"

Robert stood rooted, his mind conjuring up the image of Arianna's curvaceous body beneath her nightshift, then picturing her wet and glistening, standing at the edge of the forest pool.

Judith called to him from the doorway. "Robert!"

Seeing Rob's hesitation, Arianna called out, "Lord Warwick, please don't worry about me. I'm sure I can find some other trustworthy knight."

"No!" Rob said quickly. "No need. Will and I will gladly be your guards." Turning to Judith, he said, "We'll have our game of pall mall after the noon meal, and then, Judith, you shall have my undivided attention."

Judith's lips tightened, but she bit back her words, not wanting to seem a shrew in front of Robert. "Very well, as you wish. I'll join you then. It should prove to be quite an amusing spectacle."

The small pond sparkled in the morning sun, its shimmering water rippling gently as dragonflies darted here and there over the surface and waterbirds unfolded their wings, flying away as the small party approached. They circled patiently above the clearing waiting for the time when the pond would be theirs again.

Surrounded by a thick fringe of trees, the small forest pool was a peaceful setting, marred only by the sound of feminine laughter as Buttercup blindfolded Will and Rob.

"There now. Turn around and face the woods, me brave laddies, so's we can be sure you won't be tempted to raise your scarf for a peek at me charms."

"Hmph, I'm sure it wouldn't be the first time my brother has seen you naked, Buttercup," Judith said dryly from her seat on a fallen tree.

The two young women helped each other undress, stepping out of their clothes nervously. Arianna was uneasy to say the least, being naked in the presence of men. Their blindfolds were little comfort to her—and then there was Judith, gaping at her as if she had two heads. What had she gotten herself into?

Eager for the protection the water would provide, she grabbed Buttercup's hand and ran into the pond, squealing with delight as the cold water sprayed over her. Unhanding Buttercup, she dove under, emerging a moment later.

"Oohh, this feels so good. You don't know what you're missing, Judith."

"Catching my death, that's what I'm missing." Judith answered, watching Arianna swim gracefully through the water. Good thing the men were blindfolded—

Arianna made too pretty a picture. Realizing how quiet Will and Rob were, Judith focused on them. Will's mouth was curled into a broad grin, the only part of his face that could be seen beneath the scarf. Hmph, he's certainly enjoying himself, she thought. Rob, too, no doubt. Her eyes swept over Rob and a frown creased her forehead. Rob wasn't smiling at all; his lips were tight and grim, his body stiff and formal as if he were in pain. He looked . . . yes, curse it all, he *was* aroused. There was no doubt about it.

Judith suddenly wished she had undressed and joined the women in the water. If Rob was going to get excited over anyone, she wanted it to be her. The devil take it, she had missed the perfect opportunity.

Rob listened to Arianna's lilting voice in agony — the gentle splashing of water told him she was enjoying herself. He could see her in his mind so clearly, but wanted, indeed needed, to see her in the flesh. His manhood hardened uncomfortably and he longed to rip his clothing off and join her. Damnation, how long was this torture going to last?

Suddenly Buttercup's excited voice split the air. "Will — Robert! Arianna's disappeared under the water. I can't find her."

Rob tore off his blindfold and turned quickly toward the water, his gaze searching the surface for the spot where Arianna went under. Not a ripple or bubble could be seen. Where was she? My God, had she drowned? Tearing off his boots, he dove in, emerging the same time as Arianna and just a few inches from her.

"Rob!"

"Arianna! Buttercup thought you were drowning."

Arianna laughed softly, then fell backward, wriggling her shoulders and kicking her feet gently to stay afloat. Her breasts bobbed becomingly, floating on top of the water like delicate water lilies.

105

"You've had a bath for naught then, for I'm fine."

Rob couldn't take his eyes off her breasts — so perfect, so white — her nipples large and pink, just ripe for a mouth to close around them. She swam effortlessly on her back, moving away from him like an enchanting mermaid. He followed after her, unwilling to be parted from the mesmerizing sight.

He swam ever closer until the unbearable gap between them narrowed and he was over her, his arms stroking the water on either side of her graceful, gliding body. "Arianna, my God, if you only knew what you are doing to me. Your innocent beauty is driving me mad."

Arianna looked into Rob's eyes, hardly breathing from the excitement of being so close to him, watching as his tender gaze moved to her breasts. A sensation washed over her there, as if she had been physically touched. She wanted, need to feel his skin against her own. Compelled by an overwhelming force, she reached up to circle his neck with her arms.

In a second, his arms were around her waist drawing her up against him, their bodies melding, their legs entwining. Moaning, he pulled her under the water where no one could see and ground his mouth into hers, his hands moving over her body hungrily, cupping her breasts, her tiny waist, then traveling over deliciously rounded hips and buttocks. This was what he wanted — this is what he needed to be complete.

Arianna felt she would die with desire. Feeling his hands on her naked body, she wriggled against him, craving more. She was rewarded by the hard press of his manhood straining against his wet clothes.

Rob guided himself between her legs, too far gone to have any control.

Arianna reveled in the wondrous feel of him until a stabbing pain in her lungs told her she was out of air. She pushed against Rob and he brought her swiftly to the surface.

Facing him, Arianna gasped for breath and treaded water to stay afloat.

Rob's chest heaved, his words coming in short spurts between gasps. "Arianna. God forgive me. I couldn't help myself."

Voices from shore mingled in the air over Rob's head, but he didn't hear. Staring into blue eyes filled with as much longing as his own, he was oblivious to all but the beguiling creature before him — oblivious to all but the fierce need that overwhelmed him, the fierce need to make Arianna his own.

Chapter Nine

Nothing was proceeding as Judith had planned. Robert was not responding to her at all, his brain addled by that virginal, cow-eyed contemptress he had brought into her home. What a fool she had been this morning not to play the same canny game as Arianna! If she had gone naked into the water and pretended to drown, Robert would be gazing moon-eyed into her face now, instead of that designing little witch's.

Well, she'd make up for it. Her gauntlet was off. No little snippet from a convent could best her in the game of seduction. She'd go to Robert's chamber tonight after everyone was abed. Men were such weak creatures when it came to satisfying their sexual urges; there wasn't a one of them able to push a naked female from his bed.

Robert would be no exception. He would make love to her, of that she had no doubt, and then, good and noble knight that he was, he would feel compelled to marry her to protect her virtue. But first, she had to get through this miserable evening.

Arianna had spoiled even that for her, suggesting they have their evening musicale up here on the ramparts of the castle. Wouldn't you know—Robert and Will had immediately jumped at the idea, and so they had climbed the narrow staircase, musicians and all, to breathe in the unhealthy night air.

Everyone with their wits about them knows the night air is full of poisonous vapors, Judith reminded herself. It would serve Arianna right if she came down with some terrible sickness. Look at her, leaning against the parapet, gazing up at the stars as if she had never seen them before. And Robert watching her as if he wanted to eat her up. It was infuriating.

Gazing up at the star-filled sky, Arianna's face was alight with happiness. A few short weeks ago, she never dared dream that such a wonderful life was within her grasp—never dreamed Robert would look at her with such desire, or that she would be standing on the roof of a castle listening to music amidst the highborn lords and ladies she had always admired.

It was a dream come true and she owed it all to Will. Turning her head, she sought him out, finding him gazing at her from his seat by Judith. He winked at her and her smile widened. Gaily, she blew him a kiss which he pretended to catch and press to his mouth.

Rob's lips tightened when he saw this and he felt a stab of fear. What hold did Will have over her? Did she love him? Is that why she sought him out when she escaped from the convent? Was it too late to win her love?

"Arianna . . ."

Still wrapped in a cloud of contentment, Arianna gazed dreamily into Robert's eyes. "Yes, Robert?"

Rob saw a thousand stars dancing in her eyes and wanted them to be for him. "Are you . . . very fond of Will?"

"Very, very fond of him. He's my guardian angel."

Rob's heart began to pound. "Do you mean to marry him?"

"Marry Will? Is that what you thought? Oh, Rob, I could never do that. Will is like a brother to me, a cherished brother."

Relief swept over him and he lifted her hand, pressing it to his lips.

"Robert, please, you mustn't do that. After this morning . . . the way you touched me in the water, I blush to speak of it, and yet I must. I fear you must think me wanton, and I . . ."

"Arianna, surely you don't believe that. Don't you know how much you mean to me, how much I . . ."

Arianna placed her hand over Rob's mouth. "No, don't say any more, please. You warned me once to be wary of pretty words. You said men would use them to take advantage of me. Forsooth, I find you're right, for look at me now, after your pretty words. If Will and Buttercup hadn't been there this morning, I fear I would no longer be a virgin. I should never have left the convent. Mayhap I should ask Will to take me back."

Rob couldn't believe what he heard. "Arianna, no." Grasping her by the arm, he led her around the corner of a turret and pushed her up against the rough stone of the merlon. "You were never meant for that solitary life. Never. You were meant to be cherished, loved, protected by your husband and his deep love for you. You were meant to share his bed, bear his children . . ."

"Husband? What man would want me, the illegitimate daughter of a baron."

"What man *wouldn't* want you? What man wouldn't kill to have you? My God, Arianna, I want you so

110

much it hurts, but until I speak to Judith I have no right to say any more."

"What are you saying?"

"I'm saying that in the morning I'm going to talk to Judith and tell her there will be no marriage contract between us."

As Arianna listened to Rob, a sudden fear clutched at her heart. She was so close to getting what she wanted most in this world, it scared her. What if something went wrong? What if she won him only to lose him in sickness or in battle? She couldn't bear it, she loved him too much. Tears welled quickly in her eyes, splashing onto her cheeks when she tried to blink them back.

"Arianna, what is it? Don't you want me? My God, if you don't want me, I don't know what I'll do."

"I want you, Rob. Oh, how I want you. I've wanted you for so very long . . ."

"So very long? Foolish damsel, we've only known each other a few days, but yes, it does seem a lifetime."

Hearing voices, Rob moved quickly away from Arianna as Will and Judith, along with two of her ladies-in-waiting, came around the corner.

"Robert, we've come to take you away. Lady Miriam was just saying how she longed to hear you play the lute again." Taking his arm, Judith walked off with Rob, looking back over her shoulder to give Arianna an arrogant smile.

Will took the opportunity to talk to Arianna, whispering in her ear. "You've done your job well. And you with no practice at being a girl!"

"Oh, Will, are we doing the right thing? It seems so wrong, so deceitful, to manipulate him like this."

"Darling girl, you're doing what women have done since the beginning of time. No more, no less. It's the end result that counts: Robert wed to you and not Judith. Don't have any regrets now — the game is almost won.

It was late enough, Judith thought, as she slipped out of her clothes and wrapped a velvet cloak about her naked body. Everyone should be abed by now. She could go to Robert's chamber, climb into his bed, and claim him for her own. Then poor, sweet little Arianna would lose him for all time.

Stealthily, she opened her door and crept down the hallway toward Rob's chamber, already feeling triumphant. She turned the corner, then stopped suddenly, flattening herself against a wall. A yeoman stood outside Robert's door. She stood watching for several moments, before realizing he wasn't going to leave, anger welling up inside her. Determined to pursue her goal, she walked over to him, speaking harshly. "What unsavory business brings you to Lord Warwick's door?"

The stout young man was startled by Judith's sudden appearance and stammered, "Why, my lady, 'tis nothing like that. I'm here on Lord William's orders."

"My brother? Fie! What reason would he have to guard Lord Warwick's door? You lie."

"Oh, no, my lady. 'Tis true. Lord William gave me specific instruction not to let anyone cross Lord Warwick's threshold, especially those of the feminine gender, especially . . . you, my lady."

Judith stood staring into the yeoman's face, unable to comprehend the meaning of his words. Will was making sure she couldn't compromise Robert. But why? What objection could he have to her marrying Rob? "Well, I am countermanding his orders. You are to leave this moment. Do you hear? Leave now, or I'll

112

have my father stretch your bones upon the rack."

"Forgive me, my lady, but Lord William anticipated your reaction. He told me I was to stay right here, no matter what threats you made. And . . . Your Ladyship, if I might point out, it would be useless to appeal to your father, since he is away on a hunting trip and won't be back for many days."

Fury raged in Judith's eyes, knowing she could not change this obedient fool's mind. Storming off, she strode back to her chamber and began to pace back and forth, rage building ever stronger.

"No! No! No!" she shouted. It was more than she could bear. She couldn't sit back and let that little witch take Robert from her. Knowing what she must do, she searched the chamber. Yes, there. Her jeweled dagger.

Picking it up, she made her way to the secret panel and quickly opened the door.

With each step she took through the dark winding passageway, her mind envisioned the stroke of her dagger on Arianna's delicate white skin and the pain it would inflict. She conjured up a picture of Arianna lying across the bed with her throat slashed, and of Buttercup finding her like that. The foolish girl would probably be blamed for the murder, considering her less-than-pristine background. In any case, Arianna would be out of the way and Robert would be hers.

Judith's heart pounded as she came to the secret door to Will's chamber—the door she had used so many times to visit him in the middle of the night when her need of him drove her through it. Steeling herself she pushed the panel.

It wouldn't budge!

She pushed harder. It still wouldn't move.

Bolted! It was bolted from the inside!

113

Tears filled her eyes and spilled down her cheeks. Tears of frustration and of, oh God, yes, relief. What madness had overcome her? Thank Jesus, the door was bolted—or she'd be a murderess. She looked down at the dagger in her hand, dropping it as if it burned her. Choking back a sob, she turned and stumbled back through the passageway to her chamber.

Arianna heard a metallic sound on stone and was pulled drowsily out of a beautiful, sensuous dream about Robert. Then, eager to return to his arms, she closed her eyes and slept.

The familiar morning sounds of castlefolk at work drifted up to Arianna through the open window of her chamber. She yawned and wriggled deeper into the soft mattress, listening in contentment. The squeaking of wood on wood as a bucket was lowered into the well could be heard, along with the sharp staccato sound of wood chopping and the metallic clang of cookpans. Cheerful voices called to each other, mingling with the muted murmuring of voices from the hallway. Ah me! All was well with the world, she thought happily.

She heard the door open and someone enter her chamber. Buttercup, she thought smiling, looking for something to do as usual. Feeling impish, Arianna closed her eyes and pretended to be asleep. She'd let Buttercup await her attention for a while. It's time she realized she was to adjust to Arianna's schedule and not the other way around.

A light rustle of skirts told Arianna it wasn't Buttercup in her chamber and her eyes flew open.

"Did I wake you, Arianna? Sorry. I thought convent inmates rose at the crack of dawn."

"Lady Judith!" Arianna exclaimed, sitting up. "You

114

didn't wake me. I was just being lazy—a luxury I couldn't enjoy in the convent, as you can imagine."

"Yes, I can well imagine. Which brings me to the reason for my visit. I've brought you one of my cast-off garments. Until you can have your own made you'll need another change of clothes."

Arianna's gaze focused on Judith and the forest green gown she held; then her eyes widened as she realized it was the gown Will had convinced Judith to have made—the same gown that resembled the Queen of Scotland's.

"Oh, Judith, I don't know what to say. It's beautiful. Are you sure you want to part with it?"

"I'm quite sure. It never suited me." Judith stared at Arianna with feverish eyes, fascinated at seeing her alive when one deft stroke last evening could have caused her death. She felt compelled to come to Arianna's chamber this morning, though she knew not why. The gown was just an excuse. But truth to say, it was also a way to appease her guilt.

Arianna saw the strange way Judith looked at her and tried to shrug it off, but when she saw the twisted smile that flicked across Judith's face for a moment, she shivered as if someone had walked across her grave.

"Well, Arianna, I must leave you now to prepare sleeping accommodations for the Earl of Clinton and his entourage. They'll be here momentarily. My sly brother admitted to me this morning that he sent for him. He somehow got the idea I'd be in need of another suitor. Isn't that strange? But then, many strange things have occurred here of late." Judith headed for the door, then turned. "Wear the green today," she purred. "Will is quite fond of it. Or is it another man you wish to please?"

When the door closed behind Judith, Arianna didn't move. She had never seen Judith like that before and it frightened her. She seemed almost . . . demented. Shaking off a feeling of dread, she rose and began to dress.

Turning a corner, Judith passed Buttercup, who was carrying a tray to Arianna's chamber. The plump wench seemed to enjoy her new role as handmaiden. Judith frowned, seeing Robert headed the same way. "How nice to see you, Robbie. Were you perchance looking for me?"

"As a matter of fact, I was. I wanted to speak to you in private. I have something important to talk about."

"Robbie, you sound so serious. I can hardly wait. Come — we can go to my chamber. No one will disturb us there."

"I would rather it not be that private. Mayhap the library?"

"As you wish." Judith wended her way to the library, linking her arm in Rob's. She had a good idea what Rob wanted to tell her and it wasn't that he wanted to marry her. Well, she'd make him squirm, she thought darkly. She wasn't making it easy on him. The fool! In love with that little twit of a girl, without a parcel of land to add to his coffers. He would get what he deserved.

Entering the library, Judith sat herself prettily at a table and looked up at Robert adoringly. "Oh, Robbie, if it's what I think it is . . ."

Robert's heart sank. She thought he was going to ask for her hand. How was he going to tell her? "Ah, Judith. You know how much I admire you. As Will's sister, I've always held you with the utmost regard, but . . ."

Judith's eyelashes fluttered, "Yes, Robert . . ."

116

Rob had never seen Judith so soft or feminine. Damn it all, this would be the hardest thing he had ever done. But it had to be done. "Judith, I . . ."

Judith began to laugh, startling Robert by its sudden wickedness. "Oh, Robert, if you could only see your face. It's too funny. I wanted to see you squirm and, having accomplished that, I set you free. You may marry your little convent virgin. You deserve each other. Did you think you were my only suitor? Why, even now the Earl of Clinton is on his way to court me."

Robert heard the venom in her voice and realized for the first time what a dangerous woman she was. "Is that so? In that case, I wish you every happiness. As you know, I'm well acquainted with the Earl of Clinton. He'll be a worthy suitor."

Bowing formally, he took her hand and kissed it stiffly, then turned and left, the weight of the world falling from his shoulders as he closed the door behind him.

Judith rubbed the hand Robert had kissed as if it had been stung by a wasp. Then she walked to a bookcase and reached for a book. Opening her hand slowly and deliberately, she let it fall, enjoying the satisfying sound it made on the wooden floor. She picked up another book, then another and another, dropping each in the same way until she had cleared one shelf and then another, until the desire to plunge a dagger into Robert's chest began to fade.

Robert made his way to the castle chapel, needing to put his mind in order before speaking to Arianna and feeling a need to wipe away any lingering malevolence from his encounter with Judith. He wanted to come to

Arianna pure of thought and deed, worthy of becoming her mate.

Kneeling at the altar, he lowered his head and prayed, staying in the same position until his knees grew stiff. Then, reluctant to leave the soul-cleansing atmosphere of the chapel, he sat in a darkened pew and closed his eyes.

The creaking of the door let him know someone was entering. He looked back, surprised to see Arianna. He watched silently as she made her way up to the altar, her eyes never wavering from the gilt cross, her soft voice reaching him as she knelt to pray.

"Dear Lord, forgive me my terrible sin, I pray."

"Arianna," he said, wanting her to know he was there. "What terrible sin do you need forgiven?"

Hearing Rob's voice, Arianna buried her head in her hands and wept.

He was at her side in a moment, pulling her up and into his arms. "Forgive me for startling you, but I didn't want to overhear your terrible confession," Robert said laughing. Seeing the shocked look on her face, he quickly added, "Sweet Arianna, I'm jesting. Surely your sins are not so very bad."

Gazing into his eyes, Arianna saw so much love there and knew he deserved to know the truth. "Oh, Rob, I wish . . ."

"Sweet girl, what can you possibly need forgiveness for?"

"The sin of making you desire me." She blurted it out, glad to be rid of the weight of her guilt.

Robert began to laugh. "Is that it? Is that your terrible sin?" Taking her head in his hands, he said softly. "Darling girl, making me love you was no sin, but the kindest thing you could have done.

118

You made right a terrible wrong. If you only knew . . . I shudder to think . . ."

Arianna put her hand to his mouth to stop his speech and he kissed it, then proclaimed, "Here in this sacred place I pledge my undying love for you. I want you, no, more than that, I need you with me always, to share my home, my life, my bed. Will you do me the great honor of becoming my wife?"

Arianna's knees began to shake, hearing the words she never dared believe she would hear anywhere but in her dreams.

Robert's arms reached out to steady her. "Will you?"

Arianna couldn't speak, so tight was her throat, so deep her emotion.

Rob searched her eyes, suddenly afraid. "Arianna, what is it?"

A huge, tortuous sob escaped Arianna's throat, followed by a torrent of tears. "Oh, Rob, yes! Yes, I want to be your wife more than anything in the world."

"God's teeth, but you scared me. Don't ever do that again. I couldn't bear to lose you." His lips came down on hers, blocking out everything but his love and his need.

Still holding her tight, he said, "Gather your belongings. We leave for Everly tonight. I have to get you there quickly. I know it sounds foolish, but I'm suddenly afraid and I have no idea why."

"I know. I feel it, too, Rob. I'll be ready. Buttercup will help me."

Taking her arm, he led her out of the dimly lit chapel into the full light of the great hall where Arianna squinted, trying to adjust to the sudden brightness. Her gaze focused on a man elegantly dressed in purple velvet and she watched as Judith greeted him with a deep curtsy. No doubt this was the

Earl of Clinton.

As Rob drew her closer to the pair, Arianna suddenly turned white. Dear God, no. Please don't let it be Edmund Deveraux. Her heart raced faster as she came closer, praying every step of the way that she was wrong, that it wasn't the one person in the world who could destroy her happiness.

Robert saw her stricken look and halted. "What is it, Arianna? Why do you look so pale?" Following her gaze, he smiled. " 'Tis just the Earl of Clinton. Come, I'll make the introductions. You'll like him—he's quite a charming fellow."

"Must I meet him now? I should go to my chamber if you would have me ready this evening."

"You'll have to meet him sooner or later, darling girl, since Edmund will be your closest neighbor in Everly."

Arianna's heart sank. Edmund. It *was* Edmund! Their closest neighbor? Dear God, no! If he recognized her as the peasant girl who returned the queen's dog, all would be lost. She should have known it would never work, that she could never have her dream, that she could never have Rob. Resigned to her fate, she allowed Robert to lead her to her doom.

Chapter Ten

Edmund Deveraux listened halfheartedly as Judith filled his ears with endless chatter, his attention drawn to the exquisite woman at Warwick's side. There was something damnably familiar about her, and yet, if he had ever seen this lovely woman before, would he not remember her vividly? His eyes traveled over her while his mind searched his memory for a clue; he noted her graceful walk and her rich forest green gown. Yes, that was it!

As Warwick and the woman drew near, he called out, "Robert, old fellow. I never thought to find you here."

"Strange," Rob answered, "since I had no doubt I'd find *you* here. Wherever there's a beautiful woman, Edmund Deveraux is never far away."

"Too true, too true," Edmund said, shaking Rob's hand and patting him on the back. "And now, with two such lovely ladies under the same roof, where else could I be?" Edmund's eyes rested on Arianna's face. "Pardon, my lady. We haven't been formally introduced and yet, I do know you, do I not?"

Arianna felt a surge of fear so strong she could taste it. "You are mistaken, sir, for we have never met."

"Hmmm, I thought for sure . . . Then it must be your lovely dress. That I am sure I recognize."

"Edmund," Judith said, irritated at the attention he was paying to Arianna. " 'Tis my garment you speak of, and since I am sure I didn't have the gown when last you visited, you could never have seen it before."

"Yours, Judith? That complicates matters further."

"Not at all. You're simply mistaken. Will had this gown made for me by a local dressmaker."

"My dear Judith, believe me when I tell you on the highest authority that the Scottish Queen has a very similar dress. So much so, I cannot believe it a coincidence. Mayhap your dressmaker has seen the Scottish Queen in her gown and thought to copy it for you."

"The Scottish Queen! I should be flattered, I suppose, to think my gown comparable to a queen's. But since she is a prisoner in some dismal castle, without any idea of the latest fashions, I do not deem that a compliment."

"She has you there, Edmund," Robert said, happy he wasn't the recipient of Judith's biting tirade. "Now, if you'll excuse me, I needs must speak to my men. I'm leaving today, Judith. After our talk this morning, I think you'll agree there's no reason for me to stay any longer." Rob squeezed Arianna's hand. "I have urgent business to take care of in Everly."

Edmund's eyebrow arched knowingly. "Leaving so soon, Warwick? After so short a visit? And what of this lovely lady? I pray you, do not deprive me of her company as well."

Rob's back bristled, but his voice remained even. "I'm afraid you will have to content yourself with but one beauty, Edmund. Lady Arianna is under my protection now."

"I see," Edmund said, drawing the words out slowly. His eyes moved from Robert to Judith, and then to Arianna. A smirk played across his face. Sweeping his *toque* from his head, he bowed low to Arianna. "Then I must bid you a sad *adieu,* sweet lady, and pray that we might meet again . . . soon."

Arianna nodded to Edmund, afraid her voice would betray her nervousness if she spoke. She cringed when he reached to kiss her hand.

"Yes, my dear, we must meet again so we may continue this conversation. I'm most anxious to solve the curious puzzle of the queen's gown. You know, the more I look at you the more I see a resemblance to Mary herself. Of course, you are younger, slimmer, and far more beautiful—but in that garment, you resemble her greatly."

Arianna was filled with relief. If he believed her to look like a queen, he was far from remembering her as the peasant girl who had had an audience with Mary. Beaming, she answered. "I thank you for your kind words, sir. I've been told the queen is very beautiful. You flatter me deeply."

Turning to Judith, Arianna took her hand. "Judith, thank you for your many kindnesses. You made my stay very comfortable."

Judith blinked at the foreign touch of Arianna's hand. "Yes, well, I was happy to do so. After all, you are my brother's friend."

"Speaking of Will," Rob chimed in, "if you'll all excuse me, I have to speak with him before I leave. Arianna?"

Arianna felt Rob's hand on her elbow as he steered her away from Edmund and Judith .She was thankful she had been spared, but oh, she thought, it had been close. Too close.

"Arianna, while you're packing your things, I'll inform my people to make ready to leave. And I must speak to Will. Poor man, I don't know how he'll react to our betrothal."

Arianna felt a twinge of guilt at Rob's words, but she pushed it aside. The important thing was, Rob wasn't going to marry Judith. Suddenly, for the first time, she realized fully that Rob might belong to her. When she gazed up at him, stars danced in her eyes.

A few minutes later, Arianna opened the door to the bedchamber to find Buttercup with a jeweled dagger in her hand. "Buttercup? What are you doing with that? It belongs to Judith."

A puzzled expression crossed Buttercup's face. "Judith? That's strange. I found it on the steps, on the other side of the door that leads to Judith's chambers. You know, the one behind the tapestry."

"What were you doing opening that door?"

"I was just . . . looking for something to do. I thought to sweep the steps and knock down the cobwebs. Arianna, what do you suppose the dagger was doing there? 'Tis a precious thing, with all those jewels. Surely she didn't throw it away."

A shiver slowly wended its way up Arianna's spine as she remembered the clink of metal on stone the night before. The sound could have been the dagger dropping, but what reason would Judith have for being outside the door so late at night, and with a dagger in her hand?

"I'm sure she didn't throw it away — it's much too valuable. Just lay it on the table; Will can return it to her after I've gone."

"Gone?" Buttercup looked stricken. "Where are you going? When are you coming back?"

"Oh, Buttercup, be happy for me. I'm going to Everly to marry Rob."

Buttercup laid the dagger on the table, her shoulders hunched over, her lower lip jutting out from her round face.

"Buttercup, what is it? Aren't you happy for me?"

"Aye, I am that. It's just that I didn't expect it to happen so soon. I've been so happy here as your chambermaid, and now, you're off to Everly, leaving me behind like I was . . . a sack of grain."

"Oh Buttercup, is that what's troubling you? I wanted to ask you to come with me, but I thought you'd not want to leave your family behind. Will you come? I'd like that very much and I'm sure Will would give his permission."

"Are you sure? Do you want me, truly?"

"Truly I do. I want you, you little ninny, though I don't know why, what with you waking me so early in the morning and . . ."

"Oh, Arianna, I'll never do it again, I promise you. From now on, you can sleep as long as you like."

Arianna laughed gaily, embracing Buttercup's ample waist. "Then it's done. You shall be my very first attendant."

Buttercup squealed loudly, then said, "Oh, Lordy, I've got to go tell Ma, and what about my things? I've got to pack them, and oohhh, I'm not thinking, I've got to help you. There'll be no time to pack my things, but I don't mind, I . . ."

"Enough. Go tell your family and gather your belongings. I can manage here. I've precious few possessions to take. And . . . if you will, Buttercup . . . go to my family and say my goodbyes for me. I dare not be seen near them with Edmund Deveraux here. Tell them I love them and will visit often after I am married."

"I will that. Oh, Arianna, I know how much you'll miss them. I'll miss my Ma, too, but later, when I'm settled, mayhap I can send for them, with Lord Warwick's permission. My Ma, she can do for him, and the little ones, they're getting old enough to help . . ." Buttercup's voice faded when she saw a deep sadness fall over Arianna.

Arianna walked slowly to the window and looked down at the small village below, her eyes focusing on the small cottage that had been her home. As much as she hated the life she had led, she loved her mother and father very much. She would be starting a new life, but at what cost?

The hilly English countryside passed by quickly as the party of men and two women rode by. An uneasy feeling in the pit of his stomach kept Robert riding long past sunset, eager to put distance between them and Norbridge castle. He still could not fathom the reason for his concern.

Was it simply his passion for Arianna that fueled his anxiety? Was he afraid of losing her now that he realized how important she was? He never thought love could be so worrisome. Glancing over to Arianna riding sidesaddle on her white stallion, her hair blowing around her like a golden cloud, love burned strongly in his heart. She smiled back serenely, and he felt such pride that she could love him so soon, so easily, as if she had been waiting for him to come into her life. Maybe she had, for he knew now he had been waiting for her.

He knew the moment he laid eyes on her that first day that she was the woman he had been looking for. He knew, had always known, that his first mating and every mating thereafter would be with the woman he married. Ever since he was old enough to know about such things he believed that love between a man and woman was a sacred covenant, and their mating a holy thing — too holy to defile with casual intercourse. It was important to him to come to his wife on their wedding night in a state of grace, but never more so than now, with sweet, innocent Arianna as his bride.

His manhood throbbed, thinking of Arianna lying on his bed in naked splendor, waiting to receive him. Oh, endless days, speed on, until I have the right to make her mine.

They finally camped when it became too dark and unsafe to ride, pitching their tents in a small clearing beside a rambling brook. Their only source of light was the soft glow from the moon. After a cold supper, sentries were posted and the rest of the men lay down on their bedrolls, weary after the long hard ride.

Arianna shared a tent with Buttercup, each sleeping on her own thick, comfortable bedroll. Rob chose to lie under the stars, curled up by the fire, too restless to sleep.

Listening to the music of the night, Arianna closed her eyes and thought of the new life ahead of her. Could it be true? Was she really going to marry Rob, to become his cherished wife? Would she be a lady? She tried hard to envision that, but the image of Edmund's arrogant face kept interfering. After a long while a strong breeze stirred the trees around the clearing, seeming to whisper her name, and she was lulled into a troubled sleep.

She saw Judith, dressed all in black with a jeweled dagger in her hand, moving toward her, a look of wanton pleasure on her face. The image quickly shifted and Edmund stood in Judith's stead, his manhood thrusting toward Arianna, engorged. He moved toward her and she tried to run, but couldn't, caught in a large thick web that held her captive. Suddenly she screamed, "No! No!"

The clink of steel sounded in the night: Robert's men drawing their swords.

Buttercup cried out, "All's well. Lady Arianna was only dreaming."

Robert was at Arianna's side instantly, soothing her. "Rose Petal, I'm here. Nothing can hurt you now." Calling to his men, he said, "Go back to sleep. There's nothing amiss." Then gently touching Buttercup's shoulder, he added, "You, too,

127

Buttercup. I'll tend to your mistress."

Arianna sighed deeply, relieved it had been a dream. Then remembering Rob had called her Rose Petal, the special name her parents called her, her eyes shone brightly. "Rose Petal? You never called me that before."

"I've wanted to, but feared you'd think me foolish. But truly, you are my Rose Petal, for what else under God's heaven is so soft and delicate?"

Arianna's arms reached up to embrace Robert, pulling his head down to kiss him. "Oh, Rob, how dear you are to me. I love the name. I wish I could tell you how very much." She kissed him again and Rob responded with a low moan.

"Arianna, our marriage must be soon. I cannot bear many more days of this sweet agony—wanting you, needing you. God's blood, I never knew wanting someone could be so painful."

Arianna laughed softly. "And I would marry you right away. Before you jilt me the way you did Judith, when the next pretty face comes along."

Rob's hands moved over her hair to cup her face lovingly. "Never, my love. This union is for life. Know that now, for I warn you, after we're wed it will be too late. You'll be forever mine."

The countryside was shrouded with swirling patches of morning mist as Robert and Arianna rode through it, disappearing now and then and reappearing magically. Arianna had the feeling of riding into a new world, the old vanishing behind her in the mist, and her heart soared knowing Robert would be a part of that future.

Robert's gaze turned to Arianna often, not quite believing she was truly there. It seemed awesome to him, knowing that he had captured the heart of one so beautiful, so pure.

128

When they drew near Everly, the mists cleared long enough for Arianna to get a glimpse from a nearby hill.

"Home," Rob said, his arm sweeping outward to indicate the peaceful pastoral view.

Her eyes drank in the beautiful sight of Everly Castle high on a hill, blue and gold banners flying from every turret. The lush green hill sloped gently down to a silver ribbon of a river that wended around one side of the castle and continued on into a thick forest.

Below the castle, cottages were scattered beside green blankets of well-attended, crop-filled fields. Unlike the more congested Norbridge, Everly was a peaceful rural community and she loved it already. "Oh, Rob, it's so beautiful. I never dreamed such a lovely place existed."

"We are of like mind, for I never believed anyone as lovely as you existed." Rob reached out for her hand. "Everly is well suited to you, Rose Petal. I do believe my ancestors had second sight, for surely they built Everly with you in mind."

Arianna beamed, her heart so full of love she thought she'd burst. "It must be so, for I've seen this wondrous place in my dreams since I was a wee child." Peter and Sybille's faces flashed before her and her smile faded. Mama, Papa she whispered wistfully. If only they could be here, too, to share this perfect dream.

"What is it, Arianna? What sad thoughts have taken you away from me?"

Blinking back tears, Arianna smiled. " 'Tis nothing, my lord. You have my full attention. Take me . . . home. I'm eager to begin our new life."

Chapter Eleven

Margaret Warwick watched from her chamber window as her son's entourage approached the castle, her eyes sweeping over the blonde beauty at Robert's side in confusion. Surely this wasn't Judith of Norbridge. Though she had never met the girl, she knew Will's sister to be raven-haired.

"Fiona," she said, turning from the window. "My son is here, accompanied by a young lady. And by the way he looks at her, I'm guessing she will soon be my daughter-in-law. Join me in greeting her. I'm most curious to discover how he rode out for one bride and came back with another."

In the courtyard, Rob drew his horse to a halt, dismounted, and helped Arianna from Pasha. He saw the anxiety in her eyes and ventured, "Don't be so fearful. My mother is no dragon, but a beautiful, caring woman. She'll love you on first sight, just as I did. Mark my words."

Arianna smiled up at him shyly and took his hand as he led her to the elegant dark-haired woman standing with her attendants.

"Mother," he said, embracing her, "I want you to meet Arianna, my betrothed."

Margaret looked closely at the wide-eyed girl, seeing how truly exquisite she was and how frightened, like a skittish colt ready to bolt at the slightest provocation.

"Arianna? A beautiful name, but I don't believe I've ever heard Robert mention your name before. Do I know your family?"

Arianna squeezed Rob's hand in fright.

"Mother, Arianna's family is not important. I love her and she's to be my wife. That's all that matters."

Margaret was taken aback by her son's brusqueness and found herself answering in the same tone. "Do I take that to mean she has no title, no standing, no dowry to bestow upon you?"

"You may take it that way."

" 'Tis true? I don't understand. I send you off to win a duke's daughter and you return with a mysterious girl with no heritage, no dowry, not even a name to call her own?"

"Mother, enough of this. Can't you see you're frightening her? I love Arianna deeply and mean to make her my wife, with or without your blessing. So make up your mind to accept her here and now as your beloved daughter."

Margaret saw the determination in her son's eyes and the love that shone there so brightly for the delicate creature by his side. A lump came to her throat at the realization that Robert was truly a man now. His stance was bold, his manner protective. So much like his father.

Margaret stared deeply into Arianna's eyes and she returned her fervent gaze. Each searched the other's eyes, measuring whether they could be friends. Rob watched warily, unsure of what was happening but instinctively knowing he should remain silent.

These two were dearer to him than his life. And yet they were as different as morning is to night. His mother was tall and solidly built with dark hair and brown eyes

131

like his, while Arianna was light of hair and eyes and delicately built. Knowing instinctively that what happened between them now would set the mood for a long time to come, he grew restless as he watched.

Around him, he heard the shuffling of feet, the nervous whispers of the castlefolk, and knew that they, too, were anxious. He couldn't blame them, for it would be hard on them if they had to take sides between his mother and his wife.

After a long, uncomfortable silence, Margaret spoke. "Forgive me, Arianna. You caught me by surprise. I wasn't expecting . . . that is, for many years I thought Rob would marry . . . Well, it doesn't matter what I thought. Welcome to my home, your home, from this day forward."

Arianna exhaled suddenly, unaware that she had been holding her breath. "Thank you, Lady Margaret. I'm most happy to be here."

Hearing Arianna's shy, sweet voice, Margaret smiled warmly and embraced her new daughter. "Now, meet Fiona. She is to be your chief attendant. You'll find her most helpful. Fiona, this is . . . *Lady* Arianna."

Fiona curtsied to her new mistress. "Welcome to Everly, my lady. If you wish, I'll show you to your bedchamber and bring you water that you might freshen up."

"That would be nice, Fiona, and would you find a place for Buttercup? She's to be my attendant also."

Buttercup stepped forward and curtsied to Fiona, as if Fiona were the mistress of the castle, embarrassing the handmaiden enormously.

"Pleased to meet ye, *Fee-oona*."

Never in her life had Fiona met anyone like this wild-looking redheaded woman. It was fair hard to believe Lady Arianna would have such a creature as her attendant. Nervously, she took a step backward.

132

Seeing poor Fiona's distress, Margaret said, "Fiona, Buttercup will share your chamber along with Annie and Deirdre. You shall all attend Lady Arianna. I leave it to you to help her settle in after you've attended to Lady Arianna's needs."

Turning to the plump maid, she continued. "I think you'll be very comfortable here, my dear, and after you get to know her, you'll find our Fiona a boon companion."

Buttercup curtsied again. "Thank you, milady." Beaming, she followed gaily after Fiona, carrying Arianna's few possessions up to her chamber.

Rob breathed a sigh of relief. "Well, now that the sleeping arrangements have been settled, there's one more piece of business to attend to before my two ladies can get to know each other. Mother, would you see that Arianna is fitted with a suitable wardrobe? Your new daughter was raised in a convent, so she's in need of everything."

Margaret's eyebrow shot up. "I see." She had so many questions, but now was not the time to ask them. Robert was taking control, becoming the true Lord of Everly, and she was surprised at how much that pleased her. "I'll have the dressmaker get started this very day, and meanwhile, Arianna, I have many beautiful garments I've regrettably outgrown of late. With a few stitches here and there, they'll fit well enough. I'll have Fiona send them to your chamber."

"You're very kind, Lady Margaret."

Taking Arianna's hand, Rob started pulling her away. "If you'll excuse us, Mother, I'm going to show Arianna her new home. Shall we start with the ramparts, since you have such an affinity for high places?"

Margaret watched as the two young people ran up the stairs, their exuberant voices echoing through the courtyard. She had never seen her son so happy. That was worth a lot . . . maybe even as much as a duke's holdings.

Early next morn, Robert was out and about, cheerfully making arrangements for the day. When he was finished, he took the stairs two at a time, making his way to Arianna's chamber. Knocking lightly on the door, he whispered, "Are you still abed, my lady?"

The door opened a crack and a sleepy Buttercup stared out at him. "Milord, begging me pardon but don't you think it be a mite too early for a visit?"

"Don't be turning into an old lady, Buttercup. 'Tis the first morning Arianna will be in her new home. I'm not wasting a moment. Now, stand aside and let me in."

Rob quickly entered, striding to the bed and kneeling at Arianna's side. Taking her hand, which dangled limply over the side of the bed, he kissed it. "Rose Petal, wake up. There's much I want to share with you this morn. First we'll go hawking, then a picnic by the river, and then . . ."

Arianna's eyes flew open. "Did you say hawking, Rob? Can we? I would truly love that." Throwing off her covers, she swung her legs over the side of the bed and Rob swiftly lifted her into his arms and twirled her around, laughing. "I didn't know my plans would meet with such enthusiasm. Will you always be so easy to please, my lady?"

Arianna gazed into Rob's eyes, drowning in the warmth of them. "With you at my side, my lord? Indeed."

Standing her on the floor, Rob's arms crept around her waist, his lips pressing eagerly on hers. Buttercup cleared her throat, saying, "I'll just see to your clothing. I believe there was a hunting dress in the bundle of garments Lady Margaret sent. Just the thing for hawking."

Lost in each other's arms, neither Rob nor Arianna knew when Buttercup left. One kiss led to another, one caress fueling the desire for another. The thin nightshift Arianna wore was little protection from Rob's searching hands and he was soon breathing heavily from the sweet soft touch of her through the thin cloth.

Gently, he pushed her away, holding her at arm's length. "Arianna, how can I bear to wait? I want you so. We must marry at the earliest possible moment, for I cannot stand this agony much longer."

In a teasing mood, she answered. "Is it agony to hold me in your arms? To kiss me? Then I shall refrain from inflicting such terrible pain. You shall have no more kisses or caresses. No more . . ."

Rob pulled her tight against him, growling low in his throat. " 'Twould be unbearable agony if you were to do that. My hands have a desperate need to touch you, my mouth to drink your nectar." Finding her lips, he lost himself in her sweet softness.

Arianna was bathed in contentment. Gazing at the wide valley from atop a hill a half hour's ride from Everly, she knew the meaning of happiness. All this would belong to her soon, and Rob—Rob, too, would belong to her. Was she dreaming? Would she wake up soon and find herself back in the cottage in Norbridge?

Dressed in a beautiful tight-fitting, russet-hued jacket made from the softest leather and a matching velvet skirt, she felt every inch a lady. Sitting atop sleek, white Pasha and carrying a peregrine falcon on her gauntleted fist, she wondered what more a woman could want.

"I can't get over it, Arianna. You carry the falcon as if you were an expert. Don't tell me they let you hawk at the convent?"

"Indeed they did. Many's the day I brought home

135

game to add to the stew."

"Then we shall never starve with you around. Shall we begin? I'm eager to see what you can do."

" 'Twill be my pleasure." Handing the falcon to a yeoman while Rob helped her dismount, she took it back on her fist once she stood on the ground, speaking softly to it all the while. Bending her head close to the bird, she took one end of the leather trace between her teeth while with the fingers of her free hand she grasped the other end, pulling and lifting the crested leather hood from the bird's head. The falcon immediately ruffled his feathers, while the pupils of his eyes shrunk to small dots as he adjusted to the bright light.

Arianna always thrilled at the sight of amber fire blazing in the eyes of a hawk about to fly. Here was an animal to admire, to envy, for what creature could equal the wildness, the freedom, of a hawk or falcon in flight? In a moment the bird was spiraling skyward in search of prey, climbing so high it was but a speck against the blue sky.

Rob watched, entranced at the sure way Arianna handled the bird, and felt a tug at his heart. There was something so familiar about it . . .

Commanding the falcon with whistles and hand gestures, Arianna soon had it diving toward a grouse. She watched as the small dot in the sky grew larger and listened to the eerie sound of wind whistling through the bells attached to the peregrine's jesses as it dove toward the earth at tremendous speed. Nothing in the world sounded quite like that, and hearing it never failed to excite her. In a few moments it was all over, the grouse the first catch of the day.

"I shall never doubt your ability again, Arianna. That was marvelous. I know a falconer and his son who could learn from you."

Arianna paled, knowing Rob was talking about her

and her father. She shouldn't have shown Rob how skill-ful she was. What if he suddenly realized? But her pride had taken over, along with the joy of finally being able to hawk like the grand ladies she had seen so often. When would she ever learn that pride was not a virtue, but a sin?

Noticing how quiet she had become, Rob asked, "What is it, Arianna? You have that lost, wild look in your eyes again."

" 'Tis nothing, Rob. Nothing at all. I guess I'm not in the mood for hawking after all. Would you mind terribly if we stopped now?"

"Women! Truly it is hard to fathom the way you think. You seemed so eager for the sport, but if you wish to stop it's fine with me. Shall we adjourn to the water? A picnic lunch awaits us there."

"Mmm, sounds good. I'm famished. But what of the falcons?"

"My men will carry them back to the castle. And though I wish it were not so, Buttercup and Fiona will stay to chaperon us properly."

Rob helped Arianna up on her horse; then, holding the bridle, he led Pasha and his own horse through the woods to a small clearing by a brook.

Arianna was surprised to see an ornate tent by the wa-ter, and Buttercup and Fiona bustling about a small table set with trenchers and goblets. "Rob, how lovely. And the brook—how did you know I love to dangle my feet in water?"

"And other parts of your body as well, if I remember right, my lady."

Arianna blushed. "My lord, you are too bold."

Buttercup laughed heartily, knowing full well the meaning of his words, while Fiona looked on in wonder at the familiarity between them.

After their meal, the attendants cleared the table,

137

packed the tableware and leftover food into baskets, then withdrew at Robert's command to wait with the horses out of sight of the clearing.

"Time to dangle," Rob said, pulling Arianna to her feet and leading her to the edge of the water.

"Yes, yes, let's do. But first I have to remove my shoes and hose. Turn around. Don't look."

"Where have I heard that before?" Rob laughed. "But surely, this time it's not necessary. 'Tis only your hose you're removing—you'll be perfectly safe."

"That's true. But if you insist on watching, I'm putting you to good use." Lifting her skirt a little, she stuck out a foot and in a regal voice said, "You may remove my shoes."

Laughing, Rob knelt and lifted her small foot, pulling her shoe off and letting it fall to the ground. Arianna presented her other foot and he removed the shoe, tossing it over his shoulder playfully. But instead of putting her foot down, one masculine hand circled her ankle while the other tickled the bottom of her foot. "That'll teach you to use me as your servant. Now we'll see who's in command."

Laughing hard, Arianna held onto Rob's shoulders to keep from losing her balance. "Be careful, you'll ruin the only hose I own."

Rob's expression suddenly grew solemn. Releasing her foot, he slid his hands very slowly up her legs. Arianna stopped laughing, her expression matching his own. "Rob, no, you mustn't."

"Arianna, I'm just taking off your hose. That's all, that's all," he said soothingly, his hands moving again, slowly, up her legs, his fingers shaking a little at the exquisite rapture the touch of her gave him. Grasping the hose, he pulled it down, inch by inch, staring up into Arianna's eyes as he did so, until the soft cloth was around her ankles. Gently lifting one foot at a time, he

138

pulled the hose free.

A little shudder of desire crept through Arianna as Rob flung the hose aside and she anticipated what was yet to come.

Rob's hands moved beneath her skirt again and up her silken legs, never taking his eyes from her face. Another shudder shook Arianna and she cried, "No, please, no farther."

"Just a little farther, Rose Petal, a little farther." His hands moved up her thighs, feeling the heat of her as he reached closer to the secret part of her he yearned to touch. So close, so close. His eyes became half-closed with desire, his breathing erratic as the skin beneath his fingers grew moister, hotter . . .

"Rob, you mustn't. I have no underthings on."

His hands stopped moving as her words sank in and with a low groan he removed his hands, letting her skirt fall into place. In agony he circled her waist tightly, burying his head in the softness of her lower belly. "Oh God, I want you so."

Arianna's hands cradled his head, pulling him even tighter against her, feeling the warmth of his breath reach through the velvet to the part of her that ached for his touch. Unable to stop herself, she felt her body undulate against his head, wanting, needing more of him.

Knowing how close he was to losing control completely, Rob released himself from Arianna's grasp and stood, holding her at arm's length. His breath was constricted, his need so great he knew there was but one thing he could do now to safeguard her virginity.

Backing up, his eyes never leaving her face, Rob felt the water enter his boots.

"Rob, what are you doing?"

Backing farther into the brook, he felt the cool water creep up his legs.

"Rob, stop it! You fool, you're getting soaked."

Reaching the deepest part of the water, he lowered himself until he was sitting on the sandy bottom, the cold water easing his throbbing manhood.

Arianna's mouth flew open in astonishment; then she began to laugh, her ardor now in control. "Whatever possessed you to do such a foolish thing?"

"My innocent little angel, I vowed to protect you from amorous rogues, and upon my sword, that includes myself."

Chapter Twelve

The fire crackled and sputtered into life as Fiona stirred up the logs with a stick, her ears pricked, listening while Lord Robert entertained his mother and Arianna in the small sitting room between his chamber and Arianna's. My, but the young lord was pleased with his lady, she thought to herself. Why, the air fairly crackled with the energy of his voice, as if rent by a powerful lightning bolt.

"And the way she handled the falcon, incredible. Mother, you should have seen it. You'd never believe the skill such a small baggage as she has with such fierce birds. Next time you must join us."

Margaret bent her head low over her embroidery to hide the smile that crossed her face. Rob's happy enthusiasm was a joy to behold. She had worried often about him, wondered if he would ever be happy, and now, it was clear that he was. Arianna would be the perfect mate for him after all. "I'd like that. It's been a long time since I sported about."

"Since Father died two years ago. High time you began enjoying life again."

"And I shall, but first, I'm thinking the wedding will keep us all more than a little busy, since you're marrying so soon. Why, one would think you *had* to marry for all the haste."

Arianna's face turned red as it was wont to do since this morning by the water. Every time she thought of the intimate way Rob had touched her and the way it made her feel, she was embarrassed all over again.

"Mother! What a thing to say. Look at Arianna. Have you ever seen so innocent a girl?"

"Forgive me, Arianna. I was only jesting. Though it was a poor joke, to be sure. I know how pure you are. Don't pay any attention to me. I'm just a jealous old woman — jealous of the love that I see shining in my son's eyes. I miss my Robert looking at me as yours looks at you."

"Lady Margaret, there's no need to be jealous. A child's love for his mother can never be broken; in sooth, Rob shall love you all the more after we've wed. When he sees how it is between the two of us, he'll remember that his father felt the same about you. 'Twill make his heart grow all the larger for it."

Margaret reached over to clasp Arianna's hand. "You have been gifted with the mind of a sage. There is much truth to what you say."

"And what about the gift of beauty, Mother?"

"Aye, in that she has great wealth, son. She'll produce beautiful grandchildren, I have no doubt."

Rising from her chair, Arianna moved over to the fire, pleased but embarrassed by all the flattery. "Can we talk of something else? I fear I'll get a toothache from your sugary words."

Rob grasped Arianna's hand and pulled her down to the settee beside him. "Very well, my blushing rose. Mother, what's the latest gossip from court? It's been a while since I've heard you speak of the happenings there."

142

"And little interest you have in the subject, too. But there is some news from court that might interest even you. Edmund Deveraux, poor fellow, has become one of the queen's favorites."

"Poor fellow? Most men would give their right arm for that privilege."

"To be sure they would, son, until the queen clamps down on it with her sharp teeth. She turns her favorites into virtual prisoners, I've heard, not even allowing them the right to choose whom they marry or, for that matter, forbidding them to marry at all."

"Is that so? Then there's yet another to pity. Judith, Will's sister. She's decided that Edmund's to be her husband."

"Mayhap the queen will not mind Edmund marrying," Arianna interjected. "Why should she object?"

"Arianna, sweet, there's no accounting for the actions of a queen. But I wouldn't worry about Edmund. He'll not stay long in her favor—then he'll be free to marry as he chooses."

A light knock sounded on the door and Buttercup poked her head in. "Begging your pardons, but I've brought the mulled wine."

"Thank you, Buttercup. You may serve it now," Margaret said with a smile.

The buxom maid entered, carrying a wooden tray, and proceeded to hand a tankard to each of them. Rob watched, amused at Buttercup's continued nervousness; then his expression changed as he noticed the dagger sheathed at her waist.

"Buttercup, come here."

Fearful she had done something wrong, Buttercup made her way to Rob. "Yes, Your Lordship?"

Rob reached for the dagger, pulling it out of its sheath. "I thought so. Buttercup, what are you

143

doing with this dagger?"

"I borrowed it from Lady Arianna until I could get one of my own." Buttercup turned to Arianna, paling when she saw the distress in her mistress's eyes. "Your Ladyship, I meant no harm. I was going to return it."

Arianna's heart froze at the sight of the dagger Rob recognized as his own. She'd been a fool to bring it to Everly, but it was so precious to her she didn't have the heart to leave it behind.

"Buttercup," Rob said, becoming angry. "I gave this very dagger to you two years ago, asking you to give it to Sparrow. Now I find it in your possession. Why did you keep it for yourself? Surely you knew how much I wanted Sparrow to have it?"

Buttercup's eyes opened in horror, recognizing the dagger for the first time. She realized immediately she had put Arianna in jeopardy. "I'm so sorry, Rob, I mean, Lord Warwick. I don't know what came over me. I . . ."

Arianna knew Buttercup was trying to protect her, but she couldn't let her do it. Enough lies had been told already.

"Buttercup, don't. I'm going to tell Rob the truth."

Buttercup looked at Rob with horror and suddenly he was not sure he wanted to hear what was to come.

"Rob, Buttercup did give the dagger to Sparrow, just as you asked. She would never go against your wishes."

Rob remained silent, his uneasiness growing stronger every second.

"Oh Rob, I wish you never had to know. I'm suddenly afraid of losing you, but I have no choice — you have the right to know. Everything I've told you is a lie. Everything *Sparrow* ever told you was a lie, for you see we are one and the same."

Rob slowly shook his head in deep denial.

"Sparrow? You can't be. He . . ."

" 'Tis true. I was forced to disguise myself as a boy. It was my only protection."

"Why are you telling me this, Rose Petal? To protect Buttercup? There's no need. I'm not going to punish her for taking my dagger."

"Rob, look at me. I *am* Sparrow. Everything I told you about being in a convent was a lie. I lived at Norbridge with Peter and Sybille, my foster parents. I'm so sorry. I know what you must think of me for . . ."

Rob jumped to his feet, the blood rushing to his head as he realized the truth. "Think of *you?* What must you think of *me* for believing it all? What a fool I've been! What a complete and utter fool, treating you like a delicate flower when all along you were used to the rough company of men. Privy to their vulgar oaths, their naked bodies, and God knows how much more. And that story about the convent, why? What need did you have for that?"

Arianna cowered under Rob's onslaught. "Will thought . . ."

"Will? Was he in on it, too? Does the whole world know of this but me? My God, what a fool I've been."

Arianna's face paled to white. She stood and reached out to touch his arm. "No, Rob, you're not the fool. I am, for ever thinking I could get away with this. It's just . . . I loved you so . . . I couldn't bear the thought of you marrying Judith."

Rob raised his elbow to brush away Arianna's touch. "Love? Don't speak of love. The word sounds foreign to your tongue. You wanted me for one reason only — for the life I could give you." Throwing his tankard against the stone wall, he strode out of the small chamber, slamming the door behind him.

Arianna was stunned at Rob's anger. "Why didn't he understand, why didn't he understand? He's always been so kind, so good, why . . ."

Margaret walked over to the fireplace and warmed her hands before the flames, gathering her thoughts before she spoke. She wasn't quite sure what was going on, but one thing was clear: both young people were hurting and both loved each other deeply. "Arianna, I don't know what need you had to deceive my son, but if you're willing to tell me, I'm willing to listen. Mayhap this can all be worked out."

"Too late, too late. He'll never forgive me and I can't blame him. I'll leave in the morning. He'll never have to see me again."

"Child, surely it won't come to that. Come sit by the fire with me and tell me everything."

"Lady Margaret, how can you be so kind to me after what you've heard? You should hate me as much as I hate myself."

"Arianna, nothing in this world is all black or all white. I learned that a long time ago. Tell me your story and let me be the judge of whether I should hate you or not."

Sitting down by the fire, Arianna wiped her tears away and unburdened herself, telling Margaret everything that had happened since she moved to Norbridge with Peter and Sybille. She wanted Lady Margaret to understand what her son could not. Her voice murmured on as the fire changed from crackling flames to glowing embers, and Margaret again filled Arianna's goblet with wine to soothe her nerves.

When Arianna was done, Margaret gathered her in her arms. "You poor child, you're not to blame for any of this. 'Twill be all right, you'll see. Rob's pride is hurt now, and he feels betrayed, but after he's had time to think about it, he'll come around. Now dry your eyes and drink some more wine. It'll help you sleep. I'll call your attendants to make ready your bed."

Arianna stared into the fireplace until Buttercup led her into her bedchamber. Fiona, Deirdre, and Annie all waited solemnly, knowing something was wrong. At the sight of Arianna's tear-stained face they tried to cheer her up, laying out the prettiest nightshift from the folded pile Margaret had sent to her chamber.

After Arianna was dressed for bed, Fiona set about combing her hair while Deirdre and Annie folded back the bedcovers and Buttercup latched the window shutters. Suddenly, the door was flung open and a drunken Robert stood in the opening, swaying back and forth.

He stood there silently, aching at the tranquil scene and the beautiful woman at the center of it, his ever-present passion fueled by the sight of her looking so fragile, so feminine.

Arianna knew immediately what he wanted and so did her handmaidens. They moved quickly to surround her, barricading her from his sight.

Watching the attendants' protective movement, Rob became indignant. "Hah! She is not the one in need of protection. 'Tis I. Who will protect me from her? Who will protect my heart from breaking in two?" Waving his arms wildly and losing his balance for a moment, he shouted, "Get out, all of you. Leave me alone with your wicked mistress."

The women huddled closer.

"Out, I say. There is unsettled business here. Nights of agony to make up for, days of torture, until I couldn't think straight from wanting her. Teasing me with her body until all I wanted was to make her mine. Well, tonight I shall collect the payment long overdue."

The handmaidens moved closer to Arianna, their

eyes wide with fright. Even Buttercup was frightened, for she had never seen Robert this way before.

Arianna felt sick at heart knowing it was all because of her. She had never known fear in his presence and she felt none now. She had always felt most secure when he was near, and knowing that, she spoke soothingly, confidently to the women. "It's all right. You all may leave. I'll not come to any harm in this man's company."

With fearful glances in Rob's direction, the four young women left through the door that led to their sleeping quarters and closed the door quietly behind them.

Rob was taken aback by Arianna's brave move and floundered for a moment, but his anger overcame him once again when he remembered Sparrow standing up to him in the mews of Norbridge that first day. Staggering, he made his way to her while she slowly moved backwards until she was against the wall.

"Why don't you raise your fists to me now? Sparrow would. I showed you the proper way to hold them. Remember?"

"I remember. But you see . . . I'm not Sparrow anymore. I'll not resist," Arianna said quietly. "If you think I owe you a night in my bed, you shall have it. If all I am to you is a vessel to spend your passion in, then so be it. I won't stop you, but at morning's light, when you are done with me, my debt will be paid. I'll leave this place and you'll never see me again."

Never see her again? That wasn't an option he had considered. How could he live without her? How could he bear not holding her? Staring into her eyes, he saw tears flood them into liquid sapphires. "Damn you. Damn you to hell." Raising his fist, he slammed it into the wall behind her head, the pain in his hand easing for a moment the pain in his heart. Then he turned and left.

Arianna saw his shining eyes and knew the pain she had caused.

Enough! she thought with a shudder. He's suffered enough! No more of this!

Rob was right, he did need protection. And she would provide it . . . by leaving.

When morning came, Arianna put on a happy face for her attendants, knowing she must keep them in the dark until the last moment. They would go for a ride after breakfast, then once safely away from the castle she would send them back and head for Norbridge.

Walking past Rob's chamber, she noticed the door was ajar, and hoping for one last glimpse, peeked in. He lay splayed across the bed, fully dressed, his clothes disheveled, an empty tankard beside his head. Her selfishness had brought him to this, she thought, pain stabbing her heart. He would be better off without her.

The morning meal tasted like ashes, but she swallowed it all, knowing it would be a while before she had anything more to eat. When she was done, she mounted Pasha and with her attendants started out of the inner ward of the castle. Margaret, watching from her chamber window, waved gaily to them as they cantered through the gate.

As they made their way along the narrow road, Arianna looked back, remembering how full of hope she had been at seeing Everly for the first time. A huge lump formed in her throat. What twisted pagan gods of fate delighted in torturing her so? . . . letting her hope for a time that all would be well, only to smash her newfound happiness into a thousand pieces . . .

When they had gone far enough to assure they wouldn't be seen, Arianna drew Pasha to a halt. "But-

149

tercup, Fiona, this is where we part."

Buttercup felt a cold chill run up her spine. "My lady, what do you mean? It wouldn't be wise of you to ride by yourself. Lady Margaret would skin our hides if we let you, not to mention Robert."

"Buttercup, I'm not going for a morning jaunt, but leaving forever. I'm going back to Norbridge."

"Oh, Arianna, no!"

"Stop your wailing, Buttercup. I'm going and there's nothing you can say that will make me change my mind."

"Then I'm coming with you. 'Tis my fault you're running away and I won't let you go by yourself."

Arianna's tone softened. Buttercup wasn't responsible for any of this. "No, I want you to stay. You'll have a better life here. And you can say goodbye to Robert for me and return this to him." Arianna pulled out Rob's dagger. "It seems it's my turn to give it to him."

"Lady Arianna," Fiona said, "I don't pretend to understand, but surely you can wait until you have an escort. What need is there to run off like this?"

"What need?" Tears began to flow, and sobs shook her body. "What need? To leave whilst I still have the strength. If I look into his eyes once more, I'll never be able to go." Spurring her horse, she galloped off, leaving the women to stare after her helplessly.

Something woke Robert.

"Arianna!"

Tumbling out of bed, he staggered to the window and looked down at the courtyard below. Everything was fine, and yet, the uneasiness he felt was a physical thing. Glancing over the wall to the road beyond the castle his eyes focused on the figures on horses in the

150

distance. As they neared, he could make out Buttercup's chubby shape and Fiona's slim form riding back toward the castle. Arianna wasn't with them. Something was definitely wrong.

All signs of drunkenness were instantly gone from his body as he made his way to Arianna's chamber and pushed open the door, knowing in advance she wouldn't be there. Taking the stairs two at a time, he went down to the great hall and peered inside, scanning the room for a girl with golden hair. She wasn't there either.

Margaret saw the anxious look on her son's face. "What is it, Rob? What's happened?"

"Mother, have you seen Arianna this morning?"

Relief was evident on Margaret's face. "She went off riding with Buttercup and Fiona. They should . . ."

"My God!" Running outside, he made it to the gate just as Buttercup and Fiona rode through. One look at their faces and he felt his knees grow weak. "Where's Arianna? What's happened to her?"

"Oh Robert, I tried to stop her. I did, I did. But she wouldn't listen. She said to give you this." Buttercup handed the dagger to Robert, but he ignored it.

"Get off your horse."

Relieved, Buttercup jumped off and Robert mounted, riding off in a fury. Is this how Arianna resolves her problems, he muttered. Running off, hiding? Is this how the future Countess of Everly acts at the first sign of trouble? Fie! It's time she learned how to face problems, time she realized who she really is. Not Sparrow, not a girl from a convent, not . . .

Hearing the thundering of hooves, Rob looked up to see Pasha barreling down the road toward him, his saddle empty.

Arianna! Fear gripped him as he continued riding,

151

his eyes scanning the ground for a crumpled body. There ahead, a bundle of white lay on the road. Pulling to a halt, he leaped from the horse and ran to the pale form lying so still.

"Arianna," he cried, kneeling beside her and pulling her into his arms. "Please, Dear God, let her be all right."

A low moan escaped her lips.

"Arianna, Rose Petal, it's all right. I'm here."

"Rob," she murmured, opening her eyes. "I tried to leave you, but Pasha had other plans."

"Tried to leave me? And take my children from me?"

"Rob, are you still drunk? We have no children."

"Ah, but we will have—a dozen. If you leave now they'll never be born. Are you that cruel? Could you murder your own children?"

"Are you mad? Have I done this to you, too?"

"Oh God, Arianna, you've never done anything to me but love me. And isn't that what I've wanted all along? I don't care how you came to be with me, who your parents are, or any other bloody thing. The only thing that matters is that we be together. Marry me or pierce my heart with my dagger, for I can't be without you."

"Oh, Rob, I want to marry you more than anything in the world, but are you sure? Can you ever trust me again? For if you cannot, I'll leave."

"Never, never, never," Rob said, rocking her in his arms.

Two of Robert's yeomen rode up, leading Pasha between them.

"Is Lady Arianna all right? When we saw the horse come back with an empty saddle, we rode right out."

Rob looked up at the prancing white horse, its head tossing wildly as it tried to break loose. "Destroy him. I won't take the chance of him hurting Arianna again. She could have been killed."

Arianna drew in her breath. "No, Robert! You can't. Pasha is mine. How could you think of such a thing? I couldn't bear to have him destroyed and I don't understand how you can."

"Can't you?" Rob's voice was low and deadly earnest. "Then you don't know how much I love you."

"Oh Rob, it would be wrong to destroy this beautiful animal in the name of love. Look at him. Look at how magnificent he is. If I promise never to ride him unless you're with me, will that satisfy you?"

Rob hesitated. It would be hard to destroy something so beautiful, but . . . Gazing into Arianna's face, he saw how much she cared for Pasha. "How can I refuse, when you put it that way? And he did keep you from leaving me. All right, I concede, but it's against my better judgment. He's a dangerous animal. He's proven that twice already, but if you give me your sacred promise not to ride him unless I'm with you, then his life will be spared."

A triumphant laugh rang through the air. "Then help me up, for I'm riding him back to the castle."

Laughing, Rob pulled Arianna to her feet. "You bewitching little baggage! You still have Sparrow's spunk. I can see I'm going to have my hands full with you." Helping her into the saddle, he shook his head in awe. "I don't mind telling you, though; it eases my mind considerably knowing Sparrow was not a boy but a desirable female."

"Is that so, my lord? Well, I don't mind telling you how much I enjoyed seeing you naked when you thought I was Sparrow." With that, she dug her knees into Pasha and galloped off, leaving Rob to stare after her with a dazed expression.

153

Chapter Thirteen

Glowing fingers of red spread across the twilight sky, adding a pinkish tint to the stones of Everly Castle. Peter and Sybille Trilby arrived, accompanied by Lord William Ludlow and his entourage. Included in the colorful party were two horses gaily decorated and laden with presents for the betrothed. They had come none too soon, for the wedding would be on the morrow.

Hearing of their arrival, Arianna and Rob left the crowded great hall so that they might greet her foster mother and father outside in private. No one at Everly knew Peter and Sybille's true relationship to Arianna except Lady Margaret, Buttercup, and Fiona, and for now that was how it would remain. But Arianna was eager for the day when everyone could know the truth — she had come to hate deception of any sort.

"Glad I am to see you safely here," Rob's voice boomed. "Arianna was worried you wouldn't make it for the wedding."

Will jumped from his horse and strode up to Rob, pumping his hand eagerly. "Not make it for the wedding? Not bloody likely. We would have been here sooner, but were delayed unexpectedly. We'll talk of

154

that later. Right now, I have two people here anxious to see their daughter."

Peter and Sybille stepped forward and Arianna gloried in the sight of them. Her mother was dressed in new clothing from head to foot, and Papa's hair was trim and orderly, his quilted blue jerkin spotless. "Mama, Papa, I'm so happy you're here. Now my happiness is complete." In an instant, she had her arms around them.

"And ours, too. Now that you'll be safely wed, and to such a one as Rob," Peter said gruffly. "He'll take good care of you, I've no doubt."

Rob offered his hand to Peter, saying, "Upon my uword, of that you can be certain."

Peter was beaming as he pulled Sybille to his side. "This is my wife, Sybille. I don't believe you two have ever met."

"Not formally, but I've seen her beautiful face in Norbridge many a time."

Sybille lowered her lashes, answering with a lilting voice, "You flatter me, sir. I can see why our Arianna fell in love with you."

Seeing Rob occupied with Peter and Sybille, Will strode over to Arianna and embraced her, whispering in her ear, "Well, little Sparrow, you truly fly with the hawks now. Are you as happy as you look?"

"Oh Will, I can't tell you how happy. Even knowing the truth, Rob still wants to marry me."

Will held Arianna at arm's length and searched her face. "He knows? Then I am truly happy for you. Rob is an admirable man."

"What was that you said, Will?" Rob asked, coming up behind him. "Who is admirable?"

"Why, I am, of course, for arranging for the two of

155

you to meet. Now, if you'll have someone show my attendants where to put our things . . ."

"Of course. Arianna's women will show the way. I'm afraid we're short of help at the moment. Everyone is occupied with preparations for the wedding."

"Including the men and women we passed in the fields outside the walls? Just what are they doing there, anyway? I could swear they were chasing fireflies."

"Shhh!" Rob glanced over at Arianna, but she was talking to her mother and didn't hear. "It's a secret, a surprise for Arianna tomorrow evening."

"Hmmm, I can't imagine what it is, but knowing you, I'm sure it will be something romantic." Will's countenance suddenly became more serious. "Peter and I must speak to you in private, Rob. Where can we talk?"

"What is it, will?" Rob's eyes clouded. Confound it, what was it that made him feel so afraid of losing Arianna? She was safe in his castle and would wed him tomorrow. What could possibly happen to separate them? "We can talk in my chamber. No one will interrupt us there."

Upstairs, Will drained a tankard of wine, then wiped his face. "Before I tell you what's on my mind, Peter has something important to tell you . . . about Arianna's true parents."

"Aye, I do, but first you must promise never to reveal to a living soul what you hear this night, not even to Arianna."

"Not even Arianna? I don't understand. Why can't she know since it concerns her?"

"After I've told you, you'll understand. Will knows already. It became necessary to tell him yesterday when Queen Elizabeth made a surprise visit to Norbridge, seeking the Earl of Clinton. He's been there since you and Arianna left."

"Yes, I was sure Judith would see that he stayed a while as she has hopes of becoming his bride. But what has this to do with Queen Elizabeth?"

"The Queen is the reason we've had to hide Arianna's identity since she was born," Peter said. "You see, Arianna's father is Robert Dudley, Earl of Leicester."

Rob gave out a low whistle. "Are you serious?"

Peter nodded solemnly. "Very serious."

"Then I'm beginning to understand. If Leicester's her father, I pity the poor woman who gave birth to his child. If Elizabeth ever gets her hands on her . . ."

"You may well pity Arianna's mother, for she be Mary, Queen of Scots."

"This is no time to jest, Peter."

"He speaks the truth, Rob. Arianna's mother is the Scottish Queen."

"Arianna, the daughter of a queen? 'Tis hard to conceive of such a notion. I don't know what to say." Rob's gaze moved from Will to Peter and back again, his brown eyes reflecting his amazement. They were serious. "I was amazed enough to find out Arianna is Sparrow, but this—this is too incredible. Why haven't you told Arianna who her parents are? She has a right to know."

"Aye, that's true, but for now 'tis best she be in the dark. Elizabeth has been searching for Leicester's child since she was born. She wanted to raise her as her own, and, thwarted all these years, she now seeks revenge. We have no way of knowing what evil plan

157

she has in mind for Arianna if she's found and we can't take the chance that she'd be benevolent."

"But since she doesn't know who she is, then surely Arianna is safe."

"She has been . . . 'til now. It seems Edmund talked the queen into accompanying him and my sister Judith to Clinton castle near here, and when she heard you were going to be married, decided she'd stop in and attend the wedding. She thinks it would be a lark to surprise you like that."

"A lark? Elizabeth here? My God! We haven't any room to put her up, not with the huge entourage she travels with. Her visit will disrupt everything."

"That won't be a problem. She's staying only long enough to see you married, then she'll continue on to Edmund's."

"That's a relief. I envisioned having to ask all the wedding guests to camp in the fields while Elizabeth and her party take over the chambers." Seeing their solemn expressions, Rob sobered. "Elizabeth and Arianna together in the same castle. My God! You're afraid she'll discover who Arianna is—that's what troubles you."

"I know the chances are slim," Will answered. "Though Arianna resembles her mother greatly, Elizabeth and the Scottish Queen have never met in person, and the portraits Mary has sent of herself through the years hardly do her justice. So it would seem highly unlikely Elizabeth would see the resemblance; still, there is that fear. You see now why we can't tell Arianna yet who she is. How could she hide her nervousness tomorrow, meeting Elizabeth, if she knew the queen was searching for her, if she knew Elizabeth held her mother captive all these years because of her?"

"I see, and agree. Arianna mustn't be told. It'll be hard enough for me to hide my fears tomorrow. God's wound, if Elizabeth took her away from me . . ."

Will put his arm on Rob's shoulder. "It won't happen, Rob. Forewarned, we can make sure Elizabeth never finds out.

After a hearty supper of stew and crisp hot bread, Lady Margaret bustled around seeing to the needs of her guests. Every room in the castle was filled to overbrimming and more guests were expected on the morrow. Messengers had been sent to all the nearest lords and ladies inviting them, and they had been trickling in along with their knights and ladies and attendants all day long.

Margaret's nerves were on end trying to cope with all the details, but she managed to keep smiling for her guests, providing local musicians and madrigals to entertain in front of the fire in the great hall. Sinking wearily into a chair her son brought to her, she smiled gratefully and patted his hand. "Always the thoughtful son. Arianna is a lucky girl to win you as her husband."

"And I shall remind her of that every day of her life."

Rob's smile didn't reach his eyes, and Margaret was suddenly worried. "What is it, son? I know you well. Something is bothering you."

"Mother, 'tis nothing. I'm just anxious for tomorrow to come."

"Yes, I'm certain you are, but is that all? There's nothing amiss?"

159

"Now what could possibly be amiss? You and I have worked hard these past two weeks to make this wedding the grandest this old castle has ever seen. Stop fretting and enjoy this last evening of my bachelorhood." Rob kissed his mother's forehead, then made his way to Arianna, sitting beside her on a bench.

Was this the uneasiness he had felt since the day he asked Arianna to marry him? Elizabeth? Was she the cause of his worry? No, it was all foolishness, he assured himself. But to be safe, he would keep Elizabeth's visit secret, even from his mother. If his mother knew, she'd have a sleepless night to be sure, and after all her work, she'd need a restful sleep. And, too, it would be better for everyone to be truly surprised when Elizabeth arrived. Let her have her petty little surprise, then be on the move, out of harm's way, out of Arianna's life.

Slipping his arm around Arianna's waist, he whispered, "Just think, Rose Petal. Tomorrow night at this time, you'll be in my bed."

"And you, my lord, where will you be?" Arianna answered teasingly.

"I'll be where I've dreamt to be . . . inside you . . . inside paradise."

Arianna's face flamed. "Rob!"

Rob laughed and pulled her to her feet. "Come, there are too many people here for what I have in mind." Taking her hand, he led her outside.

Arianna shivered in the damp night air and Rob took off his mantle to wrap around her shoulders, staring down at her in a way that left no doubt in her mind what he was thinking.

Blushing once again, she looked away, her eyes

160

suddenly attentive to the strange sight before them. Men and women were running around the courtyard with outstretched hands. They seemed to be . . . chasing fireflies? Surely not . . .

Rob steered her around a corner out of their sight. He didn't want her to know what they were doing. It would spoil the surprise he had planned for their wedding night. Pressing her up against the stone wall, he kissed her tenderly.

"Are you afraid, Rose Petal?"

"Afraid? Of what?"

"Of what you and I will be doing in my bed."

Arianna gazed deep into Rob's eyes. "Nothing you could ever do would frighten me. I trust you with my life, with my soul, with the very breath I breathe."

Rob felt a hard lump in his throat. Arianna had a way of making him feel like a god, to feel there wasn't anything in the world he couldn't do. Her love made him invincible and he knew he would brave any danger for her.

Activity went on long into the night at Everly Castle, preparing for the morrow's event. Margaret sent Arianna off to her bedchamber early, accompanied by Sybille, who would be sharing her bed. The bride would need her rest.

After Fiona and Buttercup had finished preparing them for bed they left, knowing Arianna's desire to speak to Sybille alone. Arianna filled her mother in on everything that had happened to her since she left Norbridge and Sybille did the same. Then, picking up a large ornate chest, Sybille placed it on the bed and opened it. "Arianna, I've brought you a very special gown from your . . . mother."

Arianna looked at Sybille in bewilderment. "My mother! But how? Does that mean you've found her?"

"Truth to tell, we've always known where she is."

"You knew where she was but never told me? She knew where I was and never sought me out? Never cared enough to see me?"

"Arianna, your mother has always cared about you, always. 'Tis no fault of hers that she could not see you. You must believe that. The day after you left Norbridge, your father went to her and told her of your betrothal. She was so happy for you. But sad, too, that she couldn't attend. She thought if you wore this gown at your wedding, that in some small way she could be a part of it."

"A part of it? When she's chosen to ignore me all my life? If she cared for me at all she would have made herself known to me long ago."

"Sweet, believe me, that was impossible. Your mother, does not have the . . . freedom to do as she wishes."

"I don't understand."

"I wish I could tell you more, but knowing any more would put you in jeopardy."

"What kind of jeopardy? What have you been hiding from me? I'm a grown woman now. I have a right to know."

"And your mother has a right to keep you safe. Come, let's not speak of this any longer. It's a joyous time for you, let's not spoil it. Aren't you even going to look at the gown?"

"No! Take it back to Norbridge or wear it yourself! I'll not ease her conscience by wearing it."

"Oh, child, I hate to see you hurt so. Your mother

loves you as much as I do, and if she had her way she would be here for your wedding. Believe that and let go of the bitterness."

"How can I, Mother, when I don't understand. If I had a child nothing in this world would make me give it up."

Arianna tried to push all thoughts of her true mother from her mind, but late that night when everyone was asleep, she lay awake tossing and turning, her thoughts on the chest just a few feet away. Unable to fight her feelings any longer, she crept out of bed so as not to wake Sybille and made her way over to it.

Lifting the gown gently, she carried it to the window to look at it in the light of the moon. Her hands stroked the shimmering surface of the pale blue taffeta shot with threads of silver. She was in awe of its exquisite beauty. Never had she seen such a garment.

To think her own mother had worn this very gown, but where? When? She pressed her nose to the garment, inhaling the faint aroma of delicate perfume. Her mother's scent. Who was she, the woman who owned this gown?

No peasant woman ever wore a gown as dear as this. Why hadn't she been told her true mother was a gentlewoman? Why couldn't she know her, be with her? Tears came to Arianna's eyes as she pressed the exquisite fabric to her face. Tears of longing for the mother she had never known spilled from her eyes.

Chapter Fourteen

She couldn't awaken, couldn't pull herself out of the nightmare that had her in its terrifying grip. Edmund naked. Judith with a dagger. Coming for her. Reaching for her. She couldn't move, tangled in the strangling web. *No! No! Robert! Help me! I need you!*

Then, miraculously, the sound of beautiful music broke through the murderous web, dissolving it into a fine mist that floated harmlessly away. She heard the soft flurry of wings and gazing skyward, she saw two angels gliding down to her, like peregrines on an invisible current of air.

Long slender fingers grasped her arms, lifting her over the heads of Edmund and Judith, carrying her away to the safety of a high hill. Relieved, she sighed deeply, then opened her eyes.

The soft music of lutes and lyres surrounded her still — the same angelic music she heard in her dream. Rubbing her eyes, she sought the source. Annie and Deirdre sat on either side of the bed playing the soothing instruments. She smiled and sank back to her pillow, content. It was her wedding day. Soon she would be Rob's wife, safe from Edmund, safe from the nightmare he symbolized.

"My lady, you're awake at last. Lord Robert was

afraid you'd sleep the day away and asked us to wake you with soft music."

"Did he? My sweet Lancelot. 'Twas a lovely way to wake up."

"Aye, but he resembles not Sir Lancelot now," Annie said, laughing. "Be glad you won't be seeing him until the ceremony, my lady, for the very sight of him would make your stomach cleave together in one hard lump."

"What do you mean?"

"Been up since the crack of dawn, he has, running around like a whirlwind making sure everything is set for the ceremony and driving Lady Margaret crazy with his nervous behavior. Then up to the ramparts he goes, time and time again, looking out into the distance as if expecting someone. Lady Margaret told him everyone has already arrived except for the Duke of Clinton and Lady Judith of Norbridge."

Arianna's heart constricted upon hearing the names of the two people she dreamt of so often. Why did she have so many nightmares about them? There was nothing to worry about anymore. It didn't matter if Edmund suddenly remembered seeing her with the Scottish Queen. Rob knew the truth now, so Edmund couldn't hurt her anymore.

A light rap sounded on the door and Lady Margaret and Sybille walked in. "Ah, you're up. I'll send for a tray of food. After you've eaten Sybille and I will help you dress."

"Oooh, don't mention food. Suddenly, my stomach isn't feeling very well."

"That's to be expected, my dear. But you'll be fine, which is more than I can say for my son. If he doesn't slow down, he's going to be too tired to perform his duty in the marriage bed this evening."

Buttercup entered the room with Arianna's breakfast tray in time to hear Lady Margaret's remarks. "Never fear. Our Rob will do his duty, all right. Never was a man so ready. If you get my meaning. Been waiting a lifetime, you might say."

Lady Margaret looked at Buttercup askance, but Sybille's friendly laughter tamed her anger. "Don't mind about Buttercup—she's always been one to speak her mind. And if it be true he comes to Arianna a virgin, then I say she's a lucky girl indeed."

Arianna blushed at Sybille's words.

"We're embarrassing our little bride," Lady Margaret said. "Let's speak of bridal beds no more. Buttercup, fetch the tub. A nice warm bath and a cup of mead will set her right."

Lady Margaret spoke the truth. Sitting in the tub of hot water and sipping on a cup of warm mead was calming indeed, and the music Annie and Deirdre played added greatly to her tranquility.

A young boy of about nine or ten was admitted to the chamber and stood near the door, nervously looking about at all the women. "My lady, begging your pardon, I be Donald. Sent to you by my lord. He has composed a poem for you and bade me say it to you now, but . . ."

"Oohh, how wonderful. Do say it."

Pleased, he took a step toward the tub.

The ladies in the chamber began to titter.

"From where you are, if you please, Donald."

Fiona moved quickly to block the young lad's view.

"As you wish, my lady." Clearing his throat, he began, bursting the air with his nervous soprano voice.

166

Sweet velvet petal of the ivory rose
My love for thee cannot be found in prose
But in sweet notes of passion's tune
Sung in harmony beneath God's stars and moon
When crimson drop adorns our sterling sheet
Then all will know this troth be a holy feat
And like bright angels joined in glorious choir
So shall our love burn pure as heaven's fervent fire

Arianna's heart soared. Robert, her own sweet Robert had written that for her. Was ever there a man so romantic? Noticing the sudden stillness in the room, her gaze moved from woman to woman. There was no need for words. Smiling, she turned her attention to the small boy.

"Thank you, Donald. That was very well done. You may tell your lord I am greatly pleased and shall thank him properly when next we meet."

Donald's face lit up. "Yes, my lady. Thank you, my lady. I will tell him, my lady." Backing up, he stumbled over Annie's lyre, righting himself in time to keep from crushing it underfoot. Wiping his forehead with his hand, he turned and left. Arianna held back her amusement 'til he was far enough away, then laughed in delight.

She stepped out of the bath and her handmaidens wrapped her in a large linen towel. "Buttercup, fetch the pale blue gown."

"Pale blue?" Buttercup asked. "I thought ye were going to wear . . ."

Looking directly at her foster mother, she said, "The blue one, please. It has special meaning."

Sybille smiled back, nodding slowly.

"I hope you don't mind, Lady Margaret. The gown you gave me is lovely, it's just . . ."

Margaret saw the melancholy look in Arianna's bright eyes. "My dear, 'tis your wedding and should be the way you want it. Now get you dressed—a very impatient young man awaits outside."

Suddenly everyone in the room was busy, each attending to Arianna's needs. When at last they were finished, Arianna gazed in the looking glass, a deep blush suffusing her face.

Never had she felt so beautiful. The pale blue taffeta was exquisite. Shot with silver thread and adorned with a delicate white lace ruff at the neck, it flattered her enormously. Annie and Deirdre had worked on her hair for over an hour, braiding some of it to circle the crown of her head like a coronet, entwined with pearls, the rest to hang down her back in delicate curls. How many times had she dreamed of this?

As she beheld her reflection, Fiona draped a sheer silk veil over her head, covering her face in front and trailing to the floor behind her in a long train. Then Buttercup handed her a wreath made of oak leaves and acorns entwined with pale pink rosebuds to carry and, for luck, clasped a gold chain around her neck with the Scottish Queen's ring strung on it. It nestled down between her breasts comfortingly.

"Oh, Buttercup. Is that truly I?"

"Aye, my lady, it truly be," Buttercup said, sighing deeply. "Our Rob will be most pleased."

Lady Margaret was about to reprimand Buttercup for her unseemly familiarity when the sound of trumpets filled the air. Running to the window, she looked down to see a huge party approaching the castle. Her heart stopped when she saw the Queen's banners flying boldly above the riders and the Queen herself sitting regally on a dashing black charger.

"Heavenly Father, what am I to do? The Queen is here. What can she want in Everly? Ohhh, quickly everyone, we must greet her. We must make her welcome. Hurry, hurry . . ." Lady Margaret started for the door, sheer panic on her face.

The others followed after, all except Sybille who stood frozen with fright.

"Mother, think of it, Queen Elizabeth here—on my wedding day. Isn't it exciting, isn't it . . ." Seeing the frightened look on Sybille's face, Arianna's heart suddenly lurched. Something was wrong, something terrible, to judge by Sybille's expression. "What is it, Mother? Why am I suddenly frightened?"

"Arianna, dearest, I . . . 'Tis nothing. The Queen's sudden appearance took me by surprise, that's all. It seems you shall have a royal audience for your wedding." Walking slowly to the window, Sybille looked down in dread, steeling herself for the sight of the hated Queen. Her eyes opened wide when she saw the Earl of Leicester helping Elizabeth from her horse. Leicester here? A guest at his own daughter's wedding? But . . . he couldn't know that.

Arianna joined Sybille at the window. "Look at her, Mother, how regal she looks. And that man beside her, what a striking figure he is. Oh, this is like a dream come true. But, oh dear, I'll be so nervous in their presence. How will I ever get through the ceremony?"

Taking Arianna by the shoulder, Sybille led her away from the window. "You'll be fine. Just look to

169

Robert. Keep your gaze on him and you'll forget anyone else exists."

"Oh, yes, Mother. One glimpse of him and I'll be fine."

In short time, Lady Margaret returned to the chamber, unable to contain her excitement. "All is in readiness. The Queen has been seated, along with her entourage, and the chapel is filled to brimming. Thank goodness, she'll be leaving right after the ceremony. Going to the Earl of Clinton's. He's here with her, and Lady Judith as well, and the Earl of Leicester and . . ." Wiping her brow, Lady Margaret closed her eyes for a second, then continued. "I'm fairly faint with excitement. To think the Queen regards Rob so highly that she would ride to his wedding. You should feel honored, my dear."

"I do, indeed, Lady Margaret. Tell me, what is she like? Did she actually speak with you?"

"Yes, yes, truly she did. And sounding exactly as you would suppose a Queen would sound. You'll find out for yourself. I'm sure she'll want to speak with you after the ceremony."

Sybille felt a tightening in her chest.

Hearing voices in the hall, Lady Margaret opened the door, proclaiming, "It's time. Arianna, are you ready?"

Swallowing hard, Arianna scooped up the hem of her gown and said. "To marry your son? Oh, yes!"

Sybille kissed Arianna's cheek. "Remember what I told you. Look to Robert and you'll be fine." Following after Lady Margaret, she left the room as two small girls dressed as angels, complete with gauze wings, arrived. Taking Arianna's hand, they proudly led her out the door, more than pleased at being chosen for this most important task.

A double line of small girls similarly dressed waited for Arianna in the hallway. She hadn't been expecting them and was delighted they would be a part of the ceremony. Solemnly she took her place behind them and the processional began, wending its way down the curved staircase and then through the great hall, emerging on the walkway to the chapel.

Trumpets sounded when Arianna stepped out into the light and suddenly the air was filled with the crystalline soprano voices of a hundred boys. The sweet sound came from every direction. Looking up, she saw them standing on the surrounding parapet, miniature angels in white robes against the backdrop of the bright blue sky.

Oh, how beautiful, she thought joyously. Contentment swept through her as she walked slowly toward the chapel, Rob's love surrounding her like a velvet mantle. She could feel his presence everywhere.

Moving to the music of the children's voices, she stepped into the chapel.

Hundreds of candles twinkled from the gilded altar, and from the congregation. She gasped at the beauty of it all and felt a kinship to all gathered there. Then Robert was at her side, ready to escort her to the altar and she was aware of no one but him. Gazing into his warm brown eyes, her heart brimmed with love.

Rob was dressed in a white doublet trimmed with gold, looking more handsome than she had ever seen him. The light shining in his eyes reflected the thousand twinkling candles and the love he felt for her.

She took his arm, proudly, reverently, and they started down the center aisle of the chapel until Rob

brought them to a stop in front of the first row of
pews. Arianna was puzzled until she saw him bow to
the Queen. Realizing what she must do, she curtsied
deeply, holding the pose until the Queen nodded her
head slightly, accepting the tribute. They continued
walking, their eyes now focused on the officiant who
would unite them.

The children's voices reached a crescendo and then
stilled. The ceremony began.

"All here be witness to the marriage covenant between Robert Anthony Charles Warwick, Earl of Everly, and Lady Arianna Rose. This be a holy union
entered into by two who believe wholly in the Protestant faith, knowing it to be the one true religion.
With this undying faith to guide them the bond between them shall be strengthened and all offspring
that come to this union shall be sanctified."

Arianna and Robert kneeled at the clergyman's
signal and he laid his hands on the tops of their
heads in unison. Arianna felt herself drifting away. It
was as if she had left her body and was looking down
at the scene from above. She saw herself kneeling beside Rob, saw the loving way he looked at her and
she at him, saw it all from far away. This was the
culmination of all she had dreamed of, and it was as
if she were dreaming it still.

She held out her hand as the pastor asked, watching as the tiny seeds fell from his hand to hers, so
slowly it seemed as if they floated. She clutched them
tight, knowing the importance of the symbolism. She
would be fertile for Rob, would bear him the many
children he wanted, and felt great satisfaction that
none of the seeds escaped her grasp. It was a good
omen. She watched as the clergyman kissed the

172

golden ring, then handed it to Rob. As he placed it on her trembling finger, he kissed it as if to seal the pact. It was done. She was his wife. She had her dream.

The boys began to sing once more, a jubilant song that matched Arianna's spirit, and the spectators blew out their candles, then began to cheer and clap. Rob pulled her to her feet and embraced her, holding her for a long time. Then gazing into her eyes, he proclaimed, "My wife, my beloved, every breath I breathe from this day forward I breathe for you."

Eyes shiny with tears, Arianna raised Rob's hand to her mouth and kissed it. Then they were surrounded by people laughing and talking, jostling them in their enthusiasm. One woman, in her eagerness to embrace Arianna, entangled her hand in the gold chain at Arianna's neck, pulling the ring from its snug home to dangle on her chest openly.

Suddenly a hush came over the crowd. It parted, revealing Queen Elizabeth making her way to the altar. Elizabeth looked neither to the left nor the right: her eyes locked onto Arianna.

Arianna felt her knees grow weak, but the touch of Rob's hand on her arm steadied her. She curtsied deeply. "Your Grace, I'm deeply honored at your presence."

Elizabeth's eyes never blinked, never left Arianna's face. "Yes, I thought it would be a goodly surprise. And indeed, it was well worth the effort, riding over here. Quite a spectacle, I must say, with all those angelic boys and girls. Yes, quite. You do things quite differently here in the country. Charming."

Elizabeth's eyes swept over her, making Arianna feel very uncomfortable, her uneasiness growing when the Queen's penetrating gaze stopped suddenly, staring at Arianna's chest. A steely look transformed Elizabeth's face. "That ring on your chain. How did you come by it?"

Blanching, Arianna looked down. Why was the queen interested in the ring? She couldn't possibly know it came from the Scottish Queen. What was she to tell her? She couldn't speak the truth.

A deep masculine voice spoke for her.

"Ah, Elizabeth, you noticed. Since we rode here in such haste, we had no time to find a suitable wedding present for the young couple. I thought to make up for that by giving Lady Arianna the ring."

Arianna couldn't believe her ears. Who was this elegant nobleman who told such an outrageous lie? And for what reason?

"Is that so? Then, my dear, of course it is yours. You should be doubly honored by his gesture since it was I who bestowed the ring on the Earl of Leicester in the first place."

Arianna's mouth flew open and she stared at the handsome Earl. Was there another ring exactly like this one? Or did the ring truly belong to Queen Elizabeth originally? It was most puzzling, but she dare not question it, dare not reveal who gave it to her.

"I don't know what to say."

"Say nothing, my dear. A gift is a gift, is it not? But tell me, I'm puzzled as to when this gifting transpired, since the Earl has not left my side since we arrived at Everly."

Arianna was at a loss for words until Rob rescued her.

" 'Tis simple enough. The Earl gave me the ring upon your arrival, and I in turn gave it to my mother to take upstairs to Arianna. I wanted her to wear it at the ceremony to honor my gracious Queen and her noble Earl."

Elizabeth beamed at Robert. "Gallantly said. You could teach my courtiers a thing or two, I warrant, in the art of flattering a lonely Queen."

"Lonely Queen? I can't imagine that to be so, Your Grace, surrounded as you are by people who adore you."

Elizabeth laughed harshly, as if there were no joy in her heart. "Adore me? I wonder. But enough of this. Lead me to the food. I'm hungry after my long ride. Leicester, escort our blushing bride to the great hall. I'm stealing her husband for a short time." Taking Rob's arm, Elizabeth started for the door. The throng followed after, leaving Leicester alone with Arianna.

Arianna and Leicester stared at each other for a long time, she in awe of his elegance and glamour, and he with the sudden knowledge of who she was.

Speaking shyly, she said, "Thank you for rescuing me. I was at a loss as to what to tell her about my ivory ring. Do you really have one like it?"

"Like it? No, the one you have is the very one Elizabeth gave me. The one I in turn gave to yet another Queen. Somehow I think you knew that already. So you see, my lie has saved us both. Elizabeth would not be pleased to hear I gave her ring to her enemy, the beautiful Queen of Scots."

"I see. No, I don't see. I don't understand any of this. And I don't understand why you stare at me as if . . ."

"Yes?"

"As if you were my lover."

Leicester laughed softly. "No, not as a lover, but as someone deeply interested in your friendship."

Arianna drew a deep breath, feeling a sense of relief. He spoke so sincerely, she had no doubts of his sincerity. "That would be heady company for me, indeed, my lord, for raised in a convent as I was, I'm not used to such as you."

"Then I shall be happy to guide you. I hope . . . I want . . . to see more of you and your husband. I should like very much to visit you from time to time. Quietly, without the fanfare of Elizabeth's presence."

"I would like that, I think. Yes, I would like that, but now, don't you think we should join the others in the hall before the Queen steals my new husband away?" Smiling gaily, she took the Earl's arm, feeling suddenly content though she wasn't sure why, and pulled him toward the hall.

Robert Dudley, Earl of Leicester, smiled. So much like her mother, so very much like her. Caught up in her gay spirit, he laughed and moved with a sprightly step. He had found his daughter and though he might never be able to claim her publicly, from this day forward she would be an important part of his life.

All eyes turned to them as they walked into the great hall, their good spirits so obvious on their happy faces. There was an easy camaraderie about Leicester and Arianna that was delightful to see, Lady Margaret thought, but when she turned her gaze to Elizabeth, her heart stilled. Elizabeth was staring intently at Leicester and Arianna. Suddenly she feared for her new daughter-in-law.

Robert saw Elizabeth's gaze, too, and moved quickly to Arianna's side, his arms circling her waist protectively. In a low voice, he addressed Elizabeth's lover. "If you would keep my wife from harm, do not be so free with her. Elizabeth watches every move you make."

Startled, Leicester answered, "Forgive me, I didn't think . . ." Shifting his gaze to Elizabeth, he waved, and called out. "Ah, there she is." Making his way to the Queen, he kneeled and kissed her hand. "Sweet Lady, your presence lights the room with such radiance, one would think you to be the new bride. Ah, would that it were so, and after the many times you've rejected my proposals we were finally wed."

Elizabeth was caught off guard. "I haven't heard a proposal from you for a long time. Why are you suddenly taken with the urge? Though the answer must sadly be the same, I am pleased to know you still wish it so. Otherwise, I would question whether I am getting too old for you to look upon in a sultry way."

"Old? You? Never, my darling. You grow lovelier with each passing year, as you well know. Isn't that right, Edmund?"

Edmund heard his name and tore his attention away from Arianna and the puzzle of the ivory ring. He could swear Rob hadn't spent time with Leicester since they arrived and, therefore, couldn't have gotten the ring; but then, he certainly hadn't been keeping his eye on him. He had his hands full enough with Judith, what with her petulance since Elizabeth had visited him at Norbridge. It was petty jealousy, obviously. Judith hated the attention he bestowed upon the Queen.

If she were ever to become his wife, she would have to learn quickly that the Queen came first. His whole future depended upon Elizabeth's generosity

177

and he wouldn't jeopardize that for anyone.

"What did you say, Leicester?"

"I was asking you if you didn't think our Queen more radiant with each passing year."

"Indeed she is." Edmund turned his attention back to Arianna before realizing he was expected to fawn over the Queen much longer. How bothersome. The old crone was truly pathetic in her endless need for flattery. Walking over to Elizabeth, he said, "And what of her dancing ability, Leicester? Does she not have a graceful presence any swan would envy?"

Elizabeth preened, touching her red wig though unaware she was doing so. "Enough. You make my girlish heart blush."

Edmund smiled, hiding his contempt. Girlish heart? Ha! No girlish rhythm had beaten in that hard heart for lo these many years.

From a safe distance, Sybille and Peter watched the proceedings fearfully, making sure they stayed out of Edmund's line of vision. Thankfully, the crowd was so pressing it was not difficult.

Rob, too, was burdened by the knowledge of Arianna's true identity and found it hard to relax and enjoy what should have been the happiest moment in his life. And yet, despite all, it was indeed happy for Arianna belonged to him.

When the Queen's hunger was appeased sufficiently, she stood, ready to leave. Immediately the room became hushed and her ladies-in-waiting rushed to her side. Arianna caught her eye and moved quickly to the Queen. She curtsied and in a beseeching voice cried, "Do you go so soon? Say it isn't so."

Elizabeth smiled broadly. The young thing was de-

178

lightful, there was no getting around that. No fear showed in her bright eyes when she faced a Queen, which was highly unusual. It was a welcome sign, for it told her Arianna had no reason to be fearful. She was truly an innocent. How rare in this time of outrageous intrigues. "I'm afraid I must, my dear. It grows late and I still have an hour's ride to Clinton Castle."

"Then I pray you have a safe journey, Your Grace."

Elizabeth took Arianna's hand in hers, squeezing it lightly. "Thank you, my dear."

Waving to the throng surrounding her, Elizabeth made her way to the door. Before leaving, she glanced back at the young bride one last time, compelled by some mysterious force. There was something very appealing about Arianna, something aside form her fresh country sweetness. Something that made her wish Arianna had been born to her, born her own sweet daughter.

Chapter Fifteen

Once Queen Elizabeth's entourage had gone, the wedding guests were free to make merry. The celebrating began in earnest.

A few amongst them, though, held sober faces, knowing how close Arianna had come to being exposed. Each sought the gaze of the other, saying with their eyes what their lips held back in the crowded hall.

Arianna was unaware of their anxiety. Surrounded by curious folk eager to know her, she joined in friendly conversation with them all, moving from one group to the next. Rob joined her, a forced smile on his face for the crowd and for his young wife. Elizabeth's visit had drained him.

When it grew dark, torches were lit throughout the castle and the celebration escalated. With drink aplenty to wash their mouths, it wasn't long before most everyone was in a state of drunkenness. Will drank little, surprising even himself. Pulling out of his somber mood, he grasped Arianna's hand and led her out to the middle of the room to dance. Their enthusiastic dancing soon had the great hall reverberating to the clapping of the spectators as they moved to an energetic folk dance.

Seeing this, Rob shrugged off his anxiety. It was his wedding day, after all. No time for gloomy thoughts or melancholy. It was time to rejoice in his marriage to Arianna. Climbing on top of a table, he let out a loud whoop and leaped onto the floor, to the amazement of all. His feet moved swiftly, in time to the music, arms folded, back ramrod straight, showing off for his mate as men have from the beginning of time.

Arianna couldn't believe what she saw. Never had she seen Rob so full of life, so full of vitality, so . . . yes, sensual. Dropping Will's hand, she moved across the floor, her eyes locked onto Rob's, her hips swaying seductively, her arms spread wide to receive him.

Rob gathered her up into his arms and spun her round and round to the lusty cries of the spectators until, suddenly, the room became stilled as the young lovers came to a halt, gazing deeply into each other's eyes.

As one, the wedding guests began to sing a sweet melodious tune, softly, with great feeling, each knowing the meaning of the lovers' fervent gaze. Without so much as a backward glance, Rob carried his bride from the hall.

He began the long climb up the spiral staircase to the tower room with Arianna cradled in his arms, keenly aware of every muscle used in the effort. Every step, every strain of his body, was sheer joy to him, and he luxuriated in the animal power of his well-tuned muscles. In the knowledge that with that strength he could protect her, love her, mate with her. Never in his life had he been more glad to be a man.

He carried her into the circular chamber at the top of the stairs, and Arianna gasped in awe at the sight that she beheld. Animal skins stretched over the windows, darkened the room, but thousands of fireflies lit it up again, twinkling magically like tiny candles. The fireflies floated around the lovers, circling them with their fairy light, while Arianna's eyes rivaled them with a brightness that shone for Rob.

"Oh, Rob, how beautiful! You've made my day complete."

In a husky voice, he answered. "No, not complete, not yet." Setting her down, he drew her into his arms and his lips sought hers.

Arianna's arms crept around his neck, holding him tight, responding as she had feared to do before, pouring her heart into her kiss. Rob groaned and kissed her harder, his body in desperate need of her. When the kiss ended, he looked down at her, need showing so clearly in his eyes. "Shall I summon your handmaidens to help you ready for bed?"

Softly, she whispered, her lashes lowered. "I need no help but yours."

Rob swallowed hard. It was as he hoped, but now he was in uncharted territory. Never had he undressed a woman before, never had he taken one to bed. What if he were too clumsy, too bold, what if . . .

"Rob . . . husband . . ." Arianna said, turning her back to him. "Begin with the laces."

With trembling fingers, Rob began untying the knotted bow, cursing to himself when he fumbled over the knot several times before freeing it. He pulled on the laces, loosing them, and the bodice slid off her shoulders. Reaching up, he pulled it from her body, his excitement building ever faster. Next came the farthingale tied to her waist. He made short work of that, leaving her with nothing but a chemise and petticoat. Slowly, he turned her around to face him, drinking in the lovely sight of her. So feminine, so . . . His hands reached for the hem of her chemise, pulling it over her head, then dropping it to the floor at first glimpse of her beautiful breasts.

"So beautiful, Arianna, so beautiful." His hands moved slowly to cover them gently, gliding back and forth over them. Then, unable to resist any longer, his fingers sank into their silky softness. It was more than he could stand, and he pulled her to him, his kisses covering her face and neck; then he moved down to kiss each breast tenderly. My God, the feel of them, the taste of them . . . Still holding her tight, his hand moved down to remove the last of her clothing, his breath stopping when at last she stood before him naked as Eve.

The touch of Rob's hands was more exciting than she had ever imagined, and the feel of his hardness against her was compelling. She wanted to feel him without the barrier of his clothing and cried out, "My lord, fair is fair. You undressed me. Let me do the same for you."

Groaning, Rob released his hold on her and she quickly concentrated on removing his clothes. Too eager and restless to just stand there, Rob helped her with his garments and in a moment, he, too, was naked.

The young lovers stood silently, staring at each other in wonder and adoration as fireflies swirled around them, paying tribute to the purity and splendor of their love.

Rob's gaze swept over Arianna's body in fervent concentration, taking in every exquisite curve. If he could have chosen the perfect female in God's kingdom, he couldn't have chosen better than Arianna. She was perfection to his eyes and she belonged to him. Suddenly, he could wait no longer. His hand reached out the same moment Arianna's hand reached for him. No words were necessary. It was time.

They walked hand in hand to the bed in silence. Then, unexpectedly, Rob lifted her into his arms, possessively, as if to show her he was in command, and laid her on the bed. He moved over her and slowly laid his weight upon her, straddling her body. She was his. Every move he made confirmed it. His lips came down on hers, bold, hard, and suddenly he was lost, no longer in command, slave to the need that drove him.

Arianna's body trembled at his touch. Though he was as innocent as she, he knew exactly where to touch her, how to touch her, as if it were born in him to know. His hands moved over her body, in a frenzy to learn all her secrets, and she was eager to have him know. And then when he had explored the surface fully, his searching hand found the moist place between her legs and she felt a finger move slowly into her. They both gasped at the same moment, their eyes opening wide as they stared at each other.

Slowly, he began to explore that part of her. "Rob, oh Rob," she cried.

He answered with a groan, his tongue breaking through her lips, delving, seeking, blending with her own, needing to know the taste of her. Then his thoughts turned to other ways to use his tongue, other ways to taste her nectar.

Moving his lips down her neck, he kissed her breasts, sucking on each rosy nipple before continuing his journey down to her belly. His mouth circled her navel, his tongue moving into its depth; but it wasn't enough, he still needed more of her.

Gently pushing her legs apart, he kissed the inside of her velvet thighs, her musk drawing him like a bee to honey. Afraid he was going too far but unable to help himself, his tongue flicked out, needing to know

184

this last secret place that from this day forward would belong to him.

Arianna gave a little cry of pleasure, feeling the wet heat of him, and then gasped loudly as his tongue pushed inside.

"Oh, Rob."

Emboldened by her reaction, he explored further with his tongue, pushing farther into her, then retreating, circling, seeking, until he found the place that pleased her most.

Arianna opened to him like a flower to the morning dew, wanting, needing to feel him inside. "Oh, Rob, I never knew it would be like this. I need you, I need you now."

Her words were music to his ears. Moving over her, his lips found hers, and in one blessed moment he was entering her, pushing through the hot, wet tightness that surrounded him, feeling the burst of heat wash over him when he broke through her virginity.

She cried out in pain, but at the same time held him tight when he started to retreat. He moved inside her at her command, reveling in the intense excitement. Nothing could have stopped him from completion now. He was gone, lost in a world of ecstasy, lost in his need to become one with her.

Truly it was a holy thing. Every thrust of his body confirmed it. Nothing this side of heaven could compare to what he felt and from this day forward he would thank God every day for giving him this woman.

His hips moved in harmony with hers, their sensual, natural rhythm escalating in an ever-increasing spiral toward fulfillment. And then it came, the spilling of his seed, the fulfillment of his dream. He cried out, his voice sounding strange and awesome in the dark. She was his, he was hers. They belonged to each other forever.

Arianna felt Rob throbbing inside her, over and over, as his seed spilled into her. Suddenly, the unbearable ecstasy she felt culminated in an overwhelming feeling that crescendoed, her muscles contracting, drawing him in to the center of her being. Her voice mingled with his, crying out in soft little sounds that grew louder until, in one last gasp, she cried, "Rob!" and it was finished.

They lay together, gasping for breath, their bodies panting in happy exhaustion until their breathing was back to normal.

When he could breathe again, he raised himself, staring down at her in wonder. "Arianna, my God. I fear I shall wear you out with my desire, for I want nothing else in this world but to make love to you through eternity."

Arianna laughed. "I'm sure every new bridegroom feels the same."

"Is it so? Then surely it must be the world's best-kept secret, for no one ever told me how it would be. How could any man feel as I do and not shout it to the world?"

"Shout it? I pray you reconsider. It would be most embarrassing."

"Then I'll try to contain myself, but it will be known anyway by the way I strut—like a peacock or a stallion or a bull."

Arianna's laughter was muffled by Rob's mouth on hers and soon all gaiety was gone as they seriously went about making love again.

Chapter Sixteen

The air was alive with sound as crickets, toads, and other creatures added their voices to the night chorus—and to the restlessness of the dark figure who climbed the narrow stairs of the battlement. Gazing out at the lonely landscape, the faint light from flickering fireflies caught his attention, their delicacy reminding him of Arianna's fragile beauty. In torment, his mind conjured up her image, fueling the flame of desire that caused his restless need to prowl the night.

She was so beautiful, and so incredibly innocent . . . "No!" he shouted, slamming his fist on the parapet. Not any longer. Her innocence was lost. Now she lay in her marriage bed, her body plundered, defiled by the carnal touch of a rutting male. She was no longer the pure creature of his dreams, no longer the one who could elevate him from the mire that surrounded him. But, God help him, he still wanted her, still wanted . . .

"Edmund!"

He whirled, irritated that his sanctity was disturbed. Was there no place in his own castle he could have a private thought? "Judith, what do you want? I thought you were abed."

"How could I sleep until I know Elizabeth's answer? You did talk to her? You did ask her permission to marry? We agreed this was a good time to ask her, after Arianna and Robert's romantic wedding, while she was still in good humor."

Suddenly weary, Edmund answered, "We agreed, and I did ask, but she did refuse. It seems she's too fond of me to share me with you, Judith."

"I can't accept that, Edmund. We must marry. Your child grows larger inside me every day. Soon all will know I carry a bastard."

"And I tell you I cannot. We'd both spend the rest of our days locked in the tower. Is that what you want? Would that make you happy?"

"Damn you, Edmund Deveraux. You *and the Queen.* I'd like to . . ."

Edmund put his hand over her mouth. "Silence. Would you have the Queen hear your treasonous words? Stretch your pretty neck upon the block? I know of a woman who can rid you of your belly's burden. I'll send you to her. No one need ever know. Though why you worry about such as that is a puzzlement. Do you think you fool anyone by telling them you came to Clinton to visit with my two sisters? Everyone in the castle knows you share my bed."

Judith pulled Edmund's hand from her mouth, sputtering, "Everyone but your precious Queen."

"Don't threaten me, Judith. 'Twould be very dangerous. You might meet with a sudden accident. The stairs are very steep, the castle walls high. If you fell, you'd break your treacherous little neck for certain. Do you ken my meaning?"

Judith's eyes narrowed to slits, and Edmund felt a

shiver run up his spine. After a long, hostile silence she spoke, her voice full of bitterness. "I ken your meaning, my lord. I'll go to the witch. I'll get rid of your brat. In truth, it will be better off dead than to have you for a father."

"Then it's settled. Once the Queen and Leicester have left, I'll see that it's done. Now, come, 'tis late, let's go to bed. Elizabeth wants to go hawking at first light, and you know how insistent she is that everyone be ready when she is." Wrapping his arm around her, Edmund led Judith down the stairs.

Revulsion coursed through Judith at his touch. Did he think all he need do is fondle her and she'd forget what harm he'd done? The vain fool. Someday she'd have her revenge and no one, not even the Queen of England, could keep her from that.

The sun rose lazily in the sky, bathing the tower room in its warm glow. Sometime during the night Rob had pulled the skins from the windows, allowing the fireflies to escape, and he was rewarded now with a beam of light playing across Arianna's beautiful hair as she slept. Reaching out, he caressed it.

Arianna sighed, "Again, my lord? Will your lust be never sated?" She stretched prettily and opened her eyes, nuzzling her head into his neck. "I fear you are right after all. You *shall* wear me out."

Laughing, Rob pulled her up against him, delighting in the wonderful feel of her. "Are you tired of your husband already?"

Arianna snuggled even closer. "Hus . . . band . . . what a glorious word. No, husband, I could never tire of you, never get enough of you, but I fear

I'll not be able to walk, so sore am I."

"Rose Petal, I'm sorry. I should have known. I should have been more gentle. I'll not touch you this morning."

"Oh? Not touch me? Even if I tickle you with my hair?" Pulling herself from his arms, she climbed on top of him, straddling his body, and lowered her head to brush her hair over his bare chest.

"You vixen! Do you tease me still, even though I've made you my wife? Remember, the deed is done — you no longer have your virginity to shield you from my ardor."

"Ummm, no shield? Then you must give me your sword, my lord. Your long . . . hard . . . sword of steel."

Rob groaned, then pulled Arianna's head down and kissed her. "My sword doth throb in desperate need to pierce." Rolling her onto her back, he entered her quickly, too far gone to hold his passion back.

Arianna took him in, eager to be filled. Was ever there a man to pleasure a woman so? In sooth, she never would get enough of him. What splendid pleasure he wrought upon her. What intense desire. Her body moved to his command, the sweet agony escalating until she thought she'd burst, then suddenly she did. "Ohhhhhhh! Ohhhhhhh!"

Her legs encircled his hips, holding tight, while her fingers dug into his back, and still it continued. "Ohhhhhhhhhhhhhh!" Then, completely spent, she slumped back upon the pillow, releasing him.

Breathing hard, Rob kissed her over and over in fast little kisses. "I love you, Rose Petal, my little passion flower. Love you, love you, love you."

The sudden knock at the door startled the lovers

from their sensual bliss. "Yes," Rob shouted. "What is it?"

His mother's voice, muffled by the heavy door, drifted into the chamber. "Rob. Arianna. 'Tis time for the viewing. 'Twill take but a moment, then you can go back to your bed."

Arianna was puzzled. "Viewing? What does she mean?"

" 'Tis a tradition, custom if you will, to view the bloodied sheets the morning after consummation. In that way the rights of our future children will be protected. If you were a virgin on your wedding night, then any children that come will be undeniably fathered by me. 'Tis embarrassing, I know. But only my mother and your own, along with a few ladies, will be present."

"Embarrassing? 'Tis mortifying. But, since these children we speak of will be my own, then of course I would protect their future."

Rob kissed her on the forehead, then called out, "You may enter."

The door opened to Margaret, Sybille, and three other ladies she didn't know. Sybille picked up Arianna's robe and handed it to her and Margaret carried a robe to Rob. Slipping into them, the two climbed out of bed. Rob took Arianna's hand and led her over to the window.

Sybille threw back the covers and looked down at the sheets, then up at Margaret in astonishment. Though the sheet was wet, there was no blood. Her face blanched. Surely her daughter had been a virgin. An awkward silence followed, as all the women turned to look at Arianna. She saw their looks and ran over to the bed. Where was the blood? "I don't

191

understand. I was a virgin. I was."

Margaret put her arms around Arianna's shoulders, smiling. "My dear, don't despair. There is an answer. Did you use the chamber pot during the night?"

"Yes, I did, right after . . . and then again, later . . . but . . ."

Margaret nodded to Sybille, and the two women walked over to the corner and stared down into the clay pot. Their faces lit up immediately, and there was an audible sigh of relief from the rest of the ladies. One by one they walked over to the chamber pot to gaze at the perfectly formed oval of red the size of a ripe cherry that floated there.

Rob moved to Arianna and put his arm around her. Blushing bright red, she stood by his side as each lady walked up to her and pressed a sprouted acorn into her hand, repeating:

> May your womb be fruitful as this oaken seed. Your body nurturing, strong as the tree that grows from it. Your children plentiful as the leaves upon its branches.

Arianna held the acorn sprouts gently, realizing for the first time that she was more than Rob's wife. She would be mother to his children. Suddenly that was very important to her. Strong sons to carry on Rob's name. Sweet daughters to ply him with kisses.

When Arianna looked up from the acorns, the women had left.

"I know the perfect place," Rob said, taking her hand.

"Perfect place for what?"

192

"To plant the acorns. We'll do it tonight while the moon is still full. Before you know it, we'll have a child for every acorn in your hand."

"What, only five? I seem to remember you wanted a dozen."

Laughing, Rob pulled her onto the bed. "Then we needs must get started right away."

The next few days passed in blissful abandonment as Arianna came to know her husband. They spent most of the time in the little tower room, appearing in the great hall only out of politeness at mealtimes. Each time she entered the hall, Arianna felt acute embarrassment, knowing everyone there knew how she had been spending her days and nights and she wondered if she looked any different because of it. She certainly felt different. Besides the soreness that still lingered and the weakness that persisted from so many hours abed, she felt like a well-kept puss. Stroked and pampered and basking in the light of Rob's love, she fairly purred with happiness.

On the seventh day, Rob told her he would be riding the borders of his property with his knights. It was a ritual done every three weeks to make sure no one violated his land or tried to built upon it. Kissing her goodbye, his lips lingered overly long, reluctant to be parted from her.

Arianna watched from the window as Rob rode away with his knights and yeomen, waving goodbye and blowing kisses as if he were going on a long journey. When he was out of sight, she dressed, then slid the ivory ring upon her finger. She hadn't worn it since her wedding day and missed wearing it. On impulse, she kissed the ring in fond remembrance of the pale Queen who had given it to her and of the luck it brought. For it was only after the Scottish Queen had given her the ring that everything good began to happen. If only Mary could know how happy she was, married to Rob.

Making her way down the stairs alone, she shyly entered the hall, looking about for a familiar face. Peter and Sybille waved from the long table and she joined them, kissing them both on the cheek.

Peter saw the ring on her finger and said in a low voice, "Rose Petal, you mustn't wear that ring, ever. Take it from your finger."

Arianna looked at him with a pained expression. "Why? What is it about this ring that causes so much secrecy?"

"'Tis best you don't know. Not yet."

"I want to know. I have the right to know. I'm a married woman now, no longer a child. Tell me."

Peter shook his head slowly.

"Mother, will you tell me?"

Sybille took her hand. "Please, Arianna, this is the way it must be. Some day . . ."

As Arianna stood up abruptly, their eyes remained upon her. "Then I'll find out for myself." She knew she shouldn't be so harsh with her parents, but she couldn't help herself. She had been restrained all her life, kept in the dark about too many things, and now that she was a grown woman she refused to stand for it.

Leaving the hall, she made her way to the stable, ordering a boy to saddle Pasha.

There was one who could tell her the truth, one who knew the secret of the ring: the Earl of Leicester.

194

The Queen was still at Clinton Castle with Edmund. Arianna decided to ride there and settle this once and for all. With directions from the stable boy, she rode through the gate house and over the drawbridge, feeling guilty that she was breaking her sacred oath to Rob: she was riding Pasha without his company. But she consoled herself with the knowledge that her mission was a worthy one — finding the truth. If she didn't go now, she might never know the secret that had been haunting her all her life.

Riding through the countryside, she felt a sense of pride that the land she traveled belonged to Rob and to her — she who spent her life in the shadow of great castles with naught but a small thatched cottage to call her own. Hearing thundering hoofbeats, she turned in her saddle to see four of Rob's yeomen riding toward her. As they drew closer, she could see the anxious looks upon their faces.

"My lady, you must never leave the castle without an escort. Why, if my lord heard of this he would skin us alive for leaving you unprotected."

"Then we shan't tell him. It will be our secret. Agreed?"

A look of relief crossed the young man's face. "Agreed, my lady. Will you be traveling any farther, or can we turn back to Everly now?"

"No, I have business to attend to at Clinton Castle. Is it much farther?"

"Far enough. But if you seek Lord Deveraux, he and the Queen and her entourage are hunting at a spot near here. Shall I take you to them?"

Arianna was jubilant. "Please lead the way!"

Cutting across a field, the yeomen led her to the place where Elizabeth's entourage was camped.

195

Brightly decorated tents sat by the edge of a stream. Horses grazed and gentlefolk and peasants alike milled around, waiting, so it seemed, for the Queen to return from hunting. Arianna ordered her yeomen to wait and made her way on foot through the woods, led by the sound of excited voices nearby.

As she stepped around a huge tree, a strange sound like that of a giant hornet caused her to stop dead in her tracks as an arrow slapped into the tree just inches from her head. Her head jerked back in surprise and her face paled.

Edmund's angry voice broke the silence. "Damn it all, Judith! If I hadn't grabbed the bow your arrow would have hit the Lady Arianna."

"I thought she was a deer. Stupid girl, wandering into the line of fire. It would serve her right to feel the sting of my arrow."

Arianna's startled gaze moved to the green-clad hunting party and Edmund, his hand on Judith's bow. By the shocked look on their faces, she knew how close she had come to being killed.

The Earl of Leicester was at her side almost immediately. "Are you all right?"

"I'm fine. It was stupid of me to blunder through the woods like that. It's just that I needed to talk to you, sir. Privately, if I may."

The Earl looked at her strangely. "As you wish. Later, when we can be alone." Laughing out loud for the benefit of the Queen, he said, "She's fine, just a little shaken. It seems she wanted to say goodbye to the Queen, knowing she was leaving on the morrow."

Arianna let the Earl lead her to Elizabeth and, taking her cue from him, she fell to her knees at the Queen's feet. "I wanted to say fare thee well, Your

196

Majesty, and thank you once again for the honor you bestowed upon me by coming to my wedding. You enriched my day most joyfully and I will remember it all the more fondly for your presence."

Elizabeth looked down at the young woman, entranced at the eagerness and youth so lacking in her courtiers. It was pleasurable indeed to have her near. "No thanks are needed, my dear, for indeed I enjoyed it much. But what are you doing away from your husband so soon? Did he not accompany you?"

"I blush to say I came without him. He's off doing whatever lords of castles do and left me quite alone. And we married but a week! Fie! It pleased me not, and needing to be cheered I thought how nice it would be to see you once again before you left."

Elizabeth fairly preened at Arianna's words. Leaning over, she tilted Arianna's head up and kissed her forehead. "Your words match my thoughts exactly. I was thinking only this morning how much I needed to be cheered, and now I am. You must join us for our noon meal. I would hear how you adjust to married life. The roses in your cheeks do speak your happy condition, methinks, but still I would hear the details."

Taking Arianna's hand, the Queen strolled through the woods to the clearing where a long table had been set up for a sumptuous meal. The Queen insisted she sit by her and Arianna was happy to comply. She was surprised and happy to find she could relate easily to the older woman, and soon had her laughing and clapping to the stories she told about her week of marriage.

"So, that is what it is like to be married to someone you love. I envy you, child. I'd like to steal you away and take you back to London with me, but I'm much too selfish. I want you to stay natural—unspoiled by the jaded ways of my court so that when I come to visit I may find you as delightful as you are this day."

Leicester listened in worried silence. If the Queen suspected who Arianna was, she would not be so amenable. It was funny, though, how fast she took to Arianna. As if . . . Elizabeth sensed the part of Arianna that came from him, the part of him that she loved. Mayhap it was a natural thing for her to love his daughter.

After the meal was over Leicester managed to get Arianna alone, telling Elizabeth he wanted to look over Arianna's splendid stallion to give her advice on how to care for the animal. Elizabeth smiled indulgently and lay under a tree to nap, her ladies-in-waiting keeping watch as they talked in low voices.

Standing on either side of the sleek white stallion, they faced each other over the animal's unsaddled back, both caressing the horse's velvet coat as they spoke.

"All right, child, tell me what is so urgent that you must ride out after me," Leicester said urgently.

"My lord, I think you know why I'm here. The ivory ring. I need to know the truth of it."

"I was afraid that's what you wanted and I don't know how to answer you. Can you not ask the ones who raised you?"

"I've asked, 'til I'm weary, but to no avail. And now I need to know if for no other reason than to keep me safe. For unless I know the truth, how can I guard myself from whatever danger I face? You lied to the Queen for me. You protected me, though

198

from what, I have no idea. Now will you tell me the truth so I may protect myself?"

Leicester's hand ceased caressing the stallion and moved slowly to take Arianna's. Holding it tight, he gazed deeply into her eyes. "Until the day you wed I had no knowledge of you other than to know a daughter was born to me with hair of gold and eyes of brightest blue."

Arianna blinked. "You can't mean . . ."

"Aye, sweet child. You are my daughter."

"*Your* daughter?" Arianna searched Leicester's face. Somehow, she realized she had already known. She had known since her first glimpse of him, but she had denied it, thinking it impossible. He was her father. The Earl of Leicester, the most powerful man in all of England, was her father. Her hand squeezed back, transmitting the pent-up emotion she had been saving for this moment.

"My dear, it's as much a shock to me as it is to you. I knew that you existed, that your mother hid you away somewhere, but no more than that. Though I tried to make her tell me where you were, she refused. And so I never thought to find you."

"What of my mother? Tell me, please. I never dared hope I'd find my father, and now, knowing, I . . . Is it possible I shall find both my parents? Can I be so fortunate?"

Suddenly, Arianna remembered what brought her to her father. "The ivory ring. What does it have to do with all of this? It was the Queen of Scotland who gave it to me and the Queen of England who gave it to you. Can it be possible my mother is one of them?"

Leicester nodded slowly.

Arianna looked at him in amazement. "But which one?"

He started to speak, but stopped, hearing Elizabeth approach.

"Well, young lady, has my most favored male in all the world filled your head with enough about the lineage of royal blood?"

Arianna froze. Had the Queen been listening? "Your Majesty, I don't understand."

Elizabeth laughed. "You mean he hasn't been speaking of the blooded horses he owns, reciting their royal lineage to you verbatim? He takes his title of Master of the Horse quite literally, my dear. Loves them with a passion any woman might envy."

Leicester's voice boomed. "What love can compare to that which I feel for you?" Taking Elizabeth's hand, he kissed it fervently.

Arianna watched them closely, wondering if she were gazing upon her parents. It was an odd feeling, very odd. Could Elizabeth be her mother? She had taken to her so easily. And Elizabeth to her, so much so that it seemed to shock the Queen's courtiers. But then, when she had been with the Queen of Scotland she had felt close to her. She remembered well how it felt when Mary had touched her hand, as if she had felt that touch before. Which Queen had given birth to her? She had to know.

And then, with senses reeling, she heard Rob call her name. Riding into camp with a dozen of his men, he jumped from his horse and swooped her into his arms. "Arianna, thank heavens you're all right. I was worried sick when I came home to find you gone. What possessed you to ride off like that?"

"Aha, your handsome bridegroom is lonely for

you. So eager to take you in his arms, he forgets to pay homage to his Queen."

Rob immediately bent on one knee and swept his cap from his head. "Forgive me, Your Majesty. I didn't see you standing there."

Elizabeth laughed lustily. "I understand and am envious of your sweet bride. You have eyes for no other, and that pleases me. Arianna is deserving of a devoted husband. If I ever hear different from her, you'll feel my anger. Now arise and take your bride home where she belongs. It grows late and I would not have the evening air make her sick."

Arianna looked to Leicester in a panic. Leave now? Not until she knew which Queen had given birth to her. Running over to him, she curtsied deeply. "Thank you for your advice on horses, my lord, and for informing me of their splendid lineage. But tell me again which mare you were speaking of that gave birth to the little filly. The Scottish one or the English?"

Leicester smiled, perceiving her true meaning. A clever girl, his daughter. "The Scottish one, to be sure. Her filly is the very image of her."

Arianna heard the words as if through water. Mary was her mother. The Madonna Queen was her mother.

Rob knew what was happening and a cold fear crept through him. It was a dangerous game Arianna played. He knew, too, he would have a hard time controlling her now, for she would want to ride to her mother's side and he couldn't let that happen. He would keep her safe despite herself.

His eyes swept over the Queen and Leicester, with Edmund and Judith standing nearby, and his heart

201

constricted. Protecting his headstrong wife would not be easy.

Somehow he got her on her horse, and making a motion to his men, rode away. Away from Edmund, away from the Queen, away from the danger that oozed from the very ground where they had been standing.

Chapter Seventeen

Arianna's sudden knowledge of the circumstances of her birth transformed her before Rob's very eyes. She was magnificent. Sitting her horse like a queen's daughter, she was bold and regal, her hair blowing around her face in a fury that matched her fiery nature. He would have his hands full now, for without a doubt she would want to go to her mother and he would have to stop her.

He hadn't spoken a word to Arianna since they rode off, thinking she needed privacy to digest what Leicester had told her. But now, crossing the border to his land, he breathed easier; unable to contain himself any longer, he shouted, barely able to be heard above the roaring wind and the pounding of hooves on the hard-packed dirt road. "Do you have any idea of the danger you were in back there?"

Her gaze never wavering from the road, Arianna answered imperially, "I do *now*. No thanks to you." Slapping Pasha with the reins, she urged him to gallop all the faster, the swift pace never slackening until she reached the drawbridge of Everly Castle.

Reining in, she cantered through the gatehouse to the courtyard, pulling up in front of the door. Composing herself, she jumped off Pasha before Rob could help her dismount and made her way to the doorway where Sybille and Margaret waited. She saw their anxious faces and felt a twinge of guilt, but brushed it away. She had every right to do what she did.

Sybille ran up to Arianna, embracing her warmly. "We've been so worried about you. Thank heavens you're all right."

Arianna endured the embrace woodenly, her hands at her sides, her face expressionless. Then without a word she entered the castle and started up the stairs. She couldn't talk to Sybille now, no matter the hurt her silence inflicted. She couldn't talk to anyone until she had a chance to think.

Halfway up the stairs, she stopped suddenly, hearing Rob's voice from below.

"Fiona, take Pasha to your parents' cottage and keep him there until further notice. I'll settle with your father later over the cost of keeping him."

Arianna turned, glaring down at Rob. "Pasha is mine. You can't take him away from me."

Rob looked up at her, relieved that at least he had gotten a response. "You broke your promise never to ride him without me and now you must suffer the consequences."

Gripping the banister tightly, she answered, "I know what you're trying to do, Robert, and it won't work. Nothing will keep me from seeing my mother. Nothing, do you hear me? Nothing!"

Rob had known this was coming. He had known, too, that he couldn't let her endanger herself. His will would have to be stronger than hers. "Shout it to the world, why don't you? Undo all the years that Peter and Sybille have kept you safe in one careless moment. Will that bring your mother back? Will that make you any happier?"

Arianna blanched.

"Know this, Arianna Warwick. You're my wife, my property, and I'll be damned if I'll let anyone harm you, not even yourself. I'm giving orders that you are never to go outside the castle walls. If you won't protect yourself, then I and all the people of Everly will have to do it for you."

Arianna looked down at Rob in shock. He had always been the gentlest of men. It was true what the old women said: you never know a man until you marry him. Through anguished tears she made her way up to the tower room and flung herself on the bed.

Rob strode up the spiral staircase to the tower room and, clenching his teeth, pushed the door open. He expected a torrent of angry words, but found instead a subdued Arianna.

The sight of her melted his heart. He wanted to soothe her with kisses, but knew he had to be firm. Stepping into the room, he closed the door with deliberation. "What a little coward you are."

His words cut through her like a knife. She had been expecting him to take her into his arms, to comfort her with kisses, not this . . . attack.

"That's right. Coward. You dissolve into tears like a spoiled child when you find you can't see your mother on demand. She who has bravely protected you all these years, suffering God knows what in the process. Would you undo all the years she's suffered with one foolish act?"

Arianna couldn't believe her ears. Where was the understanding Rob she had always known? "How dare you tell me it is foolish to want to see the mother I have yearned for all my life. You've always had your mother. How can you possibly know what it feels like to live your whole life without ever knowing your mother?"

"You're right. I don't know what that's like, but I do know how dangerous it would be for you to attempt to see her. Whether you like it or not, I'm going to protect you from that."

"Protect me? God save me from people who would protect me. Because Peter and Sybille protected me, I was raised as a peasant, never knowing I was the daughter of a queen; because my mother protected me, I never knew her love; and now, even my husband protects me by keeping me prisoner in my own home. Oh, Rob, can't you see that I have to be free to make my own decisions and my own mistakes? How else can I ever become worthy of being the Countess of Everly?"

Sitting on the side of the bed, Robert took her head in his hands, staring deep into her eyes. "I know in my heart what you say is true, but still, I must do what I must do. Can you understand that? Can you accept that, knowing it is my great love for you that compels me?"

Arianna wanted nothing more than to melt into Rob's arms, but she steeled herself, knowing what she had to say. "I *have* to see her, Rob. I have to. I want to know what it feels like to call her Mother, to look into her eyes and see myself reflected there."

Rob tried to soothe her. "I know, I know. 'Tis a hard thing, knowing where she is but unable to go to her, but that's the way it must be. Your mother above all people wouldn't want you to jeopardize your freedom to see her for a brief moment. After you've had time to think about it, you'll know the right thing to do. But until then, I must do my best to protect you. Do you understand? Can you forgive me?"

Nuzzling her head deep into his shoulder, she answered, "I only know I cannot bear to have you angry with me. I love you so."

Rob's lips came down on hers, blotting out everything but their powerful love, enclosing her in a cocoon of desire.

The days passed slowly for Arianna, days of thinking about her mother, dreaming of what it would be like to be with her. She saw herself strolling through castle gardens with Mary, contentedly sharing amusing stories about Rob, while her mother talked of politics, mayhap even asking for her advice. She pictured herself sitting with the Queen under the shade of a huge oak surrounded by elegant nobles who regarded her with envy as she commanded her mother's full attention.

If not for Elizabeth, she would have had that life.

And now, not wanting to waste any more precious time, she needed to see her mother. It wouldn't be in the wonderful way she had hoped for, but that didn't matter. Nothing mattered but to be with her, no matter where that was. Remembering Rob's words, she knew she must find a way to see her mother that wouldn't put herself, or Rob, in danger. There had to be a way. After all, she had visited Mary once before, two years ago when she had returned her little Skye terrier. And, God willing, it could be done again. Not in the same way—that would be too dangerous now—but somehow.

Rob was off hunting with his men and Will had

left the day before, taking Peter and Sybille with him. If she were going to do something, now was the time. Before they left, Peter and Sybille had told her everything, and she loved them all the more, knowing what they had gone through to keep her safe. Moving her from town to town to be near Mary, risking their very lives in the process. She understood everything now.

Everything but the danger they believed her to be in.

Surely the Elizabeth she knew would do her no harm. Hadn't she treated her with gentle kindness at her wedding and again when she sought her out in the forest? And wasn't it ridiculous to think that after all these years she would still harbor resentment toward Leicester's daughter? She had never punished Leicester for his transgressions, so why would she punish his daughter?

Or was she playing a deadly game of cat and mouse? Waiting for the day when Arianna was found, to take revenge on Leicester. Peter believed it, and he knew the Queen better than she.

No matter. She'd be more cunning than anyone could imagine. Cunning enough to visit her mother without anyone being the wiser. But how? Who had access to Mary, to come and go as they pleased? And the authority to take her along? A shiver of excitement coursed through her when she realized the answer.

Edmund!

Edmund was her only chance. No one would question her presence if she went with him on one of his visits to the Queen. And, too, Mary's jailers moved her frequently. Without Edmund, she would never know which castle or manor the Queen was residing in at any given time. So it was certain—Edmund was important to her plans. But how could she manage it? Rob guarded her carefully, never allowing her to leave the castle grounds without him.

Striding over to the window, she looked down at the people milling around the ward. Well then, if she couldn't go to Edmund, he must come to her. Seeing Buttercup lounging on a stack of hay by the stable, absorbed in conversation with the hefty master mason, she called down to her. "Buttercup, I want to see you. Now."

In a moment, Buttercup was in the chamber and Arianna was giving her a written message to deliver to Edmund.

"But Your Ladyship, Rob will be lopping me ear off if I was to help you. And begging your pardon, I'm a mite attached to it."

"Don't be foolish, Buttercup. Rob said nothing about sending messages; he only said I was not to leave the castle. Besides, no one need know. You can simply tell the gateman that I sent you to Fiona's to see how Pasha was. No one will question you."

"It don't seem right. If there's nothing wrong with going to Lord Clinton's, then why are ye keeping it a secret from your husband?"

"Buttercup, I wish I could tell you the reason I need to see Lord Clinton, but I can't. You must trust me. It is of utmost importance. Will you do it?"

Buttercup saw the fever in Arianna's eyes and knew her mistress was suffering. "All right. I'll do it, even if it means me tender little ear, that much you mean to me."

Arianna hugged the plump girl, then kissed her cheek. "Go now, and hurry. And if all goes well, Lord Clinton will return with you."

* * *

Judith struggled to a sitting position on the bed, groaning in pain. "You're going off to Everly now? Leaving me here alone?"

Edmund gazed down at the disheveled woman. "Alone? Hardly. You have a castle full of people to attend you. I'll not be gone long. Lady Arianna invited us both to sup with her, but since you are too sick to go, I'm simply doing the neighborly thing. I'll explain why you're absent, but don't worry. I'll not tell her the true reason you're ill."

"I'm sure you won't. I'm sure you wouldn't want anyone to know that you had a witch woman abort your own child. What might they think of you then? You bastard!" Judith clutched at her abdomen as a spasm of pain hit her. "You said it wouldn't hurt. You said I would be good as new. Look at me! How I wish I could transfer the pain to you, tenfold. When will it be over? My body burns with fever. Send for my brother. He'll take care of me. He'll make the pain go away."

"I'm sorry you've had a rough time of it, but in a few days you'll be feeling better. Mark my words. I'll send for the old woman—she'll give you something to ease the pain."

"I want my brother."

"In two days time, if you're still feeling sickly. All right? Now lie back and rest. That's what your body needs. I'll be back before you know it."

Edmund closed the door behind him, needing to shut out the picture of Judith on his bed. He hadn't known it would be this terrible, getting rid of a bastard baby, hadn't known the wretched way it would make him feel. Damn it all, if he had gone to

Norbridge just a few days earlier than Robert, he wouldn't be going through this now. He would have met Arianna first, would have swept her off her feet and married her.

He knew the moment he saw her walking toward him that first day that he wanted to wed her. She represented all that was good in the world and she would have been his salvation. With her at his side he could walk the earth in pride. He hated what he had become, a fawning courtier to Elizabeth, selling his very soul to stay in favor. Losing his identity, even his freedom to do as she commanded. And for what? What had he gained?

And now, here was Arianna seeking him out. Too late, too late. And yet, even so, he would go to her and see for himself what a man's touch had done to her. Maybe then, he could put her out of his mind, maybe then he could be content to marry Judith.

Gullible wench. She really believed the Queen had forbidden his marriage to her when in reality, the Queen could not care less who he married; she had even, in fact, suggested he make an honest woman of Judith. Honest woman! What did Judith know of honesty? What did she know of chastity, or goodness, or decency? The woman was spawned by the very devil himself.

A few hours later, sitting across from Arianna in a small receiving room in Everly Castle, Edmund saw clearly the changes wrought on Arianna. Though she was still the loveliest creature he had ever seen, by far, her pure innocence had disappeared and in its place was a sensuous woman who knew well the effect she had on men. It was evident in her eyes that looked at him with awareness, in her lips that curved seductively, ripe and plump and waiting to be kissed.

211

She had been solicitous of his comfort since he arrived, plying him with Spanish wine and delicious little butter cakes. She told him she wanted to get to know her nearest neighbor better, and for the life of him he couldn't figure out what her true motive was, if indeed there was one.

"Tell me again, Edmund, how much the Queen relies on you. You must be very proud to be so important to her. Why, to think she sends you to all the manors and castles where the Queen of Scotland is held. I would think she would trust only her closest confidants for that."

"Indeed, I am very close to Elizabeth. She stayed a full week at Clinton after your wedding to Robert and consulted my opinions on decisions of great importance. The matter of Queen of Scotland is but one of the areas where she depends on me."

"But 'tis truly an important one, is it not? You must have a great talent for diplomacy to be sent by your Queen for such a delicate undertaking."

"Delicate? How true. The two queens are of the same blood, you know, and yet the bitterest of enemies. I must carefully weigh everything I say to each before I speak or suffer the consequences. They do pounce upon my every word, like a tiger with a deer."

"I see what you mean. That must be hard to do. I've always admired those who could act with great diplomacy. I have not the wile myself, though I fervently wish I did. Ah, me, 'twould be lovely to be taught diplomacy by someone so accomplished."

"My lady, if you've a mind, it would give me great pleasure to instruct you in the art of diplomacy."

"Oh, would you? Truly? I should like that very much."

"Then consider it done. Next time I visit Mary,

you shall come with me and take note. The Scottish Queen has a quick wit and nimble brain, so 'twill be a valuable lesson, you may be sure."

"I'm sure you're right, but really, I don't know if I dare go with you. She may not like the intrusion."

"Nay, I'm sure Mary would enjoy meeting you. You're quite a lot like her, you know."

Arianna paled. Was she truly so much like her mother? And if so, would Edmund realize the truth when he saw them together? Had she made a mistake in inviting him here? "It flatters me that you might think so. What woman would not like to be compared to a queen?"

"I assure you it is not flattery, but the truth. As I think of it, the first time I saw you, you were wearing a green gown almost exactly like one I have seen worn by the Scottish Queen. Strange. If I didn't know better, I would swear you were related, but, of course, I realize how impossible that is, since she has but one offspring and that a male. Still . . . I sense a bond."

Arianna's heart stopped. What had she done? It would be too easy now for Edmund to put the pieces together. "There is a bond between us. The Queen and I both have a penchant for green gowns. And from the green velvet doublet you wear this day, I'd say you, too, share that same penchant, though no one would possibly think there is a bond between you and me, would they, Edmund?"

Edmund took Arianna's hand and raised it to his lips. "I would like to think there is."

Above Edmund's bent head, Arianna's eyes sought Buttercup's, beseeching her to help.

Buttercup cleared her throat. "My lord, would you care for some wine?"

213

Edmund let go of Arianna's hand. "No wine. But if my lady would oblige, a walk in the night air to clear my head."

"Aren't you feeling well, Edmund?"

"Just a bit groggy. I fear I've overindulged in drink today. Or mayhap it is your heady presence that makes me reel."

"Edmund, I beg of you to remember you are a guest in my husband's home."

Edmund stared into Arianna's eyes. Here was a woman worthy of him. A woman who could make her husband feel like a king, a woman above reproach. And she belonged to another man. "Forgive me if I go too far, Arianna. But I am only mortal, after all. What man wouldn't forget himself in your presence?"

Flustered, Arianna walked over to the table and poured a goblet of wine. "Tell me more of your duties to the Queen. I am most eager to learn all I can, since Elizabeth has promised to visit me. What are her favorite foods? And her favorite music? What of the Scottish Queen—how do her tastes compare to Elizabeth's? I am most curious."

Edmund laughed, thankful for his reprieve. "Elizabeth and Mary are more alike than either of them could ever imagine. They both love to dance and are gifted at it. They both love to read, to educate themselves. And—each imagines herself to be the most beautiful woman in two kingdoms."

"But they've failed most miserably at that, haven't they, Edmund? My wife undoubtedly holds that title."

Robert stood in the doorway, his narrowed eyes staring at Arianna.

"Robert!" Arianna's hand shook, spilling a little wine. She set the goblet down, hiding her face from

214

her husband for a moment. Did she look as guilty as she felt? She hadn't been expecting him home until the morrow, and by the expression on his face, she knew he was not expecting to find Edmund in his home.

Striding over to her, he put his arm around her waist. "Is that not so, Edmund?"

"What? Oh, yes, indeed. Your wife is undeniably the most beautiful woman in Scotland or England. You're a lucky fellow, Rob."

"Lucky? Luck had nothing to do with it, old man. I knew what I wanted and went after it."

Edmund was beginning to feel very uncomfortable. It was not like Robert to be so arrogant. "Ah, just so. Don't blame you one bit. She is quite a prize, quite a prize."

"Prize?" Arianna blustered, her voice much too high. "You speak of me as if I were won in some infernal contest. I'll never understand the way men think. But enough of this. Let's speak of other things before I get overwrought and spoil your homecoming. Is everything all right, Rob? I wasn't expecting you until the morrow."

"Everything is fine. We finished a day early so I might get back to my new bride. Are you happy to see me?"

"You know I am."

"Then kiss me," Rob said, pulling her close. "Show me how happy you are to see me."

Arianna pushed Rob away, speaking through clenched teeth. "As soon as we're alone, I shall gladly convince you of my happiness."

Pulling her back into his arms possessively, Rob said, "I'm sure Edmund understands the needs of newlyweds and will forgive our display of affection."

Rob kissed her boldly, but Arianna felt no warmth in his kiss. He was angry at her, and Edmund, too, for that matter, and obviously showing off for his benefit.

Edmund watched as Robert kissed Arianna, infuriated at the casual way he treated her. It was clear Robert was letting him know Arianna was his property. Damn him. Damn him to hell. Clearing his throat, he said, "I believe I'll leave for home now so you two lovebirds can be alone."

Arianna's heart sank. No date had been settled upon for visiting Mary. "But . . . it's dark. Shouldn't you wait until morning to travel?"

"My dear, Edmund is quite used to traveling by night. He knows what he's doing."

"Quite so. Well, I'll say goodbye then. Next time, the two of you must come to Clinton Castle. And Arianna, I'll let you know when next I shall be visiting the Scottish Queen. How lovely that we share a common interest."

Arianna was afraid to look at Rob. After Edmund left, she stood waiting for his tirade, her eyes cast on the Turkish carpet beneath her feet.

A long silence ensued.

Aware that something was amiss, Buttercup and the other attendants left the room, closing the door softly behind them.

Still Rob said nothing.

When she could take it no longer, Arianna raised her head, looking directly at him. "Well, aren't you going to berate your disobedient wife?"

"Would it do any good?"

"No!" she said, tilting her chin up even higher.

"Then, I shall say nothing." Yawning nonchalantly, he stretched his arms over his head. "Well, if you'll

216

excuse me, I'm going to bed."

Arianna wasn't sure whether she should feel relieved or worried at Rob's genial manner. It was totally unexpected. Unwilling to start an argument, she remained quiet.

Sheepishly, she followed him up to their bedchamber, watching in astonishment as he undressed and climbed into bed, pulling the bedcovers up around his chin.

"Blow the candles out before you come to bed," he murmured, then turned on his side, leaving her to look down at him in amazement.

Obediently, she did as she was told, then undressed and climbed into bed. Rob made no move to embrace her. She was truly puzzled now, and hurt. Didn't he want her anymore? Swallowing her pride, she snuggled up against his back.

He didn't respond.

Wrapping her arm around the front of him, she slowly slid it down over his warm belly to grasp his shaft. A smile curled her lips. He was fully, gloriously aroused, ready to give her what she needed.

Long after Arianna fell asleep, sated and content, Rob lay awake, his mind working on a plan to safeguard Arianna. Rising slowly so as not to wake her, he wrapped a robe around his naked body and crept out of the bedchamber and down the spiral staircase to the sleeping quarters of his knights. Making his way through the dark room he found the man he was looking for, John Neal, and tapped him lightly on the shoulder. Neal was awake instantly.

"My lord, what is it? Are we under attack?"

"Shhh! Dress and meet me in the hallway. I have

an important mission to send you on right away."

Out in the hall, Rob paced back and forth, waiting for John to finish dressing. The man was the most trusted of all his men, and the only one he felt comfortable sending on such a delicate mission. Hearing the squeak of the door, Rob watched as the knight made his way over to him.

"What is it, my lord?"

"Johnny, you must deliver a verbal message to Lord William Ludlow at Norbridge. No other must be present when you deliver it, do you understand? It is for Will's ears alone."

"Yes, sir, I understand."

"Tell him it is imperative that he ride to London immediately. There he must seek a private audience with the Earl of Leicester. He must tell Leicester to have Edmund Deveraux sent out of the country on some pretext right away. The life of someone he holds dear will be in jeopardy if he does not succeed. Do you have it?"

"Yes, sir, I have it. You can count on me."

"I know that well. And Johnny, accompany Lord Ludlow to London so that I might know the deed is done, and report back to me as soon as you can."

Too restless to go back to sleep, Rob climbed up to the battlements and watched as John rode away. Leicester would understand the message, and he certainly had the power to have Deveraux sent out of the country. Arianna would be safe. He would protect his wife whether she liked it or not.

Smiling, he thought of the way she had looked when he went to bed without a peep about her meeting with Edmund. There was more than one way to handle a woman, it seemed, and the results could be most satisfying.

Chapter Eighteen

September 1585

The sweet, melodious music of Arianna's lute drifted lazily around the great hall, its tranquil sound mingling with the cheerful crackling of the cozy fire. A perfect September evening. Or, it would have been if Arianna hadn't been feeling so guilty. Sitting by the fire, surrounded by her attendants, she should have been content, playing her lute and singing. But 'twas that very lute that caused her so much guilt.

It started a few weeks earlier when a troubadour had come to Everly Castle and was received most warmly. For several days he played and sang for them each evening whilst he was plied with food and drink. Listening to him speak of his adventures and all the great lords and ladies he had entertained, Arianna had had a revelation: troubadours were welcome everywhere. Why couldn't she dress as one of them to gain access to her mother?

The more she thought about it, the more she liked the idea. The only drawback was she didn't know how to play an instrument, but that was soon remedied when Annie volunteered to teach her the lute—

unaware of Arianna's devious plot. And now, here she was playing as well as anyone in the castle.

Rob smiled contentedly at her from the planked table where he sat with his knights, listening while she played. Her guilt grew tenfold, knowing he would not be so calm if he knew the true reason for her sudden musical interest. But as miserable as she felt about deceiving Rob, her desire to see her mother outweighed even that feeling by far.

She had it all thought out and would implement the plan the next morning. Dressed as a boy, she would walk through the gate and over the drawbridge with no one the wiser. If she wasn't looked at too closely she was sure she could get away with it. Her only worry was Robert—and Buttercup. Remembering her as Sparrow, they wouldn't be so easily fooled by her disguise. But Rob would be busy on the morrow, overseeing new construction on the northern wall, and Buttercup would be inside the castle, out of harm's way. By the time either of them realized she was missing she would be well on her way. It would work—it had to.

Over the past few weeks she had gathered all the necessary clothing and had hidden it away. She had enough coins given to her at the wedding to see her through. Her heart pounded thinking of what lay ahead for her, but it was worth any risk to see her mother again. All her life she had wondered about the woman who had given birth to her, and now, knowing at last who she was, where she was, nothing could keep her away.

Arianna's nervousness grew with each passing hour and her stomach knotted tightly, but she hid it from Rob.

Sleep was a long time coming. So sure a short time ago that she was doing the right thing, she now wondered if she was fooling herself. No, she *was* doing the right thing. She *was* sure of it, and sure she would succeed. Hadn't she accomplished everything she set out to do so far? Hadn't she played the part of a boy for years without getting caught? Well then, she could do it again. Feeling more confident, she finally drifted off, awakening the next morning at the soft pressure of Rob's lips on her forehead. Her eyes flickered open.

"I hate to wake you, Rose Petal, but I couldn't resist one kiss before I go."

"Go? Where are you going?"

"To the north wall. Don't you remember? I told you I'd be overseeing work there this day. I've decided to get an early start so I can spend the afternoon with you. Hawking, mayhap?

Arianna blinked, then swallowed hard. So soon. He would be back so soon. That didn't leave her much time. "Don't hurry on my account, Rob. I really don't feel much like hawking. I'm feeling very lazy and will probably just loll around."

"Mmmm, I'm very tempted to loll with you, but duty calls." Rob kissed the tip of her nose, then left.

Arianna jumped out of bed, scurrying frantically for her hidden clothing. Dressing quickly, she ran to the window and scanned the courtyard below. A group of farmers were making ready to leave after delivering their produce to the kitchen. If she joined them, she'd be less conspicuous. Grabbing the sack containing her lute, she ran out the door and down the staircase.

Composing herself before she walked out to the

221

courtyard, she tugged at her leather jerkin to straighten it, then made sure her hair was tucked up into the hood properly. Slowly, she sauntered over to the farmers.

They looked at her curiously, but said nothing. The local farmers were private people, known for minding their own business, and she counted on that. After a few awkward moments, the group started for the gate. Arianna looked around furtively to see if anyone had spotted her, but all was well. Everyone was busy with morning chores. Breathing a sigh of relief, she followed the farmers out the gate and over the drawbridge.

She walked beside them for a league or so, then veered off to the woods. Fiona's family lived nearby. She would stop there for a horse. Fiona had told her that her father had one for sale and she prayed it was still there. She wished she could ride Pasha, but knew it would be unwise. He was too recognizable and she would have to identify herself to Fiona's family in order to obtain him.

Barking dogs yapped at her heels as she approached the cottage. A shutter creaked open and a ruddy-faced man stuck his head out the window. "Who goes there?"

"A friend of Fiona's."

"Is that so? Then ye be welcome here. Come in. Join us in a cup of ale for breakfast."

Arianna entered the small cottage, adjusting her eyes to the dimness. "Thank you for your hospitality."

Closing the door, Albert looked the young lad over. "How do ye know my daughter? By the looks of ye, I'd say you were a wandering minstrel. Have ye been to the castle to entertain the lords and ladies?"

"Aye, that I have. Met your daughter there. She told me you might have a horse I can buy."

"Hmm, I might have, if the price be right. Got a bay I traded for just the other morn. A gelding. He's got some years on him, but his teeth are good and his body sound."

Things were going well, Arianna thought. Surely it was an omen that she was meant to go on this journey, meant to see her mother. When a price had been agreed upon and she had drunk her friendly cup of ale with Fiona's father, she mounted the bay and started off, spurring the horse when she was out of sight of the cottage. She needed to put as much distance as she could between her and Everly Castle. With any luck, by the time Rob realized she was missing, she would be in Tutbury.

Tutbury Castle stood on a rocky hill overlooking the River Dove. Much older-looking than Everly or Norbridge, it seemed a cold and dreary place. Or did she think that because her mother was held prisoner there? The castle was ugly, oddly shaped, and ungainly, with numerous turrets and towers that neither matched nor complemented each other. Wooden palisades surrounded the castle, obscuring the moat, but she had an unobstructed view of the drawbridge leading up to the tall arched gate. Two guards in the green and white Tudor livery stood there, pikes in hand, belying the fact that this was no ordinary castle. And so it wasn't, for it held something precious: her mother.

A cold chill coursed through her. She was so close now. Her gaze shifted upward to the towers that rose above the castle's stone walls, hoping for a glimpse of Mary from one of the windows, but she could see nothing.

Moving away from the shelter of trees where she had been standing, she slowly moved toward the gate, holding tight to the neck of her lute. Her thumb nervously rubbed over the frets as she moved toward the drawbridge, producing a strange sound. But she was unaware of it, her attention focused on the stone-faced guards at the gate. Would they let her in? Would she see her mother or be sent away without a glimpse?

Taking a deep breath, she loosened her body and walked with a lighter step. She was supposed to be a gay troubadour, so she must look and act the part. Smiling broadly, she approached the gate, but stepped aside upon hearing the loud racket of hooves on wood. A large party of riders was coming over the drawbridge. Arianna gasped, recognizing the one female amongst them.

Mary, Queen of Scots.

Guarded well, Mary rode at their midst, dressed in hunter's green and carrying a peregrine falcon on her fist.

Arianna's eyes drank in the wondrous sight, her heart catching in her throat. How grand she looked, how regal. No prison could take away the dignity of her birthright, no walls restrain her spirit.

Opening her mouth to speak the one word she longed to say, she mouthed it silently instead. *Mother!* Aware of nothing but the thrilling sight, she moved ever closer toward the riders, compelled to be near Mary. A booming voice broke through the spell, stopping her in her tracks.

224

"Yield the road."

Arianna stepped back quickly, in imminent danger of being run over, and watched helplessly as her mother rode through the gate and into the inner ward. Arianna ran after her, but the iron gate slammed shut. The loud clang stabbed through her heart like a spear. Grabbing hold of the steel bars, Arianna peered through them, watching as a knight helped Mary alight.

Mary handed the falcon to one of the men, then strode toward the castle door. Suddenly, she hesitated. She stopped, her ears cocked as if listening for something, a tingling sensation creeping up her spine as she sensed . . . something. She felt a sweet sadness touch her heart and shrugged her shoulders as if trying to rid herself of a physical object. She started to look back when she felt the touch of a strong hand on her shoulder.

"Here, now, Your Majesty, no use in dallying. Time to go inside." The burly guard's touch broke the strange spell. Taking a deep breath, she entered the castle.

Mother. She had been so close; if only she had looked her way, if only . . .

Suddenly, Arianna felt a rough hand on the back of her neck.

"So, here you be, you young scoundrel! Thought you'd get away, did you? Well, no one cheats the Earl of Everly and gets away with it."

Arianna was stunned. "Rob!"

"*Rob*. Yes, that's what you did to me. And now you'll pay. You'll work off what you owe me, that's for certain."

Tears threatened, but she held them at bay. Rob

was going to spoil it for her. He was going to stop her from going through the gate and there wasn't anything she could do about it without putting herself and him in danger.

"Let me go! I'm here to entertain the castlefolk. They're expecting me."

"You'll be doing no entertaining this day or many others to come, if I have my way. Are you coming peacefully, or do I have to call my men to truss you like a pig?"

Arianna's heart sank. She had no doubt he meant what he said. "Don't do this, Rob. Don't do this to me," she said in a voice that was barely audible. "I have to see her. I have to."

"Well, if that's the way it's to be . . ." Reaching down, Rob grabbed her by the thighs and lifted her over his shoulder like a sack and began to carry her back over the drawbridge to the derisive laughter of the guards.

"Put me down! Put me down! I'll hate you forever if you stop me." Her small fists pounded against his back but Rob's pace never slackened. Before she knew it she was being thrown over the saddle of Rob's horse and they were riding off.

Safely away, Rob halted his horse and let Arianna down. She sank to the ground like a rag puppet, crying as if her heart would break. In sooth, it had, for she had been so close to her mother she could have reached up and touched her. And now she wouldn't have the chance.

Rob pulled her to her feet and enveloped her in his arms, but Arianna stiffened her back and cried, "I hate you! Why did you have to come? Why did you have to spoil it?"

226

Rob's fingers dug into her shoulders and he began to shake her. "Why? You little fool, don't you know you would have been found out? Don't you know you would have been locked away, too? Is that what you want? Do you love me so little that you could do that?"

Huge sobs racked Arianna's body. With her head against Rob's shoulder she let it all out, crying as she had never cried before. And when the crying was done and Rob had retrieved her mount from the nearby wood, he set his pale wife on her horse and brought her home.

"Three days, Mother. It's been three days since I brought her back, but still she doesn't eat anything, doesn't drink anything. She just lies there, unmoving. She won't look at me, won't speak to me. What am I to do?"

"I know, son. 'Tis a hard thing, seeing your wife pine away like that, but surely she'll snap out of it soon."

Tears glistened in Rob's eyes. She'll die soon, that's what she'll do if she doesn't take so much as a sip of water. Oh, Mother, I can't lose her. I can't."

"You won't. I know it. She's a strong girl, stronger than either of you realizes."

Buttercup couldn't bear to see the young lord so distraught. What was the matter with Arianna? Didn't she care what she was doing to him? She had a good mind to go in there and give her a scolding, servant or not. Rob was the kindest man she knew, and if Arianna couldn't see that, she didn't deserve him.

Feeling righteously indignant, Buttercup quietly left Margaret and her son sitting by the fire and went upstairs to Arianna's bedchamber. Pushing open the door, she peered in. Arianna hadn't moved from the position she had been in when she checked on her earlier. What was the matter with that girl?

Striding into the room, she made her way over to the bed and began to jiggle Arianna's limp hand. "Look at me, Arianna. I'm not your sweet husband or his gentle mother that ye can callously ignore. Ye can't get away with that with me."

Arianna turned her head slowly to look at Buttercup. "Go away."

"Ha! So you can talk. Well, I'm not going away. Not until I see me friend Sparrow staring out of those blue eyes of yours. Sparrow wouldna be laying here like a drowned kitten. Sparrow had more spirit than that."

"Sparrow doesn't exist anymore."

"But Lady Arianna Warwick does. The Countess of Everly does. And someday, when ye be a mother and your wee ones are . . ."

"Stop it! Don't talk to me of mothers and children. You don't know . . ."

Buttercup was surprised at Arianna's sudden burst of passion. She had unknowingly hit upon a sensitive subject. "Don't know what?"

"Nothing."

"Arianna, are ye with child? Is that what all this crying is about? Me Ma use to carry on something awful when she was that way. I never could understand why, but . . ."

"Will you go away? I can't take much more of your stupid prattling. I'm not with child."

228

"Are you sure, Arianna? When did you last have your monthly?"

"You wash me and dress me. You know my body as well as I do. You tell me."

Buttercup cocked her head and rolled her eyes up to the ceiling.

Arianna felt a surge of energy course through her body. How long *had* it been? Not in the two months since she had married Rob. Could it be true? Her eyes opened wide.

"I knew it, didn't I? There'll be a little Rob or Arianna squalling its head off before long unless I miss me guess. Oh Lordy, isn't that great news? Wait 'til Rob and his Ma hear."

Arianna slid her hands down to cradle her stomach. Rob's child growing there? Could it be possible? Her life had been in such turmoil since she set out to win Rob that she had had little time to think of anything else. Rob's child. Mary's grandchild! If it were true she would have a chance to remedy the wrong that had been done to her. She could raise her child. Be close to it. It would make up for all the heartache she had known yearning to know her real mother.

"Buttercup, do you really think . . . Oh, I do believe it's true! I do. Oh, my. Would you bring me my breakfast? I'm suddenly very hungry. And make sure there's a tankard of milk, heavy with cream. I'm not taking any chances. My child must be healthy and fat."

Buttercup's spirit soared. "Yes, my lady, and can I tell my lord ye wish to see him?"

"Yes! No!"

"No?"

Laughing, Arianna cried, "Not until Fiona has

brushed my hair. Will you send her in? I don't want Rob to see me looking like a wraith."

"That's my Sparrow, that's my good Sparrow. I'll send her right in."

Buttercup ran out the door, almost colliding with Annie and Fiona. "Go to your mistress. She needs you. I'm off to get her breakfast."

Buttercup flew down the stairs and through the great hall to the kitchen, huffing and puffing. She made up a tray and was starting back when she remembered Rob. Making her way to Margaret's chamber, she knocked lightly on the door.

"Enter," Margaret's voice called out.

Buttercup pushed the door open and peered in, always bashful at entering other people's rooms. Seeing Rob sitting by the fire, his head in his hands, she said, "My lord, Arianna has asked for breakfast and she wants to see ye right away."

Rob was on his feet immediately and halfway up the stairs before Buttercup could catch her breath. Smiling at Margaret, she said, " 'Twill be all right now. Our Arianna has found a reason to live."

Rob knocked lightly on the door and entered, an expectant expression on his face.

Arianna was sitting on the side of the bed while Fiona and Annie attended her. She looked up at him in surprise. "Oh, I thought you were Buttercup with my breakfast."

Rob's face fell. Didn't she want to see him after all? "Buttercup is on her way up. She said you wanted to see me."

"Did she? Couldn't wait, I see." Feeling suddenly shy, Arianna asked, "Did she tell you why?"

"No. I didn't think to ask. I was so happy you

wanted to see me. Why? What is it? You're not ill, are you?"

Arianna laughed softly. "Ill? Oh Rob, no. It's . . . I've found out . . . Oh, Rob, I think I'm going to have your child."

Joyful squeals filled the room as Arianna's hand-maidens rejoiced. As one, they turned to see how the young lord would react.

Rob stood motionless, his face turning so pale Arianna thought he'd faint. "My child? Sweet Jesus." Striding over to Arianna, he fell to his knees and buried his head in her lap. Huge sobs racked his body as he began to cry freely, relieved of the tremendous burden he had been carrying.

Chapter Nineteen

December 1585

The north wind blew through the animal skins covering the tower window, its fury sending shivers of ice through Arianna as she waited, staring out at the brilliant snow-driven landscape. She was about to turn away, too cold to stay any longer, when she spotted horsemen kicking up clouds of snow as they rode toward the castle at a fast gallop.

The one she sought rode in front, trailed by four men who could barely keep up with him. Her brow furrowed. So small an entourage for so eminent a lord? What does it mean? And why did he find a need to visit now, in such terrible weather?

Ever since a messenger had come the evening before with word that the Earl of Leicester would be visiting her this day, she had been fearful. Rob tried to convince her there was nothing unusual about a father having a sudden impulse to visit his daughter and she wanted to believe that, but now? When the roads were covered with snow? When there was danger of his horse slipping on a hidden patch of ice?

Hugging her fur mantle around her, she watched as

her father drew closer and closer, the excitement inside her building ever greater.

"Arianna, what are you doing up here? You'll catch your death."

"I wanted to watch for my father and this was the best vantage point. He's riding up now."

Rob moved up behind her and opened the skin wider. "I should have known you'd be up here watching for him."

Snaking his arms around her waist, he patted the rounded swell of her belly. "Wait 'til he beholds you. There'll be no need to announce the news of his impending title of grandfather, 'tis all too obvious. You grow deliciously rounder each day."

Nuzzling her neck, he whispered, "Mmmm, the touch of your swollen belly turns my loins to iron, knowing it was I who caused your condition. It is a potent aphrodisiac. So much so that I think I shall endeavor to keep you this way permanently."

"My lord, you are insatiable. But if the truth be known, I would have it no other way." Turning to face him, she stood on tiptoe and kissed him. "Shall we greet my father? I'm anxious to know what brings him here." Grabbing Rob's hand she led him out of the tower and down the stairs, her body still agile despite its growing dimensions.

Shaking the snow from his cloak, Leicester handed it to a servant then stamped his fur boots. Hearing Arianna's excited voice, he looked up, his smile broadening at the sight of her.

"My lord, I'm so happy to see you safely here. I was worried about your journey in this terrible weather."

Leicester's eyes traveled over Arianna in admiration, noting with great pleasure that she was with child. Overjoyed, he wanted to take her in his arms, but re-

233

strained himself, knowing he must keep his distance when others were around. "My dear lady, what a charming sight you are. And Robert, 'tis good to see you, too."

Rob took Leicester's hand, shaking it exuberantly. "Shall we retire to the library? 'Tis the warmest room, and we can have a *private* chat."

Rob escorted Leicester and Arianna into the small chamber, then went to fetch Arianna's hot mulled wine, giving father and daughter a chance to be alone.

Silently, Leicester and Arianna stared into each other's eyes, memorizing the other's face. Then, smiling gently, Leicester opened his arms and Arianna flew into them.

Leicester's arms closed around her. "Ah, you can't imagine how good it feels to hold you. These past four and a half months have been the longest in my life. I wanted to come sooner, but Elizabeth has kept me on short rein. It was impossible until now."

Arianna snuggled her head against his shoulder, breathing in his masculine smell mixed with the crispness of winter. "No need to explain, I understand. I'm happy you're here at last. I've been waiting ever so impatiently."

Leicester broke the embrace, eager to get a good look at her. Holding her at arm's length, his eyes moved down to the soft swelling of her stomach. "When is the child due?"

"The end of April."

"Are you well?"

"Oh yes, I've not had a day of sickness, not even mornings as I was told to expect. I'm as healthy as one of your brood mares."

Leicester laughed. "Are you indeed? Excellent. A grandchild. Think of it. I swear upon all that's holy I

234

shall see it raised. 'Twill help make up for the lost years with you. You've made me a happy man."

"That makes two. Rob acts as if I were the only woman in the world ever to have a baby, and he the only man capable of causing it."

"He's a fortunate man." Leicester's voice suddenly softened. "Does Mary know?"

"No. And I am forbidden to go to her." Arianna blinked back the tears. She wouldn't cry. She wouldn't spoil this happy occasion.

"I'm sorry, Arianna. I know how hard it must be for you, not seeing your mother. Mayhap, someday Elizabeth will grow weary of holding her and will set her free. Pray for that day, but until then, live in joy with your husband and child. It is the best revenge, after all."

Arianna heard a tinge of bitterness. "Is everything all right with you, Father? You're still in great favor with the Queen, aren't you?"

"Tenuously. But for the moment, yes, I'm still her favorite. Though whether I'll still be after I return from the Netherlands is uncertain."

"The Netherlands! When do you go?"

"Until a few days ago, I thought it would never happen, so many times had she changed her mind about sending me. But now, it's certain. I leave in a little more than a week. That's why I came to see you. I didn't want to leave without saying goodbye. I don't know how long I'm to be gone, but I imagine it will take some time to rout the Prince of Parma."

"Oh, no," Arianna sobbed, tears flowing down her cheeks. "You could be hurt. I couldn't bear to lose you so soon after finding you. Don't go. Tell the Queen to find someone else."

Rob entered, carrying a tray with silver goblets of

235

hot mulled wine. "Arianna, an Earl does not tell a Queen what she must do, even if he is the most powerful Earl in England."

"You speak the truth, Robert. Of late, Elizabeth has been very obstinate. To tell you the truth, I'm glad to be getting way from her awhile. I almost feel sorry for the man she has chosen to favor in my absence — Edmund Deveraux."

Rob's face darkened. "I thought . . ."

"Yes, I know. He *was* safely out of the country. But a few weeks ago Elizabeth requested his presence at court. He's just arrived."

"Damn! I had hoped we'd heard the last from him."

"Aye, but I'm thinking Elizabeth will keep him occupied. He won't have much time to meddle in other affairs."

Arianna saw the knowing looks father and husband exchanged, confirming what she had come to believe: Rob had somehow managed to have Edmund sent away so that she could not have concourse with him. Well, it mattered not anymore. In her delicate condition she would not do anything to jeopardize her unborn child. She had to believe that someday her mother would be set free, and then . . .

"Here," Rob said, offering Leciester a goblet. "Drink your wine while 'tis hot. Arianna made it herself, just to please you. I might add she used up the last of our precious oranges doing so, and spices fragrant enough for the most jaded palette."

Leicester took the goblet. "Then I shall like it all the more, knowing you made it . . . daughter."

Arianna smiled shyly. It felt so strange hearing him call her that. But she liked it well. "Shall we toast this first time together as a family? It would please me greatly."

A tender look came into Leicester's eyes. Taking Arianna's hand, he placed it in Rob's, then held the two hands tight in his own large hand. Raising the silver wine goblet high, he proclaimed, "To family. Though we be torn between two feuding queens, we three and the child that grows inside your womb shall grow stronger, happier each new day, united in the love we share, the familial love no one on God's earth can take from us."

"Here, here," Rob and Arianna cried in unison.

Taking a hearty gulp, Leicester started coughing.

Seeing Leicester's plight, Rob took a cautious sip from his goblet and grimaced as he swallowed the liquid.

"Is it that terrible?" Arianna cried, taking a sip herself. "It is. I don't understand. It tasted fine when first I made it. Mayhap it has been simmering too long on the fire."

"No, no, 'tis fine mulled wine. Just a mite hot. But verily, after the cold winter's ride, it doth feel good going down my gizzard." Leicester took a small sip to please his daughter.

Rob, too, tried to placate Arianna. "Yes, truly it is . . ."

"Yes?"

"Smooth. Yes, quite smooth."

Arianna flounced into a chair, her lower lip in a pretended pout. "I don't believe either of you for a minute. But good or not, 'tis a warm tonic for a cold night, and I expect it will give you both comfort to drink it."

Leicester and Rob looked at each other and laughed.

"Yes, little mother. You see, Leicester, she's turning motherly right before our eyes. And what a beautiful one she'll make." Rob drew her close and kissed her.

Leicester's eyes shone. "Would that I were here when that happy day comes."

Many leagues away in Windsor castle, Elizabeth's angry voice echoed through the chamber. "Out! Out! I wish to speak to the Earl of Clinton alone!"

Elizabeth's ladies flew from the room quickly, knowing well what could happen when she was in a rage over Leicester.

"So. Where is he? Did you find him?"

Edmund had never seen Elizabeth so angry. Whenever he had been in her presence she had behaved coquettishly, not like the spoiled child he was witness to now. "I could not find him anywhere, Your Grace. Not in the castle, nor in town."

"And his home? Did you check there? Did he go home to his adoring wife, Lettice?"

"No, Your Grace. I went there to see for myself. Lettice is quite alone. And if I might add, not in the best of spirits, having been told she may not accompany her husband to the Hague."

"Hah! It serves her right. She married him knowing the position he held in my court — in my heart — so let her suffer the consequences." Elizabeth raised her head, moving it back and forth haughtily.

"I can't think of anywhere else to search for him, but if it is urgent that you see him, then I shall continue my endeavors."

Waving her hand impatiently, Elizabeth replied, "No, no, he'll be here soon enough. His ship sails in less than a week. I was just curious as to his whereabouts, but since he is not with his wife, I am content."

"Then, if there is nothing else . . ."

Elizabeth's demeanor changed immediately. "Edmund, do not be in such a hurry. A game of chess would take my mind off my problems. You did say you played chess with the Scottish Queen on occasion, did you not?"

"Yes, on several occasions."

"Good. I am eager to find out if I am a better chess player than she. Set up the board, there by the fire. We shall spend a cozy evening here, playing chess."

Damn! It looked as though he wouldn't be seeing Judith alone tonight, and after all his months away, he was in need of her body. There was something different about her since his return. Something quite exciting. He had noticed it at first glimpse. He couldn't put his finger on it, and knew only one thing for certain: she was not half as eager to see him as he imagined she would be.

Women! Who could comprehend them? He remembered how angry she had been when Elizabeth had ordered her to court months ago, and now, seeing them together today, it was obvious Judith was enjoying herself. She seemed quite cozy with the Queen, laughing slyly with her as if they shared some tremendous secret. What could it be?

Placing each piece upon the marble chess board, his fingers closed around the white queen. Immediately, an image of Mary's long slender fingers flashed in his head along with the ivory ring she always wore. No, not any longer. How had it been transported from Mary's finger to Leicester's hand to a chain around Arianna's neck? He'd give his finest stallion to know the answer to that.

"Your Majesty, I was thinking about the ivory ring Leicester gave to the Earl of Everly's bride. Quite a lovely gift, but it puzzles me why he would part with a present from his Queen?"

"Curious, isn't it? But do not read anything sinister in it. Arianna is a sweet, lovely child. And it is certainly true we had no other marriage gift to offer. 'Twas probably a spontaneous gesture."

"Probably so. She does bring out a man's gallant side. I couldn't help noticing, though, how unusual the ring is. I don't believe I've seen anything like it before."

"And you never shall. It is of my own design. It was originally meant as a gift to the Scottish Queen, a symbol of the blood we share. But I changed my mind when her son James was born and gave it to Leicester instead."

"I see." So that was the significance of the ruby sliver on the ring. "Seems odd that he held onto it all those years only to give it away to a girl he'd never met."

"Odd? Not really. I remember now he wore it for a few weeks, then no more. When I asked what happened to it he told me he lost it hunting. Obviously, it was never lost, but only misplaced. Strange that he should find it after so many years."

Yes, very strange, Edmund thought, and worth looking into. Finding it hard to concentrate on the chess game, Elizabeth beat him easily, trumpeting her pleasure so all might hear.

"There now. Tell me, sir, am I not a better player than my cousin, Mary?"

"Need you ask? Mary could never best me at chess, so you are quite obviously the better player."

"Ahhhhhh. It does my heart good." Grabbing a goblet of wine, she downed it in one gulp. "The promiscuous little snippet. Someday I'll find her daughter, and when I do, Leicester shall know the bitterness I have suffered all these years."

Edmund's ears pricked up. "Daughter? The Scottish Queen? I've always believed she had but one son."

240

Elizabeth threw her empty goblet into the fire, startling Edmund with her venom.

"As does the whole world. But I know better. She dared to have a child with my creature, my . . ."

Edmund choked on his wine. Leicester: Could she be speaking of Leicester? This was too juicy. "Your Majesty, it can't be true."

"Shocks you, does it? My Lord Leicester coupling with that, that . . ."

"Am I to take it that Leicester and the Scottish Queen did sleep together, that she became pregnant by him? I never knew they had even met."

Elizabeth laughed bitterly. "Oh, they met, all right. Twice that I know about. Can you believe that's all it took? Two times. Two? Nay, not even that. She was probably caught the very first time. Fertile as a bitch dog, she is, while I . . ."

Elizabeth suddenly composed herself, realizing how she must sound. "I tell you this in strictest confidence, Edmund. No one is to know, do you hear? I won't be made a laughing stock, or a thing of pity. No. I tell you this for a reason, the reason I sent for you. You are the only one I know who has actually met this daughter of Mary's."

Edmund's heart suddenly constricted. "I, Your Majesty? Surely not."

Elizabeth paced the floor, suddenly eager for Edmund to know everything. He of all people could find Mary's daughter. "I almost had her once. At least I *think* the peasant girl who visited her was her daughter."

"Peasant girl?"

"Yes. Clever *what?* Here I've been looking for some nobleman's foster daughter when all the while she was being raised a peasant."

241

"I don't understand, Your Majesty, when did I meet . . ."

"Two years ago. You *were* there. But of course there was no way for you to know who she was."

Edmund breathed easier. He wasn't being blamed. "Where?"

"Do you not recall a peasant and his daughter who had a private audience with Mary, returning her little dog? 'Twas on my birthday — her daughter's birthday, too. That's how I knew. *That's how I knew.* Mary had a visit from her daughter on *my* birthday!"

"I remember that day well. But . . . you can't mean . . . that peasant girl was Mary's daughter?"

Elizabeth's breath grew ragged, her face pinched and white. "Tell me. What does she look like? I need to know if she doth favor Leicester?"

Edmund thought back to that day, remembering the sweet oval face of the peasant girl — then replacing it immediately by the image of Arianna. Arianna! *She* was Mary's daughter! There could be no doubt. No wonder she resembled the Queen. And the ring! The bloody ring! It wasn't Leicester who gave it to Arianna, but Mary, the very day she visited her. Mary had been wearing it when they played chess, *but not when he returned to her chamber.* And never after that. Blood rushed to his head, turning the room dark for a moment.

"Well?"

"What? Oh, yes. I'm trying to get a clear picture of her. It's been so long." Edmund was stalling for time, wanting to turn this information to his best advantage. "Let's see, I'm afraid I don't recall any resemblance to Leicester, but then I wasn't looking for any. I would have to see her again to judge that."

"Then tell me, what color hair doth she have, and

eyes? Was she tall or short, fat or thin? What do you remember?"

Edmund felt a shiver of happiness. The Queen was practically begging him, and he, *he* was the only person who could give her the information she wanted so desperately. Such power. Such tremendous power. But, power that would be gone as soon as he revealed Arianna's identity. Then what was the hurry? He could make his power last. After all, the longer Elizabeth had to wait the more she would appreciate him and his extraordinary efforts to find Mary's daughter. What a stroke of fortune. He would revel in the delicious revenge of having Elizabeth in his power, and . . . why stop there? Why not use that same power over Arianna? If he could not have her as his wife, then he would have her as his mistress.

"Sweet Jesus, Edmund, tell me what she looks like!"

"Fair, quite fair, she was, with eyes of brightest blue. Somehow . . . somehow, I feel I've seen her somewhere else as well."

"Yes, yes?" Elizabeth's voice fairly whined in anticipation.

"It escapes me. Mayhap I shall remember it later. I will think on it most intensely."

Edmund hid his glee behind a sympathetic expression as he watched Elizabeth's face. She was in his power, and soon Arianna would be, too. And he would show her no mercy.

Chapter Twenty

All too aware of the audience peering through the hole in the wall, Judith enticed Edmund into acts of lust that would greatly entertain their sole observer. It gratified her to know how upset he would be if he knew they were being watched, and that gratification more than compensated for having to accommodate his peculiar sexual needs. She would never forget the ill treatment she had received at his hand when she was carrying his child or the pain she had suffered when the old witch had rid her of the babe.

Some day, when she could forestall her revenge no longer, she would delight in telling Edmund how he had been observed performing the most intimate of acts. But for now she must content herself with knowing how ridiculous he must look to the observer.

"Now! Now! Take it in your mouth now!"

Edmund's frenzied voice pulled her from her reverie. Good. At last she could finish him off. Moving quickly, Judith slid her head down Edmund's belly to take his throbbing manhood in her mouth. He grasped her head with his hands, pushing her up against him, his body convulsing violently as he quickly came into her mouth.

Leaving the bed, she walked naked to the table and drank from a wine bottle to wash away the taste of him. At the same time, she eyed the concealed hole in the wall. Edmund's sexual performance should have Elizabeth writhing with pleasure.

Elizabeth. It was funny how much they had in common. And how much enjoyment they shared over Judith's sexual encounters. Elizabeth took great pleasure in observing Judith with the staid and powerful lords she took to her bedchamber.

The higher their status, the more pleasure it seemed to give the Queen. And when next that particular lord or earl or duke came to conduct business at court, how she would titter behind her fan, remembering the unlordly things she had observed. Though they never knew she had seen them, it still gave the Queen a further degree of power over them and Judith knew well how much the Queen thrived on power.

And now, with Edmund, Elizabeth was getting an altogether different kind of thrill. Edmund was a handsome male and Judith knew Elizabeth desired to bed him herself. Knew, too, that whilst the Queen watched Judith and Edmund making love, she would be pretending it was herself in his arms.

It was rumored Elizabeth had some terrible physical deformity that prevented her from fully making love to a man, and she could only wonder then what the Queen did when she was alone with Leicester. Surely, in some way, Elizabeth received sexual gratification from him. That was one subject, though, that she would never dare bring up to the Queen — not as long as she valued her neck!

Feeling the touch of Edmund's hand on her bare

245

breast, she brushed it away, irritated at being bothered after she was finished with him. "I'm tired, Edmund. Be a good boy and go to your own chamber."

Edmund grabbed her breast again, harder, making her wince with pain. "Don't ever talk to me like that again. I'm not a lowly serf or yeoman that you may order around."

Anger grew like wildfire in Judith's heart, but she beat it back, knowing Elizabeth might still be watching. He would have his way now, but soon, soon, it would be her turn.

The weather next day was warm and balmy, enticing the castlefolk to venture out of doors after a long siege of cold and blustery days. The Queen was no different; accompanied by her ladies-in-waiting, she walked the grounds, nodding and smiling to everyone she passed.

Taking advantage of her good mood, Edmund approached her. "Your Gracious Majesty, on such a fine day as this I thought to make good use of the favorable weather to ride over to Tutbury. I want to inquire amongst the cottagers in the surrounding area for any trace of the one you seek. Mayhap, with a few coins pressed into the right palm, someone will remember seeing her and can tell me where she is."

"Excellent idea, Edmund. It pleases me to know you are doing something about it, finally. I was beginning to wonder if your heart was in it."

"Your Grace, surely you cannot doubt my sincerity. My memory is clear enough now to get a good picture of the girl in my head and I must follow it up by pursuing her in person."

"Then by all means, do so. You have my permission to go, and may take whomever you need to accompany you."

246

"I would like Lady Judith to be included in my entourage."

Elizabeth gave a little laugh. "I don't doubt you would, but I cannot see how she can be of any help to you. Outside of your bed, that is."

Edmund had been anticipating this reaction. "You mistake my motives, Your Majesty. With the Lady Judith by my side, the simple folk will be more easily persuaded. They will not see anything sinister in my inquiry if I have a lady with me."

It didn't take Elizabeth long to conclude there was much merit in what he said. Edmund was crafty. Too crafty, mayhap. She would have to remember that. However, as long as his craftiness was used to her advantage, then she would accept it. But if ever the day came . . .

Hours later, on the road to Tutbury, a still-sulking Judith drew her horse to a halt. "I want to rest. And I want to know why we're doing this. What unsavory business are you pursuing on behalf of the Queen?"

Reining in beside her, Edmund said, "That's between the Queen and me. It seems to upset you to find you're not the only one who shares secrets with Elizabeth."

"I have no idea what you're speaking of, and I care not what secrets you share with the Queen. I'm only angry you had to involve me. What part do I play in this scheme of yours? And where is it that we go?"

"You play no part in it. It simply pleases me to have you along. After all, you are my betrothed, are you not?"

"Am I? If that's true, why don't you announce it to your precious Queen? Or am I only your betrothed when it is convenient?"

"You misjudge me as usual, Judith. What would

247

you say if I told you when this journey is successfully completed I intend to do just that? It's time I took a wife."

Judith couldn't believe her ears. Did he mean it? Was it possible he did want to marry her? Maybe she had been wrong about him. Maybe he did truly love her. "Do I have your sacred oath on that, Edmund?"

Smiling broadly, Edmund withdrew his sword from the sheath attached to his saddle and kissed the shiny blade. "I swear upon this sword that I shall claim you as my bride when my mission has been successfully completed. There. Are you happy now?"

A shiver of pleasure made its way through Judith's body — she knew the importance of such an oath. No man swore lightly by his sword. It was indeed a sacred promise. Suddenly, she felt as if the weight of the world had been lifted from her shoulders. "I hold you to it, my lord. But what of Elizabeth? What if she denies you again?"

"She won't. When I've completed her quest, she will be well pleased and give me whatever I ask."

"Then why are we waiting?" Judith galloped away, the wind catching her cape and billowing it around her, a red cloud surrounding her long dark hair.

Edmund laughed and spurred his horse, signaling to the party of knights and yeomen to speed their mounts. The world was his. Thanks to Arianna, his fondest dreams would now come true. It was clever of him to bring Judith along. She was Will's sister, and therefore would not be denied entrance to Everly Castle. If he had gone without her he was certain Arianna would have kept him out.

He knew it was thanks to Robert and Leicester that he had been sent away for those long dreary months and was happy that at last he would exact his revenge

248

through Arianna. If he hadn't been in such favor with Elizabeth, he would still be on that tiresome little island overseeing Elizabeth's political prisoners in a dank old castle.

Now, nothing would deter him from his goal. When he brought Arianna back, Elizabeth would be indebted to him and reward him accordingly. Mayhap, a title to add to his name and a castle in Wales. Yes, he would like that.

He was growing ever wearier of the Queen's presence, forever flattering her, catering to her every wish. The past few months had taught him that the power she had over him was sometimes a burden too great to bear. Let her have Leicester's daughter. Then, maybe then he would have the freedom to do what *he* wanted.

By dusk, the weather had changed. The air grew cold and rain began to fall. But rather than being dismayed, Edmund was elated, for the rain would make it all the easier to gain admittance to Everly Castle.

As he drew to a halt at the castle moat, Edmund's pulse quickened. If everything had gone according to plan, Robert would not be there, but off with his men on the western border of his land, skirmishing with the band of yeomen in Edmund's pay. He had sent the yeomen off as soon as Elizabeth granted him permission to leave, giving them a three-hour start. They had instructions to set fire to the woods so that Robert would be sure to see it and ride after them.

Gazing up at the formidable walls, he had his page sound the trumpet. Immediately, heads appeared at the castle windows. "Open the gates. The Lady Judith Ludlow of Norbridge seeks shelter for the night."

Judith looked at Edmund in astonishment. What was he up to? Why had he used her name instead of his own? An uneasiness crept through her as she real-

249

ized he was using her to gain entrance. But why? He had been friends with Robert for years.

Looking down at the large entourage, the gate-keeper was at a loss as to what to do. The earl had given him explicit instructions not to lower the draw-bridge for anyone. But Lady Judith's family were great and good friends of Lord Warwick, and it was beginning to rain hard. How could he deny sanctuary to so gentle a lady?

He was relieved of that terrible decision when Lady Arianna sent word that he should admit the Lady Judith and her entourage.

Though great with child, Arianna still moved grace-fully as she made her way out to the courtyard. Why was Judith here? Had something happened to Will? Anxious to know, her gaze found Judith's as she rode into the inner ward. She didn't see Edmund until he helped Judith down from her horse; by then, it was too late.

He was here. The only thing she could do was put on a good face and hope for the best. "Edmund. Judith. What brings you to Everly? Has anything happened to Will?"

Judith was shocked to find Arianna so large with child. Her hand involuntarily moved to cradle her own stomach. She would have been that far along if . . .

Edmund jerked his head back in surprise when he turned from attending to Judith to see Arianna standing there, so full of life. And he wanted her all the more. Wanted her on her knees, on her back, begging for mercy but receiving none. And if fortune deemed it, he would have her soon. "Fear not, Arianna, William is well. Judith and I were on our way to visit him and got caught in the rain. We seek sanctuary for the night, if you will grant it."

"Of course, Edmund. But with your own castle so near, why did you not stop there?"

"Because Everly is that much closer to Norbridge, making it a shorter ride for Judith."

The answer seemed reasonable, but Arianna couldn't help feeling uneasy. "Then you are welcome."

"Well spoken. And now, tell me, where is your husband? Why isn't he here to greet us?"

Arianna's uneasiness grew stronger. The word *husband* sounded foreign from his mouth. "He's off with his men, but I'm sure he'll be back soon."

The wicked grin that crossed Edmund's face sent a shiver up Arianna's spine. No! It couldn't be possible. Edmund couldn't have arranged for Rob to be gone. She was imagining it. But when next he spoke, she knew it was true.

"Before I forget, I wish to convey a message to you from the Earl of Leicester."

Arianna knew her father would never use Edmund for that purpose. Why was he lying? "Oh? Then you must tell me what it is."

"Walk with me and I shall. The message is for your ears alone."

Arianna felt as if she were falling into a bottomless pit. "Very well. I was just on my way to the chapel."

"The chapel? Indeed. Shall we?" Offering her his arm, he led her away.

Judith stared after them, a tight knot in the pit of her stomach. Edmund was up to no good. And it was obvious by her nervousness that Arianna knew it. What could it possibly be? She had always thought Arianna to be above reproach. What power did Edmund have over Robert's wife?

When they reached the chapel, Arianna entered and made her way to the altar. She crossed herself, deriving

251

a measure of comfort from the sacred gesture of her mother's faith. She must draw strength from this holy place, for it was the only protection she had. "Well, Edmund. What is it you wished to tell me?"

"Only that I know the secret of your birth."

Arianna tightened her jaw. "Is that so? And just what is this great secret that you know? That, in sooth, I am really a changeling? A fairy? A witch? Tell me, Edmund."

She had courage. He had to give her that much. He saw the transformation in her face, the steel that came into those perfect blue eyes, and he admired her all the more for it. "You do not give yourself enough credit, sweet one. Only a few women in this world have blood as blue as yours. If things were different you'd be a princess right now, surrounded by servants and knights who would protect you from me. But, fortunately for me, you are quite alone, with no one to help you."

So. He did know who she was. "Alone? Hardly. All I have to do is open my mouth and you will be surrounded."

"Tsk, tsk, my dear. Think again. I have enough knights and yeomen with me to take this castle easily now that we're inside. But it won't come to that. When I tell your people I was sent by the Queen, they will acquiesce most readily. If they do not, their blood will stain the ground under your feet. I'm sure you don't want that. Come with me peaceably and spare their lives."

"Where?"

Edmund smiled slyly, knowing he had the advantage. "Why, to Elizabeth, of course. You have no idea how happy she will be to see you. And when she finds out that the baby you carry is Leicester's grandchild, her happiness will be overwhelming. Denied the pleasure of raising his child, think how delighted she will be to raise his grandchild instead."

Arianna fell to her knees in front of the altar, her arms spread wide in helpless subjugation. Closing her eyes, she cried, "Dear Lord, if I have offended thee, I am truly sorry, and I will accept your punishment. But, Dear God, my child is innocent. Don't punish it for my sins. Don't separate my poor babe from its mother. I know too well what that is like. I was separated from my own mother at birth. Must my child in turn be separated from me? I pray you do not let this happen."

Edmund watched in growing anger. "You seek a way out? Ask *me,* not some invisible God. Ask *me* to spare your child. Who knows? If you grant me some boon, I may concede."

Arianna turned her head to look up at him, a spark of hope lighting her eyes. "Boon? What do you want? Ask me anything, and if it is in my power I will give it to you."

Edmund's voice came from his very depths. "Oh, you have the power to give me what I want. But will you?"

"What? What is it you want from me?"

"What women have been giving men since time began. Come to my bed. Do that for me and I may be persuaded not to tell Elizabeth who you are."

Arianna shook her head slowly, unable to believe what she heard. "Look at me, Edmund. I am huge with child. How could you ask that of me now? Wait until the child is born and I will do as you ask. 'Twill be only a week or two, three at the most before its birth, then . . ."

"Now! I want you now."

Arianna looked around her, her eyes large with

253

fright, like a rabbit seeking a way to escape the sharp talons of a hawk. Her gaze came to rest on the pale statue standing in a corner. The Virgin Madonna, cradling her infant in her arms. *Mary, Mother of God, give me strength . . . to do whatever I must to survive.*

"Well, what is your answer?"

"Here? In this holy place?"

Edmund's laughter echoed through the small room. "Even I am not that ignoble. No, my lovely madonna. I can wait until bedtime. You will come to me then."

A glimmer of hope grew in Arianna's heart. She still had time to find a way to escape. She would let him think she had acquiesced. "All right. I'll come to you after everyone's abed. I don't want anyone to know . . . what we do."

Edmund took her hand and raised it to his lips. Instead of kissing it, he used his tongue to wet each finger one at a time, his eyes locked onto hers.

Arianna held herself rigid, not moving, not expressing her utter revulsion. It would end soon, it would end soon, she could endure. She must endure.

"So it shall be." Dropping her hand, he turned and left.

Before he was out the door, she wiped her fingers on her skirt. Knowing she had but a short time, Arianna moved quickly. She knew what she had to do and what she could not do — endanger her people. Rob had taken most of his men with him, leaving but a small force to guard the castle. There would have been more than enough men to defend Everly if she had not so foolishly opened the gates to Edmund. But it was too late to think of that now. There was only one thing she could do now to keep her people safe, and protect her husband. She would run away where Edmund and Elizabeth could not find her.

Composing herself, she hurried out of the chapel. A crack of thunder rent the air, causing her to jump; the rains came down in a furious torrent, as if heaven and earth were against her, too. If only there was an ounce of mercy in Edmund's heart. But that was not to be. She was alone. Mayhap she could have stood up to Edmund, but she had not the strength to stand up to the woman he represented, the powerful English Queen.

Seeking Fiona, she found her in the kitchen. Taking her aside, she told her of her predicament. "My only hope is to wait 'til the cover of dark and escape."

"But, my lady, how? The drawbridge is up. He would hear it being lowered, and besides, it is raining terribly now."

"You forget the secret passageway in my bedchamber. It leads out to the burial ground on the other side of the castle walls. Do you think I would let the rains keep me from saving my child? Fiona, use the secret passageway now. Go to your father's and get Pasha. Bring him to the burial ground and tie him to a tree. I'll make my escape on him."

"I will, but, oh, my lady. Where will you go?"

"I don't know. I'll think of that later. All I know is I have to get away from Everly. And Fiona, tell no one. Not even Buttercup, do you understand?"

Fiona shivered, feeling the full brunt of the terrible responsibility. Never in her life had she done so brave a thing or so important a task. She must help her lady, even if it meant her very life.

Assured that Fiona was on her way to her father's, Arianna joined Judith and Edmund in the great hall, putting in an appearance to keep Edmund from being suspicious. She noted with satisfaction the relief on his face when she walked up to them.

"Arianna, you're looking pale," he said with a smile. "Here, sit by the fire and have some mead. 'Twill calm your nerves."

Arianna sat down and accepted a tankard of mead, deriving sustenance from the potent liquid. She took a deep breath, forcing herself to remain calm. "Judith, it's good to see you after so long. Are you well? What do you hear of Will?"

It was all too clear to Judith that Arianna was troubled, and for some unexplained reason that bothered her. God knows, she had reason enough to hate the girl for taking Robert from her, but surprisingly she felt no animosity toward her anymore. In fact, she felt a kind of kinship. Was it because Arianna was pregnant? "I'm well, thank you. And Will is, too. I haven't seen him for a while, but then, Elizabeth keeps me quite busy, as you might imagine. Are you all right, Arianna? You seem troubled."

"Troubled? No, not at all. In sooth, I feel like staying up late to catch up on all the news at court. You must lead a very sumptuous life, Judith. Do tell me about it."

Edmund chuckled to himself. The devious wench sought to forestall her destiny by staying up late with Judith. Just like a woman. "Your talk will have to wait. I'm sure Judith is tired after her long ride, aren't you, my dear?"

Judith's eyes narrowed. What was Edmund up to? "I *am* rather damp. 'Twill feel good to get into dry clothes."

"Forgive me, Judith," Arianna said quickly. "Where are my manners? I'll have Buttercup show you the way to your chamber."

"And I am in need of some dry clothing as well," Edmund said, giving Arianna a hard look. "I'll go to my chamber now, too." He followed after Judith and Buttercup.

The tankard Arianna held began to shake as she waited for them to disappear. She followed immediately, climbing the stairs and making her way down the hall to her bedchamber. The room was lit by a single candle — she would need it to see in the darkness of the secret passageway.

Grabbing a cloak from a hook on the wall, she started to wrap it around her when she felt a tug. It was caught on something. Turning around, her eyes grew wide in horror. Edmund stood before her, the hem of her cloak in his hand.

"Are you chilled, my lady? Is that the reason for your cloak? Then fear not. In a few moments you will be feeling much warmer. Are you ready to come to my chamber? Or do you wish to receive me in your husband's bed? It's your choice."

"Choice? You offer me little choice," Arianna retorted icily.

Taking the candle from her hand, Edmund put it down and escorted her from the room by her elbow.

Every step she took reverberated through her heart, through her womb, making her sick with fear. This can't be happening, she thought in desperation.

She heard the chamber door open, and then a few seconds later close, leaving her with no hope. Her eyes lit on the bed. It would be the torture chamber and she the ravaged victim.

"Well, my dear, what are you waiting for? Take your clothes off. The sooner it is done, the sooner you can forget it happened."

"Surely it isn't necessary for me to remove my clothes?"

257

"Ah, but it is. The best part. I want to see your swollen belly. I want to savor every minute of our little rendezvous. After all, it must be worth my while if I am to keep your secret."

"You bastard!"

"True, but I'm in good company, aren't I?" Moving up close to her, he continued. "Shall I help you undress? Will that make it easier?" Reaching out, he grabbed her arm.

"No! I can't go through with it. It would injure the child. I'm too close to my time."

Edmund's voice became a growl. "You'll not back out of this, my high and mighty lady. Go ahead, fight me. 'Twill make me all the harder." With his free hand, he grabbed her breast, pinching hard.

Arianna cried out, but Edmund muffled her voice with his hand. At the same time she could swear she heard another's muffled cry. The sound of her gown ripping pushed all thoughts from her mind save defending herself, and she struggled out of Edmund's reach.

Edmund was surprised at her strength. He went after her again, twisting her arm behind her back. She cried out, and with her free hand reached for Rob's dagger at her waist.

Behind the tapestry covering the wall, Judith listened to Arianna's struggle, a strange feeling welling up inside her. Edmund had told her to stay there and be quiet, that she would be amused by what would transpire. But this? She wasn't amused at all. This was no tryst of a consenting couple, but a poor pregnant woman being forced. It brought to mind her own recent ordeal and the humiliation she had endured, and her heart went out to Arianna. Moved by her plight, she was about to make her presence known when she heard Edmund cry out. She stood still, listening intently.

"Oh, no, Edmund. I didn't mean to do it. I didn't. You forced me. I had no choice. I couldn't let you rape me. I couldn't." In a daze, Arianna's gaze went from the dripping dagger in her hand to Edmund's bloodied form leaning against the wall.

"You bitch! You'll suffer for this. And everyone else who knows your true identity. Elizabeth will lock them all in the tower for protecting you."

In horror, Arianna dropped the dagger and fled from the room, running to her bedchamber. "Dear God, dear God," she moaned. She took her cloak and wrapped it around her, then grasping the burning candle she pushed the tapestry aside and made her way down the secret subterranean passageway. The cloying cobwebs reached for her, the dank smell assaulted her nostrils, and the darkness ahead was fearful, but she went on, knowing she still had a chance to save her child from Elizabeth. Please, Dear God, she thought, let Pasha be waiting for me.

A current of air lifted her spirits and she stepped up her pace. The sound of the rain's fury drew her forward, until, at last, she emerged and pushed aside the shrubbery that hid the opening. Fierce rain pelted Arianna's face as she stood in the graveyard, her heart jumping as a muffled sound reached her ears. Straining her eyes to see through the surrounding blackness, she cried, "Is . . . is someone there?"

She listened, her heart beating wildly, until she determined the noise she heard was the rumbling of distant thunder. No one was about. What fool would linger in the burial ground, at this hour of the night, in the middle of a soaking rain?

What fool indeed? For here she was.

A bolt of lightning pierced the sky, illuminating for a moment the rugged tombstones standing lonely and forlorn in the falling rain, and . . . something else . . . something that made her heart leap with joy. Pasha, her sleek white stallion, was tied to a tree, waiting to carry her away. Fiona had not let her down.

Pulling the black velvet mantle tight around her throat, she made her way through the tombstones and approached the horse cautiously, knowing how skittish Pasha would be in the terrible storm. The high-strung animal whinnied a nervous greeting, stamping his hooves on the sodden ground and dancing in place.

"I know, Pasha. Midnight is a strange time to be taking a ride, but it will be all right, you'll see." All right? How could anything be all right when the ride would take Arianna away from Robert and everything she held dear in the world?

Robert. What will he think when he returns and finds her gone? He vowed to protect her always, but even his powerful love couldn't save her from the wrath of a vengeful Queen. She had no choice but to flee, for if she stayed Rob would endanger his life for her and she couldn't let that happen. But, oh, how could she bear never seeing her beloved husband's face again? A shudder knifed through her as she relived the image of Edmund tearing at her clothes and of the dagger plunging into his shoulder blade, propelled by her hand. The blow had slowed him long enough for her to make her escape unharmed, but it wouldn't stop him from traveling to London. In a few hours, Queen Elizabeth would have the information she had been seeking and Arianna would be doomed.

Soothing Pasha with her voice, she put her foot in the stirrup, and using all her strength, struggled to pull herself up, but her swollen belly got in the way.

She tried again, groaning at the effort, this time succeeding, her stomach scraping against the edge of the saddle as she swung into it. Digging her knees into the animal's side, she started down the narrow path that led away from the castle and the joy-filled life she had there. She was leaving as she had come, with naught but the garments she wore.

The babe stirred inside her, a small hand or foot pushing against her side, and she thought, *not true*. She was leaving with more, for her sweet babe would be born in less than a month. Forgive me, Robert. Forgive me for taking your child away.

Looking up one last time to the faint light that seeped from the castle windows, she hunched her shoulders against the rain and began her lonely journey.

She rode astride, her protruding stomach making riding sidesaddle too precarious, fighting Pasha every step of the way. Pasha was unused to traveling in the dark, let alone in a nightmarish thunderstorm, and the muscles in her arms soon ached from trying to control him. She feared striking her head against some unseen tree limb, and was afraid the stallion might stumble and break a leg. But what was the use in thinking such things? She had no choice. She had to get away — now.

Each league she traveled seemed longer than the one before, but she struggled on, her belly rubbing against the saddle uncomfortably, her body taut with anxiety, until she drew to a halt at a fork in the road. Which direction? The way seemed unfamiliar, the landscape distorted in the moonless dark, the accursed rain making it all but impossible to see.

She started down the fork that led to the right, her vision blurred by the rain, her face stinging as if pricked by the tips of a thousand daggers. She wanted

261

to stop, to huddle under her mantle until the rain ceased, but she had to go on.

Before long, she realized the road she traveled was on a steep incline and her heart sank. The last thing she wanted was to ride through some wild hilltop forest. Pasha crested the hill, then suddenly stopped, refusing to go any further. Arianna urged him on, using her voice and knees and the reins, but still the animal would not move.

"Pasha—come, lad. There's nothing to be afeared of here."

This had happened before, always when the animal was afraid of something by the side of the road, and she knew from experience the only way to get him to move beyond that spot was to walk him past it. With a weary groan, she climbed down and grabbed hold of the bridle, pulling it hard. Pasha resisted, his eyes rolling, wild with fear, his ears laid flat.

"Stupid animal!"

Arianna faced the horse, planting her feet wide apart, then holding the leather on each side of his head, she tugged again. Still the horse would not budge.

"You son of a jackass—move!"

Pasha's velvet hide had never felt the sting of leather, but if she had had a whip she would gladly have used it. She was drenched to the skin, shivering violently from the cold, and this pampered, worthless animal wouldn't move, afraid of some imaginary thing on the road.

Jerking hard on the bridle, she stepped backward for more leverage, and with a sickening jolt felt the earth give way.

The wind gobbled up her scream as she slid down . . . down . . . her hands clawing at the embankment, grasping at earth and grass and shrubs in a desperate attempt to stop her descent. Then suddenly, miraculously, her feet touched solid ground, and pain shot up her legs at the impact, crumpling her like a rag doll.

Her arms moved quickly to cradle her stomach. "Dear God, please let the babe be all right."

As if to reassure her, the baby moved, shifting to a different position. Arianna began to cry, her tears blending with the rain to wash her face. The child still lived. All would be well.

Somewhere above her, she heard Pasha's nervous whinny and felt a shard of hope. He was still there. She could still get away. She had only to find her way up to the road. But how? She had no idea where she was. The night was so dark she could barely see more than an arm's length in front of her face.

She started to stand, then suddenly stopped. Something . . . something . . . nagged at her mind . . . telling her to be cautious. Listening to that inner voice, she slowly sank to the ground. What was it?

Instinctively she moved, turning so the earthen wall she had slid down was at her back. Then slowly, cautiously she crawled forward, feeling with her hands the rugged surface beneath her. What was it? She moved slowly forward inch by inch, foot by foot, her hands becoming numb at the touch of the cold wet ground.

Suddenly, horribly, her hand plunged through air, and she immediately backed up, sucking in her breath.

It can't be!

Her heart in her throat, she moved her other arm, slowly, stretching it out inch by inch, until it too found air.

"Holy Mother of God!"

She froze, afraid to move, afraid even to breathe,

263

listening . . . as a lonely muted sound penetrated her senses from far below. The familiar sound of surf washing against a rocky shore! As that knowledge crept through her body, registering on her unbelieving brain, her body began to shake.

She knew where she was, the only place she could be: on a ledge that hung over the great cliffs!

"Dear God, I've got to get away from here."

In a panic, she started to rise, then stopped, clutching at her stomach as a violent pain tore through her.

The babe was coming!

"God have mercy!"

Chapter Twenty-one

Striding along the edge of the cliff, Colin Colrain kept his eyes turned toward the eastern sky, drinking in its pink-stained beauty. 'Twas a grand morning to be alive. After the long miserable rain, the world looked fresh and new again. Soon the land would be blanketed with flowers and the sweet smell of spring would seep into his veins, filling him with the same great vigor he felt each April.

The keening of the wind whipping along the cliff's edge sang in his ears, blocking out the sound of everything else in its wake, but he didn't mind. The wind spoke to him. Sometimes it was the only voice he heard for days at a time.

He enjoyed these early hours of the morn the most, for it was then he felt like the only person on the face of the earth, then that he could feel at peace. Ever since his Lily had died he had been drawn more and more to the forest and to the natural order it represented. He was a huntsman, supplying deer and other game for the Earl of Everly's table, and it contented him to be just that. No more would he have to bend to the will of the Queen, no more would he have to surrender his honor to hold on to what was his.

He had been in Queen Elizabeth's favor and, next to Leicester, the one she turned to most often; he paid heavily now for that dubious honor. She had taken everything he owned when he married Lily against her wishes, falsely accusing him of crimes against the crown to cover the true reason for her action and leaving him without so much as a horse for his pregnant wife to ride. If it hadn't been for the kindness of Robert Warwick they would have starved to death.

Over the howl of the wind he heard his dog bark and turned his gaze from the sky to his giant Dane, Thor, and then to the magnificent white animal that appeared out of the low-hanging mist. "Here, now! Where did you come from, Beauty? Where is your master?"

Gazing around, he saw no sign of a rider. Must be a runaway, he thought, making his way cautiously toward the horse. Might be a reward for return of so dear an animal.

Thor barked again, darting at the horse's feet, then quickly away when Pasha lowered his head and bared his teeth.

Colin laughed. "Shame on the two of you. 'Tis too nice a day to be feeling so mean."

Clicking his tongue at the dog, he gave the command for retreat. Thor resignedly slumped his mighty head and strode over to the edge of the cliff and waited.

"Now, then, Beauty, are you hungry?" Fishing in the small sack tied to his belt, he took out an apple, wiped it on his jerkin, and took a huge bite out of it.

The horse's ears pricked up immediately.

"Hah! So you are hungry. Good. Mayhap you'll come to me then for a tasty bite of this juicy apple."

As if on command, the horse started moving slowly toward Colin, his eyes locked onto the round red fruit. Colin watched patiently until the animal was well within range, then reached up to grab the bridle. The horse's ears lay flat for just a moment, then righted as Colin pushed the apple up to its mouth. It was gone in two crunchy bites.

Colin stroked the horse's neck and soothed it with his voice. "What I wouldn't give for a beauty like you. But 'tis impossible, I know. You belong to some high and mighty lord, mayhap the earl himself. In sooth, I seem to remember hearing the young earl's wife rode a horse such as you."

Thor barked again and the horse flattened his ears. "Thor. No!" Turning his gaze to the dog, the hair on the back of his neck stood on end. The dog wasn't barking at the horse but at something below the cliff.

Thor sniffed along the edge, whimpering in a way that told him something was indeed down there, something that disturbed the dog greatly. Could it be the missing rider? Tying the horse to a tree, Colin clenched his teeth and strode to the edge to peer down, bracing himself for what he might see.

Dear God! Nothing could have prepared him for the sight on the ledge below. A woman, large with child, was straining hard, obviously in the middle of a labor pain.

"Mistress, are you all right?" he shouted over the wind.

Arianna's eyes were squeezed shut as she endured the pain, waiting for it to end. The pains were coming close together now, with little chance to rest between them.

"Mistress, I'm coming down."

Her eyes flew open, focusing on the brown-clad form on the ledge some seven feet above her. "Thank God!" Hot tears scalded her blue-tinged cheeks. "Yes, I'm all right, but my babe, it's coming! Now!"

"Hold on, you're going to be just fine."

In a matter of seconds he was beside her, taking her hand in his. "You've picked a mighty strange place to birth your babe, my lady. Mighty strange indeed."

Arianna smiled faintly through the pain, gazing at the welcome sight of her rescuer bending over her. She stared into his eyes, seeking and finding the comfort she needed. Fringed with thick copper lashes, his eyes were as blue as her own, his face ruddy-cheeked and leathery. Long curly red hair blew around his shoulders in the fury of the wind, making him look for all the world like a great, wild, Norse god. "I . . . Oh! Oh! I have to push, I have to push."

Squeezing his hand tightly, Arianna strained hard, the overwhelming desire to push overcoming any notion of retaining a ladylike demeanor for the stranger.

Fear clutched at Colin. Two years earlier he had witnessed his own Lily straining to give birth to his child—watched as she had grown weaker and weaker each time she pushed until her body was too weak to push any longer. She perished, taking the babe with her.

Fearing for this fragile girl's life, he knew he must do all he could to keep her alive. Lifting her wet

268

clothing over her stomach, he laid his warm hands on her bare skin, stroking it soothingly.

The jolt of heat had immediate results. The straining ended, and her body relaxed like butter melting on scones hot from the oven. "Ohhhh! That feels good, that feels so good. I've been so cold, so cold and . . ."

"Shhh, little one. I know, I know. Just let it come now, all right? Just let it come."

His hands moved over her stomach in continuing strokes, the life-giving heat restoring her strength, her resolve to survive. "Oh! Here comes another one. It's coming, I feel it. It's coming!"

Colin moved his hands between her legs and felt the hot wet head emerging. "Just one more push, little one, one more push and it'll be out."

"Uh. Uh. Unnnnnh!" She strained hard, thinking any second she would be torn in two, the pain so bad she thought she'd faint. And then, miraculously, it was over. She felt a gush of hot liquid spray over her legs and the babe was sliding down between her thighs, the man catching it in his hands.

Her tears turned to sobs as he held her child up.

"My babe, my sweet babe. Let me hold it."

"In a moment. This young fellow needs to be cleaned."

"I have a son?"

"A beautiful, healthy son. Praise the Lord." Taking the piece of petticoat Arianna had laid beside her, he wiped the child's face and head gently until it was clean, making sure it was breathing properly before cleaning the rest of its body. When he was finished he took the knife from the sheath at his waist and severed the still-throbbing umbilical cord.

The child immediately began to cry.

It was done. The woman lived. The child lived. In triumph he placed the babe on the young woman's naked belly.

At the first wonderful, warm touch of her babe against her skin, her stomach contracted once more, and a torrent of blood was expelled, soaking the man's clothing before forming a large puddle on the cold ground.

"Ooohh!" Arianna cried out in fright. Had she survived the long night only to die from loss of blood?

"Don't be frightened, girl. It's just the afterbirth. It's as it should be. You're fine."

Reassured, Arianna's arms cradled the squirming babe on her stomach. "Did you hear that, son? We're going to be all right." A huge shiver coursed through her and she began to shake all over.

"Aye, my lady, you'll be fine. In no time at all, I'll have you home, snug and warm in your own bed."

Arianna closed her eyes. She was so tired she wanted just to sleep, but she couldn't. She had to take care of her babe, keep it safe from Elizabeth. "I can't go to my own home. Will you take me to yours?"

Colin knew this was not the time to ask about her troubles. He had to get her out of the weather and warm her up before she died. "Aye, I will. 'Tis not very far," he said, lifting her and wrapping his cloak about her. "There. Now I must find a way to get you up to your horse. If the bank wasn't so steep I could carry you up, but . . . ah, yes, I have it. I'll climb up and reach down from the ledge, to grasp your hands. That way I can pull you up. Do you think you can stand?"

Arianna could barely lift her head, but she knew if she didn't make the effort she would die. "Yes, I can do it."

Colin shook his head. "My lady, you've got more mettle than any man I ever saw. All right. I'll take the babe up with me and . . ."

"No. Please, I . . ."

"My lady, you have nothing to fear. Trust in me. You and the child are safe in my care."

Smiling wanly, Arianna nodded. Using all her strength, she pulled herself to a sitting position, but the world turned black and she sank back to the ground.

"Here, now. Let me do all the work. You've done your part, birthing your son." Reaching under her, he lifted her and set her on the ground. Her arms clung to his neck and she felt another gush of blood rush down her legs. Turning her around to face the cliff, he said, "Are you all right? You've got to stand long enough for me to climb up."

The man's voice came to her from a far distance, though he was standing but inches away. *Stand. I must stand. I can do it. I will do it.*

"That's a good lass. Here I go, then." Colin released his hold and she stood her ground, shakily, a determined look on her pale face. Tucking the child inside his jerkin, he climbed up the face of the cliff. In a moment, he was peering over the edge, looking down at Arianna. "Here now, hold your hands over your head so I can reach them. That's a girl, that's a girl." Clasping her wrists tightly he began to pull her up, his arm muscles straining.

Feeling the strong touch of the man's hands, Arianna felt herself rising and looked up, her eyes focusing on the redheaded man. Her gaze never wavered from his face, ruddy from the strain of her weight, as he pulled her up. Her eyes closed and she felt herself slipping away. When she opened them she found herself locked in strong arms, on Pasha's sleek back. "My baby . . ."

"Safe and snug in my jerkin. Sleep. We'll be home soon."

Arianna felt herself drift off, but forced her eyes open. "I don't even know your name."

"Colin. Colin Colrain."

"Col . . . in." Her eyes fluttered, then closed, and she knew no more.

Arianna stirred for a moment, feeling herself lifted and rocked gently in strong arms as she was carried. She sighed deeply, then drifted off again. Papa would take care of her. He always carried her in his arms when she was too tired to walk. He was always there when she needed him. She felt herself lowered onto a bed and the warmth of a blanket covering her and sighed again. "Papa."

"Little one, it's Colin. Go back to sleep. You're safe now."

"Safe . . ." Drifting off, Arianna remembered blue eyes staring into hers from a tanned leather face, then oblivion closed in once more.

The baby's cry broke through her deep sleep, bringing her back to consciousness. She stirred and opened her eyes. Colin was standing over her, the baby in his arms.

"Your son's hungry as the devil. I've been trying to placate him with a sugar tit, but he's having none of

272

it. He wants the real thing, I'm thinking."

Pleasure washed over Arianna, seeing the rosy pink babe in the man's arms. "He's so beautiful." Her eyes closed, but she forced them open. She must stay awake. Must feed her son.

Colin placed the babe in her arms and she kissed the top of his downy little head, inhaling deeply of his smell. Her son. Her perfect little son. She put him to her breast, and his cries were instantly silenced. Feeling the tug at her nipple, she closed her eyes a moment, reveling in the wonder of it all.

Colin watched, his heart sweetly sad thinking of his wife, and joyous seeing this beautiful lady nurse her child. "How are you feeling?" She gazed up at him dreamily and he had his answer.

"I'm . . . so . . . weak, but I do feel better. How long did I sleep?"

Colin laughed heartily. "Two days."

"Two days? Truly? But the babe, who . . ."

"I've been taking care of him — and you."

A pink blush came to her face as she realized all that must entail. "How can I ever thank you, Colin?"

"So. You remember my name. For a while there, you thought I was your papa."

Arianna smiled sweetly. "Did I? How strange."

Studying her intensely, he said, "If we're to share a cottage, don't you think I should have a name to call you by?"

Looking up at him, her face took on a strange, sad, expression. "I'm . . . Arianna Warwick."

"I thought you might be. Do you know the whole countryside is looking for you?"

Arianna's heart pounded. "You didn't tell anyone where I was, did you?"

273

"No. I didn't, since you seemed so eager not to be found. But I don't understand why. What are you running from? As I understand from the town gossip, your husband loves you dearly. Am I wrong? Does he mistreat you? Beat you?"

"No, of course not. Rob is the kindest, gentlest . . . He's not the reason. It's . . ."

"Yes?"

Arianna gazed down at the sweet babe at her breast, then up to Colin's warm eyes. "You deserve to know the truth, and verily, I'm sick to death of all the lies. I don't want ever to lie again, or assume another's identity. I am the illegitimate daughter of Queen Mary Stuart, and Leicester, the English Queen's lover."

Whatever Colin had been expecting, it wasn't that. "The devil you say!"

"I know. 'Tis truly hard to believe. But believe me, I speak the truth."

Shaking his head, Colin said, "I don't understand. Why the need to run away then? If you're Leicester's child, why do you not seek his help? He's the most powerful man in all of England."

"Aye, but it is only Elizabeth's love for him that makes him so powerful. For some reason, the Queen wants my child to raise as her own — I suppose because it is her lover's grandchild." Arianna saw the incredulous look he gave her, and continued. "Edmund, the Earl of Clinton, found out my true identity and was going to take me to Elizabeth, but not until after he had his way with me. I . . . I stabbed him and ran away. You know the rest."

"So that's how he died?"

"Died?" Arianna felt a sinking feeling in the pit of

her stomach.

"I went to the village of Everly this morning, seeking information about you. There was a large gathering. They were talking about your disappearance, and . . . about the death of Edmund Deveraux. No one seemed to know the details. Seems like the earl wants to keep them secret. All I know for certain is Deveraux was murdered."

Arianna's eyes opened wide with fright. "Murder! No! It's not true. He can't be dead. I stabbed him only once, in the shoulder. It wasn't a serious wound."

"Shhh, now. You'll sour the wee one's milk. I can't imagine you killing someone unless you had a mighty good reason. Calm yourself. I'll not let anyone take you away."

"I don't understand. How could this happen? I never meant to kill him, only to get away. Robert! Oh, no! What must he think?"

"If he's the man you say he is, then I'm sure he'll understand."

"Understand! *You* don't understand. I can never go back to him now. Never! I can't put this burden on him, too. There'll be an inquiry. Edmund was one of the Queen's favorites — she'll be deeply interested in finding out the truth. If she ever found out . . . I can't let that happen. She would take my babe and punish me and anyone else who is close to me. I ran away to keep Rob and my child safe; now I must stay away for the same reason. Without me, no one will ever know how or why he was killed."

Arianna reached out to take his hand. "Will you help me, Colin? For just a little while. Until I can figure out what to do?"

"What man could turn away from you and still call himself a man? You'll be safe here. This cottage is deep in the woods. I seldom have visitors except for my mother and my sister, Felicity. They live on the other side of the clearing and they'll not cause you any harm. Stay as long as you like."

Squeezing his hand, she cried, "I don't know how to thank you. I . . ." Sobs shook Arianna's body as she came to terms with the terrible reality. Her life with Rob was over. She could never see him again. She must find the courage to go on, to live. If not for herself, then for her son.

It was close to dusk on the third day after Arianna had disappeared when Robert heard the last of his men ride in to camp. By the fevered pitch of the horse's hooves on the hard ground he knew, at last, he would have word of her. The deep weariness he had been feeling after days of desperate searching disappeared as John Neal reined in near him.

"What is it? What did you find? What is that in your hand?"

John handed the bloodied piece of petticoat to his lord. "It was found snagged on a twig, below a ledge on the great cliffs."

Rob took the terrible cloth in his hand, staring down at it a long time before speaking. Shaking his head, he cried, "It's not hers. It can't be hers."

Gazing down at Robert, John's heart went out to him. Rob was covered with dust and ground-in mud, his clothing torn and disheveled from his long hours of searching. He had to be close to a collapse. "Rob, look at it again. No peasant woman wore such fine cloth. It belonged to a gentlewoman for certain."

Rob's shoulders slumped. His brain knew what his heart could not accept. In a choked voice he asked, "Take me to the spot where it was found. I would see for myself."

Solemnly the men rode up the path, wending their way to the edge of the cliff. Without speaking, John dismounted and walked to the edge, pointing down to the ledge. Rob never broke his stride as he walked over and peered down. His heart lurched when he saw the blood that stained the grey rock. No one could survive the loss of so much blood.

His body swayed back and then forward, as he cried out the name of his beloved, sending it forth over the cliff to the rocks below. John grabbed him, fearing Robert would throw himself from the cliff. Nodding toward his men, he gestured for them to help him. Two men jumped from their horses and helped move Rob away from the cliff's edge.

John drew a breath of relief, then moved silently over to the mounted men. Speaking in a low voice, he ordered them to climb down to the shore line and search for any sign of Lady Arianna. A half hour later they were back, silently shaking their heads. They had found nothing.

Bracing himself, John walked over to where Rob stood and laid his hand on his shoulder. Rob's body began to shake. "I'm sorry, Robert. The men have searched the shore and there's no sign of her, no sign at all."

"Then there's hope, John. Tell me there's hope."

"I won't lie to you and you can't lie to yourself. She's gone. The sea has taken her."

"You bastard!" Rob lunged for John, propelled by

a force he couldn't overcome, slamming his fist into the knight's face.

Tears formed in John's eyes as he stood frozen, unwilling to strike back at his grief-stricken friend.

Chapter Twenty-two

July 1586

Colin leaned his back against a tree and stared sorrowfully at the moon hanging low over the dark waters of the pond. It seemed to stare back, its human-like countenance displaying a mournful expression of its own. Arianna . . . so beautiful . . . so desirable, and yet as unattainable as that heavenly orb. Three months. Three agonizing months the woman had lived with him, sharing his meals, sleeping in his bed, whilst he slept but an arm's reach away on a pallet on the floor yearning to touch her, to feel her body beneath him. How much torment must he withstand?

In the beginning, whilst she was weak and fragile, lustful thoughts had not strayed into his mind. He had cared for her and the babe like a brother to his female kin, bathing her, feeding her, seeing to her intimate needs. But now, she was the picture of health: roses in her cheeks, sparkle in her eyes, growing more desirable with each passing day. And the way she moved—oh God, the way she moved—like a goddess made for pleasure, made to adore. Even his sister's simple peasant garb could not diminish her exquisite beauty. Nay, it emphasized it all the more.

"Colin."

Hearing her lilting voice, Colin closed his eyes tight. Must she torture him even here? Was there no place he could escape this agony?

"Go back to the cottage, Arianna. Leave me be."

"What is it, Colin? Have I done something to make you angry?"

Colin turned his head away.

"Colin?" She reached out and touched his cheek.

His facial muscles quivered at her touch. Grasping her arm, he cried, "Damn it, woman, leave me alone if you would keep me from your bed."

He released his hold and she shrank back, knowing well what he meant. What woman didn't know when a man was attracted to her? The signs were so obvious, the tension in the air as palpable as the beating of her infant's heart. She knew, and yet she had still followed him out to the water. She couldn't help herself. Each night when he left her alone in the cottage, she felt the longing for Robert all the more. She needed to hear the sound of another's voice, needed to hear Colin's voice. Gruff and deeply masculine, it never failed to lift her spirits, giving her the strength to live another day.

Was that wrong? She was divorced from Robert as surely as if a document had been writ. And she knew, to keep him safe, to keep her child safe, she could never see him again. Was it wrong then to need Colin's companionship? In the weeks since she had come to live with him, she had grown to care for him more and more and she hated the tension between them. It grew stronger each day, causing them to snipe at each other like caged animals. How long could they go on like this?

280

Without another word, she turned and walked back to the cottage, the warm glow in the windows holding no comfort for her. For she would be alone there with her sleeping babe—alone to think about Robert.

And yet she couldn't blame Colin. He was a virile, masculine male with needs and desires. He deserved a woman who could fulfill him, give him the love he had every right to expect.

But what about her needs? Didn't she have the right to be loved, too? Why had she been denied the one man she could ever truly love? Desolate, she entered the cottage and threw herself on the bed, pressing her fist against her lips to keep from waking the babe with her sobs. Oh, Rob, I want you so, need you so. I cannot bear to be without you.

When her tears had dried and the babe was fed and changed and rocked to sleep in his little cradle, Arianna blew out the candle and made ready for bed. It was her habit to change into her nightshift in the dark in case Colin should come back while she was undressing. It was awkward enough sharing the small cottage with him when she was fully clothed. Mayhap that was why he left the cottage each night, so she could see to her toilette in privacy. Poor man, driven from his own home.

Climbing into bed, she heard the rustling of rain through the thatched roof. Her only change of clothing would be soaked—she had left it to dry on the limbs of a tree. Jumping from bed, she opened the door and ran outside. Running to the tree, she snatched the clothes and started back for the house just as the heavens opened up in a fury. Driven by the gusting wind, the rain slammed into her, soaking her to the skin and plastering her nightshift against her as she ran.

She made it to the cottage the same time as Colin did. He opened the door, shouting, "What a fool thing to do! Haven't you had enough of rainstorms by now?"

Pushing the door shut against the driving wind with her back, she yelled accusingly, "Well, why didn't you bring the clothes in? You were out there. You knew it was going to rain."

"Why didn't you think of it before you went to bed?"

"Mayhap I was too sick with worry over you to think about it. Did you think of that?" Arianna's chest heaved, still out of breath from the dash to the cottage, her wet body shivering with cold.

Colin breathed hard, too, but not from running. Arianna's wet nightshift was clinging to her, the nipples of her milk-gorged breasts showing pink and taut against the white cloth. He clenched his teeth and closed his eyes but her image stayed before his eyes. With a low growl, he pulled her up against his chest, the bundle of wet clothes spilling to the ground as he ground his lips on hers.

Arianna gave a little cry, then went still, offering no resistance. Encouraged, Colin kissed her again, his hand moving down the curve of her back to grasp her buttock and push it against his hardness. "Oh, God, Arianna, I have such need."

Burying her head into his shoulder, her tortured voice answered, "I know, I know."

Groaning, he held her away and looked into her eyes, seeing the affirmation he needed so desperately. Quickly, he pulled her wet nightshift over her head and dropped it to the floor. Arianna shivered, and he lifted her in his arms and carried her to the bed. "I'll

282

try to be gentle. I'll try . . . it's been so long, I've wanted you so much, I . . ."

Laying her on the bed, Colin undressed quickly, then joined her on the bed, his hands seeking her in the blackness of the night.

Arianna felt his warm touch and shivered again. She remembered that same touch on her rain-slicked and freezing body while she labored to give birth, and its wonderful lifegiving warmth and her body relaxed. He was her savior. He deserved to have whatever she could give him.

She lay quietly as Colin's hands moved slowly over her, seeking, exploring, caressing her breasts and belly and thighs. It would be all right. He would be gentle.

Colin's need drove him. He knew he should take his time, woo her gently, but he could not wait. The touch of her warm body was more than he could bear. It had been so long.

His hand moved between her legs and she instantly stiffened. "Arianna, Sweet." His finger moved slowly into her moist opening, rubbing her gently, and she began to move under him.

Arianna felt her body come alive. Her mouth sought his, her tongue his own, swirling around it, tasting it, sucking on it, as if it were a lifeline and she a drowning victim.

Colin couldn't believe it was happening at last. What he had dreamed of, agonized over each day since she arrived. The soft, silken feel of her against him drove him nearly out of his mind with desire. She would be his—unbelievably, she would be his. Moaning softly, he raised himself to enter her and heard her gasp, "Oh, yes, Rob, yes."

No other words could have stopped him. Groaning, he rolled away from her and stumbled out of bed.

Arianna suddenly realized what she had said. "Colin, I'm sorry. I'm so sorry."

A rush of air washed over her as she lay in the dark. Colin opened the door, slamming it behind him.

Sick at heart, Arianna left the bed and followed him outside. The rain was falling gently now, the night still black as pitch. "Colin, where are you? Colin."

"Get back inside."

Whirling, she faced him. "Oh, Colin, I'm truly sorry. I . . ."

His voice was brusque and cold. "It doesn't matter. At first light, I'm leaving."

"Leaving?" His words rang in her head, her heart, stabbing her with pain. "For how long?"

"I don't know. But don't worry, I'll see that you're cared for. I'll . . ."

A high-pitched keening filled the air as Arianna swayed back and forth, her naked body luminous and shiny with rain.

"Arianna!" Only once before had Colin ever heard a sound as eerie as that. The night his father died, his mother had cried that same way. "Arianna, what is it?"

Her choked, distorted voice came back to him. "I've lost everyone in the world who is dear to me, everyone I ever loved. And now you would leave me, too?"

Colin's eyes widened as hope grew in his heart. "Do you count me in the same company as those you love?"

"I . . . do."

"Then will you live with me as my wife?"

Her whispered reply, borne to him on the wind, sent his spirit soaring. "I will."

Gathering her into his arms, he held her tight against him. The rain stopped as suddenly as it had begun and the moon peeked out from behind a dark cloud, peering down at them, the only witness to their vows.

Lifting her in his arms, Colin carried her back to the cottage and laid her on the bed. Arianna held tight to him, as if in fear he would still leave. He swallowed hard, deeply moved. She did love him. She would be his wife, and in time, Robert's memory would dim and fade and she would truly belong to him.

At Everly Castle, Rob woke suddenly, his heart pierced with a sharp pain, his manhood throbbing. "Arianna," he called softly.

Climbing out of bed, he walked to the window and looked out at the moon. It stared down at him in lonely silence, increasing his sorrow. It had been three months since she died on the cliff. Three months, but it might as well have happened tonight. What had awakened him so suddenly? Why did he feel her presence so strongly just now, his need for her so great it made him ill?

Restless, he began to pace the room, but only grew more agitated. He dressed and made his way up to the ramparts. Walking to the parapet, he peered out in misery at the dark, lonely landscape.

Chapter Twenty-three

December 1586

The sound of Arianna's laughter filled Colin's heart with joy. He would never tire of hearing it. After all the sorrow she had experienced, it was evidence that she was finally healing. He watched her now as she sat on the floor with his mother and sister, playing with Robin. The babe was eight months old.

Portia Colrain, his mother, and Felicity, his sister, visited often now. They lived on the other side of the pond, no more than a ten-minute walk away. Colin had been taking care of them since his father died. The two women had grown quite fond of Arianna and Robin, staying with them whenever he was away on hunting trips. They loved the babe as much as if he were their own flesh and blood. Colin's eyes swept over the women and child in contentment. He had the family he had always wanted.

Still laughing, Arianna rose and started for the door. "I'm going to the well for water. Robin needs a bath."

Colin grabbed her hand. "Stay, I'll get it."

"No, I'll do it. You stir the fire. It'll have to be warmer in here before our young sir can be washed.

"Brrr, I feel a sudden chill. The fire must be dying." Wrapping a wool shawl around her shoulders, she took a wooden bucket from a hook on the wall and left.

Colin hadn't noticed a chill. Glancing at the fire he saw it was burning brightly. His brow furrowed. It was snug and warm in the small cottage. Mayhap she was not feeling well.

Arianna walked to the well, smiling at Robin's antics. That child was going to grow up to be a jester, or mayhap a troubadour. Attaching the bucket to the line, she began to lower it when the hair on the back of her neck stood on end. What was it? The sound of dry leaves crunching came to her then, and voices, drawing hear. She drew in her breath. Clearly they were on their way to the cottage. There could be no other reason to be traveling so deep into the forest.

Quickly, she ran around to the back of the cabin before she was spotted. She couldn't go back inside for fear it was someone who would recognize her and she couldn't take time to warn Colin. She could only pray that the visit would be short. It was cold and threatening to snow at any moment.

She heard the riders rein in beside the cottage and dismount, heard Thor barking at them in earnest, and then her heart stopped when she heard one of the travelers speak.

Rob!

No! It couldn't be!

Stunned, her hand went to her breast, covering her heart as if to protect it from the pain of hearing his beloved voice again.

The door opened, and Colin called out loudly so Arianna might hear, "Lord Warwick! What a surprise."

So it was true. Her imagination wasn't playing tricks on her. Rob was here. Arianna flattened herself against the wall, as if hoping to disappear into it, and closed her eyes tight. *Oh, Rob, Rob. Just when I was beginning to feel alive again.* If there was a God looking down at her, he must be a hateful one indeed, to tease and torture her thusly.

Inside the cottage, Colin offered Robert and the other men a cup of mead.

"No, thank you, Colin. We're plenty warm. We've been nipping from our flagons all along the ride. But let me introduce you. This is Lord William Ludlow from Norbridge, my good friend, and my most trusted knight, Sir John Neal. You've probably met him a time or two."

"Yes, indeed I have, indeed I have. What brings you my way, Lord Warwick? It's powerful cold outdoors. I'd think you'd be by a cozy fire now, warming your toes."

Rob sensed Colin was nervous, anxious for him and his friends to leave. But why? *Is he ashamed of his humble abode?* Glancing around, Rob noticed the women on the floor with a chubby babe. "I didn't know you were married, Colin."

Kneeling down, Rob patted the child's silken blonde hair. "Beautiful little boy you have. Hello there, young fellow. It looked like you've been having a good time of it."

Colin froze, watching Rob play with his son. *Would he know?*

Rob stood back up. "Aren't you going to introduce me to your wife? I'd like to meet the woman who tamed my head huntsman."

"My wife?" Blanching, Colin looked around helplessly, then reached down to grasp his sister's hand.

288

He pulled her to her feet. "Here she be. Felicity, meet Lord Warwick, our gracious Earl of Everly. It is he who has kept us from starving these past two years."

Felicity quickly composed herself, curtsying nicely to Arianna's husband. "Pleased to meet you, sir." Then her attention turned back to Lord Ludlow. Never had she met so handsome a man. Just looking at him sent shivers up her spine.

Will caught her glance and smiled. Damn, all the good ones were taken. First Arianna, and now this pretty wench. Was it his fortune in life to fall for women who were unattainable? His eyes swept over Felicity, enjoying what he saw. Her peasant clothes could not hide the curves of the body, and her hair — never had he seen such a mass of red curls.

Tearing his eyes from her, he noticed movement outside the window. Someone was looking in. The devil take it, he thought, what's that? Turning to Colin, he said, "If you'll pardon me for a moment, I fear I've drunk too much mead this day and am in need to let loose some of it."

"Of course," Colin answered. What else could he say? Besides, Arianna knew enough to stay out of sight. Turning his attention back to Lord Warwick, he noticed him staring at Robin with a strange expression.

"May I hold him for a minute? My child would have been just that age."

Colin's answer came out in a choked voice. "I'm sorry, I remember now . . . you lost your pregnant wife. Yes, please, hold him."

Portia rose and handed the babe to Rob, her eyes large and round with fear.

Rob noticed the older woman's fright. "Don't

worry, I shan't drop him. What's his name?"

Colin hesitated, then said, "Robert, but we call him Robin after our Queen's favorite, Robert Dudley, the Earl of Leicester."

"Is that so? Well, young Robin, for a minute I thought your father had named you after me, but I see you are named after a far greater lord."

Robin reached out and grabbed Rob's nose. Laughing, Rob pried loose the little fingers, then kissed them. Suddenly, an incredible sorrow fell over him, thinking of his own dead child. It might have been a beautiful boy such as this, chubby and healthy. His shoulders began to shake.

Colin knew Rob was close to breaking down. "Felicity, take your child before he dampens our benefactor."

Arianna watched through the window as Rob handed his son back to Felicity. It broke her heart to see them together. Father and son, the way it should have been. So engrossed was she that she failed to hear Will until he rounded the corner.

Will stopped dead at the sight of her, his face registering an array of emotions. Arianna was alive! He opened his mouth to speak but she silenced him with her hand.

"Please, don't call my name. Rob mustn't know."

Tears welled in his eyes as he spoke, his voice hushed in awe. "My God, Arianna, how could you do that to us? How in God's name could you let us think you were dead?"

"I had to, Will, I had to. Believe me. It was I who killed Edmund. When I found that out, I knew I could never go back to Rob. Don't you understand?"

Something nagged at the back of Will's mind, but he was too overwrought to think of it. "No, I don't understand. Do you have any idea the hell Rob has been living through thinking you dead? How could you do that to him? As much as you loved him, how could you?"

"Because I love him. Because I won't let him be imprisoned. And because of my son. I'll never let Elizabeth have him. Did you know she told Edmund that when she found me she would take away any children I had? That can never happen now. Robin is safe."

"Your son? That babe in the cottage is yours? My God! Rob's son—alive. If he only knew." Remembering suddenly the huntsman who claimed Robin as his own, he asked accusingly, "And what of Colin, what is he to you?"

"Don't look at me like that, Will. Colin is a good man. He's taken care of me. He found me on the cliff, saved my life and Robin's."

Shaking his head in wonder, he said, "What a tangled web you and I have woven. And Felicity? If she's not the babe's mother, who is she?"

"Colin's sister."

"His sister?" Will's face brightened, then grew dark as everything Arianna said registered. " 'Twas all for naught then, wasn't it? Everything we did to make you a grand lady. Here you are, a peasant once more."

"Yes. Here I am and here I'll stay. Promise me you won't tell Rob. Promise me."

"You ask too much. Robert is my friend."

"A greater friend than I?"

"That's not fair. You know how much I love you."

"If that be true, then keep my secret. If not for me, then for Robert. Help me keep him safe from Elizabeth. If I returned and admitted to killing Ed-

291

mund, she'd have me imprisoned. You know Rob would never let her take me. He'd die trying to protect me. You know that's true."

" 'Tis true. 'Tis true." Thinking about it for a moment, he said, "All right. I won't tell him. Not now, anyway. But dear God, when is all this deceit going to end? I started it all and by God, I'll find a way to end it. You and Rob belong to each other and I vow you will be together again."

Arianna wrapped her arms around Will's neck and held him tight. "My dearest Will, you always were a hopeless romantic."

Will felt a lump come to his throat as he held Arianna close. "I'll be back soon to visit. Now that I've found you, I'll not lose you again."

"I'd like that, Will. And . . . and would you do something for me? Would you let Leicester and Peter and Sybille know I'm alive? There's no reason they can't be told, now that you know. 'Tis a blessing, your coming here. I couldn't bear it any longer, not seeing any of my loved ones, having them think me dead. Would you do that for me?"

"Aye, I will. I'll find some excuse for leaving Everly for awhile. Judith and I have been staying there with Rob these past months, to help him over his . . . grief."

"Oh, Will, I've been afraid to ask how he is. Tell me he's happy. Tell me he's going on with his life."

"I'll not lie to you. He's surviving, that's all. Surviving."

"Oh, Will, it breaks my heart to hear that. If it were in my power, I'd run to him this minute. If only Edmund hadn't discovered the truth. But it seems I'm destined to live as unhappily as my mother. Have you heard word of her? Do you know how she fares?"

292

"Only that she was tried for conspiracy to kill Elizabeth. The whole country is waiting to hear the verdict."

"So, it's finally come to that. God in heaven, how can anyone believe she plotted to have the Queen killed? She's helpless to do anything, locked behind prison walls. Dear God, forgive me, but I would gladly plunge a dagger in Elizabeth's heart myself to save my mother."

Will gazed solemnly into Arianna's eyes. "Don't even think it, Arianna. You're distraught, I know, and with good reason, but you mustn't think of avenging your mother by harming the Queen. You have a child to think of now."

"I know, Will, I know. I'd never do anything to harm Robin. I didn't mean it, truly I didn't. But, oh, it's hard to be so helpless. Do you think . . . Is it possible that you can get word to my mother? Let her know I'm alive?"

"Do not worry. Peter told me no one has broken the news of your death to her. They were afraid if she heard, she'd lose all will to live."

Arianna choked back her tears. "I'm glad of that. She has enough to bear."

"Take cheer. When I've seen Leicester and Peter and Sybille I'll return and give you any messages from them. And Arianna, I am relieved to hear Felicity is not Colin's wife. She's a comely lass." Brushing her hair from her face, he smiled softly. "Now, I'd better get back in there before Rob starts searching for me." Kissing her forehead, he turned and left.

Arianna peeked through the window again, seeing Will enter the cottage. Her eyes sought Rob, finding him leading Colin toward the door.

"I almost forgot the reason for my visit. I have a

Christmas present for you, Colin. It's right outside the door."

"What? My lord, I certainly wasn't expecting a present. I have none for you."

"No matter. Come see." Opening the door, he led Colin outside. "It came to my ears that the horse you ride to deliver game to my castle is a borrowed one, that you must pay rent on it each time from your earnings. Well, no longer. The dappled mare is yours."

"My lord! I cannot accept such a gift."

"But you must. 'Tis no hardship for me, and you'll be using it in service to me, will you not? Accept it, or take the chance of offending me."

Colin walked up to the animal and patted its grey neck. "Then I shall accept it. Thank you, Lord Warwick."

"The least I can do. My God, Colin, any of us could be in your shoes right now. Elizabeth could take everything from me if she's a mind. And for very little provocation. The woman is as tyrannical as any man, but take heart, Colin, for I've heard she can be just as generous. Mayhap, someday you can gain back your title and lands. She is just as capable of giving as she is of taking."

"I don't live my life in hope anymore. I've learned to take things one day at a time, to live each day as if it were my last. And I'm happier for it."

Rob grasped Colin's shoulder. "And you have a son. I envy you that."

Colin lowered his eyes, overwhelmed by guilt. "Yes. I am a lucky man."

After Rob and his companions left, Colin cornered the cottage looking for Arianna. He knew she must be hurting, seeing her husband again. Without a

294

word he took her in his arms and she began to sob as she never had in all the eight months he had known her. He let her cry, encouraged her to cry, knowing how much she needed to. And when she was finished, he lifted her in his arms and carried her into the cottage, laying her gently on the bed.

Felicity and Portia looked on, sympathy on their faces. Arianna had seemed so happy, but it was evident that she still loved her handsome young husband very much.

"Mother, some hot mead for Arianna." Taking a blanket, he covered her then sat on the floor by her head, speaking words of comfort. Robin, thinking it a game, crawled over and climbed into his lap, babbling in his sweet baby talk.

Arianna gazed down at them and smiled. Relieved, Colin smiled back until he saw the hauntingly sad look that came into her eyes. His heart sank. Though he possessed her body, he knew he would never possess her heart.

Chapter Twenty-four

Fotheringhay, December 1586

From castle to church, tower to steeple, the bells pealed dolefully in the winter air. Mary Stuart, imprisoned Queen of Scotland and the Isles, had been tried and found guilty of conspiring to have the sovereign Queen Elizabeth killed. The sentence had been passed and read: Death to the Scottish Queen.

For a day and a half the bells ceased not, the sound traveling throughout the countryside to the furthest reaches of the kingdom. In Fotheringhay Castle, Mary listened to the mournful tolling, knowing she was hearing her own death knell. She tried to block out the deep resonant dongs echoing in her heart, but the sound was so strong it seemed to substitute even for the very beating of her heart.

Overwrought, she paced her chamber, her voice ringing out in anger. "Can you imagine the effrontery of that high and mighty Sir Amyas Paulet? First he has my Canopy of State torn down and my billiard table removed, and then he dares to sit in my presence. And with a hat upon his head to show his disregard."

Mary Seton looked upon her mistress with great compassion. "But you showed him well what a great Queen you are, putting a crucifix where the canopy had hung. You showed him and his heartless Queen that you are ruled by a much higher authority. Never was I so proud of you as at that moment."

Mary smiled, cheered by her handmaiden's words, and walked to the window. Wiping away the fingers of frost that marred her view, she looked up at the sky. "He wasn't expecting that, was he? Nor I the speech he gave me of how dangerous I am. He told me that as long as I lived, the Protestant religion was in danger of being destroyed."

Fingering the cross that hung from her neck, Mary's voice became barely more than a whisper. "At that moment, I realized fully my true destiny. But then, deep down I always knew it would be so. You remember the device I stitched into my embroideries? *En cette mort sera mon commencement.* If Elizabeth signs a death warrant I shall not die a Queen alone, but a martyr for the Catholic Church, and *in that death will be my beginning.* Indeed, I feel no pity for Elizabeth at this moment, for 'twill be upon her head that I die, upon her writ that I become exalted as a true and faithful daughter of the Catholic faith. 'Tis a heavy burden she carries."

Mary's words enthralled the listening women. Their noble queen was ready to die, her bravery an inspiration to all. In silent awe, they sat looking from one to the other while Mary continued to stare out the window. Her small Skye terrier, too long ignored, broke the silence with his sharp, staccato yaps, begging to be lifted into Mary's arms. Obliging, she scooped him up, nuzzling her head in the soft fur. "Ma petite babe, you feel it too, the pall of death. If only the accursed bells would stop. Must I be driven crazy by their incessant toll?"

As if by magic the tolling stopped, and Mary's attendants joined her in delighted laughter.

"Ah, you see, I still have some authority in this horrid land."

Later, alone with her most trusted servants, Mary sat writing letters, her quill moving quickly over the parchment pages.

"Your Grace, you've been writing for hours. I beg you stop for awhile."

"Ah, Marie, God alone knows whether I'll have another chance. I must take good advantage of the time I have left."

"Don't speak like that, I beg you," Jane Kennedy said, unnerved by the trial and Paulet's visit—and the terrible tolling of the bells. "Elizabeth dare not have you killed. She'll pardon you for certain. Everyone says so."

"So they do, and so they believe. But still, I must be prepared. One last letter, then I will stop. It is the most important letter of all—to my daughter, Arianna."

A terrible stillness fell upon the room. Noticing it, Mary looked up, her gaze taking in the stricken faces of her attendants. Her heart began to pound. "What is it? Why do you two look as if you've been to my funeral already? Tell me."

Mary Seton had been dreading this. She had withheld the news from the Queen all these months in the hope she would never have to tell her. "I cannot bear to tell you, Your Grace. I cannot bear to be the one." Bursting into tears, she hid her head in her hands.

Mary steeled herself. She had endured much sorrow in her hard life and had learned to accept it all.

"Then Jane, you must be the one to tell me. What is it? Did my daughter lose the baby she was carrying? Is that it? It was due in April and I have had no word in all this time. I reasoned with myself, convinced myself that I haven't heard because it was not safe for anyone to communicate with me. Is that it? My grandchild did not survive the birth?"

Jane Kennedy made the sign of the cross before she spoke. "It is Arianna, Your Grace."

Mary sank to the window seat, clutching its rough edges on either side, her body stiffening as she spoke. "Tell me, now, while I still have the strength."

"She is dead."

"No! No, I would have known. I would have felt it. Why do you tell me this lie? She cannot die. I could not bear to have my child die before me. I could not bear it."

Mary Seton moved quickly to comfort Mary. "Then we will not believe she's dead. It could be some horrible mistake. Her body was never found. Nothing but a bloodied piece of cloth attests to her death. We can take comfort in that, my Queen."

"No body? Then she is not dead! She did not die! I did not spend all these years as Elizabeth's prisoner rather than reveal where my daughter is only to have her die before me. We must take heart. We must believe. Until there is absolute proof we must believe she lives. You will tell me what you know and then we will speak of it no more. I will write my letter to her, just as I planned, and she *will* read it."

Long after everyone slept, Mary was still awake, her mind going over the story she had been told of Arianna's supposed death on the cliff. What connection was there to Edmund's death the same night? Had he discovered the truth? Had someone killed him so that he could not reveal Arianna's identity to Elizabeth?

Why had everything in her life turned bitter? She could count on the fingers of one hand the truly happy years she had had. She had been conspired against and even betrayed by her brother and her son. Both were under Elizabeth's influence, and neither had tried very hard to free her. Leicester, too, for he had been on the very commission that tried her. But how could she blame him? Alone, he could never have prevented the trial, and to speak up in her defense once it had begun could have cost him his life, or at least his freedom. Elizabeth would not have looked kindly on him for defending her. As for that, how could she condemn her son? She had not seen him since he was an infant. He had never known his mother's love. Blood alone was not enough, it seemed.

Blood. Elizabeth and she shared a grandfather and therefore the same blood, but it had not prevented Elizabeth from betraying her. No—blood was not enough. Then remembering the ivory rose ring with the sliver of ruby she had given to her daughter, she changed her thought. Sometimes blood is all. All her hopes and dreams lay in her daughter. Through her, she could live forever. Through the child born to her, she would have immortality. Arianna couldn't be dead. God could not be that cruel.

The bare, ice-laden limbs groaned stiffly as the gusting wind moved through the trees, circling the cottage in the clearing then moving deeper into the forest. Swirling around Pasha's enclosure, the wind's force knocked the wooden gate against the

300

fence post repeatedly, frightening the animals. The mare whinnied nervously and Pasha answered, blowing through his nostrils and tossing his magnificent head.

Speaking softly, Arianna calmed the animals and they pranced over to the fence, snorting a greeting. Arianna caressed the mare's forehead, then gave her a carrot. Pasha nudged his head under Arianna's hand and edged the mare away with his body.

"Hey, boy, that's no way to treat a lady," Colin said, moving up beside Arianna. Reaching out, he handed the stallion a carrot.

"I'm glad you've kept Pasha all these months, Colin. I thought at first you were mad to do so, for fear someone would find this hideaway and recognize him."

"If they did, what would it matter? I would just say that I found him wandering and secured him 'til I could find the owner."

"I suppose you're right. And I can't help thinking about the profit we'll make someday when the mare foals."

"Oh? Profit, is it? If I know you, you'll want to keep the foal."

Arianna laughed. "You're right. I would. At least the first one, for Robin."

A gust of wind hit Arianna, bringing with it the faint, lonely, faraway clang of a bell. "They're still at it." She shivered and drew the hood of her cloak up over her hair.

"What did you say?" Colin asked, stroking Pasha's neck.

"The bells. This is the second day they've tolled. What does it mean?"

Colin had a good idea what they meant, but he

wasn't about to tell Arianna. She had enough grief in her life. "Who knows? Probably the birth of some duke's son."

"I don't think so. Not for this long. Something to do with Queen Elizabeth, I warrant. Mayhap she's dead."

Colin laughed nervously. "If wishes could kill, indeed she would be dead, wouldn't she?"

Arianna shivered again.

"Are you cold? Shall we head back? I think we've given Will and Felicity time enough to be alone. I don't want you getting sick from being out in the cold too long."

"In a minute. Give them a little more time."

Colin laughed. "You've decided Will and Felicity belong together."

"Yes, I have. Will needs a good wife and Felicity needs someone who can . . ."

Pain clouded Colin's eyes for a moment. "Go ahead, say it. Someone who can give her a good life."

Arianna reached up to touch his face. "Colin, don't be angry with me. I was talking about Felicity, not myself."

Colin took her hand, kissing the palm. "I know. I'm sorry. It just pains me that I cannot give you the kind of life you had before. By heaven's thunder, you're the daughter of a Queen. You shouldn't be living in a hovel, working your fingers to the bone. You belong in a palace, with servants at your beck and call."

"I don't work that hard, and what I do I do for you and Robin. As for my former life, have you forgotten I was raised as a peasant? I'm used to this. But it's different with Felicity. She was raised as a gentlewoman. It would be so wonderful if she could marry Will and live like that again."

Colin studied her face, seeing what he always saw — a serene sadness in her eyes. Would she ever lose that look, would she ever be happy again?

Chapter Twenty-five

February 6, 1587

Will carried an armload of logs to the rustic fire-place and piled them on the crackling fire. "There, that'll keep us warm."

Felicity sat with Robin in her lap, bouncing him on her knee whilst he laughed and hiccuped at the same time. "Robin says thank you, don't you, sweet?" She kissed him on his rosy cheek.

Will's face took on a melancholy look. "I wish Rob could know his son. It's so unfair."

"Life is unfair, Will. I can attest to that, person-ally. I hope you're not having second thoughts about telling Rob that Arianna lives, for if you . . ."

"Never fear. I shan't tell him. But I hate keeping this secret. It seems it's my lot in life to keep se-crets from everyone."

"Oh? Does that mean you're keeping secrets from me, Lord William?" Felicity said teasingly.

Will sat beside her. "Never you. I promise that." His arm snaked around her back as he kissed her forehead at the same time. The door to the cottage opened, admitting the frigid wind along with Colin and Arianna.

Laughing, Arianna unwrapped her cloak and hung it on a hook while Colin carried the water bucket over to the table. "Will, every day for the past several weeks you've spent time alone with my sister, and I'm thinking it's about time I asked what your intentions are toward her."

Felicity blushed deeply and moved to the fireplace, where she stirred the logs, waiting for Will's answer.

Moving to Felicity's side, Will turned to face Colin and Arianna. "I've asked Felicity to be my wife and she has accepted. So, Colin, if you have any objections, raise them now."

Colin tried to make his face stern, but it didn't last. In a moment he was laughing out loud. "Object? I'm delighted to be rid of her. You have no idea how much the little baggage eats. 'Twill take nothing less than a duke's son to afford her."

Felicity threw her arms around her brother's neck. "Oh, Colin, thank you, thank you."

Holding her at arm's length, Colin stared into her eyes. "Are you sure of this, Felicity? The time you've known this man can be counted in weeks. Are you certain this is what you want?"

"I knew the minute I saw him that he was the man for me. I don't know how to explain it, but I knew."

"Then I'm happy for you, both of you. God knows life is damnably uncertain. We must take happiness when we can." His eyes moved to Arianna.

Arianna lowered her eyes a moment; then, not wanting to spoil the moment for Will and Felicity, she answered. "I agree. Marry right away. You were

305

meant to be together."

"Aye, we were," Felicity said, squeezing Will's hand. "Can we go tell Mother now? Oh Will, she'll be so happy for us. And think of it, she can live in a grand castle again, and Arianna and Colin can come visit whenever they like, and . . ."

Arianna nuzzled her head into Robin's neck to hide the tears.

After Will and Felicity left, the cottage became very quiet. Arianna fed Robin and laid him down for a nap, then sat by the fire, mending Colin's shirt. After a long time, Colin said, "You're thinking of him now, aren't you?"

Very quietly, she answered, "I'm sorry."

Without another word, Colin wrapped his cloak around his shoulders, took the axe from beside the door, and went outside. Striding to the wood pile, he swung the axe, splitting a log. The loud thwacking sound echoed through the woods, growing ever louder, ever faster, as Colin tried to tire himself, tried to keep from thinking about the hopelessness he faced. When the logs had been added to the stack of firewood, he knew what must be done.

Early the next morning, he left the cottage without waking Arianna and made his way through the woods to the horse's enclosure. He saddled the mare, then rode in the direction of Everly Castle. His jaw was tight, his blue eyes darkened to a deep, steely grey. Save the day his Lily died, this was the worst day of his life.

He couldn't go on seeing Arianna so unhappy — he loved her too much. She belonged with Lord Warwick, she and the babe. He would go to Everly Castle and see for himself whether Arianna had a

306

chance to be happy again. If Robert still loved her, if there was a way to protect her identity from Elizabeth, then he would tell the Lord that his wife still lived.

God help me, I hope I'm doing the right thing.

Conjuring Arianna's sad face, he knew it was. But, oh, it was not an easy thing to do. What would his life be without her? And Robin—the sweet babe had brought joy to his bleak life. But he couldn't think of that. He must find the strength to do what he must.

"Yoooo, stranger!"

Pulled from his reverie, Colin watched as a young man hardly more than a boy rode up, reining in beside him.

"I'm glad to see someone on this deserted road. On my way to Fortheringhay, and for the life of me, don't know which fork to take."

Colin looked around, orienting himself. Three roads diverged in three different directions.

"You see, they are not marked. Do you know which one goes to Fortheringhay?"

Colin looked over the anxious rider. Surely being lost had not caused his highly excited state. "Fotheringhay? That's where the Queen of Scotland is being held, isn't it?"

"Not for much longer. Elizabeth has finally signed the death warrant. I'm on my way there now to witness the execution. Soon the country will be free of her evil smell."

Colin's heart lurched. "You don't say. When is this execution to transpire?"

"On the morrow. In the great hall at Fotheringhay. But if you're thinking about witnessing it, forget it. Only knights and gentlemen will be allowed in, and they only with a written pass."

Colin's mind raced. What should he do? Go on to Everly Castle, or turn back and tell Arianna about her mother? He thought about his own mother. If she were imprisoned, about to be executed, he would want one last chance to see her. Robert would have to wait. Arianna deserved that chance.

Nudging his horse closer to the young gentleman, he said, "Let me see. If I remember right, the road . . ." Swift as an arrow, he reached out to grab the bridle of the stranger's horse, unsheathing the sword at his side at the same time. He pointed it at the stranger's neck.

"What the . . . what are you doing?"

"Seeing that justice is done. Obey me, and you won't be hurt. Understand?"

"Yes, yes, I understand. Take my money, my horse if you wish, but don't hurt me. My mother is a widow. I am her only child, I . . ."

"Calm down. We're going for a little ride. Over there." Colin pointed to a clump of woods on the other side of a fallow field.

"You said you wouldn't hurt me," the boy cried.

"And I won't. I'm just going to take your fine clothes and your pass. Your horse, too, so you cannot follow me to Fortheringhay."

When the lad was stripped of his clothes and the pass to Mary's execution safely transferred to his saddle bag, Colin tied the boy to a tree. "There, you'll be safe here for awhile. I've tied the rope loosely so you'll be able to work your way free. Keep your wits about you and you'll be all right.

It'll make a man out of you." Doffing his cap, Colin rode off, leading the boy's horse by the reins.

It was out of character for Colin to take advantage of someone smaller and weaker than himself, but it was a desperate situation. Arianna would see her mother one last time, and that was worth any risk.

The countryside passed by him in a blur. Soon, too soon, he was in the clearing by the cottage. With a heavy heart, he dismounted and tied the horses to a tree. Clenching his teeth, he prepared himself to tell her. The door to the cottage opened and Arianna appeared, an anxious look on her face.

"Where have you been? Why did you ride off without telling me where you were going? I was so worried. I thought . . ." She stopped, seeing the grim look on his face.

"Arianna . . ." he began.

"What is it, Colin? You're scaring me."

"Elizabeth has signed the death warrant."

Arianna slumped against the doorjamb.

With long strides, Colin made his way to her, pulling her into his arms. "I know. 'Tis hard to bear. But you must be strong. You knew it could happen."

Arianna's voice was low and emotionless. "How long does she have?"

"Until the morrow."

"Then I must hurry." Releasing herself from his hold, she went into the cottage.

Colin followed her in, perplexed at her calmness. No tears. No anger. Just a resoluteness he had never seen before. She had always been so emotional, so quick to cry over the smallest things, but

309

now . . . this new Arianna frightened him.

He told her of his encounter with the poor young man while she dressed the babe, packing clean diaper cloths in a sack. Then, taking the pilfered clothing, she dressed in them as if it were an everyday occurrence.

"Arianna, are you all right? I'm worried. You're too cool, too calm, aren't you going to cry?"

"After. After it is all over, I'll cry, but not now. I can't lose control now. I must see my mother, and for that I will need a cool head."

Colin shook his head in amazement. "You're truly your mother's daughter. Who else could be as strong?"

"I want to thank you, Colin. If I were not in your debt before, I am truly so now."

"Thank me for what?"

"For telling me about my mother's execution. For making it possible for me to go. I don't know of anyone else who would have done the same in your shoes. Rob or Will or Peter would have protected me, kept me from knowing until it was too late. Leicester, my father, too. You gave me the chance to decide for myself what I must do, and you can't imagine how important that is to me. I'll never forget it."

"Here now, enough of this. There'll be plenty of time for thanks later; right now, we've got to get you to Fortheringhay. My cousin has an inn there. He'll put us up. You'll see your mother, never fear. I wish to God it could be under better circumstances."

Smiling sadly, she touched his cheek with her hand. "You've never let me down. Always been there for me. My stalwart savior."

Flushing with pride, Colin took her hand from his cheek and kissed it fervently.

They arrived in Fortheringhay well after dark. The bitter weather had long before worked its way through the layers of clothing to seep into Arianna's bones. Aching with cold and the long hours in the saddle, she was close to collapse. Surprisingly, though, little Robin seemed not to mind the cold at all and had spent much of the trip asleep, the rhythmic movement of the horse's gait lulling him into contentment.

Ahead of them stood Fortheringhay Castle on a motte of land, the River Nene winding its way around it. There was something unsettling about the sight, but she couldn't discern just what it was. Torchlight could be seen in a few of the windows, and she wondered which one was her mother's. Concentrating hard, her brain formed a message, sending it forth through the cold hard stones of the castle's walls.

Mother. I'm here.

The babe woke as if he, too, had received the message and made sucking noises with his mouth. Arianna pulled herself from her trance and soothed him. "In a few minutes we'll be by a cozy fire and you shall have your supper," she cooed. Her eyes were drawn back to the castle, unwilling to leave the spot where her mother dwelled, and she suddenly realized what had been bothering her about the castle. "Colin. It's not fortified. It's not fortified! I don't understand. It would be easy for the Scots to rescue my mother."

"Aye, 'tis true. I've wondered about that myself. Evidently, Queen Elizabeth has no fear that a rescue will be attempted."

"But why? Why wouldn't my half-brother, James, send a mighty army here to rescue his mother?"

"I fear the answer is all too plain. James wants to be King. He does not want to share the kingdom with his mother."

"My God, can it be true? Can a son be so heartless? If only I had Rob's knights, I'd take this castle and free my mother."

"And then what? Where would you go? Where would you live? You couldn't return to Everly after that. The Queen would send her army and then not only would your mother die, but you and Rob and Robin and . . ."

"Enough. Say no more. I know how hopeless that would be. But by Jesus' blood, I will avenge my mother. Elizabeth will pay. I don't know how or when, but someday she'll pay."

Colin heard her words and shivered. "Shhh, let's hear no more of that. There's the inn, ahead. No more talk of revenge, you hear? Elizabeth's spies are everywhere."

Arianna's gaze took in the worn wooden sign that proclaimed THE DANDY LION. A corner of her mouth lifted sardonically. The Dandy Lion did not live up to its name. It wasn't that it was terribly ramshackle, but there was nothing about the inn to distinguish it from the other bleak buildings that pressed against it.

Dismounting, Arianna reluctantly handed Pasha's reins to a black boy of about ten. Pasha was indeed out of place on this dismal street, and she feared someone would steal him. Colin saw her dismay and reassured her. "Jim, here, works for my cousin. He's been with him since he was born. Pasha is safe in his care."

Colin started to take her arm, then realized how funny that would look. He must remember to treat Arianna as if she were a boy, for that was what she looked like, a boy of no more than fourteen or fifteen. Taking the lead, he opened the door.

An explosion of sound greeted them, and a swirl of hazy smoke. Colin spied his cousin standing by the bar and pushed his way through the crowd.

Alan saw him and broke out into a grin. "Colin! What are you doing here? 'Tis right good to see you."

"Alan, what is this? A party?"

"You might say that. The crowd is here to celebrate the beheading tomorrow. A little prematurely, to be sure, but 'tis the most exciting thing to happen here in many a year."

"Does that mean you have no room for me and my friend?"

"Of course I do. Most everyone is local. They'll be going back to their own homes before long."

"That's a relief. My young friend over there with the babe is ready to keel over from fatigue."

Alan looked in the direction of Colin's friend. "I'll have a room ready in a few minutes. I've got to send my servant up to change the sheets."

"Fine, fine."

"Colin Colrain. What are you doing here?"

Colin's heart lurched. Turning, he stared into Rob's drunken eyes, watching as the young lord tried to focus.

"Business matters. And you, Lord Warwick? I didn't expect to see you so far from home. Did you come to see the execution?"

"Me? No. I had no idea Mary was goin' ta be exe . . . cuded. I came on other matters. Leaving in the morn, mayhap you can a . . . accompany me back home. Make the leagues go by faster, ha?"

Colin took Robert by the arm and led him around the corner to a table. Glancing over his shoulder, he saw Arianna being led upstairs by a servant. She hadn't seen Robert.

"I'd like that, my lord, but you see, I've just gotten here. I won't be leaving for several days."

"Ohhhh, too bad. Then have a drink with me before you retire."

"I think, mayhap, you've had enough to drink, my lord. Are you staying here at the inn?"

"What inn ish this?"

"The Dandy Lion."

Robert guffawed loudly and fell over the table. An empty wine bottle clattered to the floor, smashing into pieces. "No, thish isn't my inn. I'm at the Cressshhhann."

"The what?"

"The Cressshhhinn."

"He means The Crescent, Colin." Alan kneeled down to pick up the broken glass.

"I know the place. I'm going to see you safely there, my lord." Colin wrapped Robert's arm around his shoulder and led him toward the door. "Alan, tell my friend I will be up shortly. Tell him I'm, uh, seeing to the horses. I don't want to worry him."

314

Alan watched Colin leave with the drunken noble, a perplexed look on his face.

Colin struggled down the cobblestoned street with Robert, supporting most of his weight. That had been close. If Robert hadn't been so drunk he would surely have seen Arianna. He couldn't let that happen until after Arianna had seen her mother. Right now, that took precedence over all else. But it was clear that telling him would be the right thing. Robert was sinking into oblivion. His eyes were sunken, his cheeks ashen, and he had lost weight.

Damn. Life was so unfair. Unfair to Arianna and her mother, unfair to Robert and himself, and yes, even unfair to little Robin. He had a right to be with his father. Damn, Elizabeth. Arianna had the right idea—revenge. It would be so sweet.

Through a grey haze, Rob looked up to see the entrance to the Crescent Inn. "No, I don' wanna go in."

"You don't mean that, my lord. 'Tis bitter cold out here."

Rob loosened himself from Colin's hold and stumbled backwards, almost falling. He righted himself, shouting, "No, 'tis too quiet in there, too lonely. Need to hear the sound of living people."

"Robert, I thought you were doing better. In December, when you came to my home, you seemed almost happy."

"Happy? Happy?" Harsh laughter emanated from Rob's throat. "I'll never be happy again. Can't stop thinking about her, dreaming about her. Sometimes I think my only peace will be in my grave."

The words knifed through Colin, and he agonized

315

over telling Robert this very minute that Arianna lived. But if he did, Rob would never let Arianna go to her mother's execution. He'd protect her from that, and if Colin knew anything in this world, he knew Arianna must go.

She needed to see her mother again, even if it was at her execution. A powerful force drove Arianna, more powerful than anything else in her life. She had been able to turn away from Robert to save him from Elizabeth, but she couldn't turn away from Mary to save herself.

Because he knew this, Colin stilled his tongue.

With the help of the inn's servants, he got Robert to his room and laid him on the bed. Handing each a coin, he dismissed the servants and sat by the bed. He would stay until he was sure Robert was safely asleep. His desperate words made him uneasy. Was Robert capable of killing himself? "My lord, can you hear me?"

Robert mumbled something unintelligible. His eyelids were heavy, too heavy to stay open.

Colin watched as Rob drifted off to sleep. Murmuring, he said, "If you hear me, Robert, take heart. Soon, you'll be happy. Soon your fondest wishes will come true and you'll live out the rest of your life in contentment, your wife and child by your side."

Back in the Dandy Lion, Arianna sat staring out the window at the lonely castle. If only she could be with her mother — to help her through her last night on earth. There was so much she wanted to tell her, so much she needed to hear, but that would never happen now.

She wanted to cry, but could not. Wanted to

shriek to the world of the terrible injustice, but could not. She was encased in a cocoon of ice, a cocoon that kept her from breaking down. She accepted that, knowing it was the only way to get through this terrible time, for if she shed one tear, it would turn into a flood that would be impossible to stop.

Her hands were folded in her lap, the pass to Mary's execution clutched tightly in her hand. It was the lifeline to her mother, the only way she could glimpse her one more time. But a hideous thing, all the same. Part of her wanted to tear it into a thousand pieces, to deny what it meant, but instead, she held it as if it were a precious jewel, for in a way it was. Because of it she would see her mother and she would make sure her mother saw her. If she could do nothing else for Mary, at least she could make sure she knew her daughter lived. Mayhap, Mary could take some comfort in knowing she was close by. It was pitifully little that she could do for her now, but she would do it!

Staring at the castle, she willed the walls to crumble, but they did not. She wanted to brave the walls, climb over them and find her mother. Wanted to take a sword and run through everyone who stood between her and Mary, but she knew it was impossible. She would be killed and Robin would be denied his mother, as she had been denied hers. For Robin's sake, she would act rationally. For his sake she must live.

Turning away from the window, she leaned down to kiss her sleeping child's rosebud lips. Robin. Rob's child. Mary's grandchild. In him, she still had them both. For them, she would raise him to be a

317

fine man—a man proud and brave as her mother, noble and kind as her husband. For Robin, she would go on.

Chapter Twenty-six

February 8, 1587

Watching the sun rise for the very last time,
Mary looked directly at the red sphere, gazing at it
until her eyes watered, hurting too much to stare
any longer. How could it be that dawn, the bedaz-
zling beginning of a new day, the symbolic image of
hope and dreams, now heralded the end of her life?
How could Elizabeth have signed another Queen's
death warrant?

Mercifully, she had not been told 'til yesterday
that she would die this day; though she had asked
for more time, stunned that Elizabeth had actually
decreed her death after everyone thought she would
not, she was glad now it had not been granted,
glad her travail would soon be over.

She hadn't slept at all but lay awake, preparing
herself for this morn. She wanted everything
planned perfectly, so that everyone present would remember this day forever so that it would be said of
her that she died the noble death of a Queen. Nay,
even more, that Mary, Queen of Scotland and the
Isles had died the death of a martyr.

Elizabeth little knew what service she performed

in signing the death warrant, for with that signature she had assured Mary a place in heaven. Long weary of living without freedom, without her children, the years had worn away her will to live. She had but one regret left that still ate at her innards: not seeing her daughter's face one last time.

Though Mary's servants denied it, she knew they thought Arianna was dead. They tried to hide their feelings from her, but she knew them too well. If only she could prove them wrong. If only she had some measure of proof that her daughter still lived she could go to her death with the greatest of ease. And Arianna's child, her grandchild—was it asking too much to know it survived, too? Mary swallowed hard, pushing back the tears. It would not do to break down now, so close to the end. She must make ready. They would be coming for her soon.

Calling to her women, she began the ritual of dressing, knowing it would be for the last time. How odd that felt. It was unimaginable to think she would never dress again, or eat again, or see another dawn.

But her imagination had not let her down when it came to thinking out the details of this day. Knowing what lay ahead, she had planned her wardrobe down to the smallest detail. She had witnessed enough beheadings to know how much blood would be shed and had chosen a petticoat and camisole of crimson. When her gown was stripped to bare her neck, the red would blend well with her blood.

For two hours her women worked diligently at dressing her, while she directed them. Clothed in black, she wore an elegant robe of state, edged with velvet and richest gold. No somber clothing at her execution. Let all who looked upon her know they look upon a Queen. She wore a crucifix of gold around her neck and one of ivory to hold in her hand, so all should know she died a daughter of the Catholic faith. A fashionable wig covered her thinning grey hair, and atop that was set a peaked cap with a white veil that reached to the ground.

How good it felt to dress like a Queen again, to feel the heavy weight of elegant garments on her body. She was ready now to face her enemies. Smoothing her skirt, she said, "Now, I have finished with the world. Gather around me and let us kneel and pray."

Nursing her son, Arianna's eyes closed and her breathing slowed to almost normal. For these few, precious moments she could pull herself from her numbed state and know a measure of contentment. She could tend to her son's needs before having to dress once more as a boy. Feeling Robin's milk teeth sink into her flesh, she smiled wanly. He was almost ready to be weaned. How fast time flies.

Time. Her mother had precious little left.

She wished with all her heart that Mary could know her grandchild, that Robin could grow up knowing his grandmother's love. How cruel life could be. In a few moments, she would be leaving her son in Colin's care so that she might witness her mother's death. How could she bear it?

As if reading her thoughts, Colin said, "Are you sure you can do this, Arianna? There's but one pass. I cannot be there with you."

"I can do it. I have to do it. Not just for me — so I might have one more glimpse of my mother — one glimpse to last a lifetime. I do it so she might derive some small degree of comfort in seeing me there."

"Your bravery humbles me, Arianna. In your place, I don't know if I could do the same."

With a low, sad laugh, she said, "I haven't done it yet. Save your compliments for when 'tis over." Kissing Robin's forehead, she took him from her breast. "Now, young sir, 'tis time for your mother to bind her breasts. 'Twill be much easier now that you've reduced them considerably."

Colin helped her dress, growing more uneasy with each passing minute. He wanted to tell her she couldn't go, just as Robert or Lord William would have done, but he knew how important this last gesture was to Arianna. It was a gift to Mary, the only gift Arianna could ever give her mother, and he couldn't deny her that. Mary would know her daughter lived, and what greater gift could she receive in her last moments on this earth?

"There. How do I look? Will I pass for a pampered young gentleman?" Arianna posed for Colin, trying to keep the mood light. She couldn't let him see how frightened she was or he might keep her from going to the castle.

"Aye, you'll pass. In any case, all eyes will be on Mary. Don't speak or call attention to yourself and you'll be fine. I'll ask Alan's wife to care for Robin so I can wait outside the gates for you. You'll not have to walk back here alone."

"No! I want you here with Robin. If something goes wrong and I am taken, I want you far enough

322

away so that there'll be no connection to me. Understand? For Robin's sake."

"Arianna . . ."

"And . . . in the event I am taken, I want your promise that you'll deliver Robin to his father."

"You know I will, but it won't come to that. God in heaven, I've got to believe it won't come to that. How can I let you go, otherwise?"

Arianna felt herself pulled into Colin's arms, felt the warmth of his body drawing her strength, her will to leave. She let the stiffness, the numbness move up her body to her heart, to her brain, making it possible to leave him and Robin, making it possible to survive the horror that lay ahead.

A throng of people ringed the castle entrance as Arianna made her way to the gate, her pass clutched in her hand. Peasants, burghers, men, women, children, all eager for any news of the execution. Vultures! How can they be so eager for the death of an innocent woman? Pushing her way through the crowd, she thrust the stolen pass at a guard.

With a silent nod of his head, Arianna gained admittance. Following a group of knights, she found herself in the great hall and immediately sought out the stairs leading to the scaffold—the one sure place where her mother would pass, the one sure place where she might have an unobstructed view. A frown creased her forehead when she saw a group of knights there already. Pushing her way through them, she boldly took her place in the front row. No one would stop her from seeing her mother.

The giant-sized knight she dislodged angrily boomed, "Here, there, what do you think you're doing?" Upon seeing the fragile boy, his expression changed. "You've a brave lad to jostle me. I eat little boys like you for dinner, but I am in a benevolent mood this day so I'll let it pass." Looking over the delicate boy, he commented, "You look a mite young to be witnessing a beheading, but 'twill make a man of ye for certain. This be your first execution?"

Arianna nodded silently.

"Well, I'm glad you're standing in front of me, instead of behind. In case you get sick, I mean." Laughing loudly, the man slapped Arianna's shoulder.

Arianna winced at his words and was relieved when the man turned his attention back to his companions. It galled her to think so many people were happy that Mary would be dying, treating the execution as if it were an outing. Resentment grew inside her, threatening to overpower her. Knowing she must stay calm, she pushed her anger away and looked around the hall, her eyes lighting for a moment on the blazing fire in the huge fireplace across the way. Somehow, the fire seemed out of place in this hall of death, its light and warmth belying the terrible deed that would be done.

Transfixed, she stared into the flames for a long time before daring to look up at the scaffold, so close she could reach out and touch it. It was about twelve feet square and over two feet high, covered with black cloth. In fact, everything upon the stage was black, from the low rail that ran 'round it to the chairs, to the horrid block covered with black, to the small cushion placed behind it. How thoughtful, she mused bitterly, a cushion to cradle her mother's head whilst it was being chopped off!

Tearing her eyes from the terrible sight, they lighted on something even ghastlier — the axe — leaning against the rail. Feeling her knees go weak she clutched at the railing for support.

Upstairs in her chamber, Mary heard a loud knock on the outer door and without blinking, continued her prayers. A male servant shouted to the intruders: "Her majesty is engaged in prayers."

His words were greeted with silence. Sighing, he joined his mistress in prayer. Fifteen minutes later, the pounding began again, this time louder, and the door opened. The sheriff, along with Sir Amlys Paulet, Shrewsbury, the Earl of Kent, and many others entered, shuffling restlessly, uneasy at interrupting the Scottish Queen at prayer.

In a moment, Mary stood, her gaze resting on the sheriff.

In a faltering voice, he said, "Madame, the Lords have sent me for you."

"Then, so it must be."

Immediately, the wails and cries of her servants filled the air and Mary embraced them each in turn. When two of Paulet's men came forward to take her arms and lead her out the door, Mary's serenity was broken as she realized her servants were not being allowed to accompany her.

"Surely no one can object to my poor servants witnessing my death. They would be a great comfort to me."

"That cannot be allowed," Kent replied, "for fear they might scream or faint or attempt mayhap to dip their handkerchiefs in your blood."

Mary knew there was a more devious reason why

Kent did not want her people to witness the execution. But she could not afford to leave the account of her death to her enemies or the fanatic puritans. If she was to die a martyr's death, then the whole world must know the true details.

"My lord, I give you my word, although it be all but dead, that they shall do none of these things."

"I'm sorry, I cannot allow it."

"Sir, you are too harsh. The Queen would never deny me so slight a request. You have denied me my chaplain; in this, the last hour of my life, how can you also deny me the comfort of my own people?"

She saw the uncertainty in Kent's eyes and pursued him more vigorously, pouring her anger and frustration into her words. "Remember, I am cousin to your Queen. Descended of the blood royal of Henry the Seventh. A married Queen of France, and anointed Queen of Scotland. Do you dare deny me this meager last request?"

Kent broke down. Everything she said was true, and how would it look to the watching world that in her last hour she was denied the comfort of her servants? "You may have six of your men and women."

Triumphant, she quickly chose her physician, her surgeon, her apothecary and Melville, the master of her household, along with Jane Kennedy and Elizabeth Curle. They of all her people would best tell the truth of her death when it was all over.

Now ready to face her destiny, she said, *"Allons-y! Let us go."* Bourgoigne, her French physician, stepped to her side and the procession began. Supported on either side by Paulet's men, she made her way slowly down the staircase on legs swollen and stiff with rheumatism. Andrew Melville, her master of the household, knelt on the last step, waiting for her, a reverent expression upon his face.

Deeply touched and grateful, Mary extended her hand to lift him from his knees and embrace him. The feel of his strong arms around her was unexpectedly comforting and she clung to him, willing the moment to last. Here, finally, was someone who loved her, a Scotsman, a countryman.

In a voice choked with emotion, Melville said, "It will be the saddest message that ever I carried when I shall report that my Queen and mistress is dead."

"Ah, no, dear Melville, not so. Today, I die a woman true to my religion, a true Queen of Scot land and France." Drawing herself up to her full height, she took on a majestic bearing and with great verve swept into the hall. Forgotten were the stiffness and the pain in her legs, the ache in her heart. Forgotten were the nineteen years of captivity. She was a Queen, and by God, all would know it!

A great hush fell over the hall. Arianna turned her head to the doorway, her heart stopping at the sight of her mother moving toward the scaffold stairs. Immediately, guards moved to push the crowd back and she was forced to move away from the steps, away from the point her mother would pass. Panic gripped her. She had to do something or her mother would never see her, never know she was here.

"Your Majesty," she cried, above the din. "I shall tell my infant son of this great day."

Mary stopped suddenly, remembering the voice of

her daughter. It couldn't be. Her head turned in the direction of the crowd, recognizing the face she yearned to see. The ivory crucifix fell from her hand.

Arianna moved quickly to pick it up, her hand surreptitiously touching the hem of Mary's gown in silent homage. Slowly, oh so slowly, she stood, her eyes moving up the elegant dark form, until she beheld the golden eyes of her mother. She stared into their depths, her gaze so intense that nothing on earth could have broken it. She had looked into those eyes only once before and would never do so again. This moment was all she would ever have with her mother. Reaching out, she handed Mary the ivory crucifix.

Mary gazed into clear blue eyes, drinking in the sight of her beloved daughter. Her heart soared and yet at the same time was at peace. Thank you, God, for this wonderful gift. Her hand reached out to take the crucifix, closing around Arianna's small fist and squeezing it tight.

They stood for what seemed a lifetime, the only time left to them, bestowing their love with their eyes, giving each other strength with the touching of hands, saying their silent goodbyes. And then, realizing the danger to Arianna, Mary took the crucifix and kissed it fervently. Then she walked, unaided, up the steps.

All who watched wondered at the calmness the Queen displayed and at the smile that played across her face. Sitting in the chair behind the block, she looked up at the man who held the death warrant. His voice droned on as he read the warrant, but she heard it not. Her daughter was but a few feet away. That was all that mattered now. And then it came to her . . . the words Arianna had shouted to her over the crowd . . . *"I shall tell my infant son of this great day."* A son. Arianna had a son. Though her blood would be drained from her body, soaking into this rough wood, it would never turn to dust. It flowed now through her daughter, through her grandson. She would live!

The sheriff finished reading the warrant, then rolled up the parchment and stepped back. A hush came over the crowd. Lord Shrewsbury stepped forward, clearing his throat. Speaking softly, he said, "You hear what we are commended to do?"

Rising from the chair, Mary answered him. "You will do your duty."

Fearing she was about to start praying, the fanatical Dean of Peterborough, Dr. Fletcher, began reciting Protestant rhetoric, happy for the opportunity to preach in front of such a distinguished crowd.

Mary had hoped she would be spared this last feeble attempt to have her die a Protestant. Dismayed, and determined that her death would not be turned into a triumph for the reformed church, she tried to interrupt him, to no avail. In deep frustration, she fell upon her knees and began to pray in a voice that grew ever louder, competing with the dean's thunderings. Immersing herself in the holy words that had kept her in good stead, she emphasized them all the more by striking her crucifix against her bosom over and over.

Her zeal wore Dr. Fletcher down, and he wearily mopped his brow with his handkerchief, then sat down. At last, it was her voice alone that filled the air. "Even as thy arms, O Jesus, were spread upon the cross, so receive me into thy mercy and forgive my sins."

Mary rose.

The black-clad executioners stepped forward and knelt before her begging forgiveness for what they were about to do. It was a formality, a tradition, and she took it as such, nodding her head coolly to each of them. When Bulle, the burly executioner, stood again, Mary knew it was time. Her body swayed, for just a moment, and when she righted herself, she willed her mind to drift . . . away . . . to a beautiful castle . . . in the green-clad highlands. There, yes, there, sitting beneath a huge oak tree, her grandson upon her knee.

Arianna had kept her eyes averted from Bulle and his assistant, but now whilst they knelt before Mary, she had no choice but to see them. Their very sight was hateful to her eyes. *Those loathsome creatures dared ask forgiveness for their heinous crime? Never. They will rot in hell.*

And when the executioners rose and motioned Mary's women to help her undress, and when Mary, now in crimson undergarments, stood before the throng of knights, Arianna drew deeper and deeper into herself, hiding from the horror, hiding from her deep sorrow. In a dream-like state, she saw herself sitting beneath a tree . . . a giant oak tree . . . and heard the gentle murmurings of a brook nearby. So peaceful . . . Smiling serenely, she turned her head to see her mother sitting beside her, Robin on her lap. An overwhelming feeling of love washed over her, and needing to express it, she reached out . . . to touch her mother's hand.

A burst of crimson blinded her.

330

Startled, she opened her eyes.

Oh God! The axe was coming down for the second time.

She squeezed her eyes shut, desperately seeking the oak tree, her brain sending forth a message. *Mother, where are you? Mama, Mama, don't leave me.*

Through a mist, she heard the axe one last time, and felt a sudden rush of wind through her hair. It gentled to a caressing breeze that kissed her cheek and then . . . was gone.

She could open her eyes now, for what lay upon the bloodied floor would no longer house her mother's essence. Taking in the horrific scene, she saw Bulle reach down to pick up Mary's head. Lifting it for all to see, it suddenly fell to the floor, leaving him with naught but a wig in his grasp.

A huge gasp filled the hall as the head hit the wooden floor, making a sound that would live forever in Arianna's head. She wanted to shriek, to cry, to pummel the horrid man with her fists, but she stood frozen, too shocked to move. It was more than she could bear. Dear God, it was more than she could bear!

But she was wrong.

For an instant, she was bearing much, much, more.

Bulle's men lifted Mary's body from the floor. Instantaneously, the spectators gasped as one, seeing the little Skye terrier cowering beneath Mary's skirts, his blue-grey body covered with crimson flecks. Arianna cried out, but no one heard in the pandemonium that followed. Confused and frightened, the animal ran around the perimeter of the stage seeking comfort from a familiar face. Chased

331

by the executioner's assistant, it jumped into the air, landing on Arianna's chest.

Arianna's hands moved up to cradle the dog, feeling the sticky wetness on his fur. Instantly, the numbness was gone. She felt the full fury of grief and sorrow, of anger and hatred, and cried out, "No!"

Immediately, hands were reaching out to support her falling body, others to take away the small dog.

Like everyone else in the hall, Rob had watched in horror as the terrier, grisled with the Queen's blood, ran frantically around the edge of the scaffold — watched as the animal leaped into the arms of one of the spectators, his face turning white when he recognized the form of Sparrow. It cannot be! Arianna! My Arianna!

He blinked his eyes, and when they opened again, she was gone.

Chapter Twenty-seven

Cold air wafted over Arianna's face, awakening her with a start.

"Back amongst the living are you?" Thomas set the boy down. "Can't say as how I blamed you for blacking out. Horrible thing to be covered with another's blood. You feeling better now?"

In a daze, Arianna looked down at her crimson-spattered jerkin and the horror washed over her again. Another's blood? No. Much more horrible than that. Her mother's blood.

"Do you have lodgings close by? I'll see you there."

Blinking back tears, she stammered, "The Dandy Lion."

"Well, then, come along." Thomas took the lad by the arm, seeing he was weak as a newborn foal, and started down the street.

Back in the hall, Rob bumped into one person after another as a surge of men pushed their way outside.

Deep in shock, he frantically wove his way through the throng, trying desperately to get to the other side of the scaffold. *Arianna. It had to be she. It was she. He knew it. My God, she was alive. How? How?* "Make way! Let me through! Get out of my way!"

When at last he broke free of the sea of knights and lords and made it to the other side of the scaffold, he searched the faces of the crowd looking for the familiar precious form of his wife. She wasn't there.

"Dear God, I can't lose her again."

Rushing out the door, his eyes searched for her. Where was she? Where could she have disappeared? Had he imagined it all? Then, out of the corner of his eyes, he caught a glimpse of her disappearing around the corner, accompanied by a giant of a man.

With wooden legs and hammering heart, he ran up the street and around the corner, stopping when he saw the street was empty. Had he dreamt it all? Of course he had. Arianna was dead. It had been an hallucination, that's all. Leaning against the side of a building, he buried his head in his hands. Arianna. Arianna.

"Are you all right, sir?"

Rob opened his eyes to see the man who had been with Arianna. *It wasn't a dream. If* he *exists, then so does she.* "Where is she? Where did you take her?"

The man looked at him as if he were demented. "She? Who do you mean, sir?"

"I mean he, I mean the boy. Where is the boy you were with a moment ago?"

Thomas shook his head. "I think you had better go home and sleep it off."

"What are you talking about? I'm not drunk. It's just, that boy, he's someone I haven't seen for a long time. Someone I thought was dead."

"Dead?" Thomas looked closely at the young nobleman and saw the shock and pain in his eyes. "The lad is in yon inn, and if you don't mind my saying so, I'm thinking you and your young friend are both

334

in need of a drink. You both look near to expiring."

"Which chamber is he in? Do you know?"

"That I do. Helped him there myself. Up the stairs first door to the right."

Rob pumped the man's hand vigorously. "Thank you, thank you."

Hurrying toward the inn, just a building away, a hundred thoughts crowded his head. He had to prepare himself for the fact it might just be someone who resembled Sparrow. Or, mayhap someone who doesn't resemble Sparrow at all. His imagination could be betraying him. The horrible sight of Mary being beheaded could have conjured up the image of his dead wife.

It had been brutal. Mary's death had not been swift. The first blow had only struck the back of her head, the second had not completely severed her head. If Arianna had truly been there, witnessing her mother's terrible death, she must be devastated.

Arianna alive! The thought took his breath away and he prayed it was true. Opening the door to the inn, he entered, his heart racing out of control. Glancing to the right, he saw the stairs. Taking them two at a time, he made his way to the second floor. First door to the right. First door to the right. It was a litany he repeated until he stood in front of the room. He rapped softly on the door, suddenly afraid.

"Go away. Come back later."

Rob was startled by the booming male voice and by its familiarity. He knew that voice. Who . . . ? Then he heard it. The sobbing. Arianna's sobbing. His hand reached out to grasp the door knob, his breathing becoming erratic when he discovered it wasn't locked.

Swinging the door open, he was unprepared for

the scene that greeted him. Arianna. Living, breathing Arianna, reclining in a wooden tub. Beside her, washing cloth in hand, Colin Colrain.

"Lord Warwick!"

As if through a haze Arianna heard her husband's name and opened her eyes. Rob? Here? Was she dreaming?

Myriad emotions coursed through Robert at the sight of her. Joy that Arianna was not dead, confusion at finding her naked in the tub, anger — then rage when it registered that Colin was there with his wife.

Colin, the only one capable to thinking rationally, said, "For God's sake man, come in and close the door. Arianna doesn't need an audience."

Jolted from his paralysis, Rob entered the room and shut the door. Striding over to Colin, he cried, "You bastard," and slammed his fist into Colin's face.

Colin staggered back, stumbling against the wooden tub.

In deep shock, Arianna's body went limp. Moaning softly, she sank down into the tub. Turning on her side, she drew her legs up, curling into a cocoon. No more. She could take no more.

Striding over to the tub, Rob cried, "Arianna, oh God, Arianna." Lifting her, he carried her to the bed and laid her there, his heart rejoicing at the warm touch of her. Alive! Taking a blanket from a nearby chair, he covered her up, then pulled her into his arms, the need to touch her and hold her too great to deny. Feverish kisses covered her eyes and cheeks and neck, gentle hands soothed her hair, touched her skin. "Tell me you are really here. Tell me I'm not dreaming this."

The touch of Rob's lips released a flood of emo-

336

tion. It took control of her and she cried, unable to withstand all the pain, the suffering. The loneliness without Rob, the sorrow at seeing her mother beheaded, the anger at Elizabeth, the raw hatred toward the executioner. Her sobbing grew stronger as she relived the horror of the day.

"You fool! You see what you've done? She just witnessed her mother's death. She was suffering enough. Did you have to storm in here like a . . ."

"My God! You dare to speak that way to me? I find you with my naked wife and you dare lecture me on my behavior? Get out of here before I kill you! Leave me alone with my wife. I'll take care of her."

"I'm not going anywhere. Arianna needs me."

Enraged, Rob started for Colin, then stopped dead when he heard a baby cry. His head jerked in the direction of the sound. *A baby! On the floor by the window. What? Whose? My God . . . mine!* Tears began to flow as he moved toward his child and turned to sobs when he lifted the beautiful boy, cradling him in his arms.

Hearing the baby cry, Arianna came to her senses. She stopped crying and sat up. Robin needed her.

Rob sat beside her on the bed, in control of his emotions once more. "I never dared hope . . . never dared believe . . . What is it? A daughter? A son?"

"Your son — Robert . . . after you, after my father, too. We . . . I call him Robin."

"Robin," Rob repeated softly, then he remembered the child in Colin's cottage. "The cottage. My God! You've been living there with Colin all this time."

Colin watched the scene in silence, knowing he should leave but wanting to stay to protect Arianna if need be. He needed to know how it was between

Arianna and Rob, needed to know that she would at last be happy.

Rob's tone was accusing, but Arianna accepted it, knowing what he must be feeling. "Yes," she answered quietly. "He saved my life and the babe's. Rescued me from a ledge where I gave birth. Kept me hidden from Elizabeth."

"And from *me*. *Why?*"

"Because I killed Edmund."

Stunned, Rob could only stammer, "You couldn't do something that horrible."

Arianna bit her lower lip to keep from crying. " 'Twas horrible, I know. But he was going to violate me. Going to take me to Elizabeth. He knew my true identity."

Finding it too much to comprehend, Rob's head reeled. "I can understand killing him to defend yourself, but to mutilate him like that . . . My God, how could you?"

"Mutilate? Rob, I don't know what you're talking about. I stabbed him once, in the shoulder. I don't understand what you mean."

"Once? He was stabbed repeatedly and his man part hacked off. We thought some madman had gained access to the castle, had abducted you and . . ."

Arianna was speechless with shock.

"Sweet Jesus, Rob, you can't believe Arianna would do that, even to a despicable man like Edmund Deveraux?"

Robert looked up at Colin. He had forgotten he was there, forgotten everything but his son and his wife. He shook his head to clear it. "I don't know what to believe anymore. Arianna alive, when I thought her dead. You deceiving me in your cottage, convincing me you were married to some other girl. And the babe, telling me it was yours. What am I to believe? What can I count on anymore, when I've been fed lies since the first moment I set eyes on Arianna."

Hugging his son tight, Rob stood and began to pace the room. "The only truth I know is what I hold in my arms. This is my son. I'm bringing him back to Everly with or without his mother."

Arianna felt the life drain out of her.

Colin grabbed Rob's arm, pleading, "Don't be a fool, man. Don't let your foolish pride keep you from doing the right thing. Arianna loves you. She stayed away to protect you and the babe."

Rob knocked his hand away. "Protect me? How did she protect me? By breaking my heart? By denying me my son?"

"She protected you from Elizabeth. After today, can you deny how vicious the Queen can be, having a helpless woman beheaded? Arianna's own mother? What do you think she would do to Arianna and the babe if she found out who they were? What do you think she would do to you when you tried to protect them? Arianna had no choice. Don't you see that, man?"

Colin's words sank in. Everything he said was true. "I need time. There's too much to comprehend."

"Fine," Colin answered. "Take the time, but not here. Arianna is close to the breaking point. Look at her. Take her back to Everly. Keep her safe whilst you think about it. Let her tell you what happened before you decide the future."

In a tortured voice, Rob said, "I need to know the truth. I'll not accept anything less."

A spark of hope flared inside Arianna. "Rob, be-

339

fore God, I did not kill Edmund. I know that now. When Colin told me he was dead, I wondered how I could have done it with such a shallow blow. And now, after what you said about Edmund being mutilated, I know I didn't do it."

Robert wanted to believe. Oh, God, he wanted to believe. "If that is true, there's only one way to prove it. Come back to Everly and . . ."

Arianna stood, drawing the blanket around her as a shield. "I can't go back, Rob. I can't. I've done enough harm to you. I couldn't stand it if you suffered at Elizabeth's hands because of me."

"Robin belong in Everly. If you want him, you'll have to come back."

"You can't mean that. You can't be that cruel."

Rob laughed bitterly. "Look who calls me cruel. You let me think you were dead. Let me grieve for ten agonizing months. You denied me my firstborn son, and you call *me* cruel? Lady, you are the very author of the word."

Arianna could not defend herself. Everything he said was true. "Then I am lost."

Rob's heart broke in two, hearing her sorrowful resignation. Why was she giving up so easily?

The sudden deadly silence was more than Colin could stand. "Here, now. Neither of you is thinking clearly. Understandable, considering all you've been through this terrible day. What's needed now is a way to prove Arianna's innocence. Since I'm the only one with a cool head, I'll gladly devote myself to finding out what really happened."

"Your services to this family are no longer required," Rob said coldly.

Colin shook his head, hearing the bitterness. "Think, man. If not for Arianna, then for your son.

Will you let your family be destroyed because you were too proud? Let me help you. God knows, I need to. I should have brought her back to you as soon as she was well enough to travel, but she begged me not to and I gave in. At the time, I thought it was because she would be safer with me. But now I can't help but wonder if I kept her because of my own selfish motives."

Robert wanted to hate Colin, but hearing the anguish in his voice, he could not. How could he blame him for loving Arianna? What mortal man's heart stood a chance? "Enough. If Arianna comes willingly, I'll give you the chance to prove her innocence. But after that, I never want to lay eyes on you again. Do you understand? You'll leave Everly forever."

"I understand." Colin felt the loss of Arianna already. His chest was suddenly constricted, his voice barely more than a whisper. Turning to Arianna, he asked, "Agreed?"

Arianna's gaze moved from one solemn face to the other. She had caused them both to suffer. Would she do the same to her child? A shroud of malaise fell around her, and she sank into its midst. Her nostrils were still filled with the smell of her mother's blood. She was tired, too tired to fight her dark destiny any longer. Her life was doomed from the moment she was born, just as her mother's had been. It was her fate to suffer, to die a bloody death at Elizabeth's hand. She felt the dark close 'round her, the darkness of the grave. Robin would be better off without her. Robert and Colin would be better off without her.

The feel of Rob's hands cradling her face, broke her reverie. "Arianna?"

His soft voice drew her toward the light, drew her toward life.

"Arianna, look at me."

Compelled, she opened her eyes and stared up into the light shining from the warm brown depths of his. "Rob. Oh, Rob. God help me, I want to live."

Chapter Twenty-eight

Three horses carrying the woman, babe, and two men rode eastward toward Everly, three minds adrift in separate worlds: Colin, envisioning his lonely life without Arianna; Robert, in a confused state of hope and despair; and Arianna, still absorbing her hellish experience. Theirs was a world in which helpless women were beheaded, dreams died, and a heartless queen could yet destroy those she loved.

A few short hours ago she had almost given up, but the touch of Rob's hands on her face had turned her toward life again. So many long, lonely months had passed since she had felt that wondrous touch, so many nights of yearning. Would Rob ever love her again the way he had before, totally, completely, incredibly? Would he ever believe in her?

Dressed in borrowed clothing from the innkeeper's wife and wrapped warmly in a fur-lined cloak Rob purchased before they left Fotheringhay, Arianna rode Pasha. The blood-spattered clothing, tied into a neat little bundle, hung from the saddle. Rob had tried to have the clothing burned, but she had rescued them. She couldn't tell him why; she wasn't thinking clearly enough to fathom the reason, but she knew she had to keep them.

343

Rob rode with Robin in his lap, his hand brushing the babe's cheek from time to time, as if afraid it was all a dream. His son. Alive and well. It was truly a miracle. Feeling Arianna's eyes burn into him, he looked up to see her staring over at him, the sad little smile that played across her face for one short moment breaking his heart. She was still the most beautiful woman he had ever known, and whatever the future held, he would never stop loving her.

The terrible months without her had proven that. His grief had never lessened, nor his deep love. And yet, if his love for her had been an appendage like an arm or leg or hand, he would gladly chop it off now, to be rid of it once and for all. But there would be no short, merciful end for him; no blade could cut his deep love for her, nothing short of death erase his consuming desire.

This woman he loved had slept with another man, lived with him as many months as she had lived with him. Could he forget that? Forgive that? Colin Colrain. God's teeth, but he wanted to hate the man. But try as he might, he could not. Colin had saved Arianna's life, and his son's. For that alone, he would be indebted to him the rest of his life. But even so, the very sight of him was hateful to his eyes. Every time he looked at him he thought of him in bed with Arianna, touching her, exciting her, and he wanted to cut the image from his brain.

It was too much to bear. And yet he did bear it, allowing Colin to accompany them back to Everly. Why? Because Colin could help him discover the truth about Edmund's death? Because deep inside his soul he knew he would have acted the same in his place? Or because, with Colin present, he could stay angry at Arianna and protect his heart by keeping her at a distance?

Riding around a bend on the narrow road, Rob saw the welcome sight of John Neal and a dozen knights heading their way. He raised his hand in greeting, halting in front of them.

"My lord," John shouted, "tis good to see you. I was beginning to worry. You said you'd meet us here first thing this morning. We were about to ride into Fotheringhay after you." It suddenly registered on John that Rob was not alone. Looking down at the child in Rob's arms, his eyes opened wide, then wider as he looked up in astonishment at the female rider beside him. "Arianna! My God!"

Jumping from his horse, he ran over to her, his eyes glistening with tears. Taking her hand, he kissed it tenderly, but that was not enough to express his feelings. Lifting her from the saddle, he embraced her warmly and set her on the ground.

"Forgive me, my lady, for my exuberance, but I can't begin to tell you how happy I am to see you. My God, everyone thought you were dead."

"I know, John, I know. 'Tis good to see you, too. Good to know someone is happy that I'm alive." Her eyes sought out Rob's, holding his gaze a long moment.

Seeing the tension between the lord and his lady, John's eyes swept over the third rider and his jaw tightened. Colin? With Lady Arianna? "We have some stew simmering over a hot fire at our camp. Shall we partake before heading home?"

Dismounting, Rob said, "That sounds good, John. Lead the way."

Grateful for the chance to gather his wits, John led the small party back to the camp in a small clearing in the woods. Seating Arianna on a fallen log, he personally saw to her needs.

Arianna was touched by John's concern. When he

handed her a bowl of steaming stew, she smiled graciously, a shiver coursing through her as she tasted the hot liquid. She hadn't realized how cold she was.

Rob saw her shiver, and his natural instinct was to go to her and warm her with his body, but he forced himself to turn away. If he went to her now, he would be lost.

Colin, too, wanted to give her his warmth, but knew it was no longer his place to do so. *Damn it all, Robert, forget your pride. Go to her.*

John waited a moment to see what Robert would do and when he made no move, walked over to Arianna and removed his cloak and offered it to her. "Here, take this, my lady. Wrap it around your legs and you'll feel much warmer."

"Thank you, Sir John, but I have no need of it. Besides, I don't want my favorite knight to catch his death. I may have need of your services some day, and would have you healthy."

"Are you sure? 'Tis no hardship for me."

"Very sure. This stew shall warm me and give me strength."

Rob and Colin locked eyes, each humbled by John's gallantry and Arianna's graciousness.

Later, after Robin had been tended to, John helped Arianna mount Pasha and they started for Everly. Rob rode at the head of the column, Robin on his lap. Behind him rode Sir John on one side of Arianna, Colin on the other, Robert's knights bringing up the rear. They rode through the wintry afternoon in uncomfortable silence, arriving at Everly by dusk.

With Everly Castle looming overhead, Arianna was brought back to cold reality. She would need all her strength to face what lay ahead. Somehow she must find the courage to go on, for Robin's sake. Listening to the slow, whining noise of the moving drawbridge she suddenly became strangely restless. Something inside her resisted going over the drawbridge. But what? What danger could there be in Everly Castle? Everyone there loved her.

Sensing her restlessness, Pasha began to dance in place, his head tossing wildly as he became more and more agitated.

"Whoa, boy," she murmured, patting him on his neck. "Whoa, there." She felt precarious, balancing her body sidesaddle.

Rob could see the high-strung animal was too far gone to be calmed easily, but with his small son on his lap, it would be risky to grab hold of Pasha's bridle. Out of the corner of his eye, he saw Colin steering his horse toward Arianna and his anger flared, pushing everything else from his mind. Spurring his horse, he rode quickly to Arianna's side. Holding his son tightly in one strong arm, he reached out with the other to grasp Pasha's bridle.

Spooked by Rob's sudden move, Pasha started to rear, but Rob forced his head down. In an instant Colin and John were out of their saddles and holding onto the animal.

Arianna kept her seat. Clinging to Pasha's mane, she held on and rode it out until the animal was calm once more. When Pasha was under control, she shouted passionately, "I swear right here and now, I will never ride sidesaddle again! From this day forward I ride astride, and God help anyone who tries to stop me. Do you hear?"

Rob felt a surge of joy at the fire in Arianna's eyes, and the arrogant tilt of her chin. She was coming around, returning to the land of the living, becoming the magnificent creature he knew her to be. Smiling broadly, he sought John's eyes, and then Colin's, sobering when he saw the loving

347

way Colin looked at Arianna.

Hearing the thud of the drawbridge, Rob kneed his horse and rode over it, blotting out his anguished thoughts. Hearing a loud cheer, he pulled himself from his dismal thoughts and looked around. His people were surrounding Pasha, reaching for Arianna, crying and laughing. Arianna sat her horse like a queen amongst her subjects, nodding her head and smiling.

Rob watched the touching scene, a hard lump coming to his throat. He wanted to climb from his horse and join in the adulation. Wanted to hold his wife in his arms, carry her to his chamber . . . Oh, God, what was he going to do? Needing a surge of anger to cut through his desire for Arianna, he deliberately sought Colin's gaze, finding him staring up at the parapets with a puzzled look.

Something compelled him to look up, too. Judith, dressed in a black gown and cloak, stood there looking down, the wind blowing her cloak upward like wings on a dark angel. A sudden dread coursed through him. Why was he suddenly afraid for Arianna?

Turning his head, he looked at his wife being lifted from her horse by John Neal and at his people so happy to have her back, and then back up to Judith on the parapet. He saw the black look on her face and shivered. Pushing away the feeling, he dismounted and strode over to the crowd. He was immediately surrounded, too.

Lady Margaret uttered a little cry when she saw the babe in Rob's arms and ran over to him, taking Robin. Frightened by all the noise and the strangers reaching for him, Robin began to cry. Tears streamed down Margaret's face as she held the baby.

Arianna heard her son and the crowd parted so she might go to him. Margaret handed the child to Arianna, then gently brushed the hair from Arianna's face. "I never thought I'd see your lovely face again or hold my grandchild in my arms. Welcome home, Arianna."

Taking Margaret's hand from her face, Arianna squeezed it. She started to speak when Rob's booming voice filled the air. "Arianna, Sir John, and two of his men will escort you up to the tower room."

A puzzled expression crossed Arianna's face.

"Don't worry, you'll be comfortable there. I've had glass put in the windows."

Arianna's heart ached at the harshness in Rob's voice, but she accepted it. She had brought about this awful change in him. She heard the hush fall over the crowd when Rob spoke. Margaret squeezed her hand in reassurance, and, holding her head high with Robin in her arms, she followed John Neal and his men into the castle and up the stairs.

The men set about lighting a fire in the fireplace and women bustled around making up the bed with clean linen and blankets and furs. But none of her women was amongst them. Where was Buttercup? And Fiona and Annie?

Drained of any remaining strength, she looked around in a daze and saw Rob in the doorway, staring at her. "My women . . ." she began.

"Buttercup is married to the master mason and lives outside the castle walls. The others will no longer attend you."

"But why . . ."

"Because I no longer trust anyone but John and my knights. You'll be locked in here nights and guarded by John and the men at all times."

Arianna blinked back the humiliation. "Sweet Jesus, Rob, is that necessary? Are you afraid I'll murder someone else? Is that it? You still believe I mutilated Edmund? Answer me. Is that what you believe?"

349

Rob stared at her in silence, then turned and left. If that was what she believed, then let her think it. He was hurting too much to talk to her now. He heard the door close behind him, heard it being locked, and started down the stairs with a heavy heart.

An anxious Lady Margaret stood at the bottom of the stairs. "Robert, son, why in God's name do you lock your wife and child in the tower room?"

"I have good reason."

"Then tell me so I might understand."

"Later, Mother," he said, his voice filled with emotion. "I need time to sort it all out. But until I do, no one but you or I will have access to Arianna. Do you understand?"

Margaret looked deep into his troubled eyes. "No, I don't. I cannot fathom any of this. I have so many questions."

Taking her hand, he said, "I lost her once. I won't let that happen again."

Sitting close to the fire, a wool shawl wrapped around her, Arianna listened to the howling wind rattling the windows like a wild animal trying to gain entrance to her chamber. She drew closer to the fire, seeking its warmth, feeling lonelier than she ever had. She knew all she had to do was call out and the guards would appear, but that thought didn't lessen the feeling. Robin stirred in his sleep and Arianna moved to the large chest that served as a temporary bed for him.

Robin was snug and warm, nestled into a nest of pillows and blankets. Oh, to be that content. She heard a light rap on the door and looked up to see Margaret, carrying her needlework.

No words were necessary. Margaret and Arianna closed the distance between them and embraced. Then

350

Arianna led the older woman over to the chest and Margaret peered down at her grandchild, whispering, "He's beautiful. The image of Robert when he was a babe."

"Oh, Margaret, I'm happy you can know your grandchild now. I've hated having to be parted from everyone I love. At least this one good thing has come out of this. If nothing else, at least there is that much."

"Arianna, I don't begin to understand, but surely it cannot be as bad as you make it."

"Hasn't Rob told you everything?"

"He's told me nothing. He's unable to open his heart. It's too full of pain."

"Pain. An old companion of mine."

"Child, it grieves me that you've suffered so much in your short life. I wish there was something I could do to help you, something that would ease your heart."

"Oh, Lady Margaret, you help just by being here. I was feeling so lonely just a few moments ago. Will you sit with me a while?"

"I shall do more than that. I've brought my embroideries along. We can work on them together. The time passes easier when the hands are busy."

"Aye, 'tis so."

The two women settled by the fire, needlework in their laps, and began to chat of unimportant things. Margaret knew it was what Arianna needed most — to forget for a time her troubled life. What terrible thing had happened to put such sorrow in her beautiful blue eyes?

"Is it true Buttercup is married?"

Margaret smiled. "Aye, and expecting a child, too. You'd laugh to see her. She carries on as if she were the first woman to have a child — and her husband! Oh Lordy, but he dotes on her."

Arianna laughed. "I can hardly wait to see her and

351

meet her husband. Is he truly a master mason?"

"He is, and a great deal older than she. But somehow, they make a perfect match. He's burly and gruff, but has a heart of gold, and Buttercup, why, she's in complete awe of his station in life."

"I'm happy for her. 'Tis nice to know that sometimes things work out for the better."

Margaret saw the sad expression that washed over Arianna's face. She reached out to pat her hand when the door opened and Robert stood there.

The tranquil scene before the fire startled Rob for a moment. Lost in a world of painful conflict, he wasn't expecting to see Arianna in this peaceful setting. "I came to see my son before I retire for the night."

Arianna stood, the forgotten needlework dropping to the floor.

"I shan't awaken him. I . . ." He couldn't take his eyes from her as she stood before the blazing fire. He was drawn to her, like a shivering animal to a life-giving fire. "I hope you're comfortable. Is it warm enough for you here? Do you need more blankets?" He moved closer, closing the gap between them, until he was close enough to touch her. Oh, God.

"No. Thank you. I'm sure I'll be quite warm in . . . bed."

Bed. Arianna in bed, warm, silky, soft beyond belief. "I'll just take a peek at Robin now, if you'll excuse me."

On wooden legs, Rob moved to the chest, his heart pounding wildly just being in the same room with her. What would it take to be freed from her spell?

Arianna was glad when Rob walked away. The very sight of him had her heart fluttering like a butterfly in her chest. She couldn't look at him without desiring him, without wanting to be in his arms. Would it always be so? Was there no cure for her?

352

Robin began to make little sucking sounds in his sleep and in a moment was awake, crying for his mother. Rob lifted him from the chest. "What is it, son? Your papa's here. He won't let anything hurt you."

Margaret had been watching her son and his wife, not missing a thing. These two were as much in love with each other now as they had ever been. No, more, for they knew the anguish of separation. They belonged together, and if there was any justice in this world, it would be so. "Son, I fear you cannot give the babe what he needs most right now — his mother's milk."

"Oh! I didn't think, that is . . ." Walking over to Arianna, he placed the child in her arms. The heat from the fire enhanced her fragrance, and he yearned to nuzzle his head in her neck.

Arianna took Robin and sat by the fire, undoing the laces of her bodice. Robert watched, entranced, as she lifted her chemise and held her breast out. He felt a throbbing in his groin as the babe's mouth closed round the swollen nipple.

Never had he seen a more beautiful sight. Arianna and his son. Mother and child. For a brief moment in time, all was right with the world. Everything was in its place. He breathed deeply, absorbing the dear moment, letting it sink into his heart and his brain. And he listened — to the crackling of the fire, the soft guzzling sounds the baby made taking the life-giving nourishment from his mother, and to his heart pumping hard with the passion he felt. He felt himself moving closer . . . drawn to her as he had always been.

A male voice broke the spell. It was Colin calling from the doorway.

Robert stopped. He turned and looked at the man who had slept with his wife.

"I'm sorry for interrupting," Colin said, uneasy at Robert's dark stare. "I just wanted to make sure Arianna and Robin were all right."

A few moments of potent silence passed before Robert could bring himself to speak. "Since I have already seen to their needs, there is no reason for you to stay."

Colin swallowed hard, then burying his pride, he said, "Of course. Good night, then."

Watching Colin leave, Robert felt no sense of victory. There were no winners in this situation. With a heavy heart, he turned for one last look at his wife and son. Then he left.

Chapter Twenty-nine

It was not a morning to be outdoors. Wet, freezing winds blew around the battlements of Everly Castle, leaving a slick, icy surface on the rugged stone. But Rob knew not, cared not, about the weather. Deep in troubled thought, he barely knew where he was. Looking out over the parapet to the wintry world, he saw only Arianna's face.

Will found him there. "Rob. Come down to the great hall with me. The fire is warm and welcome."

"Huh? Oh, Will. What am I doing out here when there's warmth inside and good company such as you?" Trying to sound cheerful, he added, "How are you, friend? I haven't seen much of you lately."

Will steered Rob toward the stairs. "I've been busy wooing a young lady, but I'll tell you more about that once we've warmed up."

Rob was halfway down the narrow stone stairs before it dawned on him what Will had said. "Found yourself a lady, have you? Good. 'Tis god-awful to be alone."

They entered the hall and made their way to one of the tables set up by the fire, sitting with their backs against the warmth.

"Brrr, I didn't realize how cold I was 'til just now," Rob said with a frown. "I've got to snap out of this. I seem to be going to pieces and I don't know why."

"Don't you? My God, Rob. You just found out the woman you love is alive. Of course you're falling to pieces. What man wouldn't?"

"So you know? I don't remember seeing you when we rode in yesterday, but then, I wasn't in any condition to notice anything but her and my son. Imagine that, Will. I have a son. You should see him, he's . . . But, you have seen him. That day in Colin's cottage. That was my son on the floor. My son."

"I know, Rob . . . I knew it then."

"What?"

"I saw Arianna that day. Discovered her when I went outside to relieve myself."

Rob suppressed his anger, not wanting anyone to hear the conversation, but he couldn't suppress the color that came to his face. "And you kept it from me? God's blood! I thought you were my friend."

"Rob, I am your friend, but I'm Arianna's, too. She begged me not to tell you. She wanted to protect you, keep you safe from the Queen."

"Why are you telling me this now? It would have been better if I never knew."

"You'll know in a minute, when I introduce you to my wife." Will looked across the room to a small form waiting anxiously by the door that led to the chapel. Smiling shyly, she made her way over to her husband.

Rob was still trying to comprehend Will's words when he looked up at Felicity. "Wife?"

Will stood when Felicity came to the table and Rob followed suit.

"I take it you two met at the cabin in the woods," Rob said quietly.

"I'm Colin Colrain's sister, sir. I hope you can forgive me for pretending to . . ."

"I have no quarrel with you, Felicity. I'm getting quite

356

used to duplicity. It seems to be the way of the world. Nothing is what it seems, no one who they say they are. I . . ." His words trailed off as Arianna entered the hall, Robin in her arms. Behind her, one of his knights kept watch over her.

For a long palpable moment, the hall was hushed—then suddenly it was filled with animated voices as everyone spoke at once. Arianna looked over to Rob but made no move in his direction.

Will glanced from Rob to Arianna and saw how it was between them. He went to her and, taking Robin from her arms, led her back to Rob and Felicity. "Arianna, see who's here."

"Felicity!"

"Felicity Ludlow now, Arianna. We took your advice. We married right away, not wanting to waste any of the few precious moments each of us has on this earth." Felicity looked at Rob, hoping her words had sunk in. By the way he looked at Arianna, she was sure they had.

Arianna hugged Felicity, her eyes shiny with tears. "That's wonderful news." She looked to Rob to see how he was taking all this, and saw him staring at her. "Are you happy for Will, Robert?"

Rob didn't answer, but continued to stare at her in uncomfortable silence. Will stepped in to break the spell. "Here, Rob. You hold your son. I'm thinking he's in need of a chance of his cloth."

Felicity giggled and took Robin from Will. "You can't expect a great lord to change a baby now, can you? If you'll show me the way, I'll do it."

"No, Felicity," Arianna said, taking Robin. "Stay with your new husband. I'll do it." Turning, she almost collided with Judith. Staring into Judith's eyes a moment, she smiled apologetically and continued on her way.

Judith's face was drained of color. She hadn't expected to see Arianna so soon. Then, seeing Will's arm around

357

a young woman, she paled even further.

Will opened his mouth to speak, but she didn't want to hear what he had to say. Blindly, she turned and fled.

"What was that all about?" Felicity asked. "Is your sister upset because of me?"

Will held Felicity tight. "I don't know. But I don't mind telling you all I'm worried about her. She acts stranger all the time. I think it's time to bring her back to Norbridge. Maybe there, with father, she'll be her old self again. Besides, it's time we went home, too. Time we worked on starting a family of our own. I like the way the babe looked in your arms."

Felicity blushed and lowered her lashes.

Arianna was glad to be away from everyone. She wasn't ready to face the fact that life went on no matter how much tragedy she had endured in her life. Her mother was dead and yet there was still joy in the world. Her mother was dead and yet two lovers married. Suddenly, she wanted to be alone with her grief. Opening the door, she signaled to one of the guards. "Will you tell my husband I won't be going downstairs for breakfast, after all."

"Yes, my lady. Shall I have the cook send up a tray?"

"Yes. That would be nice. Thank you."

Seeing the guard enter the hall without Arianna, Rob's heart sank. He wanted the company of his wife. He couldn't get enough of looking at her, knowing she was here. He looked around the room for Colin, hoping to fuel his anger once again, but the man was not there. Was he with Arianna? He started for the door, then stopped when he saw Colin, deep in conversation with two servants.

Colin saw Robert and led the servants over to him. "Robert, I've been making some inquiries about Edmund's death and found out an interesting thing. Did you know a small stone—an amethyst, I believe—was

358

found in one of Edmund's wounds?"

"Yes, I know. Obviously, it was dislodged from the dagger that killed Edmund."

"Do you have the dagger?"

"No, the killer must have taken it."

"Ummm. If the killer left at all."

"What are you saying, Colin? That the madman who killed Edmund is someone in the castle? That's ridiculous."

"Is it? Why did you think it was someone from outside the castle wall?"

"Because everyone believed Arianna was abducted, taken away by the . . ." Rob's eyes opened wide.

"You see? Now that you know Arianna wasn't abducted but ran away, it throws that theory right out the window. It makes sense now to think the murderer is someone in the castle."

Rob shook his head slowly, thinking about what Colin had said.

"Do you still have the stone?" Colin queried.

"I think . . . yes, somewhere."

"Good. If we can find a dagger with a stone missing, a stone that fits, we'll have our murderer."

"I think you're right. You are right, Colin. I should have thought of it, I should . . ."

"Don't berate yourself, man. You were grieving a dead wife, and in no condition to think of such things."

Rob looked into Colin's eyes. He saw the compassion there, and thought, at least, Arianna was with a kind-hearted man. At least, she didn't have to suffer at the hands of some villain.

The frigid night seemed somehow colder than any Rob had ever experienced. Huddled under layers of furs, he should have been comfortable, but instead felt as though his veins were filled with ice. If that were not enough, his mind kept wandering up the spiral staircase to the small chamber. Arianna was there. Warmth was there. His heart was there.

Throwing back the covers, Rob climbed out of bed, angry with himself for not being able to sleep, for not being able to forget what it felt like to lie with his wife. Damnation. He hadn't been able to forget her when he thought her dead. How could he forget now, knowing she was here?

Think of her and Colin together, he reflected bitterly. Think of the way she betrayed you over and over. Think of her lips, her hair, her breasts. No. Oh, God, no. Don't think. Don't think at all. It was the only way to keep from wanting her, to keep from hurting. It was all so impossible. Nothing would keep him from wanting her.

In agony, Rob dressed and left the room, in such a turmoil he knew not where he was going until he found himself outside the tower room. He told himself it was because he wanted to gaze at his small son. Yes, that was it, he wanted to see his son. Without speaking, he gestured to the guard to unlock the door and made his way into the darkened room, closing the door quietly behind him.

The makeshift crib stood under the window, the babe fast asleep. Starting toward it, he changed directions, a thin stream of moonlight guiding him to the side of Arianna's bed instead. The soft glow embellished her beauty enticingly.

Arianna. Oh, Arianna.

Kneeling beside the bed, he gazed at her, taking in the loveliness of her face in sleep. How many times he had stared at her as she was now, content just to be in her presence. Content to count the lashes on her eyelids, the very breaths she took. It had been ten long months, but it might have been today for the way he felt about her. It would be so easy to climb in bed beside her, to fold her in his arms, to continue his life with her as if nothing had happened.

No. Not true.

She had deceived him in so many ways. How could he ever trust her again? She had lied her way into his life, violated his deep love and trust. Had enticed him into falling in love with her so he wouldn't marry Judith, and yet . . . Looking at her now, he saw only goodness. And innocence and beauty. It was as if she were untouched by all that had happened, as if she were not responsible for any of it.

Could it be true? Was she blameless? Mayhap she had done the only thing she could to survive the cruelty that surrounded her. He couldn't begin to imagine what it had been like for her. He had been pampered all his life, had had a golden life from the very start. How would he have acted if he had been denied his birthright? How would he have acted if his own mother had been executed?

It had taken a great deal of courage for Arianna to go to her mother's execution. To be strong for Mary. To give her the gift of love when the rest of the world had abandoned her. If he knew nothing else about Arianna, he knew she had a deep loyalty to those she loved. And she had loved him — enough to leave him so he would be safe.

He started to rise, disturbed that he was beginning to understand her motives, that if he did understand he would have to open his heart to her and to the possibility of being hurt again.

Arianna let out a low moan, moving her arm as if warding off a blow, uncovering her naked breasts in the process. He stopped, sucking in his breath.

She tossed her head back and forth wildly, crying out,

361

"No! No! The blood! The Blood!"

His greatest desire was to take her in his arms, comfort her, calm her fears, but he couldn't . . . mustn't, or he'd be lost. He started for the door, knowing he must leave before it was too late. Turning suddenly, he strode back to the bed and lifted her into his arms. He had never been able to deny his love for her, never been able to stay away when she needed him, and he couldn't deny her now. "Arianna. It's all right. I'm here. No one can hurt you now."

His words broke through her terrible nightmare and she opened her eyes to see her beloved Robert. Instantly, her arms were around his neck, holding onto him for dear life. "Oh, Rob. It was so awful without you, so awful."

His lips came down on hers, grinding into them with all his pent-up passion. Oh God, how he had missed her! And having touched her he couldn't stop, but covered her face with kisses, murmuring between each touch of his lips. "Arianna . . . Rose Petal . . . my love, my life."

Arianna answered the only way she knew how — drawing him down to her. Her tears and his mingled as he laid his full weight on her, needing to feel her under him. His kisses became more fervent, traveling down from her face to her neck to her breast, until he had a swollen nipple between his searching lips. Hot liquid flooded his mouth, surprising him. Her sweet milk. He swallowed it eagerly and sucked at her nipple again, swallowing more.

Arianna felt the milk spurt into Rob's mouth and wanted to fill him with it. She had an overwhelming desire to nurture him, gorge him with her love.

Groaning with desire, Rob moved his head, seeking her other milk-filled breast, sucking on it as if he had been starving for the ten long months she was gone, and, in fact, he had. Starving for the one woman he was meant to love, the one woman who could make him feel this way .

He swallowed again and again, knowing the nourishment was born of their love, each drop of liquid put there by the act that had produced their beautiful son. And when his desire for her grew too strong to bear, he stood and undressed, ready to come to her.

Seeing his arousal, Arianna rose and reached out to touch him. Her trembling hand curled around his manhood, the overwhelming sensation bringing her to her knees. She took him in her mouth and Rob knew, though no words were spoken, that the spilling of his seed in her mouth was needed for the fulfillment and completion of the symbolic act he had started at her breast.

He held her head lightly as she used her mouth and tongue on him, filling him with a greater desire than he had ever known. He cried out, unable to contain the emotion.

Arianna remembered the taste of him and she was filled with joy. This was her man, her lover, her husband. She wanted and needed to be nourished by him, as he had been by her breast, and she strove for that end.

Her hungry mouth soon had Rob crying out in rapture and he held her head tighter now, as his manhood throbbed and pulsated with life, his essence spilling down her throat. She took it all and wanted more.

And he was ready to give it to her. Lifting her, he laid her on the bed, his body covering hers possessively, sensually.

He covered her body with kisses — love bites, licks of his tongue — reclaiming her as his own. Covered her with the scent of him, the touch of him, until she thought she'd die if she didn't have him inside her.

And then he was, and she was holding on to him as if

her life depended on it. And it did. Oh, yes, it did. Each deep thrust brought ecstasy and yearning for another thrust and another, deeper, deeper, her need greater than ever before. And when the supreme moment came, when their souls were united as one in blessed ecstasy, she felt such a deep abiding love for him she cried from sheer joy.

Rob looked down at Arianna through shining eyes, knowing that whatever happened, from this day forward they would be together. He would do whatever it took to keep her safe and by his side. It was their destiny to be together and no one, not even the Queen of England, would be strong enough to break their sacred bond.

Chapter Thirty

Morning came, and with it Robin's cheerful gurgling. Robert woke hearing his son's sweet voice and a satisfied smile played across his face. His son. His wife. Here, with him. He hadn't dreamt it. Arianna was really alive. Nuzzling at her neck, he kissed her awake.

Arianna opened one sleepy eye, then closed it again. Rob kissed her again and she murmured, "Mmm, I'm afraid to open my eyes and find I was only dreaming."

"Open them, Arianna. I'm here. You're here, where you belong."

A sudden sadness came over Arianna and she held tight to Rob. "Oh, Rob, I'm so afraid. What if something tears me from your arms again? I couldn't bear to go through that again. I couldn't."

"Shhh, Rose Petal. You must trust again. Somehow, everything will turn out as it should. You must believe our love is powerful enough."

"I want to believe, truly. But I don't know if I can. The Queen! What if she takes me away from you? Or Robin, what if she takes him away? How can we live under the constant threat? You should have taken Robin and left me in Fotheringhay. At least then the two of you would be safe."

"Don't ever talk like that again." Rob's hands gripped

her shoulders tight. "Why is it you can face the Queen bravely when you're alone, face a room full of her men without blinking an eye, but lose your courage when you are with me?"

"Because I love you so. Because I fear for you."

"Trust in our love, Arianna. Let it make you strong, not weak."

Arianna absorbed the words. "Do you mean what you say, Rob?"

"Of course I do."

"I don't think you do, else you wouldn't keep me locked here in the tower. Else you'd trust me to ride Pasha."

"I do it only to protect you."

"No," she answered in a quiet voice. "You do it to protect yourself."

Rob stared at her. Was there truth in what she said? Had he kept her a prisoner to protect himself from hurt if she were injured or lost? Had he kept her from Pasha for the same reason? His father had died from a fall from a horse; it wasn't unreasonable to fear for his wife, but still, it was wrong to smother her and keep her from living freely. "Have I always been so selfish?"

"You're not selfish, Rob. You just don't trust me. I can't blame you for that."

"Then, I'll blame myself." Walking to the window, he looked out at the frozen world. "I'll tell John you have no further need of a guard." Turning back to face her, he continued. "As for Pasha, that's a different story. The animal has proved time and time again he is too dangerous to ride. I'm having him put out to stud and will find a gentler horse for you. Agreed?"

Arianna threw her arms around Rob's neck. "Agreed, my lord. Pasha will be more than happy to spend his life servicing the mares."

"Good. Get dressed. I'm hungry as a bear."

"So is your son," she said, picking Robin up. "You go ahead. I want to feed him before I go down to breakfast."

Rob felt a tug at his groin. "Don't be long. I want the people of Everly to see us together. A family again."

Laughing wickedly, Arianna said, "I warrant they know already. I'm sure word has spread of where you spent the night."

Rob pulled her up against his chest. "And every night from this day forward."

Walking into the hall, Rob realized he was hungry for the first time since Arianna's disappearance. He sat at the table, joining in conversation with a group of knights, and didn't notice Judith watching him from across the hall, didn't notice when she rose and left.

Upstairs in the chamber, Arianna sat by the fire nursing her son. Absorbed, she didn't know anyone was there until she heard the rustle of skirts. Startled, she looked up—into Judith's dark eyes.

"Judith," she said, recovering her composure, "how nice of you to visit. I was feeling a mite lonely. Sit with me while I feed this young sir here."

Judith blinked in surprise. Arianna always surprised her with her warmheartedness. She always expected to be rebuffed by her, and was always received so warmly. Disconcerted, she sat, releasing her hold on the hilt of the ornate dagger at her waist.

"How are you, Judith? I've been thinking of you. I know you must still be grieving over Edmund, and I want you to know you have my deepest sympathy."

Judith's face took on a lost look and Arianna realized there was something deeply wrong with Judith. She had sensed that several times before in Norbridge, always pushing it out of her mind, but now it was too obvious to ignore.

Judith slowly reached out to touch Robin's downy head, a dreamy look on her face. "I . . . was pregnant

367

once. Did you know that, Arianna? Did you know I was carrying Edmund's child?"

Arianna felt a touch of fear. "No. I never knew."

"No one did. Edmund saw to that. He didn't want a bastard child and didn't want to marry me. He . . . sent me to a witch woman who took my child."

Arianna reached for Judith's hand. "I'm truly sorry. It must have been dreadful going through that alone."

Judith looked into Arianna's eyes and saw sincere sympathy. She swallowed hard. Why had she come up here? Her hand closed round the dagger once again.

"If ever you need to talk about it, or anything else, I'm here, Judith. Sometimes it's good to talk things out with a friend."

"Friend?"

"Are you all right, Judith? Would you like me to get Will for you?"

Judith's face grew grim. "He has a wife, you know. After everything I went through for him, keeping Edmund from telling the Queen, I lost him anyway. Now I have no one."

Arianna's heart lurched. "You saved him from the Queen?"

"Did you think it was you, Arianna? Did you think you killed Edmund with your puny blow? It took much more than that. He didn't die so easy as that. Edmund was still standing when you left, shouting that he would have Will and everyone else who knew your true identity arrested and sent to Elizabeth. I couldn't let him do that to Will." Judith gripped the dagger tighter.

"Oh, Judith," Arianna cried. Leaving her chair, she knelt beside Judith, Robin still in her arms. "Don't hate yourself for killing him. He wasn't worth it. I know how evil he was. You did it to save Will, to save me and my unborn child. If not for you, Robin would never have been born."

368

Judith looked down at Arianna in amazement, taking in her words. She looked at the babe in Arianna's arms in wonder. *If not for her* . . . It was true. Because of her, a child lived. Because of Edmund another child had died. "You don't know the agony I've been through, having no one I could confide in. Not even Will. He's lost to me, you know, lost . . . I'm lost . . . And when you came back and I looked down at you from the battlements, I wanted to hate you because you were free of Edmund, as I can never be."

Down the hall, Rob waited impatiently for Arianna. What was keeping her? He was about to go after her when Colin came over to him, an anxious look on his face.

"Robert. Buttercup is here, visiting. I talked to her in the kitchen. She told me Judith has a dagger, one with amethysts on the hilt. Buttercup found it once in the secret passageway outside Arianna's door and . . ."

The image of Judith on the battlements, her cloak spread out like wings on a dark angel swam before Rob's eyes. "Judith! Where is she?"

He hadn't known he shouted until he heard a knight answer from a nearby table. "She left the hall a while ago, my lord. Didn't you see her?"

Rob and Colin exchanged glances then headed down the hall in a run. They climbed the endless stairs and opened the door to the tower room fearing what they would see.

Arianna and Judith looked up in surprise.

Rob saw the dagger at Judith's waist, her hand tightly gripping the hilt. Arianna was on the floor kneeling beside Judith, Robin's head only inches from Judith's lap. Any sudden move and his wife or child could die.

Arianna saw the look on the men's faces. They knew about Judith. "Rob. Colin. It's all right. Do you understand? It's all right," she said pointedly.

Rob looked into his wife's eyes. Didn't she realize how close to death she was? Then looking closer, he saw that she did. And yet, she was so calm. "Arianna . . ."

"Robert," Arianna said, keeping her tone of voice light. "Can't you see Judith and I are having a woman-to woman-talk? You and Colin leave — now — please, so that we may finish." She prayed that he would listen. Prayed that for once in his life he would trust her to know the right thing to do.

Arianna's words struck deep at his heart. Leave? Leave her alone with an unstable woman? A woman who had already killed once?

He looked at Arianna and heard the words in his head. *Let our love make you strong, not weak.* Arianna was begging him with her eyes to do just that. This was the test. But oh, dear God, did it have to be such a hard one? Trust. Be strong. He had to trust her. She wouldn't ask him to leave if she thought the babe was in danger.

Taking Colin by the arm, he said, "Colin. You heard. Leave the women to their chatter."

Under his breath, Colin muttered, "I hope you know what you're doing."

Taking his arm, Rob led Colin out the door, closing it behind him. It was the hardest thing he had ever done in his life.

Arianna breathed a sigh of relief once they had left. She knew they were probably right outside the door, but that was fine, as long as Judith wasn't aware. It had been a terrible moment, fearing that Judith would strike at Robin if the men came any closer, but it would be all right now.

"Judith, would you like to come to breakfast with me and Robin? Nursing him makes me very hungry." She held her breath, waiting for Judith to answer. If she misjudged her, she would be in terrible danger.

Judith looked at Robin, still at his mother's breast.

The child she had saved by killing Edmund. "I imagine it does. Yes. You must be sure to eat enough. It would be terrible if you didn't have enough milk for the child."

Arianna choked back a sob. It was going to be all right.

Rob and Colin watched the door open, tensed and ready to strike.

Judith walked out, followed by Arianna and the baby.

They were unharmed. Thank the Lord, Rob thought gratefully. He looked into Arianna's eyes and felt great pride. This beautiful, courageous woman belonged to him.

Will stood at the bottom of the stairs, watching as Judith came down on Colin's arm. Buttercup had told him about Colin's search for a dagger with a missing stone, told him it belonged to Judith. He knew what that meant. She had always had a violent nature and he had protected her from retribution many times in the past. But Edmund's murder? He couldn't protect her from that. He felt a deep hole in his heart watching her, lovelier than ever, walking down the stairs so serenely. What would become of her? He couldn't bear to see her imprisoned.

Judith smiled and reached out to him, then stopped, her expression turning to steel when she saw the red-headed girl walk up to Will. For a moment, she had forgotten. For a moment she, too, had been free. She was at the bottom of the steps now, the door but a few feet away. Outside, in the yard, she heard the whinny of a horse calling her, beckoning her to freedom.

She ran, breaking away from Will and the others, out the door across the yard to the white horse tied to a post. It was as if the animal had been put there just for her so she could ride with the wind to freedom, to Norbridge Castle.

The white horse flattened his ears at her approach,

the whites of his eyes shining in the morning light. Good. He was eager for the ride, eager to take her away. Putting her foot in the stirrup, she pulled herself up.

Running through the doorway, Will shouted, "Noooo! Judith!"

Halfway in the saddle, Judith heard her brother's voice and turned her head toward him eagerly.

In horror, Will saw Pasha rear, the reins that tied him to the post snapping under his great strength, throwing Judith to the ground. She fell, her foot still caught in the stirrup, her neck snapping on impact. Pasha twisted his body away, but his leg was positioned wrong and he fell to the earth with a great thud.

Running into the yard, Arianna heard the terrible sound of Pasha's leg breaking and his unearthly screams of pain.

Frantic, she handed Robin to Buttercup, then ran toward Pasha. Rob and Will and Colin got there first, pulling Judith's limp body free of the horse

"Pasha, oh Pasha," she cried, going down on her knees. She couldn't bear to see him in such terrible pain. The magnificent animal tried to stand, his eyes wild with fear, and she held his head down, talking to him soothingly. Out of the corner of her eye she saw Rob take a sword from John Neal and walk toward her. She knew what he was going to do. His eyes pleaded with her to understand.

"Oh God! Nooooooo!" Colin pried her arms loose and pulled her away.

She knew when it was over . . . a terrible silence fell.

Will knelt by his sister, tears streaming down his face. He wouldn't let anyone near her until Felicity's sweet soothing voice broke through his terrible grief. John Neal touched his shoulder, then lifted Judith's lifeless body into his arms and carried her into the castle.

Will looked around as if he were lost.

Arianna called his name and ran into his arms, crying too hard to stop. Will tightened his arms around her and began sobbing, too, finally allowing himself to feel the grief he had tried to contain.

Felicity touched Will's shoulder gently, murmuring his name, and Will turned to her and drew her into his arms.

Dropping his bloody sword, Rob walked over to Arianna, afraid she would hate him for killing Pasha. Steeling himself for her rejection, he looked deep into her eyes and saw only love.

Pulling her into his arms, he buried his head in her hair. "I had to do it. He was suffering. His leg was broken. There was no other way."

Arianna put her arm around him and caressed his back as if soothing an injured child. "I know, I know."

Chapter Thirty-one

April 6, 1587

The warmth of friendly chatter permeated the cozy sitting chamber of Everly Castle, dispelling the dampness and chill of the unseasonably cold spring day. Little Robin, absorbing it all, sat on Peter's lap, his chubby baby fingers clutching the hawk his foster grandfather had carved for him from an ash tree.

Peter's booming voice rang out, drowning out all others. "Begging everyone's pardon, but I do believe Robin likes this present the best."

"I believe you're right," Rob said, handing Peter a tankard of ale. "Comes by it naturally, don't you think, considering his mother's penchant for flying hawks."

Felicity's eyes lit up. "Hawking? Oh, I would dearly love to learn how."

Will squeezed her waist. "And you shall. I know just the lad to teach you, too. An apprentice falconer named Sparrow."

Felicity was startled by the laughter that echoed through the chamber at Will's words. "Hmmm. Methinks there's something you're not telling me. What is it?"

"Some day, my darling wife, I'll tell you the story."

Arianna looked around the sitting room, a contented smile on her face. The people dearest to her in the world were gathered here to celebrate Robin's first birthday. Rob acting the proud father, Peter, doting grandfather, with Robin on his lap, beautiful Sybille at his side. Will and Felicity, Buttercup and her portly husband Dan, and Margaret, all gathered here. All her loved ones but two . . . Leicester and Colin.

She had not sent word of the birthday celebration to Leicester, in fear the correspondence might fall into the wrong hands. As for Colin, no one had heard from him since the day after Judith died. He had left without so much as a goodbye. She tried to tell herself it was better this way, but her heart ached too much to truly believe it was so.

A staccato knock sounded on the door and a yeoman burst in, looking as if he were about to expire. "My lord, forgive the intrusion, but the Queen is at the gate, demanding entrance."

Rob's heart thudded against the wall of his chest. "Well, then, by all means let her in. Don't keep her waiting." Seeking Arianna's eyes, he saw the fear there. "Stay calm, Rose Petal. We can't jump to conclusions. She may simply be seeking shelter for the night on her way to some country estate. Don't read anything sinister into this visit."

Arianna hid the horror she felt. It wouldn't do to be nervous in Elizabeth's presence. "Of course. I know. Everyone, make ready. Felicity? Come let me groom your hair, and Rob, straighten your doublet. We must look our best for the Queen. Papa? Mama? Will you stay here with Robin? I'd rather not expose him to the chill of the castle halls."

Peter and Rob exchanged looks. They both knew Arianna feared having Elizabeth anywhere near her son. "Good idea," Rob said, trying to sound nonchalant. "Besides, he's likely to pull Elizabeth's wig off if she comes within range of him. He's become quite adept at that little trick."

When Felicity's grooming was finished and Arianna could find no other reason to delay, she smoothed her skirts and cried, "Shall we greet our Queen?"

With much more bravado than she felt, she took Rob's arm and walked into the hall and down the stairs. Throwing open the door, she entered boldly. Elizabeth stood by the fireplace warming herself at the fire, a small familiar blue-grey bundle of fur in her arms.

Gazing in disbelief, Arianna choked back the fierce rage that engulfed her. *How dare she claim Mary's dog for her own? God in heaven, how much am I to endure? She will pay for this. She will pay for everything.*

Seeking to calm herself, her gaze shifted to Leicester, knowing the sight of him would ease her troubled heart. Seeing the broad smile on her father's face, she was reassured. Nothing was amiss if he could smile at her so openly. That reassurance gave her the strength to transform herself into the Arianna the Queen was familiar with, the strength to hide the rage she felt at Elizabeth for causing her mother's death, and the new fury toward her for stealing her mother's dog. With forced gaiety, she ran across the floor to greet the Queen.

As she grew closer, the little dog began to whimper and wriggle his body, eager to be freed. Annoyed, Elizabeth dropped it to the floor. The dog immediately bounded toward Arianna.

Arianna watched, her fear escalating as the dog drew closer. She tried to ignore him so Elizabeth wouldn't know he was no stranger, but the dog clamored for attention. Fearing her neglect would make her look even guiltier, she scooped the ball of fur up into her arms.

"What a friendly little fellow. Is he like that with everyone, Your Majesty?" Arianna curtsied deeply, rising at Elizabeth's command.

"No, my dear, but as you can see by his enthusiastic greeting, he has the same good taste in folk that I have." Unexpectedly, Elizabeth embraced Arianna. "My dear, dear, girl. 'Tis so good to see you."

"And you, my Queen." Elizabeth's touch penetrated Arianna's skin and a cold shiver went up her spine. "Here is your dog." Arianna kissed the little dog's head, then handed him to the Queen, hiding the reticence she felt at having to return him to her blood-stained hands.

"I don't know why I've kept him. He's not trained at all, but does his business wherever he has a mind to. If it wasn't for the fact he belonged to my dear, tragic cousin, Mary, I would have given him away long before today."

The Queen's words penetrated Arianna's senses, filling her heart with hope. Could Elizabeth be giving her the terrier? Choosing her speech carefully, she answered, "He belonged to the Scottish Queen? I don't wonder at your reluctance to keep him then."

Elizabeth looked startled at Arianna's words. "What do you mean?"

"I only thought . . . Well, it must be an awful reminder of the tragedy. I heard how angry you became when you found out Mary was dead. Some misunderstanding, wasn't there? About the death certificate? You didn't know that you had signed it? At least, that's the story I heard." *Misunderstanding indeed! The witch knew exactly what she was doing.*

"Quite right. It was all a terrible mistake. And 'tis true his presence is a constant reminder of that terrible day. That's why I thought of you. I remembered Edmund Deveraux telling me shortly before he died that you had a fondness for Skye terriers. He told me he was going to

377

give you one. Poor man never got the chance. In any case, remembering that I decided you would be the perfect one to care for my cousin's dog."

Arianna's heart was in her throat. Edmund had told Elizabeth that, but no more? Of course not. He meant to torture her first. Give her a Skye terrier just to see her cringe in fear. But it had backfired, and thanks to him, she now possessed her own mother's beloved dog. "Thank you, Your Grace. I shall take good care of him."

Triumphant, Arianna took the little dog in her arms. *Mother, oh Mother, at least I have this much of you.*

Wiping her hands as if wiping away Mary's blood, Elizabeth said, "Now you must tell me everything. When I got the news that you had died in a fall I prayed it wasn't true. And you see, God heard me and rewarded me by bringing you back to us."

"I told Her Majesty it was a miracle," Leicester said. His lips curled in the same way Arianna's did when she was amused.

"Yes, my lord, a miracle," Arianna answered, snuggling her head into the dog's fur.

Leicester stared into his beautiful daughter's eyes. "When word came that you had been found alive and safely delivered of a child, your Queen did cry. A great honor to you, my dear."

Beaming, Elizabeth purred, "Enough. You'll make her pretty little head swell out of shape. But, yes, 'tis true. I did cry for joy. And I'm glad to see you're no worse for your terrible travail. Nay, you look lovelier than ever."

"Thank you, Your Grace."

"You've had your share of troubles, haven't you? With Edmund murdered in your home by that wicked girl, and you out in the storm that very evening, giving birth all alone."

"I wasn't alone, Your Grace, but was rescued by Colin Colrain."

Elizabeth rolled her eyes. "So I heard. It seems I shall have to be nice to the man and forget my grievances. Where is he? Bring him forth so we may be done with it."

"He's not here."

"Then I am reprieved. Good. Leicester has been trying to persuade me to restore the man's property and I have been considering it. What say you on that, Arianna?"

"Your Grace, that would please me greatly. Colin is a superior man and a good one to rely on in time of trouble."

"Hmmm, you may be right. I will think on it. A Queen is always in need of strong, dependable men. But meanwhile I am most curious to hear about the night Edmund died and why you were missing for so many months."

Arianna felt the color drain from her face.

"Oh, my dear. I don't mean to upset you. Is it very painful to talk of it?"

"I want to tell you, Your Majesty, but hate to disillusion you about Edmund. I know you held him in esteem."

"Fah! I hold no man in great esteem, except of course, my Master of the Horse, the Earl of Leicester."

"It was dreadful, Your Majesty. Edmund and Judith sought refuge in the castle that night, and I, of course, granted it. Rob was away, fighting a fire with most of his men, and Edmund was drunk. He came to my chamber late that night and tried to have his way with me."

Elizabeth's eyes grew large. "And you large with child. The bastard!"

"Aye, he was perverse. So much so, he insisted Judith watch."

379

Elizabeth paled a little upon hearing that. It came too close to the arrangement she had had with Judith.

"To defend myself, I stabbed him with my husband's dagger and then escaped through the secret passageway in my chamber. I had no choice but to flee. Edmund had enough knights with him to kill every man, woman, and child in the castle."

"Enough, my dear. No need to tell me more. I would have done the same in your shoes. You did what you had to do to save yourself and your unborn child. I see now, Judith had good reason to kill him. Poor creature, dying so violently. But I don't understand the reason you were gone so long, why everyone thought you dead."

Arianna swallowed hard. "I have so little memory of that time. You see, when I fell I hurt my head. For the longest time I couldn't remember who I was. It was only over the course of several months that my memory came back. As soon as it did, Colin brought me back to Everly and my husband."

"Dear me, but you've led an exciting life for one so young. What of your health now? Are you completely well?"

"Oh, yes, Your Grace. Thank you for asking."

Turning to Robert, Elizabeth said, "Well, young man, you must be very happy to have her back."

"Indeed I am." Robert breathed deeply, freely, knowing Arianna's identity was safe. "And proud that my gracious Queen honors us with her presence."

"Oh, yes, I quite forgot the reason for my visit. I understand this is your son's first birthday."

Rob nodded, wondering what Elizabeth would say next.

"I've come bearing gifts. A pony from my own stables and a spacious castle near Wimbledon."

Arianna gasped at the Queen's largesse. "Your

Grace, you are too generous."

"Nay, my motives are purely selfish. Wimbledon is so very close to London that 'twill be easier to visit with you there."

A strange light came into Arianna's eyes. "I would like that very much, Your Grace."

"Good. I am pleased. Now take me to your son. It's time we became acquainted."

Arianna had a hard time containing the thrill of victory. Elizabeth was no longer a threat! Her identity was safe! How ironic. Elizabeth had just given Mary Stuart's grandchild a castle. And oh, she would make good use of it. She'd be very happy to visit the Queen there. Yes, very happy.

The image of her mother standing on the scaffold flashed through her brain, filling her with loathing for Elizabeth. From that very castle she would avenge herself on this haughty Queen, and one day . . . she would bring Elizabeth to her knees.

Rob's heart constricted as he watched Elizabeth and Arianna together. He knew the hatred in his wife's heart and her obsession to avenge her mother's death. And though he had vowed, in good faith, to let her lead her own life, this was asking too much of any mortal man. He would devote his life to her, devote himself to keeping her safe. *Lord, give me strength!*

DANA RANSOM'S RED-HOT HEARTFIRES!

ALEXANDRA'S ECSTASY   (2773, $3.75)
   Alexandra had known Tucker for all her seventeen years,
but all at once she realized her childhood friend was the
man capable of tempting her to leave innocence behind!

LIAR'S PROMISE   (2881, $4.25)
   Kathryn Mallory's sincere questions about her father's
ship to the disreputable Captain Brady Rogan were met
with mocking indifference. Then he noticed her trim waist,
angelic face and Kathryn won the wrong kind of attention!

LOVE'S GLORIOUS GAMBLE   (2497, $3.75)
   Nothing could match the true thrill that coursed through
Gloria Daniels when she first spotted the gambler, Sterling
Caulder. Experiencing his embrace, feeling his lips against
hers would be a risk, but she was willing to chance it all!

WILD, SAVAGE LOVE   (3055, $4.25)
   Evangeline, set free from Indians, discovered liberty had
its price to pay when her uncle sold her into marriage to
Royce Tanner. Dreaming of her return to the people she
loved, she vowed never to submit to her husband's caress.

WILD WYOMING LOVE   (3427, $4.25)
   Lucille Blessing had no time for the new marshal Sam
Zachary. His mocking and arrogant manner grated her
nerves, yet she longed to ease the tension she knew he held
inside. She knew that if he wanted her, she could never say
no!

*Available wherever paperbacks are sold, or order direct from the
Publisher. Send cover price plus 50¢ per copy for mailing and
handling to Zebra Books, Dept. 3785, 475 Park Avenue South,
New York, N.Y. 10016. Residents of New York and Tennessee
must include sales tax. DO NOT SEND CASH. For a free Zebra/
Pinnacle catalog please write to the above address.*

PASSIONATE NIGHTS FROM

PENELOPE NERI

DESERT CAPTIVE   (2447, $3.95/$4.95)
Kidnapped from her French Foreign Legion escort, indignant Alexandria had every reason to despise her nomad prince captor. But as they traveled to his isolated mountain kingdom, she found her hate melting into desire . . .

FOREVER AND BEYOND   (3115, $4.95/$5.95)
Haunted by dreams of an Indian warrior, Kelly found his touch more than intimate—it was oddly familiar. He seemed to be calling her back to another time, to a place where they would find love again . . .

FOREVER IN HIS ARMS   (3385, $4.95/$5.95)
Whispers of war between the North and South were riding the wind the summer Jenny Delaney fell in love with Tyler Mackenzie. Time was fast running out for secret trysts and lovers' dreams, and she would have to choose between the life she held so dear and the man whose passion made her burn as brightly as the evening star . . .

MIDNIGHT CAPTIVE   (2593, $3.95/$4.95)
After a poor, ragged girlhood with her gypsy kinfolk, Krissoula knew that all she wanted from life was her share of riches. There was only one way for the penniless temptress to earn a cent: fake interest in a man, drug him, and pocket everything he had! Then the seductress met dashing Esteban and unquenchable passion seared her soul . . .

SEA JEWEL   (3013, $4.50/$5.50)
Hot-tempered Alaric had long planned the humiliation of Freya, the daughter of the most hated foe. He'd make the wench from across the ocean his lowly bedchamber slave—but he never suspected she would become the mistress of his heart, his treasured sea jewel . . .

Available wherever paperbacks are sold, or order direct from the Publisher. Send cover price plus 50¢ per copy for mailing and handling to Zebra Books, Dept. 3785, 475 Park Avenue South, New York, N.Y. 10016. Residents of New York and Tennessee must include sales tax. DO NOT SEND CASH. For a free Zebra/ Pinnacle catalog please write to the above address.

FEEL THE FIRE IN CAROL FINCH'S ROMANCES!

BELOVED BETRAYAL (2346, $3.95)

Sabrina Spencer donned a gray wig and veiled hat before blackmailing rugged Ridge Tanner into guiding her to Fort Canby. But the costume soon became her prison—the beauty had fallen head over heels in love!

LOVE'S HIDDEN TREASURE (2980, $4.50)

Shandra d'Evereux felt her heart throb beneath the stolen map she'd hidden in her bodice when Nolan Elliot swept her out onto the veranda. It was hard to concentrate on her mission with that wily rogue around!

MONTANA MOONFIRE (3263, $4.95)

Just as debutante Victoria Flemming-Cassidy was about to marry an oh-so-suitable mate, the towering preacher, Dru Sullivan flung her over his shoulder and headed West! Suddenly, Tori realized she had been given the best present for a bride: a night of passion with a real man!

THUNDER'S TENDER TOUCH (2809, $4.50)

Refined Piper Malone needed bounty-hunter, Vince Logan to recover her swindled inheritance. She thought she could coolly dismiss him after he did the job, but she never counted on the hot flood of desire she felt whenever he was near!

Available wherever paperbacks are sold, or order direct from the Publisher. Send cover price plus 50¢ per copy for mailing and handling to Zebra Books, Dept. 3785, 475 Park Avenue South, New York, N.Y. 10016. Residents of New York and Tennessee must include sales tax. DO NOT SEND CASH. For a free Zebra/ Pinnacle catalog please write to the above address.